SO-AUO-906

COLORADO!

The seventh stirring book
in the WAGONS WEST series—
original, challenging adventures of
bold men and women of the wild frontier
pushing westward in their yearning
for freedom and a new life.

WAGONS WEST

COLORADO!

**The legendary new
breed of men and women who
conquer a raw new land!**

GENERAL LELAND BLAKE—
The former supreme commander of
American forces in the Oregon territory puts
his life on the line in the biggest
gamble of a long career.

CATHY BLAKE—
She must summon all of her courage and love
to meet the challenge of a mysterious
woman out to get her husband.

LIEUTENANT ANDY BRENTWOOD—
Son of one of the original wagon
train families, he must help protect the
gold and preserve the Union.

TRACY FOSTER—
Born under an unlucky star, he exchanges
his dreams of gold for a life of crime.

CAROLINE BRANDON—
A gold-digger, she thinks she knows all
the tricks—until she meets a man even
more coldly ambitious than she.

LUKE BRANDON—
A brilliant Harvard scholar, he is hopelessly
out of his depth when his wife's
infidelities force him into a fateful
confrontation.

ISAIAH ATKINS—
The young lawyer from California must choose
between a childhood sweetheart and a
fascinating new love.

CHET HARRIS—
With his partner Wong Ke, he rules
a far-flung financial empire. But San Francisco's
most eligible bachelor needs new worlds
to conquer, and a woman's love to warm him.

WADE FULTON—
The crusading publisher of the *Tribune*
declares war against the forces of evil
and corruption—and earns some
dangerous enemies.

SUSANNA FULTON—
Wade's beautiful and fearless daughter
solves the mystery of the "gray ghost"—but
not in time to prevent tragedy.

WILLIE de BERG—
Owner of the infamous Palace, a crooked
casino and bordello, he covets both his
rival's business and her soul.

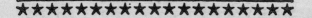

Bantam Books by Dana Fuller Ross
Ask your bookseller for the books you have missed

WAGONS WEST ★ SEVENTH IN A SERIES

COLORADO!

DANA FULLER ROSS

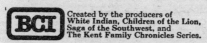

BCI Created by the producers of
White Indian, Children of the Lion,
Saga of the Southwest, and
The Kent Family Chronicles Series.

Executive Producer: Lyle Kenyon Engel

BANTAM BOOKS
TORONTO • NEW YORK • LONDON • SYDNEY • AUCKLAND

This is a work of fiction. While the general outlines of history have been faithfully followed, certain details involving setting, characters, and events may have been simplified.

COLORADO!

A Bantam Book / published by arrangement with Book Creations Inc.

PRINTING HISTORY

Bantam edition / September 1981

2nd printing	. September 1981	5th printing	... October 1982
3rd printing	. September 1981	6th printing	...... June 1983
4th printing	. September 1981	7th printing	...... July 1984

*Produced by Book Creations, Inc.
Chairman of Board: Lyle Kenyon Engel*

ISBN 0-553-24694-1

Published simultaneously in the United States and Canada

PRINTED IN THE UNITED STATES OF AMERICA

H   16 15 14 13 12 11 10 9 8

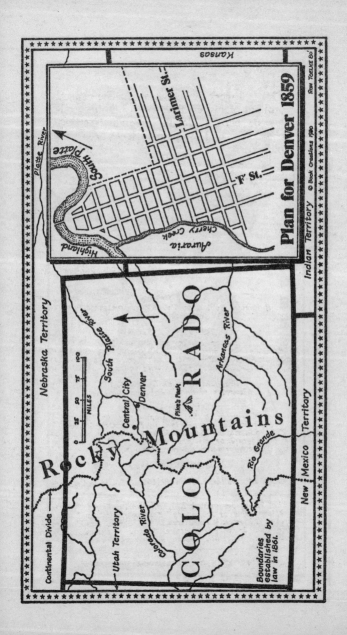

Plan for Denver 1859

Larimer St.

F St.

South Platte

Cherry Creek

Highland

Auraria

Platte River

Kansas

Ron Toelke '80 © Book Creations 1980

Indian Territory

Nebraska Territory

Rocky Mountains

COLORADO

Continental Divide

Utah Territory

Colorado River

South Platte River

Central City

Denver

Pikes Peak

Arkansas River

Rio Grande

New Mexico Territory

Boundaries
established by
law in 1861.

MILES
0   25   50   75   100

Denver in 1860

I

Tracy Foster stood at the bar of one of Sacramento's run-down saloons drinking a whiskey, his gray eyes staring off into space. Although he could have gone to an establishment in a more respectable part of town, he chose this saloon because he felt a kinship with the lonely, dispossessed men here, waiting for their luck to change for the better.

Years earlier people had come to Sacramento from all over the world to make their fortunes in the California gold rush. Once the stopping-off place for tens of thousands of gold seekers, Sacramento was now the state capital of California and a bustling, prosperous city where fortunes were being made in grain, fruit, and vegetables, not in gold.

But not everyone in Sacramento met with success. Some of the prospectors who had come out years ago to the California gold country still remained, occasionally panning for gold but more often spending what little money they had on cheap whiskey in seedy saloons. They lived in flophouses, and they went hungry, dreaming of the time when their luck would change.

Tracy Foster knew, of course, that most of these down-and-outers surrounding him in the saloon would

1

consider him a lucky man. He lived with his brother and sister in a comfortable ranch house in the Valley; he was always assured of a good, home-cooked meal; and his brother and sister were deeply concerned over his well-being. But to Tracy Foster's way of thinking, there was nothing to be thankful for.

Scott and Sarah Rose, his brother and sister, meant nothing to him. Oh, their intentions were good enough, but ever since their mother had died years ago, Tracy felt as if he had no family. What was more, Scott and Sarah Rose were more strict and demanding than parents. They expected him to work on the farm they had inherited, and he either had to toil in the orchard all day or else go into town for supplies. Well, he had done today's errands, and now he was having a drink, whether Scott and Sarah Rose liked it or not.

Suddenly there was a commotion in the corner of the bar. A young, unshaven miner wearing ragged clothes had taken the last of the hard-boiled eggs the saloon served its customers. A somewhat older miner, equally as bedraggled, said the egg belonged to him. Neither man had eaten all day, and each began shouting at the other. Then, the egg forgotten, they began to fight, tumbling onto the floor as they grappled with each other. In the melee, the egg fell to the floor, and a mangy dog that had been waiting for handouts snatched the food in its mouth before anyone could do anything. The miners stopped fighting when they saw this, and they sat up and looked on forlornly as the dog swallowed the egg in one gulp.

At that moment a man burst through the doors of the saloon. He, too, looked as if he hadn't had a good meal in a long time, and his clothes were ragged, but instead of scowling, his face was bright and excited.

"Have you heard the news!" the man exclaimed. "It's in all the papers! Gold has been discovered—a lot of it—in Colorado country!"

Suddenly everyone in the room—including the two miners who had fought over the egg—began talking excitedly. Tracy Foster put down his glass and listened. Men who hadn't eaten in days, who could barely raise themselves off their mattresses on the flophouse floor, were now jumping around the room as if they had just been let out of school. Gold! The magic word. It didn't matter that the gold strikes were in Colorado country, hundreds of miles away over some of the roughest terrain in the United States. They would go to Colorado, and maybe this time their fortunes would change.

Tracy listened intently to the excited talk about going to the new gold country, and he made up his mind. He had only been a boy during the California rush and had never seriously thought about searching for gold himself, but maybe this was what he should be doing. Just watching the unbounded enthusiasm of these miners made him think that here was something to go after, something to live for.

Tracy went over to a group of men who were making plans to set out the next day for Colorado. They didn't seem to notice him as they talked about the supplies they would need—and were willing to beg, borrow, or steal—for their trek. Suddenly Tracy broke into their conversation.

"I've got some money of my own. I'll pay you if you take me with you," he said, his gray eyes focusing on the other men.

"How much you got?" one of the men asked, now interested in the newcomer.

"A little over five dollars." Tracy showed the man some bills and loose change, a portion of which he had taken from the money his sister kept in the cookie jar at home.

"You got yourself a deal," the man said, taking the money from Tracy. "We're leavin' from here first thing tomorrow morning, at dawn. But you're gonna need yourself a horse and food and supplies of your own."

"I'll have them," Tracy said, shaking the man's hand. "And I'll be here at dawn waiting for you."

Left without funds of his own, Tracy knew he was going to have a hard time raising his own grubstake from his stingy brother and sister. Still, he wasn't going to let anything stop him from going to find gold in Colorado.

"Down at the bank just now, I heard that a prospector from Georgia—name of William Green Russell—has found gold in the highlands of the Colorado country, east of the Rockies." Chet Harris, in his mid-thirties and somewhat overweight, fingered the gold nugget that he wore on the gold watch chain spanning his waistcoat. Then, grinning at his partner, he dropped into a chair in their lavish office suite in San Francisco.

"I picked up the same story myself, and the newspapers are already screaming the news," said Wong Ke, slender and bespectacled, more than a decade older than his partner. The Chinese man, who by now had assimilated many of the ways of his adopted country and spoke a nearly perfect English, regarded Chet with his customary seriousness, but he felt the same surge of excitement. It was 1858, eight years since they had made their own fortune in the California gold fields, and in that time they had built a great financial empire. The Wong-Harris firm owned banks, real estate, newspapers, and hotels throughout the growing state of California. It was no wonder that the pair were regarded as the West's most eligible bachelors, even though they had become expert at eluding husband-seekers.

Chet pulled himself to his feet, went to the table of polished mahogany that stood near the windows overlooking San Francisco Bay, and picked up the battered tin sifting pan in which they had first found gold. He held it up to the light, then turned it over slowly. "I wonder if you're thinking what I'm thinking," he said.

"No, Chet!" Ke was emphatic. "Even if we retired today, we couldn't spend our money in our lifetimes, so I'm not going to rush off to Colorado to look for more gold."

Chet's grin broadened, but there was no humor in his eyes. "We both enjoy challenges, Ke," he said. "Our business enterprises here are thriving, and I'm feeling restless. I'm eating too much and putting on weight. You sit around so much doing paperwork that your bones are beginning to creak. Nobody knows more about gold than we do. I think we owe ourselves another taste of adventure."

Wong Ke sighed. "Last year's financial panic has put men out of work all over America," he said. "Fortune hunters from every part of the country will be going to the Colorado country by the tens of thousands. It will be the California gold rush all over again."

"Not for us. We can take security guards with us or hire them after we get there. This time we'll never go hungry, and we can afford the best accommodations—"

"If any are available." Wong Ke shook his head, then smiled faintly. "Unfortunately, I'm as lacking in common sense as you are."

"That's more like it!" Chet returned to his seat, then spoke briskly. "The way I see it, we'll use a different strategy this time. We were lucky in the California rush, but lightning isn't likely to strike again without careful planning. The surface gold is discovered very quickly, but the real pay dirt is found in the ore that needs to be smelted—which is beyond the capacity of the individual gold hunter—"

"Aha!" Ke brightened. "We establish land claims, as many as possible. We buy out individual claims when necessary."

"Exactly. The surface gold is no more than pin money to us now. We set up real mines, each with its smelter, and we'll have no trouble hiring men whose prospecting has failed." Chet hooked his thumbs in his waistcoat pockets. "How does that strike you?"

"Fine." Ke's attitude hardened, too. "The season is too far advanced for you and me to leave for Colorado now, Chet. I have no interest, at my age, in trying to cross the Rocky Mountains with winter coming. What is more, we still have a great number of business matters to settle in California before we leave. We'll send a couple of reliable advance agents ahead, with instructions to buy as much land as they can in the vicinity of the initial strike. Then, perhaps in a year's time, we will be able to set out for Colorado."

"We think alike, as always," Chet said. "By next year we'll have a much better idea where gold is to be found in sufficiently great quantities to make it worth mining. If we can handle this situation as it should be handled, we can double our fortune."

"I don't know why we're doing this—except to prove to ourselves that it can be done," Ke said. Then he laughed aloud and added, "But that's a good enough reason."

Straight rows of fruit trees stood in the Foster orchards in the Sacramento Valley, a testament to the hard work of young Scott Foster and a fitting memorial to the vision of his late father. Even a husky man in his early twenties had physical limitations, and having worked in the fields since dawn, Scott was happy to return to the ranch house at sundown.

He stopped at the well behind the house, pumped a bucketful of water for washing and another for drinking, then carried them through the back door into the kitchen, where oil lamps were already burning and delicious scents came from pots and pans on top of the wood stove.

Sarah Rose Foster, who was stirring the contents of a pan, smiled at her brother. Dark-haired, with blue eyes, she had developed into a beauty since childhood, her figure supple and slender. Her manner was reserved, quiet, and when she did speak, her voice was calm and confident. Ever since the tragic murder of her mother by a pair of outlaws during the lawless era of the California gold rush, she had become the homemaker of the little family, somehow finding the time to complete her own education, then becoming a teacher at the local Valley school.

Scott peered over her shoulder. "Mmm. Your special soup. Also, beefsteak, potatoes, and fried onions."

"With some of our own preserved peaches for dessert," Sarah Rose told him.

He poured water into the scrub-up sink, then vigorously washed his hands and face. "You ought to cook simpler meals when you've spent most of the day teaching."

Her long, shining hair seemed to dance when she shook her head. "You work harder than I do, and you deserve a good supper. Besides, this really is a simple meal. You know I throw all kinds of leftovers into the soup stock pot."

"True enough, but there was no need for you to bake bread. I can smell it."

"I felt like baking," she said, her tone indicating that she would tolerate no argument. "Now just sit down, please."

He drew up a straight-backed chair and seated himself at the kitchen table. "Where's Tracy?" he asked, referring to the brother two years his junior and a year older than Sarah Rose.

She looked at him in surprise. "I assumed he was working in the orchard with you after he got back from Sacramento today."

"He never did come back from his errands." Scott tried without success to conceal his concern.

The young woman made no reply, but she was worried, too. Tracy had become withdrawn after the death of their mother, whose murderers had been gunned down by former Valley sheriff Rick Miller,

but Tracy had continued to be erratically unpredict-
able and had shown no improvement through the
years.

"I wonder how much money he had in his pocket,"
Scott said.

Sarah Rose went to the old, cracked cookie jar that
rested on a corner of the mantel, emptied the contents
onto the kitchen table, then counted the money. "It
appears he took only a dollar and a quarter."

"Damnation!" Scott was annoyed. "That money belongs to all of us, and he has no right to help himself.
For a dollar and a quarter he can buy enough whiskey
to stay drunk for a month!"

She automatically came to Tracy's defense. "Since
we don't know that he's drinking, I see no point in
getting angry now."

Scott tried to calm himself. "You're right, I reckon.
All the same, I feel like beating the tar out of him."

She glanced at him for an instant as she returned to
the stove. "You've done that often enough, but it
hasn't stopped his drinking or made him less lazy. You
know what Rick and Melissa Miller say," she added,
referring to their neighbors, who now operated a
sprawling, prosperous ranch. "There's nothing we can
do to help Tracy or keep him out of trouble. Either
he'll grow up one of these days, or he'll be in trouble
for more years to come. And I prefer to be an optimist."

Her brother scowled. "Maybe Rick isn't as frank
with you as he is with me. After his years in the Texas
Rangers, before he took over as sheriff here, he knows
a bad penny when he sees one, and he's told me
straight out that he's afraid Tracy is moving in that
direction."

"We've fretted over him for years, and it hasn't
done us the least good. All I know for certain is that
I'm not going to wait for him and let supper spoil."
She began to ladle soup into two bowls.

They were almost finished with their first course when the kitchen door opened and Tracy came in. He bore scant resemblance to Scott or Sarah Rose. Taller than his brother and huskier, Tracy had a swarthy complexion and a reddish glint in his hair. His gray eyes, his most arresting feature, were brooding.

Sarah Rose could smell whiskey on his breath but knew that he was not intoxicated.

Scott gave his brother no opportunity to speak. "This is a private house, not a public inn that serves meals at all hours," he said angrily. "You know what time we eat supper."

"I've been busy," Tracy replied airily as he ladled soup into a bowl. "Very busy."

Scott continued to glare at him across the table, but Sarah Rose was intent on keeping the peace. "You sound very mysterious, Tracy," she said.

The younger brother smiled wryly. "Some people spend all their lives with their trees, so they have no idea what's going on in the world."

"Some people earn a living for those who are too lazy to work!" Scott retorted.

Ignoring the rebuke, Tracy calmly began to eat.

"In fact," Scott said, "some people don't even have the common courtesy to wash up before they sit at the table."

"I'll tolerate no fights in this house," Sarah Rose said firmly, "and both of you well know it!"

Not wanting to upset his sister, Scott became silent and concentrated self-consciously on eating his soup.

Tracy's gray eyes were glowing. "The news is all over town," he said. "Everybody in Sacramento is talking about the gold strike in the Colorado country."

Scott was indifferent. "One gold rush was enough to last the rest of my days," he said.

"Me, too." Sarah Rose stood at the stove, keeping watch on the cooking beef. "I was still small when the

fever hit the Sacramento Valley, but I'll never forget
those desperate, hungry men who straggled down the
road day after day."

"You never saw those who found gold," Tracy told
her. "They went off to San Francisco with their rich-
es." Something in his voice caused his brother and
sister to look at him. "I've made up my mind," he went
on. "I'm heading for the Colorado gold fields."

Scott stared harder at him. "You've got to be crazy.
Every out-of-work loafer in America will be going to
the Colorado country, and so will adventurers from all
over the world. There will be chaos just like we knew
here nine years ago."

Sarah Rose was more gentle. "Surely you're not
serious, Tracy. Our orchards earn a solid living."

"I'm not one to work from daybreak until nightfall
six or seven days a week when, with a touch of luck, I
can be rolling in wealth for the rest of my life. Scott
worries when there isn't enough rain or too much rain.
Both of you scurry like ants to put out smudge pots
when there's a cold spell. I'm as good a rifle shot as
there is, and I can ride better than most. I know the
outdoors, and I can look after myself in any company,
no matter how rough." Tracy paused, then added
defiantly, "So I'm going, and nobody is going to stop
me."

"I think you've lost your wits," his brother told
him.

"I'll tell you how serious I am. Give me the gelding
I've been riding. Give me enough cash for spare
ammunition and powder, as well as a grubstake of
flour, beans, and bacon, and I'll be on my way at
dawn tomorrow. I'll sign over my share of this property to the two of you before I go."

His brother was speechless.

"I refuse to rob you of your inheritance, Tracy,"
Sarah Rose said quietly. "As far as I'm concerned, you
can have the gelding, along with whatever money you
need. But your share of this house and the orchards

was left to you by Ma and Pa, and I won't take it from you."

"Neither will I," Scott said gruffly. "But I wish you wouldn't be in such an all-fired hurry. Crossing the Rockies at this time of year won't be easy."

"I won't be going alone," Tracy said. "There's a party of at least twenty leaving tomorrow morning. If I wait, wagon trains from the East will bring immigrants by the thousands to Colorado, and every last square foot of land in the gold fields will be claimed."

Sarah Rose brought the beefsteak to the table, and Scott carved it while she served the potatoes and fried onions.

Tracy held his knife and fork like shovels, and he began to eat as soon as his plate was filled. "I've been waiting a long time for a break like this," he said. "People who do nothing but work get old before their time."

Scott refused to rise to the bait. "I wish you the best of luck," he said, "and no one will be happier than I if you strike it rich."

Sarah Rose ate in silence for a time. She was worried about him, and his lack of stability would continue to nag at her. "Tracy," she said at last, "I hope you'll keep in touch with us."

"You'll not only be the first to know how well I'm doing," he replied, "but I'll save a big nugget, polish it myself, and hang it on a neck chain for you. Then you'll look just like the wives and daughters of those San Francisco millionaires."

His sister and brother knew it would be a waste of breath to tell him he was daydreaming.

When supper was finished, Sarah Rose gave Tracy the better part of the money from the cracked cookie jar, and he went off at once to a nearby general store that stayed open late to buy food for the long journey into the Rocky Mountains wilderness.

Scott dried the dishes as Sarah Rose washed them, and then brother and sister looked at each other uneasily. "Do you feel like taking a walk down the road to the Miller place?" she asked.

"You bet," he replied. They had no relatives, so Rick and Melissa served as family substitutes, and Scott knew his sister required comforting.

Melissa Miller was just putting her two small children to bed when the visitors arrived. "I'll be right back," she said, and added playfully, "You're in luck. I made some wonderful peach pies today, and my husband and children actually left some for company."

"It's almost impossible to resist Melissa's peach pies," the leathery-faced Rick Miller said as he stuffed tobacco into his pipe. "I ate half of one by myself."

Melissa smiled at her husband. "He eats enough for three men, and he's still as lean as he was eight years ago." Then she looked down at her children. "Now, come along, my loves; it's getting late, and it's time you were in bed." Holding their hands, she led her children out of the room. The ravishing, red-haired beauty was still as animated as she had been years earlier as a teenager in Oregon and Texas. She had experienced both hardship and joy in those years, acquiring adoring admirers, as well as suffering the cruelties of ruthless scoundrels. Not until she married Rick Miller did she know complete peace and happiness.

While Melissa put the children to bed and went to the kitchen to get coffee and dessert, Rick Miller remained in the parlor with Sarah Rose and Scott. Sitting in his armchair, slowly drawing on his pipe, he listened reflectively as Scott idly chatted about the prospects of his fruit crop this year. Rick had known the Foster children since they were youngsters, and he knew enough about human nature to realize that Scott and Sarah Rose hadn't come for a visit to talk about fruit crops. They had had a difficult life, losing their mother and, shortly thereafter, their father. Even now that they were grown up, Scott and

Sarah Rose looked up to Rick as they would to their own father, and through the years he had given them the best counsel he could. Now he decided he would ask no questions but rather would wait until Melissa returned and the two Fosters brought up what was really on their minds.

When they were all seated around the dining room table, eating their pie and drinking coffee, Sarah Rose finally spoke up. "I suppose you've heard about the gold strikes in the Colorado highlands," she said.

Rick remembered his grueling days as sheriff during the California rush and his great relief when he retired to devote all his time to ranching. "I thank the Almighty it hasn't happened here again. Once was enough."

"Amen," Melissa said.

"Tracy is leaving for the Colorado country tomorrow morning," Sarah Rose said.

Melissa was not surprised. "During that nightmare period of my life when I was forced to become a dance-hall hostess," she said, "I knew dozens of miners who were just like Tracy. Men with their heads in the clouds, on the verge of starvation, but already mentally spending the money they would never in a million years make in the gold fields."

Rick nodded, puffing on his pipe. "If I have a talk with Tracy, do you reckon I could persuade him not to go?"

Scott shook his head. "He's been bitten hard by the gold bug, Rick. He won't listen to anybody."

"That's too bad."

"Then you disapprove as much as we do," Sarah Rose said.

Rick exchanged a quick glance with his wife.

"Finding gold—and keeping it—require a special inner discipline," Melissa said. "Chet Harris kept his gold because he had a self-disciplined partner. I'm afraid Tracy will need some hard kicks in the teeth before he settles down."

Rick thought it best not to voice his own fears that Tracy was the type who might never learn. "I've seen two frontier civilizations," he said, "first in Texas and then here. And I know the Rockies from my youth, when I was privileged to meet mountain men like Jim Bridger and Kit Carson. Tracy is heading into rugged country. Aside from the usual gold-hunting riffraff, there are Ute Indians who don't like the idea of losing their hunting grounds to greedy white men. I was told just today that the prospectors who made the initial strike come from Georgia, so the presence of Southerners in free-state country is going to be another cause of tensions."

"How I wish we could persuade Tracy to stay home where he belongs," Sarah Rose said.

"You can't stop him, dear," Melissa said. "I know of no feeling more potent or persistent than gold fever."

"Look at it this way," Rick said. "You know, as we do, that Tracy is the kind of lad who has a real knack for getting into trouble. Until now, he's always had you two behind him, ready to haul him back into line. Well, he'll be on his own in Colorado. If he develops the kind of stability you two have, he'll become a far better person."

"But if he doesn't?" Sarah Rose asked.

Rick Miller shrugged, unwilling to put his reply into words.

It was ironic that Major General Winfield Scott, long the Chief of Staff of the United States Army, should live in a house at Fort Zachary Taylor, the headquarters in Washington City named for his late, lifelong rival. Taylor had served in the position to which Scott had aspired, that of President of the nation. Now that Scott was near retirement, his ambition had ebbed somewhat, but those who had served under both officers suspected that the irony continued to rankle.

One who believed it was Brigadier General Leland Blake, who recently had been relieved of his post as commandant of the Presidio in San Francisco and had been given temporary duty in Washington City. The red brick house he had been assigned on the post was comfortable, and the household staff was efficient, but Lee Blake had nevertheless been delighted to learn from General Scott's aide that the President would soon be meeting with him to discuss a new assignment. Having spent the better part of his career in the West, Lee disliked the games of politics that generals had to play in Washington City, and he was looking forward to the possibility of being transferred elsewhere.

Gray-haired and distinguished, Lee now paced up and down the walk outside the house, waiting for his wife and daughter to emerge. Beside him was his aide-de-camp, Second Lieutenant Andrew Jackson Brentwood. A member of the most recent class to be graduated from the United States Military Academy at West Point, Andy was the son of Lee's sister-in-law, Claudia, and her husband, Sam Brentwood, who had become wealthy as the owner of the principal staging depot at Independence, Missouri, where wagon trains for more than two decades had started their long journey to the Pacific. Lee's influence had inspired his nephew to seek an army career, and the young man, now carefully matching his uncle's stride, had been first captain of the corps of cadets in his final year at the academy.

"Andy, has all of Beth's luggage been loaded in the carriage?" Lee asked for the fourth or fifth time.

"Yes, sir," he responded again. As he had been taught informally at West Point, all generals had idiosyncrasies that, because of their exalted rank, had to be respected.

"What in blazes is keeping the ladies?" Lee demanded. "Railroad trains don't wait!"

"No, sir," Andy said diplomatically. He breathed a sigh of relief when the front door of the house opened.

There were flecks of gray in Cathy Blake's blonde hair now, but her chiseled features were unblemished, and her figure, beneath her fur-collared cloak, was still trim. Her daughter, Beth, who followed her, was as lovely as Cathy had been in her younger days, and Andy grinned at his young cousin. She attended Antioch College in Ohio, and he was certain that the campus was littered with the broken hearts of male students.

Beth was a flirt and couldn't resist the temptation to practice her wiles on her cousin.

"Is that the best you can do?" Andy asked her in an undertone as he offered her his arm for the brief walk to the waiting carriage. "I must know a dozen girls who really flutter their eyelashes."

Without halting or even pausing, Beth managed to kick some snow from the side of the walk onto his highly polished cavalry boots. Then she expertly fluttered her lashes at him.

"Just you wait, young lady," he muttered.

Beth was returning to college, and Cathy, despite her daughter's persistent protests that she did not need a chaperon, was accompanying her. Actually Cathy loved any excuse to travel by train. She found it thrilling to think that less than twenty-five years earlier she had traveled for weeks in a wagon to reach Ohio and now she could cover the same distance more comfortably in two days and one night on the railroad.

As Cathy settled back in the carriage she asked, "I don't suppose General Scott's aide dropped any hints regarding our new assignment."

Andy and his uncle exchanged a quick smile. It appeared that even a general's wife failed to understand the unwritten rules of army protocol. "Even if he knows, Aunt Cathy," the young man said, "it would be the worst of indiscretions to say so. An aide who makes just one mistake like that will find himself out in Ute country, in the Rockies, riding on winter cavalry patrols to discourage any Indian hostilities."

They soon arrived at the railroad station, and Cathy and Beth were made comfortable in their private quarters.

"Behave yourself, Beth," Lee said, kissing his daughter. "Depending on where I'm sent, we may not see you again before your summer vacation."

"I'll be good, Papa, and I promise I'll study hard." Then as Andy bade her farewell she grimaced and said, "Tell all your girl friends how much I hate them."

As the two officers walked briskly down the station platform to their waiting carriage, Lee laughed and shook his head. "If you weren't my aide, how would you treat Beth?"

"I'd be strongly inclined, sir, to spank the daylights out of her."

"I tried it when she was younger, without beneficial results."

Andy chuckled, too. "The man who marries Beth will never know a moment's peace. I believe she thinks she's the general in the family, so any officer of a lower rank than a full colonel would have a rough time as her husband."

"I very much doubt that she'll marry an officer. She thinks you and I—and everyone else who wears the uniform—are hopeless romantics. And, frankly, I hope she never sees the nasty side of our profession."

On the drive back to Fort Zachary Taylor, they couldn't resist the temptation to speculate on Lee's forthcoming assignment. "I have enough seniority in rank," he said, "to refuse a post here in Washington City. But, as a Northerner, I believe I'd prefer it to the command of a garrison in the South."

"Do you think there will be a war between the two sections of this country, sir?"

"I don't see how it can be avoided, Andy. General

McClellan and I were talking just the other day, and he feels as I do. The North and the South are drifting farther and farther apart, and President Buchanan seems incapable of pulling them together again. Not that I'm criticizing him for it. I doubt if any President could."

"The slavery question can't be reconciled, I'm afraid."

"The issues go beyond the problems of free states versus slave states," Lee said. "The increasingly industrialized North and the predominantly agricultural South have been developing opposing points of view on every aspect of what constitutes our society. But I can't view the problem in philosophical terms. I dread the thought of going to war against academy classmates, lifelong friends, and I'm sure you feel the same way."

His nephew nodded somberly. "It's a nightmare, and it appears that hotheads in both sections of the country may make it come true."

"All we can do is hope for the best and get ready for the worst," Lee said.

When they reached home, they found that General Blake's summons to the White House had arrived. Andy hastily called the carriage driver back to the door, then rode with his uncle. He waited in an anteroom when Lee was conducted to the President's unpretentiously furnished private office.

Throughout James Buchanan's long career as a senator from Pennsylvania, envoy to Great Britain, and secretary of state, he had been a dapper, debonair bachelor, but the almost unbearable strains of being President in a time of mounting crisis were taking their toll. He looked tired and haggard, old beyond his years, and his smile of greeting was wan as he shook his visitor's hand, then motioned him to a chair.

"I must apologize for keeping you waiting these

past weeks, General Blake," he said, "but I've been trying to cope with emergencies that never seem to end."

Lee wondered why any man would want to be President when he faced insoluble problems.

Buchanan wasted no time. "You appear to be uniquely qualified for a highly specialized assignment, General," he said. "You've had experience as a combat commander and as an intelligence officer. As a member of the first wagon train to Oregon and then as commandant of our first garrison there, you came to know wilderness living. Finally, at the Presidio in San Francisco, you had more than ample experience with boom-town conditions during the great gold rush.

"As you know, another gold rush is now under way in the Colorado country," Buchanan continued. "And the situation is complex. Part of the area is under the jurisdiction of the Kansas Territory, at least theoretically, which places it in the free-state category. But the first gold was found in the wilderness claimed by no state or territory, and the prospectors were Southerners from Georgia. According to private reports I've received, the odds favor the finding of considerable quantities of additional gold in the next year."

"I see, sir."

"This raises two problems of paramount importance," Buchanan declared. "First, the entire Colorado country must be made secure for the Union. Equally urgent is the government's need—my need—to learn how much gold is available in Colorado. I'm doing my best to avert a war between the states, but if I don't succeed, that gold will be of great value in helping the federal government finance the struggle that lies ahead. Provided there's enough of it. I must have an estimate of the quantity and quality of Colorado gold."

"I hope you realize I'm no geologist, Mr. President," Lee said.

"I'll come to that," Buchanan replied. "General, I'm hoping you'll volunteer for the assignment I have in mind. I'd be reluctant to order you to take it."

Lee leaned forward in his chair, listening intently.

"The wilderness out there is already swarming with prospectors. I'm confident that in the next year enough new lodes will have been discovered to allow a true assessment of the mineral wealth. I'd very much like you to lead a party to Colorado, General, presenting yourself as a retired army officer who may be interested in making substantial investments in gold mines. New towns are already springing up out there, so within a year's time, I daresay, decent, comfortable living quarters should be available. I mention that fact because it would be helpful in maintaining your pose if Mrs. Blake could accompany you. She also would be a volunteer, naturally."

"I have little doubt that she'd enjoy it, Mr. President."

Buchanan chuckled. "So I've gathered. Mrs. Blake appears to be a most unusual lady. You have an aide-de-camp, I presume?"

"Yes, sir."

"Take him with you. He'll wear civilian clothes, as you will, and select any other army personnel you might want to offer protection to you and the others in the party, particularly the ladies."

"Ladies, Mr. President?"

"The real purpose of your mission must be concealed from Southerners, General, and the presence of ladies in your party will help disarm the suspicious. We'll send a lawyer with you, of course. And the key member of your staff is a gentleman who has been selected with great care. Luke Brandon will pose as an investment banker from New York, but in actuality he is an expert mineralogist. I've been assured no one in the United States has better qualifications in the field. He and his wife, who is looking forward to making the journey with him, I'm told, have just arrived in Washington City, and if you accept the assignment, they'll call on you in the next day or two."

Lee did not look forward to the difficult, complicated task that had been outlined for him, but it was impossible, as a high-ranking army officer, to turn down a request from his Commander in Chief. "Of course I accept, Mr. President," he said.

James Buchanan's smile demonstrated a trace of the verve that had so long been one of his principal traits. "Splendid! I'll offer you a choice of transportation, General. You can go by one of the navy's new steamships to Panama, cross the Isthmus by the new railroad there, and then sail in another navy steamship to San Francisco, where we'll offer you a convoy from California to Colorado. Or you can go as far as Chicago by train, and then go by wagon to the Colorado highlands. Either way, I'm informed, will take you between one and two months—a fraction of the time you spent on your first wagon train crossing of the continent."

Lee smiled, too. "America shrinks as we expand, Mr. President. If I may, I'll discuss the journey with Mrs. Blake when she returns immediately after the New Year."

"There's no rush, General. You don't want to reach Colorado until the miners have fanned out and done more exploring. Now, do you have any suggestions about the plan I've outlined to you?"

"Only one, Mr. President. Unless you have an attorney in mind with special qualifications, I know an exceptional young man in California I'd like to have on my staff." He was thinking of Isaiah Atkins, an orphaned New Yorker who years ago had become the ward of his good friend, Ralph Hamilton. "His adopted father is the Chief Justice of the California Supreme Court."

"Engage him, by all means," the President said. "Luke Brandon is my only personal selection, and I

want him in your party only because I'm familiar with
his standing as a mineralogist."

After the conference came to an end, Lee rejoined
his aide and, on the drive back to Fort Zachary
Taylor, told him what the future held in store for
them.

Andy Brentwood grinned. "When my parents
learned that you had requested me as your aide, sir,
they said I'd have the most unusual job of any lieutenant in the army, and blamed if they didn't hit the
nail on the head. The assignment sounds exciting."

"We'll find out," Lee said cautiously. "Presidents
have a way of making complicated work sound simple. It wouldn't surprise me in the least if we have
some headaches in store."

The first complication arose that same evening. Lee
had invited his aide to join him for supper, and
afterward, they sat studying War Department maps of
the Colorado country. They were working in silence
in front of a blazing fire, both scribbling notes, when
they were interrupted by Cathy's attractive young
maid, Patricia, a freeborn black woman.

"General," she said, "a Mr. and Mrs. Brandon are
here to see you. They didn't say it in so many words,
but they acted as though you were expecting them."

"So I was, but not quite so soon," the surprised Lee
replied. "Please show them in, Patricia."

"Shall I clear out, sir?" Andy asked.

"Certainly not," his uncle answered. "You may as
well become acquainted with them, too."

Luke Brandon was a bluff, hearty man in his forties,
balding and bespectacled, whose well-pressed worsted suit and polished shoes would make it easy for
him to pose as an investment banker. But both Lee
and Andy were surprised by the appearance of his
wife.

Caroline Brandon could have passed as her husband's daughter. Her straight, wheat-colored hair
seemed to flow down her back, her huge green eyes

were rimmed with kohl and further accented by a pale green powder on her lids, and her pouting mouth was emphasized by scarlet lip rouge. When Andy took her coat, she was revealed in a snug-fitting silk dress with a low-cut neckline that did justice to her full but slender figure.

The young lieutenant felt uneasy as he took the visitors' coats. The far more urbane Lee greeted the couple cordially and asked if they would like refreshments.

"On a night as chilly as this, I wouldn't mind a cup of tea or coffee, General, if it's already made," Luke said.

"You'll turn into tea or coffee if you aren't careful," his wife told him, then favored Lee with a dazzling smile. "If you'll join me, General, I wouldn't object to a small glass of brandywine."

Lee had little liking for strong drink but graciously agreed, and Andy went off to tell Patricia what the guests were having.

The mineralogist caught sight of the maps as he seated himself near the fire. "Ah, you're doing your homework already, General," he said.

"Luke has been living with his maps and charts of Colorado ever since he agreed to accept President Buchanan's offer," Caroline Brandon said.

Lee couldn't decide whether he detected a hint of scorn in what appeared to be intended as good-natured raillery. "Do you think it likely that more gold will be found there, Mr. Brandon?"

"In my opinion it seems inevitable." The mineralogist picked up a map.

Andy, who came back into the room, followed by Patricia with a tray of refreshments, looked over the man's shoulder.

"Right here is where the Georgians found gold," Luke said. "On the high plateau, approximately a mile above sea level, very close to the place where a little stream called Cherry Creek flows into the South Platte

River. Other surface gold has been found in the immediate area, but I believe the most fertile ground lies farther to the west, in the rugged country on the near side of the range that extends from Longs Peak to Pikes Peak. Surface gold in such areas is merely a hint of what lies below the ground. If gold is discovered here and there, as I believe it will be, there will be far more in the ore beneath the surface. It wouldn't surprise me if silver is found there, too."

"How will we know what's there?" Lee asked.

"The prospectors will do our work for us, principally in the gullies, canyons, and small streams, General. By the time we arrive out there, the larger companies will have bought out the claims of disappointed speculators and will be digging deeper. Confidentially, I anticipate a bonanza."

"Here's to bonanzas," Caroline Brandon said, raising her glass. "I just wish that Luke would use his knowledge to establish a claim or two of our own. I wouldn't mind being filthy rich. I'd wear diamond bracelets from my wrists to my elbows."

No one joined in her deep-throated laugh, and her husband looked embarrassed.

"The gold in California and Oregon has been petering out in the past ten years," he said. "But I don't think that will happen in Colorado. New methods of crushing rock and smelting ore have been developed, and I'm inclined to believe they'll be put to good use in Colorado."

"I'd guess we're going to face some interesting challenges," Lee said.

"It appears that way," the mineralogist replied, smiling.

Caroline looked hard at Lee, her lips parted provocatively. "Here's to challenges," she said, again lifting her glass.

It was impossible for him to pretend he didn't understand her meaning. She was a guest in his house, to be sure, so he didn't want to be rude to her, but he made his attitude plain by refraining from raising his own glass in return.

The men went on with their conversation. Luke Brandon described in graphic detail the rough terrain between the Cherry Creek site and the snow-capped peaks, many of them towering above fourteen thousand feet, that lay to the west. Lee asked most of the questions, and although Andy took little active part in the conversation, he was an avid listener.

At the same time, however, he could not help noticing that Caroline Brandon concentrated her full attention on Lee. She frequently shifted her position as she directed her burning gaze at Lee, making certain he remained aware of her nearness. When Andy refilled her glass, she merely rewarded him with an absent nod of thanks.

After an hour and a half, Luke suddenly stopped and looked at his pocket watch. "Give me half a chance," he said, "and you'd think I was delivering a classroom lecture."

"You teach, Mr. Brandon?"

"Yes, at Harvard." He stood up. "I'll give you my address in Cambridge, General. Just give us a couple of weeks' notice, and we'll be ready to leave."

"I'll do better than that," Lee said. "When Mrs. Blake comes home next week, she'll write in detail to Mrs. Brandon about the kinds of clothing and equipment that will be needed in Colorado."

Caroline smiled her thanks, and when Andy went to fetch the visitors' coats, she moved close to Lee, her body grazing his. "I'm ever so much obliged to you, General," she said, "and I'm looking forward to our next meeting."

Andy approached and placed her cloak over her shoulders, making it possible for his uncle to take a discreet backward step.

After the guests had departed, the General and his

aide returned to the sitting room, and Lee dropped heavily into his chair. "Whew!" he exclaimed.

"I don't believe in hitting a woman," Andy said, "but if she were my wife I'd either beat her or walk out on her. Why do you suppose an intelligent man like Luke Brandon stands for that kind of conduct?"

Lee shrugged. "Very often, when a mature man marries a much younger, beautiful woman, he's inclined to be tolerant of her behavior."

His nephew's smile was pained. "You weren't joking, sir, when you said this assignment is going to be complicated. I'm glad Aunt Cathy wasn't here to see that exhibition."

"Never fear," Lee said. "Cathy can handle women like that. Either Caroline Brandon will change her ways fast or some very fancy fireworks are going to explode."

Wade Fulton, the publisher and owner of the Sacramento *Sun*, stood at the window of his office, turned away from the familiar view, and sighed. His long crusades on behalf of good government and law and order had been successful. Sacramento was established as the state's capital, Chief Justice Hamilton and his colleagues on the bench had brought the lawless elements under control, and it was time to move on.

Emptying the personal contents of his desk into a small sack, Fulton looked around the room, then left the building and walked briskly across the street to the modest house he occupied with his daughter. His news would be a wrench for Susanna, who worked for him as an editor and reporter.

He couldn't help feeling sorry for her. She was so bright, so lovely with her auburn hair and violet eyes, so courageous. How different her life would have been had her mother not died in childbirth; instead, Susanna was trapped in the web created by a father whose high principles gave him no rest, whose beliefs that American society be civilized and that the ideals expressed by the nation's founding fathers be the goal of all citizens drove him incessantly.

He opened the front door and found Susanna, wearing a boy's shirt and trousers, busily removing books from wall shelves, dusting them, and placing them in boxes.

She looked up from her labors, her snub nose wrinkling and the freckles on her face joining when she smiled broadly at him. "Well, Wade?" she demanded. She had called him by his first name ever since she had been a little girl.

"The deed is done," he said. "The *Sun* has been sold for five thousand dollars cash, one used Conestoga wagon, and a team of four workhorses."

"Congratulations to both of us," she said. "I guess."

Fulton suddenly felt miserable. "I'm sorry, Sue."

Susanna continued to smile steadily. "Don't apologize, Wade," she said. "The eight years we've spent here is the longest we've ever lived anywhere. I'm sure we'll like Colorado, and I'm looking forward to starting a new paper there. And judging from the number of people heading that way just from the Pacific, we'll even be able to start with a daily."

"Could be," her father said, relieved that she was accepting the news with such good humor. "What luck have you had?"

"You may not believe this," she told him, rising and perching, elflike, on top of a pile of cartons, "but you timed the sale of the *Sun* perfectly. If you're free to leave by the day after tomorrow—"

"We're free right this minute."

"Then we'll have plenty of time to finish packing. A wagon train of about a hundred and fifty people is starting out in about thirty-six hours. I had a good, long chat with the wagon master, and he's certain

the snows have melted enough in the passes by now
for us to get there. He's made the run any number of
times."

"Trust a good reporter to get all the facts." Wade
found his pipe after patting several pockets, filled it,
lit it, and leaned against the wall. "What did you find
out about our comrades on the journey?"

"Oh, most of them are gold bugs, Wade. I saw some
who looked as though they've been subsisting on odd
jobs in California since the big gold hunt here and are
ready to try their luck again."

"Any other ladies in the company?"

Susanna giggled. "I saw the female occupants of
two wagons, but even if I were being charitable, I
wouldn't call them ladies. I suspect that some of the
saloons and dance halls hereabouts will be in the
market for new hired help. Shady ladies always go
where the money flies fastest."

"Maybe," her father said, "you ought to stay behind
here until I get settled. I subjected you to frontier
conditions when we came here, but you were just a
youngster then. Now you're an exceptionally good-
looking young woman, and you might have to cope
with too much in a land of barbarians."

"Put this in your pipe and smoke it," Susanna said
sweetly. "Under no circumstances will I permit an
absent-minded, addlepated publisher to go off to that
land of barbarians alone. You're a first-rate publisher,
Wade. In a class with old William Cullen Bryant and
Horace Greeley in New York. But you can't drive a
nail into a board, and you wouldn't know how to
scramble an egg or fry a steak."

"How do you suppose I managed before you grew
up?" he demanded.

She remained calm. "We can while away the hours
on the road as I regale you with tales of your disas-
ters. One after another. If you're going to the Colorado country, so am I. And that's that."

He accepted her decision as final, and sighed.

"Now let's be practical," Susanna said. "Were the spare presses and sets of type included in your sale?"

Her father brightened. "No. They'll go with us, even though there won't be much room for furniture and things like that after we pack the presses and books."

"Furniture can be bought or made, and neither of us has ever cared much about fancy clothes. But I'll have to put in supplies of food tomorrow. The wagon master made it plain that we'll be expected to carry our own."

"Fair enough."

"You haven't mentioned newsprint."

Wade shook his head. "We'd need a second wagon just to carry the paper. I'll send off a letter to our supplier in Chicago, and he can ship a load to us by wagon freight. Don't forget that the money I've been paid for the *Sun* makes us really solvent."

"For the very first time in my life," Susanna said. "I'll take charge of the nest egg, if you don't mind, so it isn't frittered away."

He reached into an inner pocket and handed her a bank draft. "I pity the man you'll marry. Everything he does will be subject to the approval of a higher authority."

"Not if he publishes a newspaper," his daughter replied. "I happen to be the daughter of a genius, and I never question any publishing decision he makes."

He nodded, acknowledging the fact that she never interfered in matters of his professional judgment. He didn't regard himself as a genius, to be sure, but he had no intention of arguing about trifles.

Susanna changed the subject diplomatically. "Would you like to know our route of march?"

"Of course."

"The wagon master says we'll follow the Carson River route, south of Lake Tahoe. He anticipates no troubles in the Nevada country, and he showed me on a chart the trail he'll take across the Continental Divide."

"How soon will we reach the site?"

The young woman shrugged. "I didn't ask, Wade. All I know is that we'll be making our way across territory where snows are still melting, where there are rock slides, and where local Indian tribes may become ugly when they see so many outsiders invading their hunting grounds. Whenever we reach Colorado, I'll be satisfied."

"So will I." It was a relief to tell himself that he had spent years preparing Susanna for this new move. Not only was she resilient, but in an emergency she could handle firearms with the skill of any male sharpshooter. It was unlikely, in a large party, that she would be required to demonstrate her talents with her rifle or pistol, but it was a comfort to know that, if necessary, she could take care of herself.

"What will you call the new newspaper, Wade?"

"I hadn't thought about it."

"Start thinking, then!" she commanded.

She was so tiny that her earnest ferocity struck him as amusing, and he laughed.

"What's so funny?" She realized there were times when she didn't understand him as well as she sometimes thought.

"I've decided to give you the privilege of naming the new paper," he said.

Susanna stared at him, her eyes shining. Some young women in their early twenties would have preferred gold or jewels, a great mansion in which to live, or a carriage pulled by a matched team of spirited bays. But her father had just given her the most precious of gifts, and she was overwhelmed.

Jumping to the floor from the cartons of books, she ran to him and embraced him. "Wade," she said, "you're the most wonderful father in the world! Between here and Colorado I'll come up with the right name for our very last newspaper, the one that will bring you the renown you deserve!"

II

The Georgians established a small town on the south-west side of Cherry Creek, calling it Auraria, and their undisguised hostility toward prospectors from the North forced the latter to form their own community on the northeast side of the creek, under authority from officials of the Kansas Territory. They called this rapidly growing town St. Charles.

In May 1859, after gold hunters had found few traces of the precious metal in the vicinity of either community, a party led by John H. Gregory made a major strike in what would be known as Gregory Gulch on a small stream called Clear Creek, less than thirty miles west of St. Charles.

The news created national and international sensations equal to those of the great California gold rush a decade earlier. Men from the cities and farms of the Eastern Seaboard and the Middle West who had been unemployed since the financial panic of 1857 joined wagon trains heading toward the new El Dorado. Most of the early arrivals—the fifty-niners, as they were called—were those who made the far shorter journey from California and Oregon. Relatively few Southerners took part in the new gold rush, so Auraria grew slowly. But the population of St. Charles doubled almost daily, and by early summer it had a population of thousands.

Some of the new arrivals elected to live closer to the gold fields that lay to the west. Central City was founded near Gregory Gulch, and a dozen other little towns soon sprang into being. St. Charles remained the principal mecca because of its convenient location, and the huts of the first arrivals soon were replaced by more solid structures. Wood was scarce, so most buildings were made of stone, and several enterprising young men opened brick factories.

St. Charles grew at a dizzy pace, and in almost no time the community boasted saloons, gambling establishments, and more bordellos than such civic leaders as retired Brigadier General William Larimer, Jr., of the army, Samuel Curtis, and James S. Lowry cared to count. Rooming houses and hotels, restaurants and inns came into being as though by magic. Soon there were two hospitals, and because about one-third of the new arrivals were women, churches were built, dedicated, and holding worship services by midsummer. Before long, there would be schools and law courts, a headquarters for the constabulary, another for the fire department, and a jail. General Larimer and his friends made a valiant try at reserving a number of areas for public parks, but the pressures exerted by newcomers seeking housing soon defeated these efforts.

The absence of local authority constituted a problem that was difficult to overcome. Kansas Territory lay far to the east and appointed no judges. Volunteers were asked to serve in the constabulary, but few sought such unpopular work, and at least ten or fifteen men were wounded in nightly gunfights. The situation threatened to become chaotic, so the town dwellers, including the bakers, butchers, tailors, and the proprietors of hotels, inns, restaurants, and saloons

formed their own law courts, hastily appointing the
literate as judges. The miners, not to be outdone,
formed their own summary courts.

In an effort to win aid from Kansas, General Larimer and his associates changed the name of St.
Charles to Denver, naming it for James W. Denver,
the territorial governor of Kansas. Another year would
pass before Auraria was incorporated into the still-
mushrooming city.

Wade Fulton and his daughter, Susanna, had ar-
rrived by wagon train early in the summer and had
hired miners and prospectors who were down on their
luck to build a handsome, two-story stone building
that served as the offices of their newspaper, the
Denver *Tribune*, and as their home. Nearby was the
impressive new city hall, as yet unoccupied because no
local elections had been organized. A short distance
away, on Larimer Street, stood the mammoth Apollo
Hall; on its ground floor were a restaurant, a saloon,
and a gambling hall, and upstairs there was a large
theater. Traveling companies of actors occasionally
presented plays by Shakespeare and other classics
there, but the acoustics were far from perfect. In fact,
so much noise rose through the floorboards from the
saloon and gambling hall that the actors had to shout
at the tops of their voices to make themselves heard.

Denver stood a mile above sea level, and the rainfall was slight, which was helpful to Tracy Foster and
others who were homeless, for it made it easier for
them to sleep in the open during the warm weather.
But the location of the rapidly expanding city was far
from perfect, and the site had its drawbacks. Chief
among them was its distance from the established
travel routes between East and West. All supplies,
from food and medicine to lumber and hardware, had
to be transported there by twenty-mule-team wagons
traveling in trains and guarded by outriders to ward
off hostile Indian attacks. Deliveries of the necessities

of life were erratic until W. H. Russell, one of the
nation's leading freighters, established the headquarters of a new firm, the Central Overland California
and Pikes Peak Express Company, in Denver.

"Right now we're the far end of the earth," said
Prudence Adams, a middle-aged New Englander who
had been en route to California with several wagon-
loads of merchandise and decided to settle in Denver
instead. "But all that will change. This town is here to
stay!"

Prudence stood in the dirt road, keeping a sharp
watch on the construction of the two-story stone
building that would house her general store on the
ground floor and her living quarters above it. No
detail of work being done by a crew of luckless,
unemployed miners escaped her attention, and suddenly she sucked in her breath. "Ezekiel," she said, "I
do believe that tall man yonder is stealing a hammer."

Ezekiel, a broad-shouldered black giant, was an
escaped slave whom Prudence Adams had befriended
while pausing at Independence, Missouri, on her
westward journey. Her only permanent employee, he
was supervising the building of the structure, sometimes pitching in when his brawn was needed. He had
already noted the attempted theft and moved forward
with a speed and agility unusual in a man of his
size.

"You!" he said, grasping the tall miner by the collar
of his faded shirt. "You take something not belong to
you."

Tracy Foster was annoyed at having been caught
and resented the black man's grasp. "Get your hands
off me!"

Ezekiel's hold tightened. "You make big mistake.
Give back hammer."

"Who says I took a hammer?" Tracy blustered.

Suddenly a long, razor-sharp butcher's knife appeared in Ezekiel's massive hand. He made no further

comment as he brandished it under the young Californian's nose, but his expression indicated that he had every intention of using it.

Prudence decided to intervene. Other workers had stopped to watch, and she called to them as she moved forward. "Go on about your business!"

Her tone permitted no argument, and all were aware of the menacing presence of the knife-wielding man, so they picked up their trowels again, and some began to move heavy stones into place.

"Young man," the woman said sharply, "much as you need your whiskers removed, I don't rightly believe you want Ezekiel to shave you. So return my property to him this instant."

His expression surly, Tracy reached inside his shirt and handed Ezekiel the hammer.

The giant's manner changed instantly. His knife vanished, he released his grip, and his smile actually was amiable.

"That's better," Prudence said, her attitude still stern and uncompromising. "Now, why on earth would anybody in his right mind be foolish enough to take a hammer?"

Tracy was too weary and dispirited to explain that he was desperate. He was the only survivor of a party that had suffered endless agonies crossing the Sierra Nevadas and the Rockies, and only his will to live had enabled him to reach Colorado. Then he had plunged headlong into yet another nightmare. For months his prospecting had been fruitless as he had ranged through the rugged mountains west of Denver. Others panning for gold in icy streams had found nuggets and dust, but his pan always had been empty. Now he had been reduced to taking odd jobs wherever he could find them, augmenting his meager wages by stealing small objects whenever he had the opportunity. At present, he was one of the crew working for Prudence Adams.

"I—I'm hungry," he said at last, his voice surly as he stared down at the ground.

She studied him for a long moment, her eyes still hard, and all at once she softened. "Ezekiel," she said, "bring him some meat and bread."

Her helper hesitated, unwilling to reward someone who had tried to steal, but her word was law. "Yes, Miss Prue," he said, then went quickly to the wagons that stood at the rear of the property, behind the partly constructed building.

Certainly it was true that Tracy was hungry. He ate ravenously, scarcely pausing to chew his bread and meat.

Prudence watched him. "There," she said. "That should give you the energy to do a decent day's work. We'll say no more about this matter, and tonight you'll get a full day's pay."

Tracy mumbled his thanks, then returned to his labors. He was grateful for the woman's unexpected kindness and would not try to steal from her again, but his despair remained. Like so many others who had come to Colorado with high hopes—and who were still pouring into Denver by the thousands—he knew he had no real future here. Gold seekers were everywhere in the land of steep slopes, swift-running creeks, and deep gorges. As he had already learned, his chances of making a strike were virtually non-existent.

A very few sites were being purchased by men who were hiring others to dig below the earth's crust on their behalf, but Tracy had spent only two days on such a job. Digging tunnels and shoring them up with timbers was back-breaking work, and when gold was actually discovered, which happened infrequently, the owners of the mine took most of it. Others might be willing to take the risk of earning a pittance in return for such exhausting labor, but Tracy Foster was not one of them.

His pride would not permit him to return to California and admit to his brother and sister that he had failed. So he was condemning himself to remain here and, somehow, get his hands on enough money to buy food, obtain comfortable lodgings, and replenish his ragged wardrobe. Again and again he had been tempted to sell his gelding and his rifle, but they were his only assets, so he clung to them. Sooner or later his luck would change.

At the end of his day's work for Prudence Adams, he took his pay from a glowering Ezekiel, picked up his rifle, and slowly made his way to the corral where he had left his horse. As he rode past a large, noisy establishment, a sign over the entrance identifying it as De Berg's Palace, Tracy realized he was hungry again, and thirsty. On sudden impulse, he left his horse in the Palace's corral and went inside.

After buying a large schooner of beer for a nickel, Tracy wandered aimlessly through the establishment, fascinated by the heavily made-up young women wearing revealing, strapless, corsetlike garments and black net stockings who perched on the arms of chairs occupied by men playing cards at a half-dozen tables.

A burly, dark-haired man with a bristling mustache approached Tracy and clapped him on the shoulder, smiling jovially, although his dark eyes were rock-hard. "Let Willie de Berg treat you to a shot of whiskey, friend," he said.

Tracy was startled by the unexpected hospitality. "That's right nice of you, Mr. de Berg."

"My pleasure." De Berg signaled to one of the scantily clad women, who promptly brought the young patron a small glass of whiskey.

Tracy raised it in salute, then downed it.

"Try your hand at poker, friend," the still-smiling de Berg said, "and maybe Helen here will bring you luck."

"My name's Betty," the woman said to de Berg

sullenly, then immediately led Tracy to an empty place at one of the tables.

Before the young man quite realized what he was doing, he exchanged the two dollars in his pocket for a pile of chips. This was his eating money, but he was conscious of the woman's strong perfume and of her body as she sat on the arm of his chair; they destroyed his judgment. A reckless mood overcame him, and he decided he would gamble every penny. His luck recently couldn't have been worse, and just this once it might improve.

Poker hand by poker hand, Tracy lost consistently. Almost miraculously, however, each time his chips were almost depleted, he won a small amount, and this encouraged him to continue. Ultimately the inevitable happened, and the dealer scooped up the last of his chips.

"Buy another stack," the woman suggested, leaning hard against him.

"I wish I could," Tracy replied, "but I'm cleaned out."

"No more money?" she asked, drawing back and standing.

"No more money," he replied, but by that time she had gone.

Berating himself for his stupidity, Tracy walked out of Willie de Berg's gambling hall, collecting his rifle from the attendant. The night was young, but his pockets were still empty, and even though he was famished, he would need to put in another day of hard work before he could earn enough money to buy himself a meal.

Thinking over the hands he'd played, it suddenly occurred to Tracy that he had most likely been cheated. Somehow, the dealer had seemed to know precisely what cards he had held, hand by hand. All at once Tracy understood. The overly friendly young woman seated on the arm of his chair had probably signaled his cards to the dealer. "Foster," he told himself angrily, "you're a goddamn fool."

His hunger deepening his despair, he made his way slowly toward the corral, carefully avoiding the other saloons and gambling halls. The mere scent of food, he knew, would be too much for him. He remembered the wonderful meals Sarah Rose had cooked back home.

The principal thoroughfares were crowded, but the side streets were virtually deserted, and the young Californian welcomed the solitude. As he drew closer to the corral, he saw someone coming toward him, weaving unsteadily, and he knew the approaching figure was drunk.

Suddenly, without thinking about it, Tracy raised his rifle and pointed it at the man's chest.

The drunken miner halted, blinking at him.

"I'll take your money," Tracy said harshly. "Hand it over, with no tricks, and you won't get hurt."

The man began to curse, but the muzzle of the rifle jabbed him in the pit of the stomach.

"I don't take kindly to abuse," Tracy said. "Give me the money and be quick, or you'll be blown to kingdom come!"

"Hey, now," the miner said thickly. "I just got paid for two weeks o' breakin' my tail!" Instinctively he reached toward his shirt pocket to protect his funds.

Reacting swiftly, Tracy reversed his rifle. Using the butt as a club, he struck the miner a sharp blow across the side of the head. The man fell to the ground, groggy and helpless, but still conscious.

Reaching into the pocket, Tracy snatched a wad of bills, then took to his heels, racing around a corner and running hard until he reached the corral.

Not until Tracy rode to the outskirts of the town did he halt, then count the money he still held in his hand. He found himself in possession of forty dollars, a small fortune, more money than he had seen at any one time since he had left California.

"We eat tonight," he told the gelding in a hoarse voice. "A pail of genuine oats instead of grass for you, and a beefsteak for me!"

The miner, he reflected, had been too drunk to identify him. Besides, Denver didn't yet boast a constabulary. Highly pleased with himself, Tracy knew he had found a new, easy way to make his living. Circumstances had forced him to become a robber, but his conscience didn't bother him, and he promised himself that never again would he go hungry. He had found his career.

In a few days her store would be open for business, and Prudence Adams looked at her new building with a sense of pleasure, then transferred her gaze to the men who were cutting shelves of cedar under Ezekiel's supervision, the fine timber having been brought down from the mountains at great expense. Her own apartment on the second floor was completed, and she had moved into it the previous day. By tonight Ezekiel's quarters at the rear of the ground floor would be done, too.

Someone was approaching slowly down the street, and Prudence Adams stiffened. The woman was in her mid-thirties, still pretty enough, with brown hair and eyes, her gait confident. She actually carried a gold-handled walking stick, and Prudence disapproved of such showing off, just as she disliked the woman's use of cosmetics, even though they had been applied with deft discretion.

To Prudence's amazement the woman came directly up to her and spoke. "Miss Adams?"

The older woman nodded stiffly.

"I'm Clara Lou Hadley, your new neighbor down the street, or I will be after my building is done."

Prudence was unyielding. "What can I do for you, Miss Hadley?"

"*Mrs.* Hadley. I hope you won't think I'm presumptuous, and I realize you haven't opened your store yet, but there's a shortage of saws and kegs of nails in town at present, and I'd very much like to buy some supplies from you."

Prudence hesitated.

"I'm well able to pay," Clara Lou Hadley said, reaching into her commodious handbag.

Prudence noticed a large diamond ring sparkling on the woman's little finger. Still stalling, she said, "I've noted that your entire building is made of wood. A mite expensive when stone is so plentiful hereabouts."

"I think wood provides a warmer, more homelike atmosphere for my customers."

The older woman made up her mind. "I'm sorry, Mrs. Hadley. I'll sell to most people, but I won't lift a finger to help anyone who operates a—a house of assignation."

Clara Lou Hadley's clear soprano laugh attracted the attention of the workmen, who stared at her. "So that's what you think I'm building. I should have known. You may rest easy, Miss Adams. I intend to open a gambling hall. A clean, honest place, where a man can buy a drink or eat a good meal at reasonable prices. But I assure you that no prostitute will be allowed on the premises."

"Not that it's any of my business, Mrs. Hadley, but how do you expect to earn a living in a place that doesn't have half-naked young women running around?" Prudence asked, scrutinizing her.

"I did it in California, and I'll do it here," Clara Lou said. "When the men learn they won't be cheated at my gaming tables, I'll soon be turning away customers."

"You can truly earn a living in an honest gaming house?"

"Indeed." A dimple appeared in Clara Lou's cheek when she smiled. "The people who operate saloons and brothels in conjunction with gambling houses are greedy, and they give the rest of us a bad name. I'll let you in on a little-known secret of the trade, Miss Adams. Every now and again a customer enjoys a lucky streak, but the odds at a gaming table, no matter what the game, always favor the house. So I never mind paying off a lucky winner. He brags to his friends, and the very next night they show up—and lose far more to me than he has won."

Prudence changed her mind, and called, "Ezekiel!"

Thinking Prudence was in trouble, he drew his butcher knife as he approached.

"Ezekiel, go to Mrs. Hadley's foreman down the street and find out his needs. I can spare a dozen saws and two or three kegs of nails."

Ezekiel hurried off down the dirt road with the speed and grace of a panther.

"You can settle with me later, Mrs. Hadley." The statement was as close as Prudence could come to offering an apology.

"I'm obliged to you, Miss Adams! I'm using a double crew because I want to open for business as soon as I can. And when my own quarters are ready, you must join me for supper there."

"I think I'd like that," Prudence said. "But I must warn you—I never gamble."

"Neither do I, Miss Adams," the younger woman said, laughing. "I know the odds too well, so I take as few risks as I can." Clara Lou raised her walking stick in salute, then strolled back to her own construction site.

A dark man with a mustache, wearing a broad-brimmed hat and a scarlet and yellow waistcoat beneath his swallow-tailed coat, stood nearby, watching Clara Lou Hadley's crew at work. He seemed unaware of the woman's approach, but as she drew close he said, "Mrs. Hadley, I'm Willie de Berg."

"How do," she replied formally.

"I'm your neighbor around the corner."

"I'm sure everyone in Denver knows your place, Mr. de Berg."

"Willie to my friends, and I hope you'll be one." He peered hard at her beneath the brim of his hat. "How come you're going into competition with me, practically in my backyard?"

"Oh, I won't be competing, Mr. de Berg. My cook will prepare only a few simple dishes. My bartender will sell only quality liquors—and wine, once my supplier in Chicago sends me the cases I've ordered. I won't be selling women, either."

"What do you take me for?" the hard-faced man demanded. "I never heard of a gambling house that didn't have women."

"Now you've heard of one," Clara Lou told him flatly, her grip on her walking stick tightening.

"I never ask favors," he said. "I pay for what I want. Sell this property, lady. With real estate prices climbing as high as Pikes Peak, you'll get double what you paid for it. Come to work with me. Run my bordello, and I'll give you one-third of the take. I'll cut you in on five percent of the liquor profits and ten percent of what I make on gambling. You couldn't ask for a fairer deal."

"Indeed I couldn't," Clara Lou said quietly. "But I don't take money from whores, I don't believe in watering liquor, and I'm opposed in both principle and practice to cheating customers at cards. There's plenty of room in a boom town like Denver for both of us, Mr. de Berg."

"Not around the corner from each other!" he rasped. "If you know what's good for you, you'll accept my offer!"

Her slow smile told him she refused to be intimidated. "I hope you're not threatening me, Mr. de Berg. I'm not a newcomer to this business."

"Then you ought to know I never make idle threats. Folks who have brains in their heads accept good offers from me, or they soon learn to regret turning me down."

"I hope all your dealers draw nothing but aces

tonight, Mr. de Berg," she said sweetly, then turned away from him. He stared at her for a long moment, then stamped off.

Clara Lou put the unpleasant incident out of her mind as best she could. At noon she walked the short distance to the dining room of one of the best of the new hotels, the Harry Allen House, one of the few public places in town where a lady could eat alone without being molested. She had enjoyed her years in California, but she felt certain she would like Denver even more. After eating a light meal, she strolled back to her construction site, enjoying the warmth of the sun.

Clara Lou stopped short and gasped. Her own work crew had vanished, and four total strangers were piling her paneling of exorbitantly expensive Oregon oak into a cart. "What do you think you're doing?" she called. "That's my property you're taking!"

The four men ignored her as they took more planks from the stack of wood.

Furiously angry, Clara Lou took a six-shooter from her handbag and fired a warning shot into the air.

The men paused briefly, then continued loading the planks into the cart.

Someone raced down the dirt road toward her, and Clara Lou quickly recognized Ezekiel, who was clutching his butcher knife in one huge hand.

"They're stealing my oak," she told him.

The men looked smug, apparently certain that she would not find the courage to fire at them.

"No take!" Ezekiel roared, charging toward the quartet.

The thieves had no intention of facing this knife-wielding wild man and fled from the scene, scattering as they raced away, leaving their cart behind. Ezekiel halted beside the stack of lumber and did not give chase.

Prudence Adams strode briskly down the street, her skirts gathered. "I just knew something was amiss," she said. "That man who talked to you this morning showed up again, and next thing I knew, your work crew just dropped their tools and walked away."

"De Berg bought them off," Clara Lou said, speaking more to herself than to the other woman.

"Then those four showed up, and next thing I knew, here you were." Prudence looked hard at her. "Would you really have shot them?"

"I don't know."

"Well, don't worry yourself," Prudence said. "We'll leave Ezekiel right here until I can get one of my regular guards to take his place. Nobody has touched your tools and nails, and your lumber is going to stay safe."

"Thank you," Clara Lou said, aware that Willie de Berg was a determined and ruthless enemy. "And thanks most of all to you, Ezekiel!" she called.

He grinned at her as he tested the sharpness of his blade with his thumb. "Too bad thieves run away. Long time now since I have big fight."

"With the two of you on my side," Clara Lou said, "it appears I don't have too much to fear."

"That's what neighbors are for, child," Prudence said. "My work crew finishes today, so you can hire them to start work tomorrow morning. Ezekiel will have a private word with them, and I think it unlikely they'll walk off the job without as much as a fare-thee-well."

Clara Lou Hadley was so relieved that she didn't know whether to laugh or weep.

Chet Harris and Wong Ke traveled in a style befitting men of wealth and stature. A seasoned guide conducted their party from San Francisco to Denver, and they were accompanied by eight heavily armed security guards. The journey through the mountain passes was pleasant, game was plentiful, and the two partners were encouraged by the last report they had received from their advance agent. At a cost of only a few hundred dollars per parcel, he had already purchased a considerable quantity of land in the area around Central City, and faithful to his instructions, he was continuing to buy from those who had lost their small amounts of capital.

The trouble started when the partners reached Denver. The Harry Allen House was fully occupied, and although a number of transients were expected to move on in the near future, several suites were being held for an army general and his party from the East, who were expected to arrive at any time. Chet and Ke tried several other habitable hotels and were turned down by all of them.

"This is mighty strange," the perplexed Chet said. "I'll be damned if we're going to move into some fleabag. But I can't believe that all the rooms are taken in the good hotels."

"They aren't," Ke said dryly. "Didn't you see the face of the manager in that last place we tried?"

"I must be missing something."

"You're being obtuse, Chet. They have no quarters for us because I'm Chinese."

"You're joking!"

"I'm not, unfortunately. You've become accustomed to the tolerance of San Francisco. Apparently you paid no attention to the shantytown area we rode through to get to the center of town. It was almost exclusively Chinese. I'd guess that a large number of my former countrymen have come to Denver, but they're dead broke, so they work for coolie wages. And they aren't being accepted in polite society."

"To hell with polite society, whatever that may be." Chet halted his horse and looked around. "What part of town is this?"

Ke shrugged. "I'm a stranger here, too."

"Look there, down the street." Chet pointed toward a three-story stone building, into which workmen were moving brass beds they were taking from a large wagon, then assembling. "Come on!" He spurred forward again, with the bewildered Ke and the security guards following.

A middle-aged couple stood in the road near the workmen, and the thoroughly aroused Chet hailed them. "What is this place?"

"A brand new boardinghouse," the man said proudly. "Our furniture is being moved in today, and by tomorrow we'll be open for customers."

"You own the house, eh?" The woman nodded happily, and Chet's eyelids drooped slightly, a sure sign to his partner that he was intending to negotiate a deal. Wong Ke tried to intervene, but the angry Chet silenced him with a glare.

"How many rooms?" Chet asked.

"Twelve bedchambers, a parlor, and a dining room," the man replied. "And a kitchen built into the house instead of being a separate building."

"With everything brand-new," the woman added, "except for the dining room set and the pots and pans we brought with us from Iowa. All the rest has been sent to us from Chicago and St. Louis."

"You looking for quarters?" the man asked, eying Wong Ke surreptitiously.

"Not exactly," Chet said, giving the couple no chance to insult his partner by refusing to rent them rooms. "How much do you want for the place?"

Husband and wife gaped at him. Ke was astonished, too.

"The whole works," Chet said. "Property deed, the building, and everything in it. How much do you want?"

The proprietor of the new boardinghouse was stunned. "If this is your idea of a joke, mister—"

"I'm talking hard cash," Chet replied, cutting him off. "I'll give you five thousand." He opened a leather purse suspended from his belt and removed a thick wad of one-thousand-dollar bills.

The offer was generous, obviously profitable, but as the owner recovered from his initial surprise, he became greedy. "Make it seven thousand, mister, and you have a deal."

"I'll give you six," Chet said curtly. He counted out the bills and, leaning down from his saddle, waved them in front of the man's face. "Take it or leave it."

"Taken," the proprietor replied.

Following them into the house to make out a simple bill of sale, Chet grinned at his partner. "Now," he said, "we have us a nice place to live—with plenty of room for the guards until they head back to California."

Ke sighed gently. Chet's occasional impulsiveness in purchasing various business enterprises had made them as wealthy as had his own far more cautious approach, and he could not complain. "Well," he said, "anytime one of us is bored with his room, he can move to another."

A short time later the former proprietor and his wife departed, the security guards helped the workmen move furniture into the house, and the new owners wandered into the parlor, with Chet jingling a set of house keys. "Now we have a base of operations in Denver," he said. "I noticed there was nothing to eat in the kitchen, and obviously there's no one here to cook for us; I suggest we go out for some supper. I don't know about you, but I'm hungry."

"So am I," Ke said. "But I prefer not to go to one of the restaurants we saw in the hotel and business district."

"Sure," Chet said, realizing he didn't want to run the risk of being subjected to additional snubs. "Where do you suggest we go?"

"The Chinese neighborhood," Ke replied. "I saw several eating places there, and we can find the cleanest of them."

A half-hour later they were seated at a small corner

table of a tiny restaurant, where an exceptionally pretty Chinese waitress in her early twenties, speaking in broken English, offered them a choice of broiled, fried, or baked steak.

Wong Ke addressed her in Mandarin, and when it was obvious she could not understand, he tried the Cantonese dialect. "You serve only American dishes?"

The young woman smiled. "One American dish: steak. And not a good quality of beef, either. Most of our countrymen here are too poor to order anything except rice or noodles, but I would not insult two grand gentlemen by offering them peasant fare."

Chet had gleaned enough Cantonese during the years of his partnership to make himself understood in the language, and he surprised the waitress by saying, "We'll have noodles, if you please, as well as fried steak."

The startled young woman hurried off to the tiny kitchen, then returned and stood nearby as they waited for the meal to be cooked.

Ke was curious about her, and they fell into conversation. Few customers came into the restaurant, the woman said, and the owner, who also did the cooking, was planning to take a job in the mines.

"Then you'll be out of work?" Ke asked.

She shrugged. "It has happened many times since I have come to America. My mother and father died of the terrible disease that took so many on the ship that brought us to San Francisco. Since that time, for almost two years, I have worked in many places. A few weeks here, a few there."

"Where will you go now?"

Again she shrugged, but her face became bleak. "There are few positions open to a woman from China in this new city. Next, I think, I must go to Willie de Berg's Palace."

"We have just arrived in Denver this very afternoon," Chet said, "so we don't yet know the town. What is this palace, as you call it?"

"Girls of many races and nations work there," she said, then fled to the kitchen.

The startled partners exchanged glances; each knew the mind of the other.

The waitress brought their meal, and before she could hurry away again, Ke motioned her to a chair.

"Sit with us for a time, please," he said.

She shook her head indignantly.

"You misunderstood," he declared. Then he rose with great dignity, drew up a chair for her, and deliberately took his double-edged knife from his sheath, placing it on the table in front of her chair. "If we give you offense," he said, "feel free to use this blade."

She hesitated, then dropped into the chair.

"Do we gather correctly that you do not wish to work in the bordello you mentioned?" Ke asked, his voice gentle.

She blinked away her tears. "For two years I have fought to live up to the principles of my ancestors, but when a woman must sell her body so she does not starve, she sells it."

Again the partners exchanged glances, silently assuring each other they had judged her character correctly.

Wong Ke gravely introduced his partner and himself, then asked, "What are you called?"

"Wing Mei-lo."

"And you are about twenty years old?"

"I have known twenty-two summers."

"What positions have you held?"

She couldn't understand why she was being questioned, but she remained polite. "In Canton I cooked in the restaurant of my parents. Since that time I have worked as a chambermaid in a San Francisco hotel and— It doesn't matter. I have held too many positions, all for very short periods."

The men nodded, waiting for her to continue.

"You do not eat," Wing Mei-lo said. "Soon your meal will grow cold."

"It doesn't matter," Chet said, and deferred to his partner.

"This very day," Wong Ke said, "we bought a large, new house. We will live there because one of my race is not welcome in most of this city's hotels."

"I know," Mei-lo murmured.

"We must attend to much business here," Ke continued. "We have no time to prepare our own meals and look after the dwelling."

"We offer you the position of our housekeeper," Chet said, "and we are prepared to pay you fair wages."

Wing Mei-lo jumped to her feet, her eyes blazing. "I am not yet that kind of a woman!"

"If we sought that kind," Ke said quietly, "we would go to the bordello about which you told us. Neither of us seeks a mistress."

"We're in need of a competent housekeeper, no more and no less," Chet added firmly. "We have much business to attend to here, so we have no time to buy and cook food, make beds, and clean a house."

"You may select your own quarters, as far from our sleeping rooms as you wish," Ke said, his manner still solemn, even though a gleam of humor appeared in his eyes. "The door can be bolted from the inside. If you wish, we will gladly present you with a pistol and a knife. And if it will make you feel safer, I will even have a Cantonese warrior's sword made for you."

A laugh welled up within her, and she relaxed.

"All we ask of you," Chet said, "is that you operate an efficient household."

"Decide what you regard as fair wages, and we will pay accordingly," Ke added. "Tell us what you need for food and whatever else is required, and you shall have it."

Mei-lo was overwhelmed. "Why do you offer all this?"

"Your needs and our needs match each other," Ke said. "Nothing is hidden."

She thought hard for a moment, then made up her mind. "I will do it," she said, "and Teng Hai will be happy I have found new work because he can no longer afford to pay my wages here." She left the dining room quickly.

The meal had cooled, but Chet and Ke were too hungry to care. As they were finishing, Wing Mei-lo reappeared, carrying a carpetbag that contained all her possessions. She accepted payment for their supper, taking the money to the kitchen and bidding farewell to the cook.

"I think we're in luck," Chet said.

Wong Ke nodded solemnly. "In the land of my birth," he said, "people believe that when a small bird makes a nest in the eaves of a dwelling, that family enjoys good fortune. Wing Mei-lo is such a bird."

Oregon was admitted to the Union as a state in 1859, and its steady growth was emphasized dramatically by the changes in the ranch owned by Whip and Eulalia Holt. When the leader of the first wagon train to reach the area and his bride had settled on their property two decades earlier, they had built their substantial home in the wilderness. Now the expansion of the city of Portland was so rapid that the area near the Holt home was becoming heavily populated and developed. Whip regularly received offers for the property from men who wanted to carve it into building lots, but he just as regularly refused.

"Not in my lifetime," the former mountain man told his still-attractive, brunette wife.

"I agree," she replied. "You and I need breathing room. The children can do as they please after we're gone."

Not yet ten years old, their daughter, Cindy, was interested in her friends and her schoolwork and had little else on her mind, but their son, Toby, as tall and sinewy as his father and endowed with his mother's

bubbling personality, was deeply concerned about the
future of the ranch. He was emphatic on the subject
while he was home for his summer vacation from
the far-off University of Michigan, one of the nation's
few institutions of higher learning that offered de-
grees in engineering. "Raising horses has earned this
family a good living for twenty years," he told his
parents at the breakfast table. "And horses are going
to be around for a long time to come."

Whip couldn't resist teasing the youth. "You mean
they won't be replaced by all the railroads you aim to
build?"

"I didn't say that, Pa. All I know is that I'd rather
sell horses than go traipsing off to the Colorado country to search for gold, the way so many damn fools are
doing."

Smiling in approval because the boy had such solid
common sense, Eulalia sipped her coffee and watched
her son devour a platter of bacon and eggs, then take
a heaping stack of pancakes.

"I wouldn't mind putting up an experimental barn
where I could tinker with a new kind of steam engine
I have in mind," the young man added thoughtfully,
"but that's a long way off. Right now I have something else on my mind."

Whip and Eulalia looked at their son, waiting for
him to continue.

"Ma, Pa," Toby began cautiously, "I've been thinking of enlisting in the United States Army."

Eulalia felt a shock run through her, and she didn't
wait for Toby to say any more. "How can you think of
such a thing? You're going to school now; you can't
just up and quit."

"Let the boy continue," Whip said to his wife, then
turned to Toby. "You were saying, son?"

"I was saying that I've been thinking of enlisting if
there's a war between the North and the South. I want
to fight for the Union. But of course I'd go back to

school after the war was over and get my engineering degree."

Tears came to Eulalia's eyes as she thought of her only son going off to war. Whip put his hand on hers and spoke softly.

"Now, Lalie, Toby isn't going to enlist right away. Besides, there may not even be a war."

"Everyone is talking as though there will be one," Eulalia said, calmer now. "And I don't want our son going out to fight a war that has nothing to do with us here in Oregon."

"Ma," Toby said, "the problems in the country today affect everybody. I can't just sit back and let somebody else do the fighting."

"Toby has a point, Eulalia," Whip said.

"And it's not as if I'm going off right away," Toby went on. "I'd only enlist if my country needs me."

"I tell you what," Whip said. "Give your mother and me a little time to digest what you've just told us. We want you to do the right thing, but it may take us a little while to get used to the idea of your enlisting." Whip looked at his wife. "What do you say to that, honey?"

"Yes, you're right, Whip," she said, squeezing her husband's hand. "In time, I'm sure I'll feel better about the whole idea." Then looking at their son, she added, "I just pray there won't be any war!"

Cathy Blake had made it emphatically clear that, having twice made long journeys in wagon trains, she preferred other means of transportation. So she, her husband, his aide, and her maid had sailed with Caroline and Luke Brandon to Panama in a navy steamship, crossed the once-primitive jungle of the Isthmus by comfortable train, and then transferred to another navy vessel for the voyage to San Francisco. There the Blakes were entertained by old friends, including Rick and Melissa Miller. And in San Francisco there were two additions to the Colorado-bound party.

Isaiah Atkins was happy to take a leave from his law firm to advise General Blake on the legal aspects of land claims in the Colorado gold fields. And Sergeant Major Hector Mullins jumped at the opportunity to rejoin the officer under whom he had served for so long. He had not accompanied Lee Blake to Washington since, as the General explained, the assignment was not definite. But Hector Mullins was delighted to be joining him now, even if briefly. Had he wished, Hector could have taken his wife, Ginny, and their children with him, but he appeared alone, in appropriate civilian attire, for the journey. "Me and Ginny decided that both of our youngsters are too little for life in a new boom town where the gold fever raises the temperature," he said. "We did it here in San Francisco, and Ginny would rather stay on at the Presidio until I either come back or take her and the youngsters on to my next post."

Cathy was sorry, knowing she would miss Ginny's company, but she respected her old friend's decision.

Lee and young Andy were surprised and relieved when, contrary to their expectations, Caroline Brandon's behavior was that of a lady. Although her flamboyant clothes and lavish use of cosmetics caused Cathy to raise an eyebrow, she was mild-mannered and decorous, never stepping out of line and not once throwing herself at Lee. On both the Atlantic and Pacific voyages, she acted the role of a devoted wife.

Patricia, Cathy's maid, was leery, however. "Confidentially, Mrs. Blake," she said, "that's a wild one. I've watched her when she thinks nobody is paying any attention to her. She leaves the General alone because she's afraid of you, but she's the kind who'll wrap herself around any man who pays heed to her."

A matter far more important than Caroline Brandon's conduct weighed on Cathy's mind, and she finally decided that Beth, who was visiting the Brentwoods for her summer vacation, should return directly to school from there. "Beth is too attractive and too mischievous a girl to be subjected to a gold town," she told Lee.

"I believe you're right," he replied. "We'd be asking for trouble if we brought her to Denver."

The new commandant of the Presidio insisted on supplying his predecessor with a cavalry escort for the journey across the mountains. Arrangements were made, too, for tents, food, cooking utensils, and other supplies, in addition to the travelers' clothes, to be carried in horse-drawn carts. Lee's decision to ride horseback made Cathy happy. "I much prefer to ride, especially at this season, when there's so little rain," she said. "After covering almost five thousand miles in wagon trains, I'll leave those thrills to others."

The tall, good-looking Isaiah Atkins joined the party late on the eve of their departure. Caroline Brandon did not meet him until the group gathered for a very early breakfast. She came to life at once, and for the first days on the trail, she rode beside him whenever possible, flirted with him surreptitiously but steadily, and spoke to him at meals with great vivacity. Isaiah was embarrassed, but since he was a gentleman, he could not ignore her. The others pretended that nothing out of the ordinary was happening.

On the fourth night of the journey, when a halt was called near the border between California and the Nevada country, Luke Brandon finally felt compelled to have words with his wife after they retired to their tent. "Caroline," he said, "I thought—at least I hoped—that by now you'd realize you aren't irresistible."

She flipped back her long blonde hair and looked at him, her kohl-rimmed eyes innocent.

"You're throwing yourself at young Atkins," he said. "You and I know you're just amusing yourself harmlessly, but he and the Blakes don't realize it."

"Is it a crime that I enjoy his company?" she demanded.

"Not at all. But you needn't give him the impression that you'd love to go to bed with him."

"You're being insulting, Luke!" she cried.

Experience had taught him that such discussions always followed the same pattern: ultimately Caroline would weep, he would forgive her, and the next day she would resume her flirtation. That pattern had to be broken. "I've accepted a difficult, complicated assignment at the request of the President of the United States," he said. "Your little flirtations with Harvard faculty members have been meaningless, but Cambridge isn't a rough gold town, and the people with whom we're dealing now aren't colleagues of mine who know you're playing a game and abide by the rules. You behaved well until a few days ago, and I want you to start acting that way again."

"You don't trust me," she said, pouting.

"My trust is irrelevant. Either you'll behave yourself, or I'm sending you back to Cambridge!"

Rarely had he treated her with such firmness, and Caroline took her husband's warning seriously. To the relief of everyone else in the company, particularly Isaiah Atkins, she kept her distance from him.

Isaiah was becoming friendly with Andy and confided in him. "I was afraid," he said, "that I'd have an irate husband taking potshots at me, even though I've gone out of my way to avoid the lady."

"How can you call Caroline Brandon a lady?" the young officer demanded.

Isaiah shook his head, his manner suddenly grim. "Well, she'd better start behaving like one," he said. "I was growing up during the California rush, and I was old enough to know what was going on around me. The people pouring into Colorado must be pretty much the same kind, and all I can say is that any woman who isn't a lady will get what's coming to her!"

Caroline remained on her good behavior for the rest of the journey. There was virtually no rainfall, and the weather was warm during the day, although it became chilly at night in the mountains. So many travelers were using the trail for the Colorado country that game had become scarce, and it was necessary to buy bacon, jerked beef, salt fish, and other supplies at mountain trading posts. Potentially troublesome Indians kept their distance because of the protective cordon thrown around the party by the cavalry troop, and robbers who preyed on the unwary had no desire to do battle with the soldiers, either, so the march was peaceful.

All the same, everyone breathed more easily when the group rode through the passes that took them through the last chain of snow-topped mountains. Two and a half days later they came to the outskirts of Denver, and Lee dismissed the cavalry with his thanks. He and his companions went on to the Harry Allen House, where they found their quarters waiting for them. Only the grizzled Hector Mullins felt ill at ease in the elegant surroundings, and with Lee's readily granted permission, he went off on his own to find a more modest place to dine.

The others met in the lobby of the hotel, and as they entered the dining room, they came face to face with a departing group of men. One, gray-haired and erect, stopped short. "Lee Blake!"

Lee was not surprised to see General Larimer, one of the new community's leaders. "Good to see you, Bill," he said, then introduced his wife, the Brandons, Isaiah, and Andy.

"What are you doing here?" Larimer asked.

"I may do what you're doing, Bill." Lee was deliberately vague.

"Ah, I take it you've retired from the army, too. And

no doubt you're thinking of looking into the gold business out here." Larimer smiled broadly. "Well, welcome to Denver. We can use men of your caliber here, Lee." He scribbled his address on a piece of paper. "Drop in tomorrow, at any time. I can't tell you where to find gold, but I sure can steer you away from the places where there is none."

Lee took his former colleague at his word, called on him early the next morning, and obtained some valuable maps showing the places where gold had already been found. Luke Brandon was eager to see the area himself, so the other men went with him. The women were left with the responsibility of trying to find more permanent quarters than the hotel rooms.

Caroline chose to remain in her suite and primp, but Cathy had expected little help from her and set out on her own, accompanied by Patricia. Experience in growing communities, both in Oregon and Texas, sent her first to the two-story building occupied by Denver's newspaper, the *Tribune*.

Wade Fulton was in the rear with a journeyman printer, turning out a new edition on the hand press.

The front room was large, its walls bare except for a big poster that had become the slogan of almost everyone who came to Colorado: "Pikes Peak or Bust!" There were several plain desks arranged in an orderly row, but only one was occupied. A young woman with short hair, dressed in a boy's shirt and work trousers, was writing, her quill pen scratching furiously.

Susanna Fulton looked up and smiled, then stood as Cathy introduced herself. "I didn't know General Blake had come to Denver," she said. "Will he allow me to interview him?"

"He's never been one to seek publicity," Cathy replied.

"I do a regular column on prominent new arrivals in town, and I'd like to include the General. But I'll ask his permission first, naturally. Where are you staying, Mrs. Blake?"

"At the Allen House. Temporarily. That's why I'm here. Our party includes an investment banker and his wife, and a lawyer, among others. I'm hoping we can find a house large enough to accommodate all of us while my husband decides whether he and his colleagues in a new company want to invest in potential gold-field properties." Cathy had practiced her little speech, and the words rolled out smoothly.

Susanna whistled under her breath and ran a hand through her hair. "Housing is scarce, as hard to find as gold. Just about everyone who comes to Denver builds his own place."

"That wouldn't be practical for us," Cathy said. "We'll be staying only until the General decides what recommendations to make to his partners back East. We'd prefer to rent by the month, or even by the week."

"That's a tall order, Mrs. Blake. The *Tribune* won't be accepting advertising until we're established, so I have no leads for you. But I do have a suggestion."

"I'll appreciate it, Miss Fulton."

"There's a new general store, just around the corner, owned by a lady named Adams. She seems to know everything that goes on in town. I'm a reporter by profession, but I'm not in her class. I actually get leads on stories from her. Miss Adams is your best bet."

A few minutes later Cathy and Patricia walked into the general store, which was even more cluttered than usual because a freight wagon had just arrived from Chicago with supplies.

Ezekiel stood on a high ladder, storing merchandise on shelves, and looked surreptitiously but carefully at Patricia. She was equally aware of him but pretended not to notice his interest. Meanwhile, Cathy introduced herself to Prudence Adams and explained her problem.

"Dear me," the New England spinster said. "I do know of one place, across Cherry Creek in what some folks still call Auraria. It's a right big house, but the owners are asking an exorbitant rental fee."

"What do you mean by exorbitant?"

"Four hundred dollars per month," Prudence said with a sniff.

"That's outlandish!" the shocked Cathy cried.

"Everything here is outlandish, ma'am," Prudence replied. "Those who strike gold don't care what they pay, and those who don't, have such empty pockets they can't buy anything." She picked up a round tin pie pan from the counter. "Back in Connecticut or Rhode Island, you can buy one of these tins for fifteen cents. Granted the transportation costs are high, but I get three dollars for a pan, and I can't keep them in stock!"

Cathy knew that the War Department, which was actually paying the costs of the party's stay in Denver, was not generous in ladling out funds, even to someone engaged in a presidential mission. "It may be we won't be staying in Denver as long as I had anticipated," she said faintly.

"Don't lose heart, dearie," Prudence said. "I'll keep my ears open for you. The godless may flourish like the green bay tree in a heathen city like this, but the righteous eventually triumph."

The grateful Cathy thanked her and took her leave. Ezekiel kept his eyes on Patricia until she walked out the door.

Uncertain where to inquire next, the pair started slowly up the street. Cathy looked far younger than a woman in her forties, Patricia was very pretty, and most of the men walking in the opposite direction had comments to make, many of them rude.

"I hate to give up so soon," Cathy said, "but I wonder if we should go back to the hotel. All these leering men make me uncomfortable."

"They can't drive us into hiding, Mrs. Blake," Patricia replied. "You have a long, sharp pin in your hat, and I always carry a pair of shears in my handbag."

Cathy laughed. "You're right, Patricia," she said. "On we go!"

They turned the corner, and although they didn't know where they were heading, they increased their pace as they passed a gaudy saloon.

Suddenly a portly, well-dressed man blocked their path. "I thought my eyes were deceiving me, but I reckon I don't need spectacles yet!"

Cathy attempted to ignore the man, and Patricia took her shears from her handbag.

"I refuse to believe you've become uppity, Cathy Blake," the man said.

Startled when she heard herself addressed by name, Cathy looked at him for the first time. "Chet Harris! Put away your scissors, Patricia. Chet and I crossed the country all the way to Oregon in the same wagon train, and his mother is one of my dearest friends. We came to know him well in San Francisco, too. What are you doing in Denver, Chet?"

"Wong Ke and I are sniffing out gold. What about you?"

"Lee is doing the same thing. As a potential investor, that is. He has no intention of owning and operating a mine."

"It could be I can help him. Where are you staying?"

"The Allen House."

"Then I'll walk you two back there," he said. "The vicinity of Willie de Berg's place isn't the safest for ladies." He guided them firmly in the direction from which they had come.

"We didn't know," Patricia said.

"That's plain enough," he said, chuckling. "This street is safe enough, most of the time, but the street around the corner isn't. Until you come to know Denver, be careful where you go for your strolls."

Cathy explained they hadn't been walking aimlessly and told him their mission.

Chet stopped short and let loose the war cry of the Cheyenne Indians, which he and his close boyhood friend, Danny Taylor, had learned on the wagon train trail as adolescents.

His companions stared at him, and so did several passersby.

"Cathy," he said, "you're in luck—and so am I. Ke and I just bought a boardinghouse and hired a housekeeper. We've been rattling around in the place. We have more than enough room for your whole party."

"Thank you, Chet, but we wouldn't want to inconvenience you."

"We'd love it, and there's no inconvenience. We'll hire an assistant for Mei-lo, our housekeeper. Will Lee be back for supper tonight?"

"Oh, yes."

"Then come to the house for supper." He took a gold pencil and leather notebook from an inner pocket and scribbled the address. "Come whenever it's convenient, and unless you can't tolerate the house—which I think unlikely because everything in it is new and unused—your search for a place to live is over."

After he left them at the hotel, they went to their suite and ordered a light meal sent to them. Then Cathy sprawled happily in a chair and said, "Imagine running into Chet and solving our problem, just like that. It's almost too good to be true."

"You and the General seem to know people wherever you go," Patricia observed.

"I never thought of it, but I suppose we do. That's what comes of having lived in so many places. Oh, dear." Cathy paused and frowned. "Susanna Fulton and that sweet Miss Adams were so nice that I really owe it to them to tell them our house hunting seems to have come to an end."

"Why don't you stay here, Mrs. Blake, and let me go off and tell them? I'll be back in no time."

"Thank you, Patricia. That's exactly what I'll do. And I really must get off a letter to Beth, as well as one to my sister."

Patricia left the suite, went down the stairs, and walked quickly into the street, first stopping a few doors away to tell the news to Susanna Fulton.

"I appreciate your consideration," Susanna said. "Do you happen to know the address of your new place? I don't want to lose my interview with General Blake."

"Mr. Harris wrote it down, but I didn't even look at it," Patricia said. "It's a boardinghouse owned by a man named Chet Harris."

"That's good enough for me," Susanna said, giving her an elfin smile.

Patricia waved, then went on to the general store, where she halted abruptly when she saw Ezekiel standing alone behind the counter. He grinned at her.

"I'd like a word with Miss Adams, please," Patricia said, her manner haughty.

"Not here. Eating dinner. I in charge now." He continued to grin at her.

For reasons she herself couldn't quite understand, she refused to unbend. He was attractive, powerfully built, and didn't hide his attraction for her. But something perverse in her nature prevented her from acknowledging his obvious interest in her and responding to it. Her expression wooden and her voice clipped, she gave him the message for his employer, nodded curtly, and walked out into the street.

Ezekiel was hurt and somewhat bewildered by her, and his smile faded slowly.

As Patricia moved away from the entrance to the general store, she realized she should have looked carefully before emerging into the open. Coming toward her from the direction of the saloon around the corner were a half-dozen men, all in rough miners' garb, and before she had a chance to retreat, they surrounded her.

"She's for me," a bearded man declared, rubbing his hands together. "I like her better than any of them women in Willie's joint."

"I saw her first," another protested.

"We'll share her!"

Patricia tried to edge away, but there was no place to go. The men were closing in on her, and when one reached for her, she shrank from him, only to back into one of his companions. Brawny arms closed around her, holding her firmly. Afraid her captors would become violent if she screamed, she tried to free herself from the miner's grasp.

"You're gonna like what I do to you," he told her, and one hairy hand began to paw her.

Her panic increasing, she clawed at her tormentor, but he tightened his grip and slapped her hard with his free hand.

"Don't make me get rough with you," he said.

Suddenly two of the miners were sprawled on the ground, and the others were menaced by a blazing-eyed giant who brandished a razor-sharp butcher's knife.

"Let go of lady!" Ezekiel roared.

The man who held Patricia in his grasp stared at the angry demon. Ezekiel did not hesitate for an instant. His blade ripped swiftly through the fabric of the miner's sleeve.

Howling in pain, the man released the terrified woman. He and his companions had no desire to fight the enraged Ezekiel, who had murder in his eyes and a dangerous instrument of death in his hand. Two of the miners took to their heels, and one of the fallen managed to scramble to his feet and follow them.

The miner who had been attacked saw his blood reddening his slashed shirt-sleeve and stared at his wound.

"I kill you first," Ezekiel said. "Then I kill other no-good scum."

The three remaining miners had heard enough.

There was no doubt in their minds that the giant fully intended to carry out his threat, so they, too, fled ignominiously.

For a moment Patricia thought she would faint, then Ezekiel's strong arm encircled her, gently supporting her. She regained her equilibrium, and her smile was tremulous as she turned to him.

He released her instantly. "You feel better now?"

"Yes, thanks to you," she said. "I'm in your debt, and I—I apologize for being rude to you."

Shyness overcame him. His knife vanished inside his shirt, and no longer able to meet Patricia's gaze, he looked down at the ground. "Any time scum bother you, I fix," he muttered.

"I won't forget your kindness."

His self-consciousness robbed him of the power of speech. She thanked him again, then started off down the street to the hotel, aware of his steady gaze and knowing she would not be molested again while he stood watch over her.

III

Danny Taylor carved the meat while his pretty, red-haired wife, Heather, placed steaming bowls of vegetables and potatoes on the dining room table. When he carried the platter to the table, he walked with a slight limp, the result of the prosthesis that he wore after losing his leg during the war with Mexico.

"This is a wonderful supper," Melissa Miller said.

Heather Taylor beamed. All the produce had come from her own garden on the farm that she and Danny had made into one of the most prosperous in the Valley. And she was always happy to receive praise from Melissa Miller, who was an outstanding cook and her best friend. They had become close during the difficult days of the California gold rush, and together they had grown into mature, self-confident women. Heather was one of the few people who knew all the details of Melissa's past, but Melissa knew that her friend would never betray her trust.

"What's the occasion?" Rick asked.

Danny nodded toward the other guests, Scott and Sarah Rose Foster. "Heather and I figured that the four of us might be able to talk some sense into these youngsters."

"You're good neighbors and even better friends, all

of you," Sarah Rose declared, "but Scott and I have made up our minds."

"We haven't heard a single word from Tracy since he went off to Colorado," Scott said. "Not a letter in all these months. We're worried. It's no secret to you folks that he became—well, kind of peculiar after Ma was killed. If anything, he became even more sullen after Pa died, shortly after Ma. There's no telling what could have happened to him."

"I can understand your concern," Rick said, helping himself to one of the steaming rolls Heather had baked. "But you've got to be sensible. The Colorado gold fields cover a pretty large area, and you could search for a long time without finding your brother."

"We've got to try," Sarah Rose said. "There was no way we could stop Tracy from going off to Colorado and searching for gold. But it may be that he's lost his taste for adventure and will be willing to come home with us. Melissa, you wouldn't let your children go wandering off without supervision. Neither would you, Heather. Well, Tracy may be a grown man, but in some ways he's like a child. He's needed Scott and me to keep an eye on him, and we just hope he's lost his taste for adventure and will agree quietly to come back home with us."

"What about your work?" Melissa asked.

"The principal has agreed to give me a leave of absence from the school," Sarah Rose said.

"We'll close up the house," Scott said. "I've brought in a good profit from our last crop, so we'll have no money problems. And I've offered Danny a deal. He and his hired hands can take over the orchards while we're gone, and I'll split the profits with him."

"I'm reluctant to accept," Danny said. "Not that I object to the extra income. Far from it. But I think you're going off on a wild-goose chase and that no good can come of it."

Brother and sister looked at each other. "You may be right," Scott said.

"It could be we'll regret it," Sarah Rose said.

"We know what Pa and Ma would have done if they were still alive," her brother added, a stubborn ring in his voice. "We've always been a close family, and our consciences wouldn't let us rest easy if we stayed here when Tracy may be in trouble and need our help. We figure we have no choice."

Rick had to admire their loyalty, even though he didn't agree with them. "How are you fixed for firearms?"

"I've got my rifle and my six-shooter, of course," Scott said. "They're reliable weapons."

"What about you, Sarah Rose?" the former law enforcement officer wanted to know.

"My rifle has a strong kick, but I've learned to handle it," she replied.

Melissa smiled. "A rifle is all well and good on the trail, but you won't want to go traipsing around Denver with it. I'll lend you the light six-shooter that Rick gave me last year. The one Colt has been manufacturing especially for ladies and youngsters."

"Thank you, but I wouldn't want to deprive you—"

"Please. I really don't need it." Melissa and Rick exchanged glances. They both remembered how Rick's first wife had been murdered. "Life has been peaceful here; there hasn't been trouble for years."

"Melissa's right," Rick said. "California is a civilized state now. And if you insist on going into a barbarian land where every man makes his own laws and every woman is fair game, you'll need all the protection you can get!"

Wandering unobtrusively around Denver in her boy's attire, Susanna was able to escape the intense male scrutiny directed at all young, attractive members of her sex. Consequently, she could go into neighborhoods that otherwise would have been dangerous, and with no one paying particular attention to her, she was able to unearth stories for the new *Tribune* that befitted the crusading image she and her father were trying to build.

One such story, which attracted considerable attention in the East and spurred an investigation by a Congressional committee, concerned the plight of the Chinese who came to Denver. Unable to speak English and bewildered by alien New World customs, they were the natural victims of unscrupulous "labor suppliers" in San Francisco. These entrepreneurs shipped them by wagon train to Colorado, where they were given meager housing in the worst of Denver's slums and were "rented" to mine owners and hotel proprietors. In return for the menial tasks they performed, they were paid substandard wages and even then could keep only a fraction of what they earned.

Susanna's long article on coolie labor won overnight respect for the *Tribune*. It also created enemies for the newspaper and for the reporter herself. "If she ever sets foot on my property," one mine owner who employed a large number of Chinese laborers declared, "I'll put a bullet between her eyes!"

Susanna was undaunted by the threat.

The steady rise in circulation of the daily newspaper made it possible for Wade Fulton to order new presses from Philadelphia, hire a second full-time printer, and add two more members to his editorial staff. "If we could get more paper and be assured of regular delivery," he told his daughter one day when she came into his tiny, cluttered private office, "we could start printing eight pages per issue instead of four."

"Don't be impatient, Wade," she told him. "We're off to a great start. But there's trouble on the doorstep. Right now. There's a visitor here to see you. I tried to put him off, but he won't budge."

Her efforts to protect him from unwanted intruders caused him to smile. "Someone important?"

"Willie de Berg, who owns that big saloon, gambling house, and brothel. One of these days I'd like to get a big story on him. I've heard rumors that he cheats his customers. The women not only give signals to the dealers, but according to my sources, they're under orders to empty the pockets of the really drunk customers they take upstairs."

"What does Willie de Berg want with me?"

"He wouldn't tell me, Wade. He insists on a private talk with you."

"In all my years as a publisher, I've never refused to see any citizen, even a crooked one. So you'd best send him in."

Susanna sighed in exasperation. "You're too kind for your own good," she said as she hurried out of the cubicle.

Willie de Berg shoved his broad-brimmed hat onto the back of his head as he came into the room, then extended his hand and grinned broadly. "This is a real pleasure, Mr. Fulton," he said. "It's high time that two of Denver's leading citizens get to say how-do to each other!"

Wade shook his hand, then cleared a clutter of papers from his visitor's chair so his guest would have a place to sit.

"You're doing just great," Willie said, still exuding synthetic charm. "It amazes me that just about everybody hereabouts who knows how to read is buying your newspaper."

"Yes, we seem to be building a solid circulation base rather quickly," Wade replied cautiously.

"Well, this is a terrific town for anybody out to make a dollar. I wasn't old enough to get my cut from the miners out in California ten years ago, but I'm more than making up for lost time now. Blame near every last newcomer to Denver heads straight for Willie de Berg's Palace. Have you dropped in yet?"

Wade's smile was remote. "I don't play cards or roll dice, Mr. de Berg."

"That don't matter. Come over anytime at all and take your pick of the girls. On the house."

"Very generous of you, but I wouldn't want one of your young ladies to—ah—destroy the objectivity that the editor and publisher of any newspaper needs."

Willie had no idea what he was talking about but continued to smile steadily. "Our food isn't all that bad, and I keep some decent whiskey hidden away for friends, so let me treat you to supper."

"I appreciate your generosity, but I live upstairs with my daughter, who always cooks supper for me."

"I got to admit," Willie said, "that the Palace isn't a place where a real lady would feel at home. Most of my girls know how to act fancy, but a lady would know them from the genuine article."

Wade told himself that he would have to make certain Susanna kept away from de Berg's establishment, even in the interests of good newspaper reporting. "Did you just drop in to become acquainted, or is there something I can do for you, Mr. de Berg?"

"Willie to my friends." The man's geniality faded, and he scowled. "The minute a fellow starts making a heap of money, he has a passel of imitators. In the last month alone there must be a dozen new saloons have opened their doors. None in my class and none near as big, mind you, but they take away a few customers here, a few there, so my receipts have dropped a mite. Seeing as how the *Tribune* has so many readers, I'm hoping you'll let me place some advertisements in your paper."

There was no need to insult the man by telling him that a respectable newspaper trying to establish itself as a civic force in a community did not and could not accept advertising from brothels. "The *Tribune*'s policy," Wade said, "has been to accept no advertising from anyone."

"I'll gladly pay top rate!"

"I have no objection to accepting advertising money, but I won't be in a position to change the policy until our newsprint supplier can guarantee enough paper to double the size of each edition. As I'm sure you understand, I can't break my rule for any one client. A dozen potential advertisers would break down my front door. It's frustrating to know that a paper shortage limits my income, but there doesn't seem to be much I can do about it yet."

"Sure, I know what you mean. If I could find a half-dozen more girls good-looking enough, I could make one hell of a lot more money, too."

Wade had to admit that the man was candid, but in him the quality wasn't necessarily a virtue.

"A couple of weeks ago your daughter, I guess it was, wrote an article about some of the new businesses opening in Denver. She mentioned a small restaurant down the street from me, and she said the food was good there and that a man gets his money's worth. Until her article was printed, that restaurant was dying a quick death. But every day at noon when I walk past it, every last table is taken. Thanks to what the *Tribune* said."

"I'm delighted to hear we have that much influence." Wade braced himself for what he guessed was coming.

"I have no idea what that hole-in-the-wall paid you for giving them a hand, but you can name your own fee if you'll print something about the Palace being the greatest in town."

"That restaurant paid us nothing," Wade said firmly. "Our editorial columns aren't for sale. At any price."

Willie de Berg stared hard at him. "You really mean that, huh?"

"Indeed I do! If a newspaper hopes to provide service for a community, it must maintain integrity, no matter what the cost."

The publisher's attitude was so alien to Willie de Berg that he found it incomprehensible. He stood, retrieved his hat, and jammed it onto his head. "Anytime you change your mind, friend, I'll be waiting—

with a stack of dollar bills in my wallet for you." He shook hands, then departed quickly, the untied holster of his six-shooter slapping against his thigh.

Wade waited until the man left the building, then went to the door of his small office and beckoned.

Susanna quickly joined him. "You look as though you've eaten something that doesn't agree with you," she said, grinning.

"You're right," her father replied. "I have a case of serious indigestion. De Berg wanted to place some advertising in the *Tribune*, and when I told him we aren't accepting any as yet, he offered me a bribe for an article that would praise his gambling hall—brothel to the skies."

Susanna absorbed the information. "I told you. I just know the man is as dishonest as he is smug. One of these days I'll write that story, just as soon as I get a little more evidence."

"I want you to promise me you won't do anything rash—like prying around Willie de Berg's establishment. You could get in serious trouble."

"You think it's that rough, Wade?"

"In the early days of the California boom, when you were just a child in school, I met many men like Willie de Berg. He's ruthless, and he's the kind who'll hire strong-arm thugs to do his dirty work for him. I can promise you he'd be furious if he knew you were spying on him. He'd believe I sent you there because he offered me a bribe."

"Maybe we should just forget about doing the article, Wade."

The publisher shook his head. "Have you ever known threats—genuine, potential, or imagined—to stop me from getting at the truth?"

Susanna looked at him with admiration. "Never," she replied softly. "And I beg your pardon for suggesting it now."

"I simply want you to promise to use caution and tact, that's all. It would be too easy to put a bullet into a girl who weighs only one hundred and five pounds, and dump her body in an alleyway."

"I promise I won't go snooping around his place, but sooner or later I'll get the information I need." Susanna smiled and winked at her father.

Wade Fulton felt enormous pride. As long as he and his daughter lived and worked, the *Tribune* would expose the practices of the evil, the greedy, and the wicked.

Tracy Foster lurked silently in the shadows of the abandoned shack near the road that led from Central City to Denver. This was payday for the miners, who were coming to the city's saloons, brothels, and gambling halls after a week of hard labor below the surface of the earth, and this was the one day of the week that Tracy was active.

That single day of activity was enough for him to live extremely well. He had learned to select his robbery victims with care, always choosing those who looked as though they could be intimidated, always changing the place of his encounters so he never struck twice in the same spot.

Occasionally, to be sure, his judgment was faulty. The first miner he had robbed today was a small, wiry fellow who had pulled a knife on him, and Tracy had found it necessary to beat the man until he lost consciousness. Well, perhaps he had given the miner a few extra licks for daring to defy him. In any event, the little man was either dead by now or had been found by others on the road and had been taken to one of Denver's new hospitals.

Tracy really didn't care what became of his victims after he took their cash from them. His only concern was their money, and he had done exceptionally well today. His purse was bulging with bills and gold coins, giving him funds to eat where he pleased, visit the most expensive bordello in Denver whenever he felt the urge, and, if he wished, go to the new tailor in town for another suit of fine clothes.

Ah. A single horseman was approaching alone on the road, with no one ahead of him or behind him. He appeared to be in his thirties, it was obvious that he had been drinking, and his rifle rested in a hard-to-reach sling attached to the rear of his saddle. Tracy waited until the rider was only a few paces away, then stepped out of the shadows into the road, his six-shooter aimed at the man's chest.

"Get down," he ordered, his voice cordial. "Nice and easy, and if you as much as reach for that rifle, you're a dead man."

The miner blinked at the assailant whose face was concealed beneath the broad brim of his forward-tilted hat.

"Don't make me tell you again," Tracy said.

The man silently dismounted, then raised his hands over his head.

Tracy kicked the man's gelding, and the startled beast shied, then trotted off back down the road. This act enraged the miner, who sprang at the robber.

The alert Tracy sidestepped. Preferring not to fire his pistol because the sound might attract others in the vicinity, he grasped the weapon by the barrel, then brought down the butt with full force on the back of the miner's head. The miner crumpled, lying face down in the road, a trickle of blood oozing from his head.

Tracy realized he had killed the man, but this was no time to suffer regrets. He quickly searched his victim's pockets after turning him over, and when he felt a wad of bills, he stuffed them into his own purse.

Now he moved even more rapidly. Not glancing at his victim again, he returned to the far side of the abandoned shack, where he had tethered his own spirited gelding, and within moments he was galloping across the rough terrain in the direction of the

South Platte River, taking care to avoid the dirt roads that appeared here and there.

Although he knew he had escaped undetected, he preferred to take no chances, so he did not slow his pace until he reached terrain so rough that his mount might have broken a leg had Tracy not drawn the reins. Night was falling, and he felt contented, but he would not count his loot until he arrived home.

His horse slowly descended one side of a steep canyon, then laboriously began to climb the far slope. Eventually Tracy had to dismount, and he unhesitatingly led the gelding past a huge boulder. Then, man and animal seemed to vanish.

Behind the boulder stood a door of thick, heavy wood that Tracy had made himself, and he unlocked it, then led his mount into the cave that was their home. A few small holes in the ceiling at the far end allowed fresh air to enter, and an underground stream provided an endless supply of fresh, clear mountain water.

First bolting the door behind him, Tracy lighted an oil lamp, unsaddled the gelding, and gave the animal a feedbag of oats. Then he moved to his sleeping quarters, where a cot stood on a shelf at one side of the cave. Pouring his day's loot onto the blanket, he counted it with slow relish.

As he had guessed, this had been a good day, and one of his four victims apparently had been someone other than an ordinary miner. The day's booty amounted to slightly in excess of two hundred dollars, more than a miner could earn in five weeks of hard labor.

Grinning quietly, Tracy took a stiff drink of whiskey from a bottle, then prepared himself a simple meal of cold meat and bread. The tensions of the day had sharpened his appetite, and he ate heartily. There was nothing to prevent him from going into Denver tonight, but he didn't want to push his luck, so he dropped off to sleep, still wearing the clothes in which he had been dressed all day.

In the morning he felt refreshed, alive after a sound sleep. Hiding his stolen money in a crevice where he kept his loot, he opened the door to admit daylight, took his horse into the open, and groomed the animal carefully. Then he made a fire beneath the air holes at the rear of the cave, and after eating, he heated enough water for a bath and a shave.

He polished his best pair of boots, then dressed with care in a suit of dark gray, which he wore with a white shirt and black cravat, knowing he suddenly acquired the appearance of an alert young business-man. He selected a gray hat with a medium brim, then led the horse to a place at the base of the canyon, where he could mount in safety.

After a leisurely ride he reached Denver, where he took his mount to a corral and cheerfully gave the attendant ten cents. He wandered to the tailor shop, where he ordered another suit made for twenty dol-lars, and feeling in a spending mood, he also bought two more shirts and several pairs of socks. Laundry had become a nuisance, and he found it simpler to throw underclothes and socks away rather than wash them.

His next stop was the shop of a gunsmith, where he studied the wares critically. A new supply of pistols had come in from New England, but none was better than his own six-shooter. He saw a double-edged knife, eight inches long, that interested him. The blade was of tempered steel, so he bought it, knowing he would hone it himself when he returned to the cave.

His stomach told him he was past due for a meal, so he continued to wander until he came to a small restaurant where the noon crowd was thinning. Sev-eral tables were empty, and he chose one adjacent to that at which an exceptionally pretty, petite young

woman and a man old enough to be her father were
eating. After ordering his meal, he sat back in his
chair and eavesdropped shamelessly.

It took only a short time for Tracy to discover that,
although the woman addressed the man by his first
name, he actually was her father. Tracy's soup arrived, and as he ate it ravenously, he gleaned that the
man was the owner of the local newspaper, at which
he himself glanced only to see if any of his various
robberies were reported. It was apparent, too, that the
young woman worked for her father.

Tracy's beefsteak arrived, and he began to eat.

"I've got to get back to the office to interview that
new reporter candidate, Susanna," Wade Fulton said.
"But there's no need for you to rush. I know you don't
like your coffee too hot, so take your time, and I'll see
you at the office." He paid their bill and left.

Tracy waited for what he regarded as a respectable
interval before he addressed the woman. "The *Tribune*," he said carefully, "is a good newspaper, and it
gets better with every issue."

Susanna Fulton was startled. "How did you know I
work for the *Tribune*?"

"I couldn't help hearing you and your father talking," he said, "and seeing that I read and admire the
paper, I had to speak up. I hope you don't think I'm
too forward."

"Not at all," she replied graciously.

Perhaps, Tracy thought, he could interest this attractive woman in accompanying him to a hotel room
for the afternoon. The possible adventure was a more
exciting prospect than the brothel visit he had
planned.

Quietly studying him, Susanna reflected that the
young man was clean-cut, meticulously dressed, and
good-looking, but she instinctively disliked him. The
reason, she decided, was the expression in his eyes.
They were hard and searching, failing to match his

warm smile, and soon he looked away, for some reason unable to meet her steady gaze.

Inventing a new name, as he frequently did, Tracy introduced himself. No one in Denver knew his real identity, and he had no intention of revealing it, particularly to the daughter of the local newspaper publisher. The fewer people who really knew him, the longer he would be able to perpetrate his robberies without fear of being detected.

Making up her mind to terminate the casual conversation as quickly as possible, Susanna refrained from telling him her own name and drained her coffee, even though it was still hotter than she liked. Then she rose, smiled fleetingly, and made her way out of the restaurant.

Tracy's eyes narrowed as he watched her until she vanished from sight. Her snub had been deliberate, and he felt a strong urge to strike back at her in some way. How he would enjoy humiliating her, forcing her to apologize to him! But this was not the right time for such a gesture. There were too many people on the streets, and he would be taking too great a risk if he tried to isolate her in broad daylight. Nevertheless, he promised himself, he would encounter the young woman again and would force her to accord him the respect that he demanded.

Susanna put the chance encounter out of her mind, not realizing she had made a potentially dangerous enemy. She walked back to the *Tribune* office, eager to begin work on a new article she wanted to write. No sooner had she settled herself at her desk, however, when a visitor came into the room.

He was tall and slender, wearing the dark suit of a professional man, and his direct gaze was friendly. It was odd, she thought, that she habitually judged character by what she saw in a person's eyes. "May I help you?" she asked.

"Miss Fulton," he said, "you don't know me, but

I've been an admirer of your father's in Sacramento. I'm an attorney, Isaiah Atkins, and I'm the adopted son of Chief Justice Hamilton of California."

She asked him to sit.

"I've come to Colorado with General Blake. He and our investment banker, Luke Brandon, are out in the field, inspecting some mining properties recently purchased by a pair of our fellow Californians, Chet Harris and Wong Ke."

"Harris and Wong have a long list of achievements in California behind them, and I daresay they'll do as well here." Susanna felt at ease with the young lawyer.

"Ever since I've been old enough to read newspapers," he said, "I've applauded the crusading spirit of Wade Fulton. That's why I'm here now. General Blake and Luke Brandon are trying to make a survey of the mines already in operation to the west of Denver, but I'm finding it unexpectedly difficult to persuade a good many mine owners to open their properties for inspection. I'm hoping the *Tribune* can help me."

"We may be able to give you a hand, Mr. Atkins," Susanna said, smiling, "and perhaps you could do me a favor in return. I happen to know a little about you, too. I know that General Blake's party is living in a large house that Harris and Wong purchased a short time ago. I've made several attempts to interview General Blake, but Mrs. Blake has repeatedly turned me away—politely, to be sure. I'm eager to see him because he's one of the most distinguished men who has come to Denver. But, for some reason, he has refused to talk with me."

Isaiah well understood Lee Blake's reluctance to be interviewed by the press. In actuality, he was not a retired officer engaging in a business venture but was still on active duty, performing an important presidential mission. Realizing he had no authority to reveal the real reason for Lee's presence in Colorado, Isaiah nevertheless thought that this pretty reporter's request was fair.

"I can't promise you that the General will consent to be interviewed in the near future, Miss Fulton," he said. "On the contrary, he'll continue to avoid talking to you. But I hope you'll be patient. If you'll agree to wait, in due time you'll have a much bigger story than an article about a retired military officer and his syndicate of mining investors."

Susanna raised a delicate eyebrow.

"It isn't my place to say anything more," he said. "You have no reason to trust the word of a stranger, but I'll do my best, and at the appropriate time I believe I can persuade General Blake to give you a story that will make headlines."

She weighed his statement and finally decided to take a chance. "Obviously you aren't being mysterious for the pleasure of it, Mr. Atkins," she said. "All right. I'll go along with you. I'll make no further attempt to interview General Blake. But in the meantime I'll gladly cooperate with you."

"You understand that I may not be able to keep my end of the bargain. I'll tell Lee Blake about our meeting today, and he may or may not consent to have an off-the-record chat with you. He's a man who makes his own decisions."

"Understood and agreed." Susanna smiled and stood. "I've been accumulating data for an article I'm not ready to write yet. Let me get it for you."

As she crossed the room, Isaiah couldn't help noting that, although she was tiny, she had a perfect, rounded figure.

Susanna returned with a file folder. "So far," she said, "I've been investigating three mining companies that have gone underground rather than just try their luck in open pits. Their reason for not giving General Blake access to their mines is obvious, although I can't yet prove it." She handed him the folder.

Isaiah glanced at her notes.

"You probably can't read my writing," she said. "I have a horrible scribble. What I'm trying to nail down, in essence, is that these people are operating unsafe mines. They're so greedy to haul out as much gold as they can that they don't shore up their tunnels carefully. One of these days there will be a major cave-in, and a lot of hard-working miners will be injured and killed."

Isaiah read the notes more carefully, jotting down the names of the companies for himself. "The problem," he said, "is that there are no laws at present that compel mine owners to observe safety regulations. The federal government won't be in a position to intervene until Colorado officially becomes a territory. These mines lie beyond the jurisdiction of Kansas, and even the land east of Cherry Creek—where there is no gold—is too far from Kansas for any effective controls to be exerted."

"Thanks for the background," she said, then added, "Now what exactly can the *Tribune* do for you?"

"What I have in mind," Isaiah said, hooking his thumbs in his waistcoat pockets, "is to threaten the mine owners with adverse publicity in the *Tribune* if they refuse to allow General Blake and Luke Brandon entry into the mines. Are you agreeable to such a scheme?"

"There's nothing I'd like better."

"Are you acquainted with any of these mine owners yourself?" he asked.

Susanna shook her head. "I've been in touch with their managers, but I've never seen or met the owners."

"In that case," he suggested, "once they've been forced to allow us to inspect their properties and obtain permission for Luke Brandon to take ore samples, you might want to join our inspection parties."

"I'd love it!" Susanna became excited. "I had just about given up hope of seeing the inside of those tunnels."

"It seems to me that's the least I can do for you," he declared, grinning at her.

She returned his smile. "We make a good team. Between us we should be able to find out all we want to know, you for your purposes and I for mine."

Isaiah held out his hand, and a sudden tingle shot through him when she shook it firmly.

"My father will be very much interested in this arrangement," Susanna said. "Are you free to join us for supper this evening?"

"There's nothing I'd enjoy more," Isaiah replied, somewhat surprised by the depth of his own sincerity.

Wong Ke took Lee Blake and Luke Brandon for a visit of several days' duration to the mines in the vicinity of Central City and the other villages that were coming into existence west of Denver. Chet Harris remained in the city to continue the negotiations for several additional properties that he and his partner hoped to buy. So far they had found limited quantities of gold in one mine and were busily digging shafts on other properties. Their approach was methodical, and both were convinced that, in time, their efforts would be handsomely repaid.

Returning to the boardinghouse late one afternoon from a meeting, Chet heard himself hailed from the parlor. Caroline Brandon, wearing one of her low-necked, form-hugging dresses, was beckoning.

"At last, another member of the human race!" she said, smiling broadly.

"Where is everyone?"

"Well, Cathy Blake and Patricia have gone off to a dressmaker's for some clothes that Cathy is sending her daughter. Mei-lo and her new helper are cooking supper in the kitchen. Lieutenant Brentwood and Sergeant Mullins are off in the gold country with General Blake and my husband. And that leaves me. I've been reluctant to wander around town without any specific place to go because there are so many rough men on the streets looking for trouble." She sighed dramatically. "I've been reading the first installment of that new novel by Charles Dickens, *A Tale of Two Cities*, until I'm bleary-eyed. And frankly, I'm bored stiff." She paused, her eyes limpid, then asked bluntly, "Will you join me in a drink?"

"I gave up liquor a long time ago," Chet replied, "but I'll be glad to fix something for you." He went to a sideboard. "What would you like?"

"A little whiskey, please, diluted with water."

He knew few ladies who drank anything stronger than sack or wine and was surprised by her request, but he nevertheless prepared her drink and handed it to her.

Caroline thanked him with an inviting smile, sat on a sofa, and patted the adjacent cushion. It would have been rude to refuse, so Chet sat, too.

"Forgive my curiosity, but I've never met a man who won't drink liquor. May I ask why you gave it up?"

"I couldn't handle it," Chet said. "One drink always led to another, and before I knew what was happening, I found myself in trouble. The old story of too much wine and women, without the songs that go with such activities."

"You're so staid and sedate, Chet. I can't imagine you being a woman chaser."

"I've reformed," he replied, smiling.

Caroline felt the stirring of a familiar sense of challenge. Here was a man of considerable wealth and power, admittedly interested in women, who had been unfailingly polite to her since she had moved into the boardinghouse, but otherwise had appeared unaware of her existence. "You must have an unusual degree of self-control," she said, raising her glass to him.

"Willpower, I discovered, is an acquired characteristic." He had no desire to talk about himself.

In Caroline's experience all men were self-centered, so she persisted. "What do you do for entertainment?"

"I've had very little time for indulgence in the past ten years," he replied.

"Oh, dear. You make your life sound so grim." She began to flirt with him subtly, prepared to draw back if he rebuffed her.

In spite of his original intentions, Chet began to relax. "People find their amusements in different ways. I've enjoyed working, and so has my partner. We've invested in a number of businesses, and supervising them takes up just about all of my time."

She regarded him with mock solemnity. "So you became rich, and now you're even wealthier." Taking a long swallow of her drink, she looked at him over the rim of her glass.

"Something like that," he admitted.

Caroline thrust the glass at him. "If you don't mind, I'd like a teeny bit more whiskey. There's so much water that I can't taste anything else."

Trying to be obliging, he went back to the sideboard and added whiskey to her glass, not noticing that she edged closer to his side of the sofa. When he returned to his place, however, he discovered that she was sitting uncomfortably close to him, so close that he could smell the strong scent she was wearing.

"Do you like my perfume?"

"Very much," he said politely.

Her shoulder and knee brushed against his. "This is none of my business, really, but how does it happen that you've never married?" She was wide-eyed.

"I reckon I've never found the woman I wanted to marry." That wasn't true, but he saw no point in revealing that many years earlier, before Melissa Miller had married Rick, he had imagined himself in love with her but had given up his suit after she confessed she didn't love him.

"Finding the right person isn't as easy as it sounds." Her sigh was plaintive. "I was so young when I married Luke, and by the time I learned we were wrong for each other, it was too late. But there isn't much a woman can do when she finds herself in that situation. I've read that people can get divorces on many different grounds in some European countries, but it isn't possible here."

Chet was embarrassed. Luke Brandon was an honorable man whose intellect he respected and whose company he enjoyed. He preferred not to be told about the marital problems of the Brandons.

Aware that he had stiffened, she shifted the emphasis back to him. "In your position," she said softly, "you may never want to marry. You're able to have your cake and eat it, too."

He was amused. "What makes you think so?"

"You don't need me to tell you that you have the kind of personality that acts as a magnet on every woman you ever meet."

He shook his head and smiled. "If that's the case, I've been unaware of it."

"Any woman who isn't drawn to you, any woman who fails to find you irresistible must be deaf, dumb, and blind." She leaned against him.

Chet had already withdrawn to the far end of the sofa, and further retreat was physically impossible. Conscious of this sensuous young woman's ultrafeminine warmth, aware of her deep cleavage, he read the invitation in her shining eyes, telling him he could do what he pleased with her.

This was the moment to strike, and Caroline well knew it. She leaned still closer to him, her full, rouged lips parted.

In spite of Chet's intentions, his desire for her overwhelmed him, and he took her in his arms. She returned his embrace fervently, and her hand, pressing the back of his head, brought his mouth to hers.

She was so intent, so passionate he could no longer think clearly, and their kiss obliterated everything else from his mind. Then, suddenly, the realization struck him that he would be incapable of taking this woman into the bed she shared with her husband.

Wrenching himself free, Chet leaped to his feet. "Sorry," he said in a harsh voice, "but I don't engage in affairs with married women. That's one of my cardinal rules." Unable to return her gaze, he hurried toward the door, calling over his shoulder, "Tell Meilo I won't be here for supper."

Quickly regaining her composure, Caroline watched him as he fled. She had made greater progress with him than she had anticipated, and at their next private encounter she would handle him with greater understanding and aplomb. Somehow she would make certain that his principles didn't prevent him from making love to her.

The shaken Chet barely remembered in time to take his hat and his six-shooter, encased in a holster belt, from a table in the front hall as he raced out of the house. For a time he wandered aimlessly, the fresh air gradually cooling his ardor. Bitterly angry, he was annoyed with himself but could not blame Caroline Brandon. Obviously she was a harlot, but that was her problem—and her husband's. He himself should have known better than to allow her to entrap him, especially when he had recognized her aims before almost succumbing to her.

When Chet came to his senses, he realized he had blundered into a slum district where flimsy shacks made of discarded building materials, stray rocks, and even mud lined both sides of a narrow dirt lane. This shantytown was the home of independent mining prospectors, men who had come to Colorado from all parts of the United States and the world beyond its borders. Unsuccessful in their search for gold, they were desperate and hungry, and many would gladly rob a well-dressed man of middle years who was alone.

Taking care not to appear to be in too much of a hurry, Chet walked briskly toward the center of town.

Not until he left the slums behind him did he dare to take his gold watch from his pocket, and he was startled by the discovery that he had been wandering for the better part of two hours. His stomach told him that he had eaten nothing since an early breakfast.

Not wanting to encounter any of the people with whom he had business dealings, he avoided the hotel dining rooms and larger restaurants, but his hunger was acute, and he wanted a good meal. Paying no attention to the waves of sound emanating from Willie de Berg's Palace, he rounded the corner, slowing his pace as he approached a smaller, far more elegant gambling establishment, where meals were served. Several acquaintances had told him the food there was exceptional, so he opened the door and walked in.

Two card games and a dice game were in progress in the outer room, but the players, most of them in business suits, were quiet and well-behaved. A handsome woman in her thirties, discreetly dressed, smiled as she approached him.

"There's an opening at one of the poker tables if you'd care to try your luck," she said.

He shook his head. "I'm in search of supper, ma'am, and I'm told you serve the best in Colorado."

"That's good to hear." She led him to a room in the rear, where there were a dozen small tables, most of them occupied. Seating him at a vacant table, she handed him a small menu that Susanna Fulton, as a favor, had printed for her on the *Tribune*'s press. She left as he picked it up.

Soon a waiter appeared, and the hungry Chet ordered a simple but hearty meal. The barley soup was hot and delicious, and the steak, broiled rather than fried in the usual Western country-style, was the best he had been served in a long time.

Clara Lou Hadley reappeared as he was eating his main course. "We have only a small selection, but I buy only the best of liquors. Would you like a bottle —or a single drink, perhaps?"

He shook his head. "I never touch booze, Miss Hadley." He had seen the name of the proprietress on the menu.

She did not tell him she was *Mrs.* Hadley. This customer was unusual; never before had someone who neither drank nor gambled come to her place. "You look familiar," she said. "I wonder if you ever ate at my old gambling house near Sacramento."

"Could be, ma'am," he replied, grinning. "I spent a heap of time in the Sacramento Valley gold fields before I settled in San Francisco. Name of Chet Harris." Feeling more at ease, he rose and held a chair for her.

Clara Lou seated herself. "Everyone in California knows who you are, Mr. Harris. I never forget faces, and I'd swear you ate at my old place. Maybe played cards there, too."

"I won't deny the possibility," he said, going on with his meal. "Most nights I was too drunk to know where I was, and I sure dropped too many bundles at the gaming tables. That's why I gave up liquor and gaming."

She nodded. "What brings you to Denver, Mr. Harris?"

"The same thing that's brought you and just about everyone else," he replied. "My partner and I are buying mining properties. One or two major strikes is all we want. You might say we're indulging in a furlough from our real work."

"I thought I had enough rough-and-tumble in California myself, but I know how you feel. Instead of retiring, I came here and opened this place."

Both soon discovered they were acquainted with Rick and Melissa Miller, and Clara Lou asked if he knew the Millers' neighbors, the Taylors.

"Danny is my oldest and best friend," Chet said proudly. "We rode together in the first wagon train to Oregon. Later, in the war with Mexico, Danny lost his leg."

As Chet finished his meal, they reminisced about life in the California gold country.

"Somehow it's different here," Chet said. "The chance of an independent prospector making a strike on his own is pretty remote. His best bet is to go to work with someone else—like me—and take a percentage if he hits gold."

She changed the subject briefly. "I can recommend the hot apple pie."

Chet laughed and patted his slight paunch. "I've given up desserts, too. I don't get that much exercise anymore."

Clara Lou looked disappointed but refrained from comment. Chet was quick to understand. "You baked it yourself."

She nodded.

He summoned the waiter, ordered pie, and, when it was served, became dreamy-eyed as he tasted it. "This is worth putting on more pounds. Not even my mother makes pies like this. Or did, before my stepfather became a congressman from Oregon. Anytime you want to give up a gambling house, you can earn a good living as a pie baker, Miss Hadley."

"I don't think the profits would be as high," she said, then added, "*Mrs.* Hadley."

It was his turn to be disappointed. "There's a Mr. Hadley?"

Although Clara Lou didn't realize it, she smiled bitterly, then shrugged.

Chet knew better than to ask more questions. He was only slightly acquainted with the lady but felt a strong desire to know her better. So, on sudden impulse, he said, "I noticed a poster over at the Apollo, saying that Joseph Jefferson is giving a performance in a new play, *The Octoroon*, two nights from now. If you ever leave this place for an evening, I'd be honored if you'd have dinner and see the play with me."

"I'll be delighted," Clara Lou replied promptly,

flattered by the offer of a social evening. Most of the men she encountered proposed only assignations.

Later, as Chet walked home, he told himself that his luck was still good. If he hadn't fled from Caroline Brandon, he wouldn't have had the good fortune to meet Clara Lou Hadley, whose company he thoroughly enjoyed.

The five men left Central City early in the morning, their saddlebags filled with ore samples from the mines purchased by Harris and Wong. Andy Brentwood and Hector Mullins were in the lead, with the grizzled Sergeant Major necessarily concealing the contempt he felt for any newly commissioned officer. He had served in the army before Lieutenant Brentwood had been born.

Bringing up the rear were Luke Brandon, Lee Blake, and Wong Ke, and all three were engaged in earnest conversation.

"I'm optimistic about these samples," Luke said, "but I won't know for sure that there's any gold in them until we crush the rocks and put them through a smelter. Most people believe that gold is found in pure veins. It sometimes happens, of course, but most frequently it appears in tiny bits and pieces that only the smelting process reveals."

"This raises something of a problem," Lee said. He looked at the Chinese entrepreneur. "You said your big smelter can't handle samples this small, Ke. Is there someone in Denver who would be willing to rent us a little smelter for Luke's tests?"

"By this time next year I'm sure there will be dozens of smelters built for testing purposes," Ke replied. "At the present time, however, I know of none."

Luke was upset. "I can make tests without a smelter, of course, but it will take weeks to learn what we otherwise can find out in a day or two."

Ke remained unconcerned. "I see no problem," he said. "The backyard behind the boardinghouse has more than enough space for a miniature smelter. Chet and I can hire some men early tomorrow morning, and if you wish, Luke, you can supervise the construction job yourself. It will take only a short time to build what we need for our purposes."

"You're very kind," Luke Brandon said.

"I'm never kind," the Chinese replied emphatically, then smiled. "Your needs are our needs. Chet and I are even more eager than you to learn the quality of the ore in the mines we've bought so far—including the one that has been producing a steady yield of gold in these past weeks."

"I can understand why you and Chet have made fortunes. Your thinking is always a jump ahead of other people's." Lee laughed, then sobered quickly when he heard the thunder of approaching hoofbeats on the hard-packed dirt road.

Approaching from the rear was a party of a half-dozen armed horsemen, all of them masked. Ke shouted a warning, and Lee Blake instantly drew his pistol and fired a warning shot over the heads of the approaching riders.

Sergeant Mullins reversed his mount and rode to a place behind General Blake, where he could act as a shield. Lieutenant Brentwood followed and took up a similar position.

The masked horsemen continued to approach in formation at a rapid canter, and it became plain that they planned to smash through the ranks of the party that awaited them, separating and isolating each individual.

"It appears to me we'll have to break this up in a hurry," Andy Brentwood said as he reached for his rifle. Swinging it to his shoulder, he took quick but careful aim, then squeezed the trigger.

His shot at a moving target was phenomenal, his

bullet boring a hole in the center of the forehead of a would-be robber. The man toppled forward and sprawled dead on the ground, his mount swerving wildly, then galloping away.

Hector Mullins fired his rifle a second later, and his shot was effective, although less accurate. One of the other masked men dropped his rifle, grasped his shoulder, and, in obvious pain, turned away and rode off in the direction of Central City. The remaining robbers continued to press forward.

Wong Ke emptied his six-shooter, but he was no marksman, and all of his shots went wild. The unarmed Luke Brandon had paled but remained calm and quiet during the emergency.

Lee Blake waited until the bandits drew still closer before firing his pistol again. He had fought in too many battles to lose his composure.

Lieutenant Brentwood reloaded with astonishing speed, then fired again. He demonstrated that the accuracy of his aim had not been accidental by dispatching a second of the masked men.

Their numbers now reduced by half, the robbers turned and fled, with Hector Mullins sending them on their way with a shot that wounded another of them.

"Not bad, Lieutenant," Lee said, smiling, then added graciously, "You were more than adequate, Mullins."

The young officer and the Sergeant Major resumed their places at the head of the line, and the party rode on toward Denver.

Luke was bewildered. "Aren't we going to do what we can to identify the bodies of those dead men?"

"We're in a rough part of the world, Luke," Lee said, "and we've got to act accordingly. If we linger too long trying to identify these men, the friends of the dead may come back—with reinforcements. It doesn't pay to be charitable in these parts. I suggest we continue on without delay."

The geologist nodded slowly. The Colorado mountains were far from the civilized world of Cambridge, Massachusetts.

"You can be sure their bodies will be rifled of clothes and valuables," Ke said in disgust. "The buzzards will take care of the rest."

For a long time Sergeant Major Hector Mullins rode in a tight-lipped silence. Then he said, "Lieutenant, were you taught marksmanship at the military academy?"

"Not really," Andy replied, smiling. "When I was born in Independence, Missouri, it was still a frontier town. So the son of Sam Brentwood learned to ride and shoot as soon as he could walk."

Hector was relieved, and his concept of the natural order reasserted itself. A sergeant major with several decades of army experience under his belt was superior to newly commissioned academy graduates in every aspect of military life. The fact that Lieutenant Brentwood was a superb, incomparable marksman was irrelevant to his training at West Point.

IV

Clara Lou Hadley, wearing one of her more expensive, but modest, silk dresses, and the conservatively attired Chet Harris were having the time of their lives. They had been mutually attracted at their first meeting, and two nights later, dining in elegant splendor at the Harry Allen House, they discovered they were truly kindred spirits. Both knew the ways of the world, but they shed their cares and cynicism for a few hours, and all through the splendid dinner they chatted incessantly, laughing and giggling like a pair of teenagers.

They walked the short distance to the Apollo, where a large crowd was climbing the stairs to the second-floor theater. Chet had bought a pair of the most expensive seats, in the front rows, and they were surrounded by the rapidly growing community's civic leaders, most of whom were accompanied by their wives. A few rakes were escorting gaudily dressed trollops, but the respectable succeeded in not seeing these women or the men with them.

The rest of the theater was filled with entertainment-hungry miners who could afford the price of a seat. They knew nothing about the play itself, and most had never heard of the playwright, the celebrat-

ed Dion Boucicault, a master of melodrama. It was
enough for them that they were seeing Joseph Jefferson, acclaimed as one of the great actors of the era,
who had achieved a great success in New York with
The Octoroon.

The subject of the drama was the ill-fated love
affair of a man and a woman who, although he didn't
know it, was part black. During various scenes, which
intended to invoke sympathy for the mulatto heroine,
prolonged boos erupted from one side of the theater,
and miners on the other side angrily demanded quiet.

Clara Lou and Chet remained in their seats during
the intermission. "It appears," he said quietly, "that
there's a considerable delegation of Georgians and
other Southerners from what used to be Auraria in the
audience."

"So it seems," she replied. "It must be difficult for
the actors to work through all that noise."

"I don't like the attitude in the back," Chet said.
"Most of the miners have gone to the saloon downstairs for some quick drinks during the intermission,
and they'll be in an even uglier mood when they come
back to their seats. Would you like to leave now?"

"Only if you do," Clara Lou replied, giving him a
quick smile. "I don't scare easy."

"Neither do I," he said, admiring her. "If things get
nasty, stay close to me. I always carry my six-shooter."

"I'll stick to you like ox-hoof glue," she promised.
"Anyway, I always go armed, too. It's a habit I picked
up during the California gold madness." She opened
her handbag and showed him a small pearl-handled
pistol.

Chet was impressed, but there was a hint of skepti-
cism in his voice as he asked, "Can you shoot?"

Clara Lou's reply was laconic. "I'm as good as most
and better than many."

His admiration for her increased. He had known
few women other than his mother, Cathy Blake, the

amazing Eulalia Holt, and the other redoubtable pioneer wagon train ladies, who could handle firearms.

There was no further chance for conversation. The oil lamps in the auditorium were dimmed, and they settled in their seats for the last acts of the five-act play.

Boucicault's flair for the melodramatic aroused the already emotional miners. The boos and jeers became louder and more sustained, as did the efforts of others to silence them. Ultimately Joseph Jefferson stepped forward to the footlights and asked the audience to allow the performance to continue unimpeded.

A number of the civic leaders in the front rows were uneasy. Chet and Clara Lou exchanged a quick smile, and he patted her hand reassuringly. Neither wanted to leave, particularly as it would have been necessary to walk up the center aisle past the miners. Both realized their departure might trigger unpleasantness.

The audience was fairly restrained during the final portion of the play, but after the actors took their bows and the lights became brighter, sudden pandemonium erupted. Men on both sides of the aisle lunged at their detractors on the opposite side, and a dozen violent fights erupted simultaneously. Within moments scores of miners were engaged in the melee, which was developing into a full-scale riot. The growing hatred between Northerners and Southerners was the root of the disturbance, and men clubbed each other with abandon. Many were bleeding, and although no weapons had been fired as yet, it was only a matter of time before the shooting began. It was too much to expect that armed men would have the good sense to refrain from using their guns.

The fighting spread to all parts of the auditorium as the miners shouted, cursed, and shoved, using their fists as well as the butts of their weapons.

Chet's first concern was Clara Lou's safety. The

struggling fighters surged through the front rows, and many leaped onto the stage as they engaged in combat. No part of the theater was safe.

"Should we wait until this dies down?" Clara Lou shouted above the uproar.

Chet shook his head. "I'm afraid you'll be trampled. And God knows what will happen when the shooting starts." He drew his six-shooter.

Displaying remarkable calm, she took her pearl-handled pistol from her handbag and cocked it.

"We'll try to run the gauntlet," he told her. "Just remember, easy does it."

She understood what he meant. They would have to exercise care not to appear to be menacing any individual or group, or they, too, would be attacked.

Chet put an arm around Clara Lou's shoulder, his six-shooter in his other hand, and started up the aisle with her. A rifle butt missed his head by inches, but he did not flinch and continued to move slowly toward the exit.

An enraged, red-eyed miner on Clara Lou's side of the aisle was startled when he saw the attractive woman so near to him. The fight momentarily driven from his mind, he lunged toward her.

She pointed the small pistol at him. "I wouldn't, if I were you," she told him.

The man hesitated, and Chet's grip on Clara Lou tightened. He realized that the miner's pause was only momentary, so he acted swiftly, clubbing the man with his own pistol butt. The miner slumped, sprawling over the back of a theater seat.

Again Chet propelled his companion toward the stairs at the rear of the auditorium. When they reached that place, however, they became aware of a new complication. Other miners, spreading out as the riot went out of control, were fighting on the narrow staircase.

It was far too dangerous to remain in the theater, and Chet knew he had no alternative. "Stay close behind me," he shouted to Clara Lou. "Somehow we'll get to the bottom of the stairs!"

Bracing himself, he made his way down, one step at a time, and could feel Clara Lou clutching the back of his coat. Four miners, fighting in earnest, blocked their path now, and Chet realized he had to take the risk of moving them out of his way. They were beyond reason, so he knew it would be useless to appeal to them. Instead, he raised his six-shooter, grasping it firmly by the barrel, then struck repeatedly at the miners, aiming his blows at their heads. One of the men, struck on the temple, tumbled down the stairs to the bottom.

Chet's aim was hurried, and his second blow caught a miner on the shoulder. Losing interest in the fight, the man clapped a hand to his shoulder, then shrank back against the wall on one side of the staircase. The remaining pair turned together to face the assailant who had surprised them.

Chet quickly spun his six-shooter so he held it by the butt. "Let us pass, and be quick about it," he said in a voice of sharp command, "or I'll kill you."

They heard the authority in his tone, and the expression in his eyes told them he meant every word.

Then Clara Lou raised her own pistol. "We're not joking," she said flatly.

The sight of the earnest, armed woman convinced the brawlers they would be wise to obey. Panting from their exertions, their own enmities momentarily forgotten, they squeezed against the wall in order to make space for the grim couple.

Chet increased his pace, and with Clara Lou still close behind him, they reached the street without further difficulty. But the fight had spread to the occupants of the saloon on the ground floor, some of whom had spilled out into the open.

Again putting an arm around Clara Lou, Chet made his way as rapidly as he could away from the riot. They did not halt until they had gone about a block from the scene of the senseless disturbance. As they stopped, they heard the sound of gunfire erupting in the theater. They had made their escape just in time. Now men would die needlessly, others would be severely wounded or maimed, and the absence of an organized constabulary in the community meant the fight would continue until both sides were exhausted.

They were still too close for comfort, so Chet led his companion farther from the scene before they halted. He didn't realize it, but his arm still encircled Clara Lou's shoulders. She looked up at him when they paused, breathless from exertion.

Suddenly, with one accord, they embraced and kissed. Perhaps the spontaneous reaction was caused by their realization that they were safe; possibly the mutual attraction they had felt had been heightened by the danger they had suffered together. Whatever the reason, their kiss was impulsive, a natural, unthinking gesture.

When they drew apart, they were shaken. Both were sexually experienced, and both knew at once that this intimacy had been no ordinary kiss. At the same time, however, neither was as yet prepared for a close relationship that might involve more complications than they were prepared to face.

"If we were drinkers," Chet said, "this would be the right time for a strong dose of whiskey."

"I suggest coffee instead," Clara Lou replied. "My place will still be open for another hour or two, and there's always a pot bubbling on the stove."

She took his arm, and they resumed their walk, paying no further heed to the sounds of gunfire behind them. They knew, as veteran frontier dwellers, that they could do nothing to halt the riot; their only alternative was to ignore it.

Others obviously felt as they did. Men emerged from saloons and gambling halls to find out what was happening, and the scantily clad inmates of a brothel

appeared briefly in the street, too. Then, being real-
ists, all returned to their own activities.

For a time neither Chet nor Clara Lou spoke again,
but finally she said, "You were great back there."

"You were pretty wonderful yourself," he replied,
grinning.

"Well," she said, "a body can't afford to panic when
the chips are down. I've seen too many poker players
lose the whole stack of chips that way."

He chuckled, appreciating her good sense.

When they drew closer to Willie de Berg's Palace,
they saw that a number of the men and corseted
women had come into the street to find out the cause
of the gunfire and were now drifting back into the
establishment.

De Berg himself caught sight of the couple and
stayed behind to watch them. His eyes narrowed
when he recognized Clara Lou. "Enjoy the fireworks?" he asked her, then laughed.

She nodded coldly, scarcely admitting that she
knew him, and de Berg transferred his attention to
Chet, studying him carefully.

Never had Chet seen such evil, such hatred in any
man's eyes. He returned the stare quietly, persisting
until the saloonkeeper looked away and returned to
his establishment.

"He thinks of me as competition," Clara Lou said.
"He offered me a job as a madam, and he hasn't
thought too highly of me since I turned him down
flat."

"That man is your enemy," Chet said. "If looks
could kill, you'd be dead now."

"He didn't appear to be any too fond of you,
either," she said. "Willie de Berg has a vicious reputation in the gambling hall business, so you may decide
you don't want to associate with me."

He stopped short outside the entrance to her establishment and stared at her. "If I knew you better,

Clara Lou Hadley, I'd spank you until you took that back!"

"I take it back," she replied hastily.

"You better. And if this de Berg starts being mean to you—or tries to force you to close down—just let me know. Money talks loud and clear, and I have ways of not only backing him into a corner but driving him clean out of business."

Chet didn't realize it, she thought, but it was his determination, combined with the sort of stubborn courage he had displayed when he had extricated her from the riot, that made him formidable. "We'd better go drink that coffee," she said quietly, "before it gets so strong it'll keep us awake all night."

All of the evening's customers had departed from the dining room, so they carried their mugs of coffee to a table, enjoying the privacy. The strains of the evening had taken a toll, and neither was in a mood for conversation, but they enjoyed sitting together, exchanging a few words.

Suddenly Chet said, "Tell me to shut up if you want, but there's something that's nagging at me. You mentioned something the other night about having a husband."

"We've had a hundred years crammed into one evening," Clara Lou replied, "so I guess I know you well enough. There isn't much to tell. When I got married, I was young and foolish, but it didn't take long for me to learn I'd made a mistake. I worked, and he lived off my earnings for a year. Then I threw him out. After I opened my own hall, he showed up every now and again, always wheedling and whining for money—which I gave him to get rid of him. But I haven't seen him in years, and I don't know if he's alive or dead. I shouldn't say this about any human being, but he's such a mean, craven soul that I can't help hoping he's passed away."

"Thank you for confiding in me," Chet said soberly. "I'm flattered."

"I kept it bottled up inside me for too long. You're the first person I've ever told. Now I feel better, so let me be the one to thank you."

Chet reached across the table and took her hand. "You deserve better in life than what you've had."

She did not withdraw from his touch. "I have no complaints."

"No, you're not the type to complain. If anybody asks me—and I'll be glad to tell them even if they don't ask—you're a wonderful woman, Mrs. Hadley."

"Between your sweet talk and this coffee, I won't sleep a wink all night. Go along home, Chet."

"I will, on one condition," he said. "Come to dinner at our house tomorrow. I want you to meet my partner and some of my oldest friends."

Suddenly shy and insecure, Clara Lou could only nod her acceptance.

The shielded candles provided only faint illumination, but the party following the mine owner through the tunnel could make out more than enough. In places the timbers of the roofing that had been erected to prevent cave-ins were structurally sound, but in others they formed a mere skeleton, threatening those who worked there.

The visitors did not linger long in any one place. Lee Blake accompanied the proprietor, and Luke Brandon, carrying a burlap sack, paused occasionally to obtain an ore sample from one of the grimy, dirt-spattered miners. Susanna Fulton brought up the rear with Isaiah Atkins and Lieutenant Andrew Brentwood, and all three remained silent. Occasionally the young woman studied the timbers but took care to commit what she wanted to know to memory. Had she taken notes, she might have given away her purpose in accompanying the group.

Even Lee, who had the ability to remain calm no

matter what the circumstances, was relieved when they emerged into the open again.

"Whew." Susanna brushed a layer of dust from her clothes. "How I'd hate to spend twelve hours a day working down there."

"Seeing a mine from the inside," Andy Brentwood said, "makes you realize why the men who work there drink and play so hard when they come into Denver for a night and day of relaxation."

"I hadn't thought of it that way, but you're right." Susanna gave him a bright smile.

Isaiah felt an unwarranted stab of jealousy. He had spent several evenings in Susanna's company, but that did not give him a proprietary claim on her, and he had no right to object if she and Andy enjoyed each other's company. The problem was that they had taken to each other from the time of their first meeting and were too all-fired friendly.

On the other hand, Isaiah had to admit, Susanna was equally attentive to him, so he had no call to protest. Perhaps she was one of those unusual women whose interest in any young man of substance was genuine. The realization that he might be falling in love with her struck him with considerable force, but for the moment, at least, there was nothing he could do about it.

"A person can't help feeling a greater sympathy for the miners," he said, then felt foolish when he realized they were talking about something else now.

Sergeant Major Mullins appeared, insisting that he put Luke's samples in his saddlebag, and his presence provided something of a diversion. Isaiah couldn't help feeling relieved that he had interrupted the private talk of Susanna and Andy.

Lee said good-bye to the mine owner, thanking him for his courtesy, then joined the others. "I think the hazards of the road are fairly severe after dark," he said, "and it's too late now to reach Denver before early morning. If you have no objection, Miss Fulton,

I suggest we camp out in the open. I can offer you a warm blanket and the protection of a strong and competent escort detachment."

"That's fine with me, General," she said. "I wasn't expecting to get back to town tonight, and I've brought my own things for an overnight stay in the open."

Lee laughed. "I should have guessed," he said. "You're like my daughter—the resourceful type who looks ahead."

Andy Brentwood told himself that Beth Blake would be fortunate if she turned out to be as well-balanced, sensible, and attractive as Susanna Fulton. He had known few girls during his formative years in Independence and still fewer while he had been a cadet at the military academy, but he was already convinced that Susanna was unique.

"May I help prepare supper?" she asked.

"No, miss." Hector Mullins was polite but firm. "Guests of the General aren't permitted to do any of the work. I've already started the fire at the site I picked on the far side of that hill, and I'll do the cooking."

"Do you cook, Sergeant?"

"Miss," he replied, "after a lifetime in the army, I can do blame near anything."

The whole party laughed as they mounted their horses. Isaiah and Andy both edged closer to Susanna, hoping to escort her to the site, but Lee unexpectedly thwarted them. "Ride with me, Miss Fulton," he invited. "I'd like a private word with you."

"Of course, General." She moved up beside him.

He waited until they started before he addressed her again. "I'm sure you've been frustrated by my refusal to grant you an interview," he said. "I must apologize for any annoyance I've caused you."

Susanna was caught by surprise and said something polite to the effect that it didn't matter.

"Of course it matters, or you wouldn't be a competent reporter. Which you are. I've been reading some of your articles in the *Tribune*, and I like them."

"Thank you." She knew he was leading up to something.

"I've also observed you rather carefully on the occasions Isaiah has brought you to the house for a meal. And if I hadn't been conscious of your desire for an interview, Isaiah has remedied that deficiency. Lately Andy has been adding his voice to the clamor, too." He did not mention that she apparently had to be more than a good reporter; her conquests of two splendid young men indicated that she had any number of other admirable traits.

Susanna saw his expression, guessed what he was thinking, and flushed.

"I don't mean to embarrass you, Miss Fulton," he assured her hastily.

"I'm not really embarrassed," she said, giving him an elfin grin, and she spoke the truth. Actually, she was pleased by the attentions of Isaiah and Andy and hoped she wouldn't become a block to their growing friendship.

"Miss Fulton," Lee said, his manner becoming solemn, "I've decided to take you into my confidence. To an extent."

"Yes, General?" Perhaps he intended to reveal the big news story she had been so anxiously awaiting.

"I must ask you to print nothing about it in the *Tribune*. Not now, nor at any other time in the foreseeable future."

"May I ask why?"

"I must rely on your patriotism as well as your own innate sense of discretion."

She was stunned. "My patriotism, General?"

"You're bound to stumble onto a portion of the truth yourself. No, not stumble. You're bright enough to analyze certain facts. I'm sure you already know that my nephew is a recent graduate of the military academy at West Point, and you're bound to realize that new lieutenants do not retire from the army after being graduated. Andy is on active duty. Sergeant Major Mullins is still in the service." He paused, then added quickly, "So am I."

"I see," Susanna said, then shook her head. "Actually, I don't see at all."

"I've come to Colorado on a mission vital to the interests of the United States," Lee said. "That much you would have either guessed or divined, so I tell you no state secret in divulging it. After my task here is completed, I'll do what I can to obtain the approval of higher authority to give you the information necessary for an article. I'm sorry, but that's all I can divulge to you at present."

Susanna was silent for a moment. "Thank you for your confidence, General. May I explain the situation to my father?"

"I'd be the last to request any daughter to withhold information from a father." Lee knew he had judged the young woman correctly and grinned at her.

"Naturally," she said, "the *Tribune* will abide by your wishes. I just hope you won't forget me when the time comes that you can make your story public."

"Miss Fulton," he said with great sincerity, "you aren't the kind of a young woman whom any man in his right mind is likely to forget."

They pulled up at the campsite, where Hector Mullins's roaring fire was dying down to the coals needed for cooking. Before Lee could dismount and help Susanna, Andy and Isaiah leaped from their mounts and raced toward her, each subtly jockeying for the right to assist her.

Lee smiled, remembering the days when he had courted Cathy. Her smile had caused the sun to shine, and any lack of interest in him, real or imagined, had cast a pall of gloom around him.

Susanna was too quick for either of the young men.

Her light laugh impartial, she dismounted before either of them could come close to her.

Lee laughed silently, then watched as they almost literally stumbled over each other.

She solved that problem, too. "No matter what Sergeant Mullins says," she declared, "I intend to help him fix supper. It isn't right for an able-bodied woman to stand aside and allow a man to do all the cooking."

Isaiah and Andy looked at each other, their expressions a blend of frustration and sympathy.

Hector gruffly accepted Susanna's assistance. The meal was a typical army mess of beef stew and baked beans, and the coffee, which the Sergeant Major insisted on brewing by himself, was dark and bitter.

After supper Susanna offered to do the dishes, but both Isaiah and Andy claimed the privilege of washing the dishes for her. She suggested they perform the task together, which they did. Suddenly Susanna caught General Blake looking at her and smiling faintly, and she had the audacity to wink at him.

Lee had to turn away to avoid laughing aloud. She continued to remind him of Beth, and he thought that if either of her suitors was successful, he wouldn't know a dull moment for the rest of his life.

Soon after the meal ended, the older men retired, rolling up in their blankets. Susanna thought it only polite to wait until the younger men finished doing the dishes, since she had suggested the idea to them. So she sat on the far side of the fire, looking into it. The day had been anything but wasted, she reflected. The material she had accumulated on the need for greater protection in the gold mines was valuable and would make a major contribution to the exposé she intended to write.

As for General Blake's revelation that he was still on active army service, she knew she would be forced to wait until he told her the whole story. Until then, she preferred not to speculate on his reason for coming to Colorado. She loved her country and consequently was honor-bound to print nothing until she received his permission.

Their task accomplished, Isaiah and Andy came to her, placing their rifles on the ground and sitting on either side of her. Both clamored for her attention: the attorney was indirect, quietly trying to steer the conversation into channels that would put him in a favorable light, while the army officer was more blunt but equally persistent.

Never before had Susanna been subjected to such double-barreled attentions, and she enjoyed herself thoroughly. As a matter of principle she didn't believe in flirtation, so she was surprised to find herself smiling coquettishly and fluttering her lashes, first at one and then at the other.

I'm a witch and should be ashamed of what I'm doing, she told herself sternly, but that didn't deter her.

The lively, friendly competition went on, with neither of the young men ready to give up. Susanna was becoming sleepy, but her admirers were still wide awake, and ultimately it dawned on her that neither was willing to retire and leave her alone with the other. She would have to take matters into her own hands.

"I don't know about you two," she said, "but we were up early this morning, and I suspect Sergeant Mullins will awaken us at dawn. So I'm going to sleep."

Andy cut some pine boughs with his knife, then wrapped them in his blanket so she could use it as a pillow. "The night is quite warm," he said. "I'll be just fine without it."

Isaiah was not to be outdone. "I'm never cold," he declared. "Take my blanket. Just in case you need an extra one, Susanna."

Having no real choice, she accepted the loan of both blankets, even though the air was frosty and she knew the two young men would be shivering before the night ended. Later, as she was dozing off, she thought she could hear the sound of their teeth chattering, and she had to stifle a giggle.

Then, in the distance, she heard the long-drawn, mournful wail of a coyote, and she sobered. It was comforting to know that Isaiah and Andy were on either side of her, both of them armed with rifles they knew how to use.

The occupants of the boardinghouse owned by Chet Harris and Wong Ke were just sitting down to their noon dinner when a knock sounded at the front door. Mei-lo answered the summons, then came to the dining room and addressed Isaiah.

"A young lady and a young man are asking for you," she said. "I told them you were just sitting down to dinner, and they said they would wait. From the appearance of the dust on their boots, they have ridden far."

"I'll go out to see them," Isaiah said, dropping his napkin on the table and rising.

"Show them in," Ke said to the young attorney. "Perhaps they would like to dine with us."

Isaiah left the room and went into the hall where Sarah Rose and Scott Foster were waiting. He hadn't seen them in some time, although they had been childhood friends, and he welcomed them warmly.

"We didn't mean to interrupt your meal," Scott said, "but we just arrived from Sacramento today and spent all morning trying to find you. Rick Miller told us you were staying in Denver at the Harry Allen House, and at the hotel they told us you had moved here."

Isaiah escorted Sarah and Scott into the dining room and introduced them to everyone. Lee and Cathy Blake remembered meeting them on several occasions when they had visited Rick and Melissa, and along with Wong Ke, they insisted that the newcomers join them for the meal.

The competent Mei-lo took their mounts to the small corral that stood adjacent to the miniature smelter that had been built to test Luke Brandon's samples. After washing up, the brother and sister came to the table.

Sarah Rose ate carefully, as befitted a young lady who wanted to gain no weight, but Scott's appetite was prodigious, and he not only ate something of every dish but went back for second portions. Caroline Brandon eyed him speculatively, but he was not aware of her interest.

"Don't tell me you two caught the gold fever," Isaiah said.

"Hardly." Scott's voice was dry. "After what we saw in California—and the tragedy we suffered when our mother was murdered by a couple of crazy miners— we'd be just as happy never to see gold country again. But we couldn't help coming here. We had to come."

"Our brother, Tracy, caught the fever and came here last year," Sarah Rose said. "We haven't heard a word from him in all this time, so we felt we had to come here and look for him."

"Tracy Foster," Andy mused. "I haven't heard the name, but I have a friend at the local newspaper, and I'll see if she can give me any leads."

Isaiah glared at him.

"When a man is prospecting for gold," Chet said, "it isn't too easy for him to write letters. I neglected my mother and stepfather shamefully when Ke and I were searching in the California fields a decade ago."

"I realize that, and so does Scott," Sarah Rose said, and hesitated. "You see, Tracy is inclined to be—well, peculiar. His conduct has been—erratic—ever since our mother was killed, so we're worried about him."

"We'll do all we can to help you," Ke said.

"Where will you stay?" Cathy asked.

Scott shrugged. "We haven't even started to look for a place. Since we were told Isaiah was here, we thought we'd look him up before doing anything else."

"You're welcome to stay with us," Chet told them. "We have ample room."

Brother and sister exchanged a quick look. "You're very kind, sir," Scott said, "but we don't know how long we'll have to stay here. And if our search for Tracy takes any length of time, we'll have to find work to support ourselves. I'm afraid our funds are limited."

"Pay us whatever you wish," Chet replied. "We bought this house for our own convenience, and we aren't trying to make a profit on it."

Scott was speechless, and Sarah Rose had to speak for both of them. "Thank you for being so generous. We gladly accept."

"What sort of work do you do?" Cathy asked her.

"I teach school."

Everyone at the table smiled and nodded.

"Then you'll have no problem," Lee told her. "Two schools are already in operation here, and two others are being organized. There's an acute shortage of qualified teachers, and I'm certain they'll not only hire you but put you to work immediately."

As Isaiah listened to the conversation involving his old friends, he was struck by Sarah Rose's beauty. She had been a pretty child, but now, as an adult, she was striking, and he was dazzled by her. The realization confused him, and he wondered how he could be so strongly attracted to her when he was in love with Susanna Fulton—or imagined himself in love with her, which was virtually the same thing.

This was not the time to analyze his feelings. Perhaps he could find some way to help the Fosters while at the same time further ingratiating himself with Susanna. His trained lawyer's mind worked rapidly, methodically, and his voice was casual as he asked, "You're still operating your family orchards, Scott?"

His old friend nodded.

"There are no orchards in this part of Colorado," Isaiah said, "but a successful fruit grower has to be a good businessman, too. I bring this up because I may know of a good opening for you. Wade Fulton, the owner and publisher of the newspaper here, the *Tribune*, has been enjoying such a smashing success that he's looking for an assistant."

"I know nothing about newspapers," Scott replied.

"You'd be dealing with business matters exclusively. As I understand it, you'd keep the books, handle the payrolls, buy the paper and ink they need, and, when the *Tribune* starts accepting advertising in the near future, run that department, too."

Scott brightened. "I know I could handle those functions."

"It would also be helpful to you in your search for your brother. A newspaper has many resources, and the expanding editorial department can ask all of its reporters to assist you in hunting for him, which they could do while performing their regular duties."

"I'm definitely interested," Scott said.

"Then come with me after dinner. We'll go down to the paper, and I'll introduce you to Wade Fulton and his daughter. They'll be delighted to meet a hardworking individual like yourself."

Andy Brentwood stared for a moment at the young attorney. He understood Isaiah's motives and was irritated because his rival for Susanna's affections was scoring an impressive point.

Caroline Brandon's boredom was so excruciating that she wanted to scream. Luke was spending most of his time in the gold fields, collecting ore samples, and when he came back to Denver, he was busily analyzing rocks and testing them in his miniature smelter. He seemed to have forgotten his wife existed, and she was sorry she had come to Colorado. Back in Massachusetts there were any number of men who would have been able to add a little spice to her life.

Chet Harris was hopeless, and she had given him up after he had started paying attention to the woman who operated a small gambling hall. What he saw in Clara Lou Hadley, who was at least ten years her senior, was beyond her, but she didn't care. Andy Brentwood and Isaiah Atkins were personable and good-looking, but they had other interests. The tall, craggy Scott Foster could have been exciting, but he was spending all of his time working at his new position on the *Tribune* or searching for his missing brother, and it was obvious that he had no time to spare for a young woman whose need for attention was overwhelming.

Caroline had been intermittently unfaithful to Luke during the few years of their marriage, which he didn't know, of course, and his ignorance would not harm either of them. An affair, as such, didn't much matter to her, but what she wanted and needed—desperately—was a conquest that would bolster her conviction that she was irresistibly alluring. Her vanity periodically demanded such reassurance, and without it she was miserable. But none of the men in the boardinghouse owned by Harris and Wong seemed aware of her existence.

Had there been anything for her to do in this wild pioneer town, she might have been able to forget herself for a time. But she had read so much that she had lost interest in books, and shopping in Denver for anything other than mining tools, hardware, building equipment, and firearms was a joke.

To be sure, men ogled her incessantly on her forays into the center of the city, and a great many rough miners bombarded her with propositions and suggestive remarks. But she regarded herself as being far above such boors, and their interest in her did nothing to improve her mood. Any woman who was young, understood the use of cosmetics, and dressed with a flair would be certain to create a stir in the ranks of these lonely, sex-hungry men. What she needed was a conquest of substance.

When Luke went off once again with General Blake

and the other men of his party to the mines, Caroline decided that enough was enough. She dressed in one of her more provocative gowns, applied makeup liberally, and after telling Mei-lo she wouldn't be home for dinner, went off to the heart of Denver.

No sooner did she reach the busy center of town, however, than she wondered whether she was making a mistake. Miners and others of the lower classes wouldn't leave her alone and overwhelmed her with their crude comments. She went into a number of shops merely to escape them, but she had no use for any of the wares being offered and soon found herself on the street again. She was tempted to take refuge in one of the saloons, but she had the good sense to know that no lady would dream of entering such a place without an escort. Then she might suffer even more acute complications.

Her uneasiness in no way mitigated Caroline's boredom, but she nevertheless took care never to look in the direction of the miners who called to her. But as she approached what she had been told was one of the more notorious saloons in town, Willie de Berg's Palace, a man standing in front of the establishment, smoking a long, thin cheroot, attracted her attention, and she studied him surreptitiously. His handsome suit obviously had been made to measure, his boots had cost a small fortune, and even his broad-brimmed hat was expensive. Granted that no gentleman in Massachusetts would have worn a multicolored waistcoat or a green and yellow cravat that was held in place by a flashing diamond stickpin. But she was in Denver, the heart and soul of the gold-mining boom country now, not in Massachusetts.

The man looked at her, so she quickly averted her gaze. All the same, she could feel him scrutinizing her with an intensity that sent a shiver up her spine. And after she swept past him, seeming not to notice him, she realized he had fallen in behind her and was following her.

Caroline's pulse raced, and she didn't know whether to flee from the scene or encourage her admirer. Curiosity overcame her good sense, and she slowed her pace almost imperceptibly. Then she saw the sign identifying the Harry Allen House ahead and quickly decided to go into the dining room for a cup of tea. Fear and hope mingling, she knew the man was only a few paces behind her as she entered the hotel.

No sooner had she seated herself at a table than he came up to her, removing his hat. "May I join you?" Willie de Berg asked, exerting his utmost charm and good manners. "Please don't think me presumptuous, but no man enjoys the privilege of seeing such rare beauty more than once or twice in his lifetime."

He had struck precisely the right note, and her smile was as radiant as her nod of assent was gracious.

Willie de Berg introduced himself, and his identity surprised her. She had imagined that the proprietor of a saloon-gambling hall would be vulgar and uncouth, but his manners were those of a gentleman. "I am Caroline Brandon," she told him.

"Mrs. or Miss?"

She realized she had forgotten to remove her wedding ring before setting out on her venture, so it was useless to lie. "Mrs. My husband is—ah—an investment banker who has come to Denver to investigate the possibilities of interesting a financial syndicate back East in putting money in some of the mines out this way."

Willie smiled. "Let me guess. He spends most of his time out in the mining country and leaves you with time to burn."

"You must be clairvoyant!"

"Something like that," he replied nonchalantly, then told the waiter who came to the table to bring a pot of tea.

"You really must be a mind reader," Caroline said earnestly. "You even knew what I intended to order."

He had no intention of revealing that nothing but tea or coffee was served in this dining room between meals. "Ordinarily I'm not this acute," he said. "But it was more than your amazing beauty that attracted me. I knew instinctively that there was an unusual flow of mutual understanding that you and I would share—once we came to know each other."

He was saying just the right words, and she preened for his benefit. Knowing what was required, he admired her in silence for a long time before he murmured, "Extraordinary."

Caroline flushed, then shifted her position slightly so he could see her face and breasts in profile.

The silly wench was an easy mark, just begging to be seduced, Willie told himself. And he would be pleased to accommodate her. Several of the trollops who were in his employ were equally pretty and had figures as ripe, but they sold their bodies to any man who could pay for the privilege, while here was a woman who was inexperienced and naive. He could not resist the challenge to subdue her.

Their tea was served, and Caroline, after first making certain that she knew no one else in the dining room, flirted outrageously with her admirer, enjoying herself when she saw his interest quicken and deepen.

She was the type, Willie reflected, who might entertain second thoughts or suffer cold feet if he allowed her to get away, so it was preferable to maneuver her into a liaison without delay. He chatted with her as they drank their tea, his gaze adoring, and after they were done, as he left the money for their bill and a handsome tip on the table, he asked, "Have you ever seen a gambling hall?"

She shook her head.

"I'd like nothing better than to give you a tour of my modest place," he said.

Caroline hesitated. "I'm a married woman, remember, and I do happen to be acquainted with a number of people in Denver."

"Trust me," Willie said, his manner becoming solemn.

"It's strange," she told him earnestly, "but I do."

When they reached the street, she found the courage to take his arm. If the prissy Cathy Blake happened to see them, that was just too bad. This experience was the first real excitement she had known in months.

Instead of entering the Palace through the front door, Willie led the way down a narrow alleyway adjoining his building, and together they walked past a back staircase into a huge chamber, filled with tobacco smoke, where the roar of voices sounded like waves breaking on a beach.

At least a score of hard-eyed men were standing at a long bar, drinking, and when they stared at Caroline, her instinct prompted her to move closer to her escort. Willie de Berg promptly put an arm around her waist.

She leaned against him gratefully as she took in the other sights. Grim men, none apparently enjoying themselves, were playing cards or shooting dice at a number of tables. And everywhere, either perched on the arms of the players' chairs or wandering around, were young women wearing gaudily colored strapless corselets, black net stockings, and absurd high-heeled shoes.

"Surely those women aren't customers," she said.

Her naiveté was astonishing. "One of their jobs is to encourage the players," Willie said, summoning a nearby brunette. "Cassie," he directed, "say how-do to the lady."

The woman slowly looked Caroline up and down, her smile insolent. "You joining the happy family, dearie?" she inquired.

Before Caroline could reply, Willie shook his head. "Tell the lady how you like working here, Cassie."

"It ain't bad," she said. "I've knowed worse."

Willie glared at her.

Cassie knew there would be trouble if she didn't

change her tune. "Willie is real good to us," she said, "and the pay is prompt. Sometimes, when a miner has made a strike, we get little nuggets as presents."

Willie waved her away and conducted his guest to the staircase, his arm still encircling her, his hand creeping upward until it cupped a breast.

Caroline was nervous now but refrained from drawing away from him for fear he would find her lacking in sophistication. It was plain to her now that the many women here were prostitutes, and it was startling to realize that one of them had just been chatting with her.

The atmosphere in a considerably smaller second-floor room was far different from that in the main saloon. There were only four card tables here, some of the players were well-dressed, and the women who brought them drinks and submitted to their casual caresses were attired in daring evening gowns, even though it wasn't yet noon. It was difficult for Caroline to concentrate on the scene, however, when she believed that at any moment Willie's hand would dart inside her low-cut dress.

Taking his time as he allowed her to absorb the atmosphere of his high-stakes room, of which he was proud, Willie thought fleetingly that Caroline would fit in perfectly here. She had the figure and bearing for the kind of clothes his top-ranking trollops wore, and many of the well-heeled customers enjoyed the company of a woman whose manners were ladylike.

Aware of Caroline's tension, he took her through the room, strolling toward a door on the far side.

Caroline reflected that, by allowing herself to be fondled in public, she was behaving like an abandoned woman. To her surprise, she discovered that she was relishing the unusual sensation.

Once again, Willie realized, he had judged her correctly. Every woman he knew could be fitted into a category, and this one was no exception.

The door closed behind them, and Caroline saw

they were standing in a small, compactly furnished office. Conspicuous on rows of pegs along one wall was a collection of rifles, pistols, and whips.

Willie released her and poured a brown liquid from a decanter into two glasses. "We need a whiskey toast to celebrate finding each other," he said.

Never had she taken liquor this early in the day, and never had she even tasted it until it had been diluted with water. For the second time, however, she told herself not to protest; she wanted nothing to dim the expression of sheer adoration in his eyes when he gazed at her.

He raised his glass. "To you and me," he said, then drained the contents.

"To you and me," she echoed, then followed his example. The whiskey burned as it slid down her throat, and a fiery column made its way to her stomach. She gasped, then coughed.

Willie managed to look concerned.

"I'm just fine," Caroline gasped.

He did not dwell on the state of her health. "This is my office," he said. Opening an inner door, he added, "And this is where I live."

The huge room was a combination bedchamber and living quarters, with a large four-poster bed on one side and a leather sofa with matching chairs on the other. No expense had been spared on the furniture, draperies, and thick rug. "This is lovely," Caroline said, aware that he had shown good taste.

"So are you," he replied, pouring more whiskey into her glass.

She already felt the liquor and knew it would be unwise to drink more when she had as yet eaten no solid foods since the previous night, but what she had first consumed made her reckless, and she gulped the contents of the glass.

Willie stood near her, smiling as he watched her, and Caroline could not resist the temptation to strike a provocative pose for him. She stood with her feet slightly apart, her breasts thrust forward, open invitation in her eyes.

Suddenly she was in his arms, and he kissed her savagely, his bold hands roaming at will. She realized he was treating her as he did the harlots in his employ, and she was momentarily stunned. Luke had always been a complete gentleman, as had her handful of other lovers, but Willie de Berg was brutal and demanding, showing her no respect. All at once she knew she was enjoying the unique experience, that he was arousing her in spite of a determined effort she was making to remain calm.

He undressed her swiftly, expertly removing her clothes, and then he kissed her entire body, his lips gliding and pausing as they moved from her neck to her lower thighs, then worked upward again. She trembled and moaned.

He picked her up, deposited her on the bed, and after quickly disrobing, he made love to her in earnest.

He was a barbarian, she thought, thrilling to his touch. From time to time he subjected her to techniques she hadn't known previously, and because of her unfamiliarity with them, she tried to halt him. Each time, however, he tore her hands away and slapped her smartly across the buttocks. She soon learned she had to allow him to do whatever he pleased, to subject herself totally to his will.

When he took her, she was already overcome with desire, and his driving, relentless thrusts emptied her mind. When she could tolerate no more, her fingernails raked his back, and a scream of ecstasy was torn from her throat.

Then, when he released her, she realized she was not yet satiated. "More," she moaned. "Don't stop now."

He made love to her a second time. And a third. Finally, drowsy and exhausted, she drifted off into a deep sleep.

She did not awaken until a fully clad Willie de Berg stood over her. He was speaking, and with an effort she opened her eyes.

"You've slept the better part of the afternoon," he told her. "I figured you'd want to get home before dark."

"Yes, I must." She struggled to a sitting position, and in a mirror on the wall beside her, she saw her reflection. Her long, wheat-colored hair was tangled, and her face was smeared with cosmetics. Her lips were bruised and swollen, and her whole body ached. "Whatever am I going to do?" she cried. "I can't go anywhere looking like this."

"I'll send somebody to help you," Willie said, and went off.

Caroline tried to curb the panic that welled up within her.

Soon the door opened and a dark-haired young woman in a corselet and black net stockings came into the chamber, carrying a tray of cosmetics. "I'm Bessie," she announced. "Willie says you need some help." She looked at the naked figure huddled on the bed, then laughed hoarsely. "Oh, sweetie doll, do you ever!"

Caroline was too weary to feel embarrassed by her nudity in the presence of a total stranger. "I—I can make myself up," she said.

"Like hell you can. Your hands are shakin'. Just sit still, and I'll do the rest." Bessie went to work, wiping away the makeup smears, then starting anew as Caroline submitted to the ministrations.

"You got one of Willie's special treatments, huh?" Bessie asked, her hard eyes wise.

"I don't know what you mean."

"He has all kinds of special treatments."

"All I know," Caroline said, trying to recover her dignity, "is that he's wonderful."

The woman put down her rouge pot and grasped Caroline's naked shoulders with both hands. "Sweetie doll," she said urgently, "if you know what's good for you, don't fall for Willie. There's a lot of us will tell you the same thing, and believe me, we got our reasons."

Caroline told herself the trollop had to be jealous of her, so she made no reply.

"You ain't joinin' the club?"

Caroline shook her head.

"You're luckier than you know. When you get out of here, don't come back. Ever. Don't even look back over your shoulder."

The advice was absurd, Caroline told herself. Her experience had been unique, her gratification boundless.

Bessie completed her task with a comb and brush, then stepped backward to inspect her handiwork. Smiling broadly, she picked up the rouge pot again.

To Caroline's amazement, Bessie began smearing rouge on her nipples, and she drew back. "Whatever do you think you're doing to me?"

"Willie likes his women to look like that. Remember it, if you're stupid enough to come back."

"I am not one of his women." Refusing to give Bessie the satisfaction of seeing her wipe away the smears, she reached for her clothes, which were piled on a chair. "Where is Willie?"

"He said to tell you good-bye. This is his busy time of day." Bessie winked, pinched the still-nude Caroline hard on a buttock, and left the chamber, her hips swaying.

Caroline dressed hastily. She decided she would pass muster when she returned home, and after making certain she had left nothing behind, she went through the suite, walked as quickly as she could through the room where the games of chance for high stakes were still being played, and descended the stairs.

She wanted to see Willie again before she departed, but her courage deserted her when she thought of entering the huge room where the bar was located. She would choose another time, she thought as she slipped out through the alley door. Yes, she would select a more convenient hour, when he was less busy, probably the same time she had first encountered him today.

For a few moments Willie de Berg watched her through a small window, chuckling quietly at the haughty demeanor. As he had proved so conclusively, that one was no lady. He deliberately had refrained from bidding her farewell, knowing she would be all the more eager to seek him again. Oh, she'd return, all right; his conquest had been complete. It wouldn't be long before she'd become a nuisance and he would be forced to turn her away.

Wandering into the bar, Willie absently fondled one of his harlots, then strolled toward a poker table where an argument was beginning to surge. He permitted no brawls under the roof of the Palace, and anyone who disobeyed his rules would be thrown into the street.

It was Sunday, and the young people riding through the rough country west of Denver were in a holiday mood. They had left the city early for their picnic, the sun was rising in a clear sky, warming the air, and no wind was blowing down from the Rockies. It was a perfect day for an outing.

Lieutenant Andrew Brentwood and Scott Foster were in the lead, each with a rifle under one arm, and they scanned the horizon silently as they rode. Bandits and other ruffians rarely came this close to Denver, but the pair were taking no risks—not with young ladies in the party.

Sarah Rose Foster and Susanna Fulton brought up the rear, with Isaiah Atkins riding between them. Sarah Rose's femininity had inspired Susanna to wear a dress, too, which made it necessary for her to ride

sidesaddle. She did it well, Andy thought, just as she
looked confounded pretty in a dress. He had to admit
she was just about perfect.

Both young women laughed aloud as Isaiah finished
telling them a story. Inspired by their appreciation of
his humor, he launched into another tale.

Andy was quietly annoyed. Isaiah was a good fellow and a smart, enterprising lawyer. Having discovered that his work on General Blake's behalf required
only a small portion of his time, he was picking up a
local practice and already had more clients than he
could service. But he was a blamed show-off when
women were involved. Certainly he had no right to be
hogging the company of both Susanna and Sarah
Rose.

Scott slowed his pace and raised a hand to shield
his eyes from the sun as he peered off intently toward
the southeast.

"See something?" Andy asked.

"One rider."

Andy reached for his binoculars, which were suspended from his neck on a leather thong. Focusing
quickly, Andy found the subject.

"Young fellow with dark hair," he said. "Dressed
like a dude in a fancy suit, a hard-brimmed hat, and
shiny boots. He carries a rifle, of course, but he
doesn't look like the kind who would try to do us
harm. Besides, he's headed away from us, going toward the canyon yonder."

Scott nodded and relaxed. He had no way of knowing that, had he looked through the binoculars, his
search for the missing Tracy would have come to an
abrupt end.

Susanna and Sarah Rose were giggling again, and
Andy increased his pace, putting the lone rider out of
his mind in his desire to reach the picnic site as soon
as possible.

Scott knew he was irritated but asked no questions.
Andy was his kind of man, slow-spoken and careful of

what he said. If he decided to talk about what was bothering him, that would be the time to listen to his complaint.

They rode up a hill to a plateau, and after a short ride, they reached the bank of a small but swift-flowing stream. The creek had overflowed its banks during the spring floods the previous year, uprooting several trees nearby, so there was more than enough firewood at hand. The view from the plateau was unimpeded in every direction, which made it virtually impossible for bandits or stray, hostile Indians to sneak up on the party.

Andy dismounted quickly, but since Susanna was on the ground before he could reach her side, he lifted Sarah Rose from her saddle. Isaiah's quick frown pleased him.

The three men chopped firewood, a task they completed in a short time, and started the cooking fire. In the meantime, the women had unpacked a variety of delicacies, including the produce they had recently purchased.

"I mixed some mustard with the yolks of these hard-boiled eggs," Sarah Rose said. "I hope everyone likes mustard."

Andy knew that Easterners called the dish deviled eggs, but he didn't want to show off, so he kept the knowledge to himself.

"Here are some cucumber sandwiches," Susanna said.

The others stared at her in surprise.

"I had to try them as an experiment after reading about them in one of the English newspapers my father receives. The *Times* of London, I think it was. There's nothing in them except bread, butter, and sliced cucumbers that have been wilted in salt water and then rinsed."

"I'll be big and brave," Scott said, reaching for one of the dainty sandwiches, which he popped into his mouth. "Say, this is good." He grinned at Susanna.

Soon the cucumber sandwiches and deviled eggs vanished.

"Do you suppose we should give them any of the cheese now?" Sarah Rose asked.

Susanna shook her head. "Growing boys will eat rocks if they're encouraged."

"Quite true. Give them enough and they'll spoil their appetites for what's coming." Sarah Rose sat upright. "Scott Foster, don't you dare rummage in that saddlebag! That's where we've packed the desserts!"

Scott would have paid no attention to his sister's order, but he knew Susanna was looking at him, too, so he desisted.

Soon the young men bickered at length, each of them claiming the right to prepare the beefsteaks.

Susanna settled the argument. "Sarah Rose and I will cook the meat," she said. "If you're so anxious to help, you can scrub the potatoes in the creek—right now, because they've got to start baking in the coals."

The young men began their work scrubbing the potatoes, and Sarah Rose brought over to them another filled basket. "You may rinse these tomatoes, too, but don't bruise them," she said.

Isaiah was horrified. "Tomatoes? You mean love apples?"

The women were unruffled. "That's what many people call them," Susanna said.

"But they're poisonous! Everyone knows that!"

Sarah Rose sniffed disdainfully. "Many people, including a lawyer I know—but won't name because I wouldn't want to embarrass him—are ignorant and superstitious. We grow tomatoes at home, and we eat them often."

Scott confirmed his sister's statement. "The tomato is a fruit, not a vegetable," he said. "And I've been told they've been grown and eaten in China for thousands of years."

"I don't know anything about the eating habits of the Chinese," Susanna declared. "I do know that

Sarah Rose and I were lucky to find these tomatoes when we went marketing yesterday. I'm surprised that someone who hails from the Sacramento Valley has never eaten a tomato."

The uncomfortable Isaiah had no reply, and Andy was pleased. Both women had discredited his rival.

But Isaiah refused to stay squelched. After they had cleaned the produce and were waiting for enough coals to form in the fire before baking the potatoes, he recovered his ebullience as he took several tin pans from his saddlebag. "If any of you are interested," he said, "we can pass the time by panning for gold."

The entire group showed an immediate interest in the pastime. Taking a pan, Isaiah dropped to one knee beside the creek. "All you need," he said, "is a little patience and an ability to tolerate the cold water." He dipped his pan to the bottom of the stream, bringing up a quantity of mud and gravel. "That's the first step. Now you gradually wash away the mud, little by little." He placed the pan just below the surface, agitating it gently. Eventually only gravel covered the bottom of the pan.

The others peered at the contents.

Isaiah separated the grains with a forefinger, spreading them. "No luck," he said. "So the process is repeated."

"How do you know when you see gold?" Sarah Rose asked.

He grinned at her. "A nugget practically jumps out of the pan," he said. "You've got to look carefully for smaller particles. I doubt that we'll find anything substantial here. A creek this close to Denver has been worked by dozens and dozens of miners, and if they had come across anything of value, you can bet that a land claim would have been established. But you never can tell. That's the fascination of searching for gold. A hundred people can pan in some spot and find nothing, and the one hundred and first is in luck."

They all went to work in earnest, and for a time no

one spoke. Susanna broke the silence. "My fingers are freezing!"

"Mine, too," Sarah Rose declared. "Oh-oh!"

The others crowded around her.

She pointed to several tiny yellow flecks at the bottom of her pan.

"You've done it!" Andy said. "You've found gold."

"How much is it worth?"

Isaiah laughed. "That small a quantity has almost no worth. Many miners carry little vials for flecks and gold dust, and a full vial may bring quite a few dollars. But it takes many days to collect that much."

"I do believe I'll put the potatoes on the coals now," she said.

They laughed but continued to scoop up mud and gravel.

Susanna was the next to find a few microscopic bits of gold in her pan, and she, too, was satisfied.

The men continued to pan without success until it was time to put the meat on the fire. Andy, who had learned the art of cooking in the open as a small boy, attempted to instruct the girls in the preparation of the steaks but was silenced by a scowl from Susanna.

"This meal is delicious," Scott said as they ate. "I can begin to understand the lure of the gold fields now."

Isaiah nodded. "Unfortunately, most of the men who try their luck start with limited funds. Or none at all. Sometimes they live on a steady diet of nothing but bacon, beans, and water biscuits. And there are far too many who go hungry."

They consumed all of the food they had brought with them, including the homemade jam tarts that Sarah Rose had secreted in the saddlebag, and the men insisted on washing the utensils and dishes in the creek. Then, after Scott lighted his pipe, Susanna drew him aside.

"In the weeks since you've been working at the *Tribune*," she said, "I've heard you describe your missing brother to various people. Again and again. Well, something dawned on me a couple of days ago. I've hesitated to mention it to you, but that wouldn't be fair."

Clenching his pipe between his teeth, he stared at her. She opened the bag she was carrying. "Ever since we began publishing the newspaper here," she said, "I've been reporting about a series of robberies in the area. I've also been interviewing the victims of the crimes, but so far I've picked up only snippets and bits of information. Not enough for an authoritative news article. But something has struck me rather forcibly as I've made condensations of those interviews. Here's one miner's description of the thief who robbed him at gunpoint."

Scott took the paper she handed him and read it. The robber had been tall and well-built; he had been dark, with a prominent chin, and had kept his broad-brimmed hat pulled low to conceal his face. But the victim had caught a brief glimpse of his eyes, which had been gray and cold.

"Here are condensed descriptions of the man who robbed four other miners," Susanna said. "Apparently the same man. You'll note that all of them mention his eyes, which they describe as gray, ruthless, and menacing."

Scott looked through the additional papers, a lump forming in the pit of his stomach.

"Lately," Susanna said, "the men who travel between the mines and Denver call this particular robber the gray ghost. They're so afraid of him that they're riding in groups whenever possible. I believe I'll soon have enough material to do a news story on the gray ghost."

The fire died in Scott's pipe, but he didn't realize it. "There's nothing definite here," he said, "but I've got to admit the possibility that this gray ghost could be my brother. He's dark and tall, with a build similar to mine, only huskier. He has a prominent chin, and his eyes are gray. Just the thought of it makes me sick, but it could be that Tracy has become a robber."

"I'm sorry," Susanna said sympathetically, "but I felt I had to call this to your attention."

"Thank you." Scott glanced at Sarah Rose, who was engaging in an animated conversation with Andy and Isaiah. "Don't mention this to my sister. I don't want to spoil her outing."

"Of course." Having raised the subject, Susanna felt compelled to pursue it. "Something you won't find in my notes," she said, "is that the gray ghost perpetrates his robberies only on the miners' payday. Apparently he's established a definite pattern of operations. He appears suddenly, approaching his victim in some desolate, deserted stretch of countryside, and then he vanishes again just as swiftly."

"Have the men who have been robbed indicated any specific direction that he takes when he leaves them?"

"I'm sorry to say that no two miners tell the same story about that," Susanna replied. "I guess they're in a state of shock and confusion after being threatened and losing their pay. All they say is that he disappears rapidly."

"Even if Tracy is this gray ghost," Scott said, "I don't know where to search for him."

"I'll let you know at once if I learn anything new," Susanna said. "But cheer up. All we have right now are some hazy suppositions, and your brother may be completely innocent."

"Sure," Scott said, but his agreement was halfhearted. He and Sarah Rose long had been upset by the expression in Tracy's eyes, and in his own mind there was little doubt that their brother had become a robber.

V

Tracy Foster changed his clothes slowly, removing his fine new suit, then dressing in the nondescript shirt and trousers he always wore when he needed to replenish his funds. For the first time in many weeks, he felt uneasy, and after placing his new footgear on a natural shelf in the cave and donning his worn work boots, he went out onto the ledge beyond the cave entrance. There he lighted a cheroot and evaluated his situation.

Until now, he had enjoyed a phenomenal good fortune, never having encountered serious difficulties. As yet little information had appeared in the *Tribune* about the robber who had stolen from miners traveling from the gold fields to Denver. And he felt reasonably certain that none of his victims, if confronting him again, would be able to identify him.

All the same, something out of the ordinary was happening. Last week, on the miners' payday, he had waited for hours without finding a suitable victim because no man had been riding from the Central City area to Denver alone. Precisely the same thing had happened yesterday.

Tracy could only surmise that reports of a lone robber had spread and that, as a result, the miners now were making the journey in groups. Possibly he could handle two of them under the right conditions, but he would be taking a far greater risk. And under no circumstances would he contemplate attacking a party of three or four.

His unvarying success had spoiled him, he realized, but he had grown accustomed to certain luxuries: good meals in Denver, visits to various bordellos, the purchase of new clothes whenever he felt like splurging. He found it difficult to contemplate the possibility that the source of his income was evaporating.

That was the case, however, and he had to revise his operations accordingly. He had been too successful, perhaps, and the miners now were taking precautions to avoid being robbed. Very well, he would prove to his own satisfaction that he could be equally resourceful.

The sameness of his robberies was destroying his sense of achievement, so the time had come for him to begin utilizing a new technique. Denver was filled with establishments of all kinds that catered to the public and were earning fortunes. One burglary, if he picked the right place, would bring him rewards greater than he could make in a month of robbing miners.

From what he had seen of the gambling halls, he had to be careful. Granted that they kept huge amounts of money on hand and that a single theft would bring him a fortune, but he knew better than to burglarize one of them. Their proprietors took many precautions, including the hiring of armed guards who were expert shots; it would be best to avoid them. The large, heavily frequented brothels also had tough, armed men on their payrolls.

In recent days Tracy had canvassed a number of stores as well as restaurants, where the presence of patrons might make a burglary attempt dangerous. The place that best suited his purposes was the general store owned by Prudence Adams. In the past week he had paid three visits to the establishment where, he thought ironically, he had begun his life of crime so many months ago by stealing a hammer. On these visits he had bought a new frying pan, a container of lamp oil, and some odds and ends he hadn't really needed, and he had learned all he needed to know.

The store was a prime target. Miss Adams kept all of her cash in a small box beneath a counter at the rear of the main room. She herself retired early every evening. Presumably her helper, the huge black man who had nabbed Tracy when he had stolen the hammer, slept somewhere on the premises, but the man was just a lug and would be no match for Tracy's stealth and wit.

What made the store particularly tempting was a side window that remained open day and night. When the cold weather came it would be closed, so it would be unwise to delay. Twice Tracy had studied that window at night, and he knew it would be easy to climb in through it. He would need no light to reach the money box under the counter a few paces away, and in moments he would be in the open again, free and clear, ready to mount his horse and ride away. The entire operation would be absurdly simple and would be even less of a risk than robbing a miner somewhere in the open wilderness.

The evening hours would be best for his purposes because the eating places were busy and the streets were filled with the patrons of gambling halls and brothels. Those crowds would provide him with protective covering in the unlikely event that Miss Adams heard him moving around on the ground floor of her place.

He waited until nightfall, fortifying himself with the cold meat and bread he always ate before going off on a mission. His double-edged knife rested in a sheath hanging from his belt and gave him a feeling of security. This was one task that wouldn't require the use of firearms; he carried his rifle only for his own protection on the road. He saddled his horse, led the animal to the far side of the steep canyon, then rode to town.

He was gratified to see that the front door of the store was closed and locked and that no lights were burning inside. The second floor was dark, too, so he figured that Miss Adams was asleep, and he congratulated himself on his careful planning. Drawing to a halt only a few feet from the open side window, he looped his reins over the head of his docile horse and propped his rifle against the side of the building. There were a number of men in the street behind him, but they ignored him, and he smiled quietly. A no-risk burglary was far easier than holding up a miner at dusk.

Boosting himself up to the sill, Tracy climbed in through the open window. The interior of the general store was darker than he had anticipated, so he stood still, waiting until his eyes became accustomed to the gloom. After a time he could see the portion of the counter that was his goal, and he made his way toward it slowly, pausing after each step and treading lightly to keep the floorboards from creaking. He had covered about half the distance when the silence was shattered by a deep voice sounding from the cubicle at the rear of the store.

"Who there?" Ezekiel called.

The black man's hearing had to be exceptionally acute, Tracy thought. He caught his breath and stood very still.

Ezekiel spoke a second time. "Somebody out there! Who is it?"

Tracy drew his knife from his belt. He could withdraw without being detected, but that meant he would be forced to abandon the loot he had promised himself. Perhaps, if he waited, Miss Adams's helper would drop off to sleep again. It would be foolish to give up the enterprise when that cash-filled box was almost within reach.

All at once Tracy sensed someone behind him. Gripping the hilt of his knife, he whirled and lunged at the man who was trying to surprise him.

A hamlike hand closed around Tracy's wrist, immobilizing him and throwing him off balance, and at almost the same instant a razor-sharp butcher's knife cut through the fabric of his worn work shirt and gashed his shoulder.

The pain was excruciating, but he managed to bite back the scream that welled up within him. Now his panic was real, and his terror gave him greater strength. He managed to wrench free of his assailant's grasp. Then, using the double-edged knife as he would have wielded a sword, he cut and slashed at the giant repeatedly, holding him at bay while backing toward the window.

Summoning his reserves of energy, Tracy climbed to the sill, then tumbled to the ground, losing his hat as he sprawled. He was on his feet again in an instant, snatching his rifle and vaulting into the saddle while his pursuer was trying to squeeze his greater bulk through the open window.

Not until Tracy reached the street and managed to lose himself in the crowds of riders and pedestrians did he realize that the left side of his shirt was soaked with blood. His shoulder was throbbing unmercifully, and when he tried to raise his left arm, it refused to respond.

Sick and dizzy, his whole body now aching, he had no idea whether Ezekiel was chasing him—and he had no intention of finding out. Spurring his horse to a trot, then a canter, he rode with increasingly reckless abandon through the surprised crowds.

Men shouted at him, and some cursed him, but they nevertheless cleared a path for him. Riding wildly, he left Denver and headed across the rough open countryside toward his sanctuary. He needed almost all of his remaining strength to twist in his seat, look back over his shoulder, and assure himself that he was not being followed. Then he slumped in his saddle and fell unconscious.

Only his horse's homing instinct saved the wounded rider. Tracy came to his senses as his mount reached the base of the canyon and began to struggle up the far slope.

Somehow Tracy managed to dismount. Gripping the reins with his right hand, his rifle slung over his uninjured shoulder, he began the difficult ascent. He slipped and fell repeatedly, and waves of pain rolled over him every time he jarred his wounded shoulder. All he knew was that he would not be safe until he reached his cave, and he concentrated on making his way there. The stars swam dizzily in the clear Colorado sky above him as he climbed laboriously, each step an agony so intense that he was afraid he would black out again.

By the time he reached his door, hidden behind the large boulder, he scarcely knew what he was doing. In a pain-wracked stupor he managed to unlock it, pull his mount into the cave, and then bolt the door. He lacked the strength to remove the horse's saddle, and he crawled on the ground toward his bunk, favoring his injured shoulder as he inched toward it.

He had stopped bleeding, he knew, because the blood was caking on his stiff shirt, and that was a good sign. His luck had turned tonight, his attempted burglary ending in catastrophe, but he wasn't beaten. Not by a damnsight.

He would survive. He would recover, regain his strength, and rid the world of the giant who had maimed him. Only the weak and craven admitted defeat, and Tracy Foster was determined to win a fresh triumph, no matter how great the odds against him.

At last he reached his cot and collapsed on it, his semiconscious moan echoing through the quiet cave.

*　　*　　*

Luke Brandon made his final ore sample tests, then submitted the results to Lee Blake, who committed them to paper in a secret report that he would hand in person to President Buchanan. Cathy had gone into town with Patricia, so the two men discussed the report behind the closed door of the Blake bedroom.

"You're certain of what you've told me, Luke?" Lee asked.

"I'm willing to stake my entire professional reputation on it," the geologist declared. "There's not only gold worth millions of dollars in the Colorado mountains, but there's so much silver, too, that I can't even estimate the quantity. On one of the properties owned by Chet and Ke—which they haven't begun to mine yet—there's enough silver to earn them a whole new fortune. Too bad I'm not authorized to tell them what's in store for them."

"They'll be pleasantly surprised when they begin to mine the property," Lee replied. "But as you know, they're in good financial shape, so it won't matter if they don't learn about their new fortune for another year or two."

"I realize that if our information became public the rush of fortune hunters to Colorado would double and treble."

"That must not happen," Lee said quietly but firmly. "The data we've gathered is strictly and exclusively for the information of the President. Even in this remote corner of the United States, there is a lot of tension between Northern and Southern supporters. Any leak of our information might make Colorado a prewar battleground."

"Yes, I can see that saboteurs might try to blow up the mines."

"That's just one of a hundred possibilities," Lee said. "We'll hand our report to the President, personally, and he'll do with it as he sees fit. All I know for sure is that he'll be relieved to know that, if a war between the states breaks out, there's enough gold and silver here to buy all the cannons and build all the warships the Union will need."

"I'm no politician," Luke said. "I've noted that immigrants from the North have outnumbered those from the South by at least twenty to one—"

"Ah, that's the key to the situation," Lee said, interrupting him. "There's a strong groundswell right now in favor of making Colorado a federal territory, and it will happen within the next year. Congress will make it a free-state territory, which will keep it in the Union camp, but there will still be many Southern sympathizers in Colorado. That's why, with the balance between peace and war so precarious, you and I are sitting on a huge barrel of gunpowder. The sooner we can take our report to Washington City the happier I'll be about it!"

"My final tests will be completed in a few weeks' time," Luke said. "I can hurry them, if you wish."

"No, we're doing a thorough job, and a few extra weeks won't make all that much difference. But don't let on to anyone, not even your wife, that we'll be leaving Colorado in the very near future. When we go, I intend to leave Isaiah Atkins here to provide cover for us, and ultimately it won't matter if the results of our fact-finding mission leak out. But secrecy must be observed until we've paid our visit to the White House!"

Cathy Blake and Patricia attended to their errands, then went on to the general store, where Ezekiel was unpacking a crate of merchandise that had just arrived and Prudence Adams was adding a column of figures.

Patricia greeted Ezekiel with such a dazzling smile that he dropped his crowbar.

"Have you learned anything more about the intrud-

er who came here the other evening, Miss Adams?"
Cathy asked.

"Not a thing, Mrs. Blake, I'm sorry to say. The hat
he left behind is the only evidence he was even here,
aside from the bloodstains he left on the counter over
there. The hat is so old and battered that there's no
way of telling where it was made, or by whom."

"That's a pity," Cathy said.

The older woman shrugged. "It wouldn't do much
good even if we knew. I doubt if Denver will have
a real police force for another six months to a year."

"You were telling me that some of you merchants
might band together to hire a constabulary of your
own."

"I'm all in favor of it," Prudence said, "but some of
the others won't spend the money. Come upstairs for
a cup of tea, and I'll tell you all about what I'm trying
to organize. You, too, Patricia."

"If you don't mind, ma'am," she said, "I'll stay down
here and chat with Ezekiel."

"Goodness knows you'll be safe," Prudence said as
she led Cathy to the staircase. "He's the best one-man
constabulary in all of Colorado."

The flustered Ezekiel continued to pry apart the
slats of the crate as Patricia smiled at him. "Mrs.
Blake told me about your exploit of the other night,"
she said. "Goodness, but I was impressed."

"I don't do much," he muttered.

"You drove a burglar away!" she exclaimed. "I call
that quite an accomplishment."

"Part of my job," he said. "Miss Prue good to me. So
I don't let anybody steal from her. Kill first."

"Yes, I believe you would." Patricia regarded him
steadily. "Weren't you afraid?"

He considered her question for a moment, and his
slow grin was his only response.

Patricia had never known anyone quite like him.
"Aren't you ever afraid? Of anything?" He nodded. "I
don't believe you," she said, teasing him.

Ezekiel's expression became solemn. "Afraid of Patricia," he muttered. It was her turn to become flustered, and she didn't know what to reply.

He misinterpreted her silence. "You laugh at me?" he demanded.

Patricia was thunderstruck. "Never!"

Ezekiel stared at her, his confusion genuine. "You grand lady," he said. "Why you bother to talk to me?"

She could not curb the laugh that rose within her, even though she was afraid he would misunderstand. "I talk to you because I admire you," she said. "You're —an honest, fearless man. And the reason I'm laughing is because I earn my living as a lady's maid. A grand lady, indeed!"

"You very grand," he said stubbornly. "You know how to read and write."

"I could teach you to read, write, and improve your grammar," Patricia said. "I'm sure you'd learn quickly."

Ezekiel's arms fell to his sides, and he looked hard at her. "You not joke?" he asked in a whisper. "You really teach?"

"Of course," she said gently. "I'd never joke about anything that important."

To her astonishment tears came to his eyes, and he brushed them away angrily with the back of a huge hand. "I born in mud cabin," he said, his tone defensive. "Mama slave, Papa slave. I slave, too, before I run away. Always want to read, always want to write."

His confession overwhelmed her, and she instinctively put a hand on his arm. "Ezekiel," she said, "I give you my solemn word of honor that I will help you."

A light appeared in his eyes, and his smile was radiant. Then he became aware of Patricia's touch and froze.

She slowly withdrew her hand. It was bad enough that she herself knew she had lost her heart to this gentle, unassuming man. Under no circumstances did

she want him to learn her feelings prematurely or,
even worse, to think she was forward.

Willie de Berg dressed quickly, but the nude young
woman clutched him before he could leave.

"Make love to me again," Caroline Brandon begged.

He had already spent two hours with the wench,
but her demands were insatiable, and he sighed. He
couldn't help wondering how far she would go to
please him, so he said brusquely, "Dance for me."

Caroline obligingly rose from the bed, painted
rouge on her nipples, and gyrated sensuously before
him.

Willie smiled faintly, then tugged at the bell rope.
Caroline continued her dance.

"Send Bessie up here," he told the woman who
answered his summons. Then he added to the already
breathless Caroline, "Keep dancing."

She continued to move seductively after the dark-
haired Bessie joined them.

"Bess," Willie said, smirking, "this one says she'll do
anything that'll make me happy. Do you believe that?"

Hiding her contempt and dismay, Bessie shrugged.

"Just look at her dancing around the room," Willie
said. Then, addressing Caroline, he laughed and
asked, "How do you like dancing for us, Caroline?"

She was biting her lower lip so she wouldn't weep.
"If it makes you happy," she said without looking at
Bessie, "I don't mind. Too much."

That wasn't the response he had expected, so he
cursed her, then stalked out of the suite, slamming the
door behind him.

Now tears came to her eyes. "What did I do
wrong?" Caroline cried.

The revolted Bessie came up to her. "If it would do
any good," she said bitterly, "I'd beat some sense into
you, sweetie doll. My God, don't you know by now

that the more you do what Willie wants, the less he thinks of you? Get some sense into your empty head."

Caroline sobbed.

The exasperated Bessie took hold of her shoulders and shook her. "Stop that! You're makin' yourself a doormat for him. I warned you weeks ago, but you wouldn't listen to me! You keep comin' around here, eatin' the dirt that Willie shovels your way. And what have you got to show for it?"

Caroline tried to control herself, and the other woman finally released her. "Just look at you! What a mess. How'd you get that mark on your face? Don't tell me. Willie hit you."

Caroline could only nod.

Bessie slumped wearily into a chair. "That was me. Last year. And a lot of the others, who have had the same treatment from him."

"I can cover the mark with cosmetics," Caroline said, beginning to dress. "No one else will know."

"You'll know," Bessie told her fiercely. "Where the hell is your pride?"

Caroline paused in the act of pulling her low-necked dress over her head. "I—I don't know," she admitted. "I keep wanting Willie so much that nothing else matters."

"If you ain't careful, sweetie doll, you'll end up like the rest of us. Here, let me help." Bessie reached for the tray of cosmetics and covered the bruise on Caroline's cheekbone. "There, that's better. How much longer are you goin' to be hangin' around Denver?"

"I don't know. I hadn't thought about it." Caroline ran a comb through her snarled hair, then touched up her bruised lips with rouge.

"If you got any brains left," Bessie told her, "you'll clear out in the next wagon train."

"I—I couldn't."

"Willie de Berg is plain no good. For you, or for any other woman."

Caroline slumped wearily, lowering herself to the edge of the bed. "He was so charming when I first met him. And the—the way he made love was so wonderful. Now I don't seem to be able to satisfy him. No matter how hard I try, no matter what I do, he just humiliates me."

"You ain't tellin' me what I don't already know. Me and Frieda and Jane and Esther. I could name you as many as you got fingers and toes."

"Every time I leave this place," Caroline said, "I swear I'm never coming back. Then I begin to think about how Willie acts when I first get here. And I—I haven't got the strength to stay away. No matter what my good intentions, I show up here."

Bessie shook her head. "There ain't no use talkin' to you, sweetie. You got it bad. As bad as any I ever seen. You got a husband, right?"

Caroline nodded. Luke no longer meant anything to her, and she didn't care if she ever saw him again.

"Chain yourself to him. Fix the chain with a good, strong lock, and then throw away the key. I'd give my soul to be in your shoes." Bessie sighed and rose to her feet. "If I still had a soul, which ain't likely." She walked out quickly, shaking her head.

Caroline finished patching up her face, and as she departed she wondered if she might encounter Willie again. Perhaps, if she walked slowly, she might see him, if only for a fleeting moment.

"We'll be leaving Denver in the next week or two," Lee Blake told Cathy. "We're finishing our work here, and we'll travel with a military wagon convoy that will be coming this way from California. We'll go by way of Independence, and we'll take the train from St. Louis to Washington City. Perhaps we can also make a stop in Ohio and visit Beth at school."

"That will be wonderful," she said. "How long will

we be able to stay in Independence with Claudia and Sam?"

"A few days. Andy will have a chance to see his parents, too, so everything will work out well for all of us. I'll have to send Hector Mullins back to his family at the Presidio, of course. I borrowed him from the San Francisco garrison, and I won't be able to send for him until I've made my report to the President and the War Department gives me a new assignment."

Delighted by the prospect of paying a visit to her sister and brother-in-law and also seeing Beth, who was now well into her second year at Antioch, Cathy broke the news to Patricia.

To her surprise the maid burst into tears. "This is awful, Mrs. Blake," she said, the tears running down her face. "I knew we wouldn't be here forever, but I've been thinking—at least hoping—that you weren't planning to go East for another month or two."

"Ezekiel?" Cathy asked gently.

Patricia nodded. "I—I've fallen in love with him. And I believe—I'm almost certain—that he feels the same way about me. But he's so shy that goodness only knows how many months it might take him to work up the courage to propose to me."

"I wouldn't stand in the way of your happiness for anything in the world, Patricia," Cathy said. "But I don't know of any way we can change our plans to help you. We'll be traveling with an army unit that will give us protection on the trail from bandits and Indian attacks. So we'll have to accommodate ourselves to their schedule."

Patricia pondered in silence, then raised her head. "Do you suppose Miss Prue is doing enough business in her store to hire me?"

"I believe so. She's mentioned to me several times that she has a need for more, reliable help."

"Then, if it's all right with you, Mrs. Blake, I'll ask her for a job."

Cathy smiled. "It's not only all right with me, but I'll pave the way for you. Why don't we go to the store right now? I'll speak to her first."

"Just let me wash my face. I don't want Ezekiel to know I've been crying."

Soon they went off together to the center of town, and when they reached the general store, Cathy took Prudence Adams off to a corner for a private talk.

Their quiet conversation aroused Ezekiel's curiosity. "Why they whisper?"

Patricia explained that the Blakes were leaving for the East in the near future. "But I—ah—like Denver," she went on, trying to sound casual. "So we're hoping that Miss Prue will hire me. That way I could stay here."

To her astonishment Ezekiel scowled, but just at that moment Prudence beckoned, and the shaken woman went to her.

"I understand your situation, Patricia," the smiling Prudence said. "I not only approve, but I can think of no one I'd rather have on my staff. I'll give you room, board, and pay of ten dollars a week."

"But that's more than the standard wage, Miss Prue," Patricia protested. "You're being too generous."

"I've had my eye on you, and with Mrs. Blake's glowing recommendation, I have no doubt you'll more than earn your way." Prudence linked her arm through Cathy's, and they discreetly went upstairs in order to give Patricia the opportunity to break the news privately to Ezekiel.

She went to him at once, her manner defiant. "I've been hired," she said. His scowl deepened, but Patricia pretended not to notice. "We haven't settled the details yet," she said, "but I suppose I'll start when Mrs. Blake leaves."

"Not good," Ezekiel declared.

She found it difficult to control her temper. "You don't approve!"

"Not right!" he said emphatically.

"I thought you'd be pleased," she said, her anger rising. "But if you're going to be that way about it—"

"You very pretty," Ezekiel said. "Many bad men in Denver. Make plenty much trouble for you."

"Oh." Now that she understood the reason for his disapproval, her temper cooled, and she realized she might be able to utilize the situation to her advantage.

"Pretty girl need husband to protect her," Ezekiel said, folding his arms across his chest and glaring at her.

Patricia knew there was no way she could prod him into proposing to her, so she had to take the initiative herself. "I think that could be arranged," she said softly.

He was so stunned that he reacted as though she had slapped him.

"You have no wife," she said. "You're strong and big and fearless. And I'm sure that if you married me, no other man in Denver would dare to come near me."

Ezekiel swallowed hard and blinked at her. "You would marry runaway slave?" he demanded incredulously.

"I'd be very proud and happy to become your wife." There. She had actually proposed to him in so many words, and there was nothing more that she could do.

Ezekiel digested her flat statement, his astonishment slowly giving way to far more complicated feelings. A grin spread across his face, and as a man of action rather than words, he knew now what had to be done, what he had so much yearned to do. Still struggling to overcome his bashfulness, he took a single, tentative step toward her, and Patricia melted into his arms.

When Cathy and Prudence came down the stairs a short time later, the issue was settled.

"General Blake and I will arrange the wedding," a highly pleased Cathy said.

Prudence Adams turned to her helper, her voice

sharp. "You'll do no lazing around here for the next few days, Ezekiel. You can't expect Patricia to share that tiny room. I want you to build proper quarters for a wife at the rear of the building. A living room, a bedroom, and a kitchen large enough for her to move around in. Hire as many people as you'll need to have the work done properly, and see that the new addition is completed before the end of the week!"

White silk was in short supply in Denver, but the dressmaker Cathy had been patronizing finally found a length suitable for a wedding dress. Chet Harris bought an appropriate suit for Ezekiel, and Wong Ke, enthusiastically seconded by Mei-lo, arranged an elaborate, celebratory feast at the boardinghouse.

The ceremony was held in one of the city's churches, which was so new that the interior had not yet been painted. Lee Blake gave away the bride, and at their own request, Andy Brentwood and Susanna Fulton served as best man and bridesmaid. The wedding party adjourned to the boardinghouse, and Isaiah Atkins initiated the festivities by offering a long, rambling toast to the bride and groom.

"I thought he'd never finish," Scott Foster murmured to Susanna.

Many varieties of meat and produce weren't always available in the remote, raw community that depended on freight wagon trains for supplies, but Mei-lo worked wonders, and the dining room table was laden with vegetable and fruit salads as well as assorted meats, pies, and the wedding cake that she had baked earlier in the day.

"You are a magician," Ke told her. "Your feat today is equal to that of the jade goddess of the western mountain who brought a meal of many courses to the people of a starving village who had prayed to her for help."

Clara Lou Hadley knew nothing about Chinese mythology but agreed heartily with Ke. "Anytime you get tired of your job here," she said to Mei-lo, "you have a position waiting for you as chief cook at my parlor."

"She will not leave us," the alarmed Ke said. "I will double her wages."

"See that he does, Mei-lo," Clara Lou said, and a laughing Chet nodded vigorously.

Perhaps the romantic atmosphere of a wedding reception was responsible for Clara Lou's mood, but she felt even closer to Chet than she had during the many weeks of their growing relationship.

Chet sensed the softening in Clara's attitude. He could tell it in her smile, in the way she looked at him, in the way her shoulder touched his when they stood side by side. This realization created a problem for him.

He wanted her, and the desire had been mounting within him as their friendship had deepened. It was possible that when he escorted her to her home after the reception, she well might agree to allow him to spend the night with her. But his regard for her was too great, and he forced himself to curb his urge. Perhaps her husband was still alive somewhere, and Chet had come to know Clara Lou sufficiently well to feel certain she would be overcome by a sense of guilt if she engaged in an affair. Granted that she had no love left within her for her missing husband, but she was still a married woman and insisted on living accordingly. Her code of conduct would not permit her to yield more than temporarily, and later she would regret her weakness. So, for her sake, he had to behave circumspectly.

At Sarah Rose Foster's suggestion, the younger people escorted the bride and groom to their just-completed quarters behind the general store, and they cheered as Ezekiel carried Patricia across the threshold.

Then, as the group returned to the party, Susanna touched Scott's arm, and they dropped behind the others.

"I just wanted you to know," she said, "that I've written my article for tomorrow's edition about the robber whom the miners have been calling the gray ghost. He hasn't been active lately, or so it appears, so I want to print the piece while it's still news."

"Fair enough, and thank you for telling me," Scott said. It was a relief to him that this robber—who might very well turn out to be his missing brother—had apparently committed no more crimes. He had not told Sarah Rose his suspicions about Tracy, and maybe with luck they could locate their brother before he got into more trouble. "For all we know, he may have even left the area by now," Scott told Susanna.

After the young people reached the boardinghouse, Prudence Adams, who had been invited to stay for the night, finally gave in to her feelings. She had remained calm, almost stony-faced, in the presence of Patricia and Ezekiel, but now she wept. "Don't any of you ever breathe a word of my disgraceful conduct to the bride and groom," she said curtly as she struggled to regain her composure. "I'd hate them to know I could be so confounded soft!"

Only one person did not enjoy the festivities. Caroline Brandon had been brooding ever since she had learned that her husband had completed his mission and that they would leave Denver in the near future, going first to Washington City and then returning to Massachusetts. Her heart sank at the prospect of terminating what she still regarded as a glorious adventure.

Certainly she realized that Willie de Berg had treated her cruelly, but she had managed to convince herself that he equated her with the harlots in his employ only because he didn't know her well enough to appreciate her true worth. None of his other women were ladies, and he would gain an understanding of her stature only when he spent enough time with her other than in lovemaking. Now, having persuaded herself that what she wanted was right, she made up her mind to act accordingly.

She was quiet and withdrawn during the festivities, saying little to anyone. Biding her time, she waited until the party ended and Luke escorted her to their bedroom. Then, as soon as he closed the door behind them, she said, "I want to talk to you."

"Of course." Luke had enjoyed himself, relaxing after his weeks of hard work in the gold fields.

"I'm not going back to Cambridge with you," Caroline told him.

He was so startled he couldn't believe he had heard her correctly.

"You must have guessed that our marriage is ended," she said. "We haven't as much as kissed or touched for a long, long time. In fact, when you've been in town, we've slept at opposite sides of the bed."

"That's been your doing, not mine," the dazed Luke replied.

"So it has. Because our marriage has been a mistake from the beginning. I've been bored from the start. I hate Cambridge. I hate the academic life. I hate all the dry little jokes. I want to live—really live—and I've just discovered it recently!"

"What awakened you to this remarkable discovery?" he demanded.

"I've met someone else. A man who has blood flowing through his veins!"

"Do I know him?"

She shook her head.

"I have the right to be told."

"All right." Caroline looked at him proudly. "Willie de Berg, the owner of the Palace."

Luke felt as though a mule had kicked him in the stomach. The Palace had the dubious distinction of being the most notorious establishment in a town filled with gambling halls and brothels that cheated their customers. "You've taken leave of your wits," he said.

Caroline laughed. "I've finally come to my senses," she said as she went off to the small adjoining dressing room to change.

He felt rooted to the spot. Eventually Caroline reappeared in a nightgown and, climbing into bed, did not deign to address him again. Luke walked slowly into the dressing room, where a single candle was burning, and lowered himself into the small armchair there. For hours he sat unmoving, even when the candle stub finally melted in a small pool of wax.

In a sense, he reflected, he had only himself to blame. Ever conscious of Caroline's youth and sensitive to the difference in their ages, he had indulged her whims. He had told himself that her endless flirtations were harmless, but now, when it was too late, he knew better. She had married him only because of the prestige that his profession offered her.

Or was he being too harsh in his judgments? Perhaps. Caroline had been a coquette when he had married her, but her amusement had been harmless. Willie de Berg, obviously a man of the world, had taken advantage of her youth, her inexperience, her desire to be admired, and had turned her head. Yes, Willie de Berg was to blame.

As the hours passed, a cold rage formed within Luke Brandon, growing gradually until it possessed him. He had been passive long enough, and now he had to do something. His honor, his manhood, demanded action. Scarcely aware of what he was doing, he strapped on his pistol belt, made certain the weapon was loaded, and crept out of the bedchamber, where Caroline's even breathing told him she was asleep.

He made his way down the dark stairs, vaguely aware that everyone in the boardinghouse had retired for the night. His errand wouldn't take him all that long, and then he would return. He had no clear idea of his intentions and could only respond to the incessant clamor of an inner voice that demanded satisfaction from the man who was threatening to ruin Caroline's life.

Tracy Foster was amazed by the patience he had shown during his convalescence. He realized that his youth and rugged physical condition had been in his favor, saving his life, and he had been content to regain his strength little by little, day by day. His wound had healed fairly rapidly because, although deep, it had not cut into a bone. Now the ugly scar that he knew he would carry for the rest of his days was the only physical reminder of the incident that had almost cost him his life.

His recuperation was gradual, and he engaged in a strenuous rehabilitation program that had restored his mobility. He had left his cave only long enough to buy food staples for himself and oats for his horse, but now his waiting time had come to an end. He was as strong and agile as he had ever been.

But his need for funds was urgent, and he faced a dilemma. His harrowing experience at Prudence Adams's general store had taught him that burglary was far too dangerous a pastime, and he was reluctant, too, to test his luck by returning to his former occupation of robbing miners on their payday.

His long hours of solitude had enabled him to explore his potential future in detail, and he had evolved a new scheme. Every gambling house and brothel that he had visited in Denver employed armed guards, and although he had no idea how much such positions might pay, it could do no harm to find out. Provided he could earn a reasonable income, he would be willing to tolerate the boredom of a regular position until a new opportunity to make a quick dollar presented itself.

After mulling over the matter at length, he decided to ride into town and start making inquiries. Obviously the first place to try was Willie de Berg's place, the largest in the city. Donning one of the expensive suits he had bought when he had been flush, Tracy decided to wait until later in the night before departing, knowing that the supper hour was de Berg's busiest time.

He left his horse in the corral behind the Palace after he arrived, and then he wandered into the main room, where a dozen drinkers were still standing at the bar. Two card games and a dice game were in progress, but the crowd had thinned, and only a few of the corselet-clad women were in evidence. Presumably the others had gone upstairs with customers.

Willie de Berg was standing at the far end of the bar, alert for possible trouble. The shank of the evening, when some of the customers had been drinking for hours, was potentially the most dangerous.

Tracy went to him at once. "Remember me, Willie?"

The proprietor looked the ruggedly built, well-dressed young man up and down, thought him vaguely familiar, and shrugged.

"I've come here from time to time when I've been flush, but my luck has run out for the moment, and I need a job."

"What can you do?"

"I'm a better shot than any guard on your payroll. And I'm strong enough to heave even the biggest drunk clear across the street," Tracy said confidently.

Willie liked his approach and smiled. "We'll meet in my office in about an hour, after the last of the crowd clears out, and we'll have us a little talk." He turned away, then called over his shoulder, "Second floor, last door on your right. I'll send for you when I'm ready."

Tracy ordered a beer, then carried it to the nearest of a number of unoccupied tables. A previous customer had left a copy of the *Tribune* on the table, and Tracy picked it up absently, realizing he hadn't seen the newspaper in many days.

One of the corselet-clad women immediately approached him. "Hello," she said, giving him a broad smile. "I'm Bessie. Want to buy me a drink?"

Tracy grinned at her. "I'd like to do a heap more than buy you that drink," he said, "but I'm dead broke."

"Another time, sweetie doll." She wandered away.

Sipping his beer, he glanced idly through the newspaper to pass the time. He saw nothing on the first page that caught his interest, but when he opened the paper a headline leaped out at him:

GRAY GHOST
ROBS MINERS

Scanning the article quickly, Tracy was appalled and simultaneously flattered to discover he was reading about himself. The writer of the piece obviously had done careful research, and the facts about a number of his robberies were surprisingly accurate. His collar was damp by the time he read the article a second time, word for word.

Glancing around the room, Tracy saw that no one was paying any attention to him, and he breathed more easily. Taking a swallow of his drink, he knew that a door had been slammed in his face. Only his own caution had prevented him from returning to his previous pastime, but now it was too dangerous. The miners had established their own vigilante law courts pending action by the United States Congress to make Colorado a federal territory, and the justice they dispensed was rude and swift. A federal law court would take pains to establish the guilt or innocence of a suspect, but the miners' courts were inclined to hang a man first, then ask questions.

So, at least for the present, he could not run the risk

of holding up lone miners in the wilderness between Denver and the gold-mining country. Now he needed a job more than ever.

Tempted to buy himself another drink, Tracy refrained. His funds were so low now that every five-cent piece counted. Even though beer was a mild beverage, he hadn't consumed any alcoholic drink in a long time, and he wanted to be clearheaded when he was interviewed by Willie de Berg. So he remained at the table, smoking one of the last of his cheroots and waiting with increasing impatience.

Bessie returned to his table. "You're the one Willie wants to see?" she demanded. "Come along."

Folding the *Tribune* and carrying it under his arm, he followed her, aware of her swaying hips and, beneath her black net stockings, her firmly rounded thighs and long legs.

"You coming to work here, sweetie?" she asked.

"I hope so."

"Willie treats his roughnecks pretty good," she had to admit. "But you don't look like that crowd."

"I can, when it's necessary."

"Well," she said, "maybe he's got somethin' special in mind for you." She smiled as she pointed to the office door. "Just remember that us women give a special discount to any fellow on the payroll."

"I won't forget," he promised, then tapped at the door.

Willie ordered him to enter and sit. "You've got the size, and it looks like you have the muscle to do the kind of work that's needed hereabouts," he said. "Frankly, I can use more help. But being just as frank, I'm not sure you're the right man."

"Why the hell not?" Tracy demanded.

"Maybe it's because you have pretty fair manners and look like a gent. In a place like this, the strong-arm boys sometimes have some pretty nasty jobs that the squeamish wouldn't like. Are you a stickler for obeying the law?"

Tracy grinned and shook his head.

"Sometimes, when a man is hungry, he'll tell any lie to get himself a job."

Realizing he was taking a risk, Tracy nevertheless unfolded the *Tribune* and pointed to the article about the gray ghost.

Noting that the younger man's eyes were a deep gray, Willie quickly read the article. "Is that you?"

"I'm not saying it is, and I'm not saying it isn't." Tracy's expression was insolent. "Regardless, supposing it's true, do you think for one minute that I'd be stupid enough to admit it—and give somebody a hold over me?"

Willie laughed and slapped the desk. "I begin to like your style. What's your name?"

"Invent a new one for me. I don't like the name my parents picked."

Before Willie could reply, the door burst open and a mild-looking middle-aged man burst into the office, brandishing a pistol. The expression in his eyes was wild, and his face was as red as the beets grown on the eastern Colorado farms.

"De Berg," he shouted, "I demand an accounting from you."

Tracy started to rise, pleased by the opportunity to subdue the man, but Willie calmly waved him back to his seat. "I'll handle this," he said. "Who the hell are you, mister?"

"Luke Brandon!"

"Never heard of you."

"Caroline Brandon is my wife!"

"Ah, yes. Dear Caroline." A smile touched the corners of Willie's mouth, but his eyes remained cold.

"You're ruining her life!" Luke shouted.

"If anyone is ruining her life, she's doing it herself. As for you, Mr. Brandon, don't run around pointing pistols at people. They've been known to go off." Willie rose slowly, then lunged across the desk and wrenched the pistol from Luke's grasp.

The half-crazed Luke came around the desk and grappled with him, but the academician was no match for the muscular Willie de Berg, who was long accustomed to manhandling drunks and others who became obstreperous and disturbed the relative peace of the Palace. Easily subduing the physically weaker man, Willie quickly tired of the sport and struck him a sharp blow across the temple with the butt of his own pistol.

Luke lost consciousness, slumping to the floor.

"The crazy bastard," Willie muttered, annoyed. An outraged husband who was determined to make trouble could cause infinite problems.

"You want me to heave him out?" Tracy asked.

Willie stared at him for a moment, then looked down at the inert figure on the floor. "He can create too many headaches for me, so I want you to do more than that. Let's see if you're the kind of fellow I need to take care of nasty jobs and delicate assignments. Are you interested in picking up a quick five hundred dollars?"

"Am I!"

"All right. Take the old fool out of town and get rid of him. Permanently. So he can never come back here, never make another scene or threaten me again. Do we understand each other?"

"You bet," Tracy replied, his voice tight.

"Do this job the way it should be done," Willie told him, "and you'll have no more financial worries."

Tracy hesitated for no more than an instant. "For something special like this," he said, "I should be paid half in advance."

The saloonkeeper chuckled. "I already told you I like your style," he said, reaching into his pocket for a roll of bills and peeling off several. "Do you have a horse?"

Tracy knew what he had in mind. "In your corral right this minute. Chestnut gelding with a white diamond on his forehead."

"I'll have him brought to the side door, and I'll make certain there's no one in the outer room and that the staircase is clear. The rest is up to you. I'm heading back to the main room, where there will be witnesses who can swear I never left the place all night. When you're done, no matter what the time, come back for the rest of your pay. And an extra reward." He darted out of the office.

Tracy looked down at the unconscious middle-aged stranger on the floor, feeling neither pity nor contempt. As nearly as he had gleaned, the man had been involved in some kind of domestic dispute with Willie de Berg, but that had been his misfortune. Taking no risks, Tracy cut two strips of leather from a cat-o'-nine-tails hanging on a wall peg, then bound the victim's wrists and ankles with them. As a final precaution he stuffed a bandanna into the man's mouth.

Scarcely had he finished than the door opened and Willie silently signaled to him.

Throwing the unconscious man over his shoulder, Tracy sped through the outer room, then hurried down the stairs to the side entrance, seeing no one. He mounted his horse, placing the dead weight across the saddle behind him, then rode cautiously into the street.

The hour was very late, so there were few people abroad, but lights were still burning in a number of brothel windows, and there was always the possibility that a stray drunk might wander across his path.

Proceeding with great care for a short distance, Tracy took a shortcut past the side of Prudence Adams's general store, a maneuver that enabled him to avoid the better part of the downtown district. Breathing a trifle more easily, he made his way through several residential areas, then increased his pace abruptly when he came to the open countryside and took the familiar dirt road that led to Central City.

He knew this region better than any other, feeling

more at home in these steep hills. But a glance at the sky told him he didn't have too much time. The night was waning, and he couldn't ride as far as he wished for fear that early travelers heading toward the mines might see him. So, after riding in the open for no more than twenty minutes, he pulled to a halt behind a large boulder, and there he dismounted, dragging the unconscious man a short distance. The sight of the bandanna reminded him of the victim's helplessness, so he removed it from the man's mouth and cast it aside.

The best method of execution would have been with his rifle, which he could have fired from a distance, but he had left it in the Palace checkroom. That left a six-shooter or his knife, and Tracy quickly decided the latter was safer. The sound of one or more shots might arouse the curiosity of a chance passerby.

Drawing his double-edged blade, he dropped to his knees, straddling his victim.

Luke Brandon opened his eyes, blinked, and then met the steady, merciless gaze of the gray-eyed man looming above him. He recalled having seen the young man in the office of Willie de Berg. "Who are you?" he asked hoarsely. "And what are you doing to me?" Only now did Luke discover that his hands and feet were tightly bound.

Tracy made no reply, but there was no need for him to speak: Luke read death in the dark gray eyes. Then he caught sight of the blade that glinted in his attacker's hand. "For God's sake, have mercy on me!" he begged. "I've done nothing that deserves—"

The sentence he tried to speak remained unfinished for all time. Tracy slit his throat and, as life drained from the man's body, stabbed him repeatedly in the chest to make sure the task was completed.

Sightless, terror-stricken eyes stared up at the sky, where the first streaks of dawn were beginning to appear.

Tracy leaped to his feet so the blood streaming from his victim's body would not soil his expensive suit. Then, realizing he was still clutching his knife, he threw it onto the ground. He knew Denver still had no police force, but common sense told him to get rid of the murder weapon. Besides, now he could afford to buy as many knives as he might want.

He started to turn away, but a sudden thought struck him, so he flipped the man's body onto the stomach, then reached into a rear trouser pocket and removed a wallet. This was the night his luck turned for the better! He found more than two hundred dollars and hastily pocketed the money before dropping the empty wallet to the ground. It was best to let anyone who found the man's body think that robbery had been the motive for the killing. Besides, he had no intention of leaving that large a sum behind.

Pleased by the bonanza, Tracy rode back into Denver. It was day now, and he passed several people on the road, among them miners. When he reached the center of town he saw a brothel owner who might have recognized him, but he looked past the man and turned into the Palace, leaving his horse in the corral and entering through the side door.

Willie de Berg sat at a table, drinking with a pair of the security guards and several of the young women in corselets. Otherwise, the place was deserted.

Tracy grinned but said nothing.

Willie gestured the newcomer to go upstairs while he remained behind, saying something in a low voice, and Tracy preceded him to the office.

Willie had the ability to walk silently and made no sound as he came in through the open door. "Well?" he demanded brusquely.

The younger man's air was jaunty. "When I start a job," he said, "I finish it."

"So?" Willie's eyes narrowed. "I got rid of the pistol," he said. "I hope you had the sense to leave any other belongings you may have found."

"I have plenty of sense," Tracy replied. "I didn't touch the pocket watch or fob, and as far as I'm concerned, our friend can take his wallet to the grave with him—if anybody ever finds the body and bothers to dig a grave." He made no mention of having emptied the wallet.

"No details, if you please," Willie said, his manner suddenly fastidious.

"You bet."

Reaching for his roll of bills, Willie counted out an additional two hundred and fifty dollars. "When I give my word," he said, "I keep it."

"So I notice. I enjoy doing business with you."

"From now on, come around every day. I'll put you on a retainer fee, but I'll use you for—ah—odd jobs that will be useful to me. That's better than putting you on the security guard staff. I don't want to know your name, and on days when I have no work for you, I don't want you hanging around here. It's best if most of my people don't become too well acquainted with you. Is all this agreeable to you?"

"Sure," Tracy said. "It sounds like a fine deal."

Willie extended his hand. "There are exceptions to every rule, of course, and later it might prove helpful if you can account for this past night."

Slightly confused, even though he realized what his new employer was saying to him and understood the reasons, Tracy decided this might not be the best time to mention the reward that he had been promised.

"You may never need an alibi," Willie said. "On the other hand, it can do no harm to have one."

"You're the boss."

"We'll continue to get along well as long as you remember it. Don't leave here until noon, at the earliest, and when you go, use the side door. Always use it in the future. I'll have your horse fed and watered."

"Thanks." Tracy craved a strong drink, but he knew he would need rest after his long night, too, and he didn't want to spend the hours before noon sitting in an almost empty bar. "Is there someplace where I can get a little sleep?"

"Go to the far end of the corridor opposite the gaming room," Willie said. "The middle door."

As Tracy walked slowly down the hall, he had to admit that de Berg was thorough, thinking of everything. The young man came to a wing where there were many doors. This, he told himself, had to be the part of the establishment where the bordello was located. The sounds emanating from a chamber confirmed his guess.

Tracy walked to the far end of the corridor and opened the middle door.

The woman called Bessie was slouched wearily in a chair, but she looked up at him with what she hoped was a provocative smile. "Willie said to tell you I'm your reward," she declared, and handed him a glass filled with whiskey.

As Tracy had just realized, Willie de Berg indeed thought of everything.

VI

Caroline Brandon was undisturbed when she awakened in the morning and found that her husband had not occupied his side of the bed during the night. She began to be concerned, however, when she discovered he had not slept in the tiny dressing room. Then, when she went to the dining room for breakfast and Lee Blake inquired about Luke's whereabouts, she realized she had to make some comment, even though she had no intention—under any circumstances—of revealing the contents of her last dramatic conversation with him.

"He was reading in the dressing room when I fell asleep," she said innocently. "I assumed he felt restless and came downstairs, for he didn't get to bed at all. But he doesn't seem to be anywhere in the house."

"That's odd," Lee said, frowning.

"I just can't imagine where he could have gone." She remained wide-eyed and incredulous.

"Was he upset in any way?" Chet Harris asked.

Caroline shook her head. "Not in the least," she lied. "He told me how much he enjoyed the wedding feast, and when I went off to bed because I felt sleepy after all the excitement, he said he thought he'd read

166

for a while." There was no need to simulate her growing concern. Luke had been stunned by the news that she planned to leave him for Willie de Berg, and the tenuousness of her relationship with Willie caused her to hope that her husband hadn't gone to the Palace, made a fool of himself, and brought about new problems for her.

A sense of uneasiness pervaded the whole company as they finished breakfast, but no one knew of anything specific that could be done to alleviate the situation. "Perhaps," Ke said, "Luke went out for an early morning walk."

"That's possible," Caroline replied quickly. "I imagine he'll come back soon."

Scott Foster was one of the first to leave the table because he had a busy day ahead at the *Tribune,* where he had to make estimates of the newsprint and ink needs for the months ahead. He continued to think about Luke as he walked to the office in the center of the city, and for some reason he couldn't define, he felt that Caroline knew more than she had revealed. He guessed he just plain felt sorry for Luke, who had to be an unhappy man because he was burdened by a giddy, flighty wife, a woman apparently unable to refrain from flirting with every man she met.

Other members of the staff were just arriving for work, too, and Scott paused, as he always did, for a few extra words of greeting with Susanna Fulton.

"I had to go out on an early errand," she told him, "and a half-dozen people stopped me on the street. The article about the gray ghost has really caused a sensation."

"I knew it would," he replied.

"Cheer up," she said. "I'm making a pot of coffee because of all the wine we drank at the wedding party last night, and I'll pour you a cup. That will improve your spirits."

He was grateful to her as he went to his own desk in the far corner of the large room. Susanna was a wonderful woman, always thoughtful, always considerate of others, and any man who won her as his bride would be fortunate. He soon became immersed in his work and was so lost in thought that he did not hear or see Susanna when she placed a steaming mug of coffee on his desk.

A few minutes later, when he became aware of it, he looked across the room and smiled his thanks.

She grinned at him in return, then began to write one of the small feature articles that the *Tribune* printed when there was a dearth of news. She looked up when someone loomed at the far side of her desk, and she saw a middle-aged man, conservatively attired in a business suit.

"Miss Fulton," he said, "you don't know me, but I'm Ben Wheeler."

"Sit down, Mr. Wheeler. What can the *Tribune* do for you?"

"Maybe nothing, maybe something. It happens that I run one of the more expensive red-light houses in town." He made the statement flatly, without apology.

"I read the story in yesterday's paper about the fellow you called the gray ghost," he said. "If I'm wrong in what I want to tell you, that's that—and forget it. But if I'm right, I don't want any credit. If you know what I mean."

She raised an eyebrow.

"People in my line of work don't get their names in print when it can be avoided. It isn't good for business. See?"

She nodded, well able to understand.

"I got to thinking about that story you printed yesterday. It happens I have a fairly regular customer, a fellow I hadn't seen in the past few weeks, who fits the description of the gray ghost that you printed. Especially what the paper said about his eyes. They're a deep gray, and there's a look in them that sometimes send chills up my spine. It does the same thing to my stable of girls, too."

"One moment, Mr. Wheeler," Susanna said. "Why are you telling me all this?"

"Because I'm a respectable citizen," he replied indignantly. "I run an honest business, where I give my customers what they want for a fair price."

She had to conceal a smile, never having heard a bordello described in such terms.

"What's more," he said, "a house like mine is vulnerable to robbers. A lot of us in the business are. I keep a small, exclusive stable, my clients are gents, and I have no need for a strong-arm man to keep the peace. So I'd be an easy mark for a robber, if you see what I mean."

"Indeed I do."

"Well, ma'am," he said, "earlier this morning, around daybreak, I was riding home after I closed up the house for the night. I keep my wife and our youngster as far from my business as I can, so we live out on the edge of town. Anyway, I passed this customer of mine, wearing one of his fancy suits."

"I fail to grasp the significance of what you're trying to tell me, Mr. Wheeler," Susanna said.

"You'll latch on quick enough." The man lowered his voice. "He was riding in from the open country. And he was on the road from Central City!"

In spite of her attempt to remain calm, she felt a surge of excitement.

"Maybe that doesn't mean anything. But his horse looked fresh, so it was plain he hadn't come all the way from Central City. Besides, only an idiot would make that long a ride late at night. That would just be asking for trouble from bandits." He paused.

"Go on," Susanna urged.

"What makes it all so strange is that this fellow didn't even speak to me. Those gray eyes of his looked at me for a second, real quick, and then looked away again. I'm positive he knew me as well as I knew him. But he pretended not to see me."

"Mmm." His story was beginning to make a great deal of sense.

"Anyway, I got to wondering. Why wouldn't he want to know me or say good morning to me? Then I remembered the story in the *Tribune* that said all those robberies happened between Denver and Central City. So I thought maybe he was heading back into the city after a robbery." His manner changed, and he added hastily, "I'm not trying to be a good citizen, Miss Fulton, and I don't usually go blabbing about things that are none of my business. But I wouldn't want that fellow with the weird look in his gray eyes sticking a gun into my face."

"I can't blame you for feeling that way, Mr. Wheeler," she said.

Ben Wheeler sighed and rubbed his eyes. "I rode all the way back here to tell you all this because I started to get a scared feeling. If we had a police force in Denver, I would have gone to them, but we don't. So I figured the newspaper would be the next best place." He rose to his feet. "Anyway, I've told you what little I know, for whatever it may be worth. Now I've got to get a few hours of sleep before it's time to open the house again."

Susanna thanked him, and after he departed, she thought hard before going to Scott Foster's desk. "Do you have any time to spare today?"

"Not really," Scott said, "but if it's important I can always make the time and work a little later this evening."

She repeated what Ben Wheeler had told her, and Scott's face became somber as he listened. He well realized that the man with the cold gray eyes might not only be the gray ghost but also his brother.

"I can't ride out on the Central City road by myself," Susanna said. "But I wondered if you might want to come with me. I'm just playing a hunch. We might be wasting a couple of hours."

"Let's go," Scott said. "The newsprint and ink orders can wait."

They went together to the stable behind the building, and Scott saddled two of Wade Fulton's horses. Conversation lagged as the couple headed out of Denver and took the Central City trail.

"What exactly do you expect to find?" Scott asked.

"I have no real idea," Susanna replied honestly. "If there has been a robbery during the night, I'm hoping we'll run across someone who may have heard about it. The miners have been on the trail for several hours now, heading toward the gold mines, so there may be no sign of anyone who was robbed before daybreak."

The traffic flowing in the direction of the mining country had slowed to a trickle, and as this was an ordinary weekday, no one was coming toward Denver. Scott was not looking for anything specific, and more than once the thought occurred to him that he had accompanied Susanna on a wild-goose chase. But he said nothing until they had ridden for slightly more than an hour.

"I reckon we've come far enough," he said. "We've seen no sign of any trouble, and if there's something up ahead, plenty of others would have found it by now."

"I suppose you're right," Susanna replied. She turned back reluctantly.

They rode about half the distance to Denver when Scott caught sight of something unusual behind a large boulder, realizing that the stone had hidden it from view when he and his companion had been heading in the opposite direction. Saying nothing, he pointed. As nearly as he could judge, a pair of man's boots protruded into the open.

Susanna spurred forward, then faltered, afraid of what she might find.

"Wait here," Scott told her. "I'll go ahead." He rode on alone.

When he drew close to the boulder, he circled behind it, then came to an abrupt halt and dismounted, feeling ill. The body of Luke Brandon was stretched on the ground, ankles and wrists tightly bound with strips of leather, the man's open wallet nearby. Blood was caked on the front of his shirt and neck.

Susanna followed, and when she, too, recognized Luke, she gasped, then covered her face with her hands. "Oh, the poor man," she murmured. "What a frightful way to die."

Scott put an arm around her shoulders to steady her. "One thing is plain," he said. "The killer wanted to make mighty sure he was dead. Luke was stabbed a half-dozen times—and his throat was cut, too."

The reporter who had decided to play the role of a detective needed several long moments to regain even partial composure. "What do you imagine he was doing out here in the open country?"

"He didn't come here," Scott said. "He was brought here. Notice his ankles and wrists, then look yonder."

She stared at the ground, which was thick with dust, then looked up inquiringly.

"There's only one set of hoof prints," Scott said. "It appears to me that the killer tied him, brought him here, and murdered him in cold blood."

"Not for his money, surely!"

Scott examined the empty wallet. "Well, his money is gone, that's sure. But it beats me why a robber would go to all the trouble of tying and transporting him here first."

"Luke couldn't have known what was in store for him," Susanna said. "He was so jolly at the party last night." She shuddered, then added, "That Mr. Wheeler's hunch was right. This must have been done by the gray ghost!"

As Scott and Susanna well knew, if the gray ghost was indeed Tracy Foster, then Scott's brother was not only a thief but a murderer, as well.

The gruesome story of Luke Brandon's murder filled two columns in the following day's *Tribune,* and the demand for copies was so great that a double edition had to be printed. Denver residents discussed nothing else, or so it seemed, and thousands speculated on the identity of the gray ghost.

Tracy Foster cursed Susanna Fulton when he read the article. He not only should have bedded her, but he would have done himself a favor had he done away with the wench as effectively as he had killed Luke Brandon. Now the damage was done, but at least no one could prove he had committed the crime.

Caroline Brandon became hysterical when Susanna and Scott first broke the news to her. Then she settled into an icy, unnatural calm, responding in monosyllables when others offered her their condolences.

A graveside funeral service was conducted by the clergyman who had married Patricia and Ezekiel, and the same people who had been present at the wedding were in attendance, along with several mine owners with whom Luke had established cordial relations. The widow, clad in black, with a heavy black veil procured for her by Prudence Adams covering her head and face, did not weep.

She began to recover from the initial shock after returning to the boardinghouse, and the realization that she was free to live her life in her own way drove everything else from her mind. She entertained few doubts that Willie de Berg had been responsible for the murder, possibly because Luke might have goaded the hotheaded saloonkeeper beyond endurance. Whatever the details, she felt certain she had attained a hold over Willie at last, and when she reached the privacy of her bedchamber, she permitted herself the luxury of a tight smile. She would wait until General Blake and his prissy wife left Denver, and then she would look after her future as she saw fit.

The departure of Lee and Cathy took place even sooner than they had anticipated. In mid-afternoon on the day of Luke's funeral, the military convoy that would escort them as far as Independence, Missouri, arrived in Denver. "I hope I'm not causing you an inconvenience, General," the colonel in command of the unit said. "But I'd like us to be on our way early tomorrow morning, if that's at all possible."

"We'll be ready," Lee said.

The last-minute preparations were hectic. Hector Mullins made arrangements to go to San Francisco with a small party that included a carrier taking several packhorses heavily laden with sacks of mail to California. Patricia came from the general store to help Cathy pack, and Ezekiel, who accompanied her, built a crate to hold the samples of refined ore that Lee would take with him to Washington City.

Isaiah Atkins announced that he would remain in Denver for the present, and he was very pleased by an independent decision made by the partners in the firm of Harris and Wong.

"The sales agreements for the properties we're buying here are becoming more and more complicated," Chet told him. "We need a lawyer we can trust, so both Ke and I would be very happy if you'd handle our Colorado legal affairs for us."

Isaiah agreed at once, knowing that if he did well he would have an opportunity to gain some portion of the even more lucrative legal work at the San Francisco headquarters of Harris and Wong when all of them returned to California.

"Unless I make some monumental mistakes—which I'm going to avoid—my future in the law is assured," he told Sarah Rose in private.

"I'm so pleased for you," she said sincerely.

Isaiah looked hard at her, wondering whether she or Susanna thought more highly of him.

The imminence of departure cleared Andy Brentwood's mind, and the young officer knew, quite suddenly, that although he found Sarah Rose attractive, he was even more strongly drawn to Susanna Fulton. The packing of his own belongings would take only a short time, and as General Blake had no immediate need of his services, he walked quickly to the *Tribune* office.

Susanna, who had gone back to work after the funeral, as had Scott, was startled by the news that Andy was leaving the next morning. "I'm so sorry to hear it," she said.

"So am I," Scott declared, but privately he was pleased to be rid of a potential rival.

Andy hesitated for no more than an instant. "Could you spare a half-hour to have tea with me at the Allen House, Sue?"

"Of course," she replied, and they left the office together.

Scott felt a quick pang of jealousy but consoled himself with the thought that, as of the next day, only Isaiah would stand between him and Susanna—assuming that Isaiah actually knew where he stood, which was unlikely.

At the restaurant, Andy held Susanna's chair for her, then sat opposite her. "I hope," he said after they ordered tea, "that you don't believe in that old saying, 'Out of sight, out of mind.'"

She smiled and shook her head. "I've never put much stock in old sayings."

"You mean you'll remember me, Sue?"

Susanna's smile remained steady. "You'd be a very difficult person to forget, Andy."

He looked hard at her, his expression earnest. "I want to get some thoughts off my chest, and I hope I won't embarrass you."

"You won't."

"I've never been one for fancy words. My father has always favored doing things, not talking about them. That's how I was reared, and my education at the military academy confirmed that way of life for me." He hesitated. "Just a little while ago, when I found out I'm leaving tomorrow morning, something came over me with great force. I haven't even had a chance to think of the right words yet, so I'll have to say it to you plainly. Sue, I'm in love with you."

The sudden, blunt expression of his feelings startled her.

"I don't expect an answer from you," Andy told her. "We haven't spent much time alone with each other, so I know you couldn't possibly love me, too."

Struggling for words herself, she flushed. "Thank you for understanding, Andy. You're right, of course. I've had very little opportunity to fall in love with you, although I must admit I'm already quite fond of you."

He nodded, then said gruffly, "Then there's Scott. You see him every day, and anyone who looks at him knows he's smitten with you."

"Let's say I've guessed it." Susanna laughed, then sobered. "You've been candid with me, Andy, and I want to be equally frank with you. I like Scott. A great deal. I enjoy his company, just as I enjoy yours, but I'm no more in love with him than I am with you. If someone put a gun to my head and forced me to choose between you, I couldn't do it."

He listened intently, satisfied that at least his suit was not lost.

"The fact of the matter," she went on, "is that I'm not in love with anyone right now. The challenge of establishing the *Tribune* here has been so absorbing that most of my thought has gone into my work. I'm not saying I won't fall in love with you someday. I might, just as I might fall in love with Scott. Or with someone I haven't yet met."

"But not Isaiah?" he asked, his voice dry.

A giggle welled up within her and came to the surface. "Most definitely not Isaiah Atkins," she replied. "He's not my type."

"Well," he said, "that eliminates one rival."

"One who hasn't been in the running." She reached across the table and put a hand on his arm. "I hope you don't think I'm being evasive, Andy."

"You're being honest with me, and I appreciate it." He shook his head. "My problem is my profession. An army officer doesn't know where he'll be from one day to the next."

"I realize that."

"Maybe so, but only to an extent. I'll try to explain. In a few months my tour of duty as aide-de-camp to my uncle will expire, and I'll move on to a new assignment. I was trained for the cavalry, so I might be made second in command of a troop, possibly in one of the trouble states like South Carolina. Or, since I'll have service as an aide on my record, the War Department may have me flagged for work as a staff officer. I might be stuck in Washington City for years. Or I could come straight back to Denver when a garrison is established here, which is sure to happen once Colorado becomes a federal territory. And if a war breaks out between the North and South—and so far I can see no signs of compromise on either side— the odds favor a combat assignment. The only good in a war is that I'd be promoted more rapidly because the need for academy graduates will be greater. But that won't necessarily bring me any closer to you."

"You make it sound so unlikely that we'll see each other again," she said, and her regret was genuine.

"Oh, we will," he assured her. "But there's no telling when. I get a month's leave of absence every year. So if I were stationed at one of the Nebraska or Kansas forts, for instance, I'd come here to see you. But there wouldn't be time if I should be stationed in some place like the new Washington Territory, north of Oregon. Not unless they build the transcontinental railroad a lot sooner than anyone can reasonably expect."

"I'm sure we'll see each other again," Susanna said, "and don't ask me why I'm so positive. Call it woman's intuition; call it anything you like."

"Where there's a will there's a way, and I have the will," Andy said. "But all I can promise you right now is that I'll write you regularly, Sue."

"You have my promise in return that I'll answer every letter promptly. I won't play games with you, and I won't be coy. If there's any quality in members of my sex I despise, it's coyness."

He thanked her, then added, "All I really ask is that I have a chance to win you."

"You have it, Andy," she said.

Mei-lo prepared a gala dinner for the departing guests, and she and her assistant had so little time that, to Chet's amusement, Ke rolled up his sleeves and helped in the kitchen. When Mei-lo gave him orders, he obeyed promptly and efficiently, and she was surprised.

"I didn't know you could cook," she said.

Ke grinned at her, suddenly looking far younger than his years. "Chet could have told you," he said. "Until we struck it rich, both of us lived on my cooking for a long time. But I'll never be in your class."

"There's no reason you should be," Mei-lo replied. "You have better and more important things to keep you busy."

"Not today," he said, then laughed.

The atmosphere at dinner was subdued because Luke Brandon's funeral had been held the same day, but a concerted effort was made to concentrate on the living rather than the dead. To the surprise of the entire party, Caroline Brandon cast aside the black dress she had worn earlier in the day and appeared in one of her more daring gowns, with cosmetics generously applied to her face, including a velvet beauty patch on one cheek. The more charitable believed she was making a gallant effort for the sake of the whole company.

Chet and Ke alternated in offering toasts, first to Cathy, then to Lee, and then to Andy. Hesitating for a moment, the Chinese financier turned at last to Caroline. "We wish you an early end to your grief and as much peace as you can find after your return to Massachusetts," he said.

Caroline waited until the toast was drunk and then said calmly, "This is as good a time as any to announce that I'm not going with the convoy tomorrow."

Everyone stared at her, and Sarah Rose was the first to find her voice. "Where will you go?"

Caroline relished the quiet sensation she was creating. "I'm staying in Denver."

Cathy was incredulous. "What will you do here?"

"Live!" Caroline replied emphatically, then decided it was the better part of discretion to amplify her remark. "I expect to inherit very little from Luke's estate," she said. "I'll sell the little house in Cambridge and the furniture for whatever they'll bring me, but there's nothing else. And I just couldn't tolerate going back to that house. I'm sure you understand."

Still sympathizing with the widow, they imagined they understood.

Lee nevertheless felt compelled to protest. "Denver is still a rough, wild town," he said. "I'm not sure that a lady will be completely safe here."

"I had no problems in all the time that you and Luke spent in the gold fields," she said, "and I'm quite certain I'll have none in the future."

"You'll need an income," Ke said.

"Oh, I expect to earn my own way. Please, I don't want anyone worrying about me. I'm more resourceful than any of you may think."

"Maybe Clara Lou can make a position for you at her place," Chet said. "I can ask her when I see her this evening, if you wish."

"Thank you," Caroline said sweetly, "but I've heard her gaming house is so tiny that it couldn't bring in a decent living for more than one person. Believe me, I'll manage!"

She was so firm that the others dropped the subject. As Isaiah remarked later to Sarah Rose and Scott, Caroline was an adult and couldn't be forced to return to Massachusetts.

"In a way I can't blame her," Sarah Rose said. "It would be lonely for her there, and going back to the same house she shared with Luke might be too difficult for her."

"I don't know about that part." The young attorney had to win every argument. "How would you like to be alone in Denver these days?"

"I couldn't do it," Sarah Rose replied promptly, "even though I can handle a pistol and I'm not too bad a rifle shot. I've got to hand it to Caroline, though. I've sometimes thought she was silly, but she has far more courage than I imagined."

The news that Caroline planned to stay in Denver preyed on Lee Blake's mind, too, as he and Cathy retired. He extinguished the oil lamp beside their bed, then said, "You know, my dear, I can't help wondering if the tragedy of Luke's murder has unhinged Caroline Brandon's mind."

"Don't give her another thought, not that one." Cathy laughed, then yawned. "She has the calm, collected poise of a snake that's about to strike. Now that I think about it, the analogy is quite appropriate. The way she wraps herself around any man who holds still long enough makes me think of a boa constrictor in action. Not that I've ever seen one." She paused for a time, then spoke more drowsily. "I'm willing to wager she's already found poor Luke Brandon's replacement."

She was asleep before the bemused Lee had the chance to continue the conversation.

The following morning, when the commander of the convoy and a score of troopers arrived at dawn to escort the Blakes and Andy, everyone in the boardinghouse with the exception of Caroline was on hand to bid the trio farewell.

"Be sure you write to us before your next trip to California," Chet told the Blakes. "Ke and I will arrange a party for all of your old friends."

Andy took the liberty of kissing Sarah Rose lightly on the cheek, then shook hands with Isaiah and turned to Scott. "I hope you find your missing brother soon," he said. "And—ah—good luck to you in everything else."

"The same to you," Scott said, knowing that "everything else" referred to Susanna Fulton.

They gripped hands, grinned, and then Andy walked out to mount his horse. "Never fear, my friend," he called over his shoulder, "we'll meet again!"

As the horses clattered off down the quiet road, Mei-lo sighed. "We'll miss General and Mrs. Blake," she said in her ever-improving English. "They're lovely people."

Ke looked as though he wanted to console her but felt constrained in the presence of others. Not even his partner had yet guessed the growing extent of his emotional involvement with the young woman they had hired as their housekeeper.

As Lee Blake had departed, he had given Scott a sealed envelope addressed to Susanna Fulton, and when the young Californian went to work, he handed the woman the communication. She read the brief note eagerly: *I haven't forgotten your news story and will send you the pertinent information as soon as I obtain the necessary clearance. You have my pledge that the* Tribune *will be the first newspaper to receive the story.*

General Blake really was a man of his word, Susanna thought to herself, and she couldn't help wondering if the murder of Luke Brandon was connected in some way with Lee Blake's secret mission in Colorado. Then she dismissed the thought as she reflected that the General seemed as bewildered as anyone else and that he couldn't explain—any more than she could—why the poor fellow had been trussed and then taken off into the wilds to be stabbed. No, her first surmise had been correct: Luke Brandon was murdered by the gray ghost.

"Sooner or later," Susanna said aloud, looking up from her desk, "I hope to learn the whereabouts of the gray ghost."

"If anyone learns it, I'm sure it will be you," Scott said, almost positive by now that the gray ghost was Tracy. Scott had long believed that Tracy would eventually get into trouble, but what he could do for Tracy even if his whereabouts were discovered remained uncertain. "You may want to keep an eye on Mrs. Brandon," Scott said, changing the subject. "She announced at supper last night that she was staying in Denver, and she didn't leave with the Blakes this morning."

"That's odd."

"Very. I see more of her than you do," Scott added. "She has supper at the boardinghouse just about every night, and as often as not she comes down to breakfast, too, so I'll let you know right off if I notice anything out of the ordinary."

Caroline Brandon might have been disturbed had she known that the young couple intended to keep her under surveillance, but perhaps not even that realization would have dampened her high spirits. Luke had been an encumbrance, but he was gone for all time,

and after she gave away his clothes, she would have
no reason to think of him again. General Blake had
taken his documents and research references, so she
would have no more reminders of her unhappy marriage to plague her in the bright future she envisioned
for herself.

Taking her time, she applied cosmetics with even
greater than usual care, and although the day was
cool, she elected to wear a revealing dress of tissue-
thin silk. Gazing with satisfaction at her reflection in
the mirror on the bedchamber wall, she decided to
cover the gown with a thin cape when she left the
boardinghouse. There was no need to ask for trouble
with miners and other rough men she might pass on
the streets, and she could remove the cloak when she
confronted Willie de Berg. She was already relishing
that encounter with keen anticipation.

Waiting until late morning, when she knew he
would be less active than at any other time, she
walked quickly to the Palace, and only a lingering
sense of discretion persuaded her to use the side door
rather than the main entrance. Then she went straight
to the second floor, where several of the women clad
in evening gowns were sitting at one of the card
tables, sipping coffee and gossiping as they awaited
the first of the customers who would gamble for high
stakes.

One of the young women was Bessie, and Caroline
greeted her. "Congratulations," she said. "I see you've
been promoted and don't have to wear one of those
foolish corselets."

"I do what I'm told, so I've been rewarded. But you
sure don't have much sense, showin' up here again."

"Oh, everything is going to be very different now.
I've gained the upper hand."

Bessie's laugh was skeptical. "You think so, huh?"

"You'll see. Where's Willie?"

Bessie nodded toward the far door, then shook her

head as she rejoined her colleagues. It was plain to her that some women didn't know when they were well off.

Willie de Berg was sitting with his feet on his desk, smoking a cheroot as he added a column of figures. He looked up from his work as the door opened, and there was alarm and anger in his face. His feet landed on the floor with a thud, and he demanded, "What the hell are you doing here? Get out and stay out!"

Caroline closed the door behind her, simultaneously whipping off her cloak and turning slowly for his benefit. "Gracious," she said, her voice saccharine. "You're not being very hospitable this morning, darling. I was certain you'd be just delighted to see me."

His obvious appreciation of her body was far outweighed by other feelings. "You must be crazy, coming here dressed like that! Thanks to that story in the newspaper, the whole town knows you're a widow! Anybody who happens to see you coming in or out will start talking!"

"I didn't know you paid any attention to what people say," she replied, enjoying herself.

Willie continued to glower. "All right," he said. "You think you have a couple of aces up your sleeve. Play them."

"As you can easily see," Caroline declared, "I have nothing up my sleeves but a pair of very pretty arms. Darling, you went a bit too far."

His expression remained unchanged, but he wondered how much she knew.

"The other night," she said, "I told my husband about you and me, and I have no doubt that he came here to have a showdown with you. He was even carrying his pistol, which he usually wore only when he went off to the mines. It was missing when his body was found, but your bullies forgot to remove his holster, too."

"That's no proof he came here," he declared loudly.

She smiled at him. "You wouldn't soil your hands by killing him yourself. But you were responsible."

"Don't make charges you can't prove," he said sharply.

"There's no need for me to prove anything," Caroline replied calmly. "All I need to do is go down the street to the *Tribune* office and tell them you tried and tried to seduce me and that my husband came here to protect my honor. Think of the story they'll print. And that's just the beginning. Some of your customers think you've swindled and cheated them. If I go to the people at the *Tribune* and say that you told me all about your gambling operation, you'll soon have a lot of enemies in this town. I'm sure you must know it wouldn't take very long for a lynch mob to form. What I'll tell the *Tribune* might not stand up in a law court, but you must realize, darling, that lynch mobs don't demand the evidence that the courts want."

Willie sank back in his chair, his hard eyes veiled. "Tell me plain what you want, Caroline."

"Gladly. You'll put aside a couple of hours for me every day at this time. And you'll treat me as I want to be treated. No more punches or other abuse. You'll treat me like a lady when you make love to me. And you won't dare to abuse me, either, because I'll tell the *Tribune* you brought me here under false pretenses after first getting rid of my husband. Admit I've maneuvered you into a tight corner, Willie de Berg."

He chewed on his cheroot. "I admit it," he said guardedly.

Her high-pitched laugh of triumph filled the room. "For the sake of appearances, I'll stay at the boardinghouse, at least for a time. Then we'll start being seen in public together, little by little, so no one will be surprised when the Brandon widow and the dashing bachelor are married."

Willie could only gape at her, but eventually he found his voice. "The idea of getting married—to anybody—has never crossed my mind!"

"From now on you'll think of it often because I know you'll want to make an honest woman of me. By the way, darling, I need fifty dollars."

"For what?"

"My room and board bill, with enough left over to buy a new dress that will celebrate the beginning of our wonderful new relationship."

He peeled some bills from his roll. He wanted to throw them at her but refrained and, instead, quietly handed her the money.

"There, you see how sweet you can be without exerting any strenuous effort?" Caroline beamed at him, striking an arch pose. "I hope you're ready for a little lovemaking right about now."

Willie pulled himself to his feet. "I'll be back in a couple of minutes. I'll have to tell my floor managers I don't want to be disturbed."

"I'll be right here, darling, waiting for you," Caroline told him.

He opened and closed the door, his temper still under control, and then suddenly he hurled his cheroot to the floor and ground it beneath his heel.

Bessie, still sitting at the far side of the outer room, caught a glimpse of the look in his eyes and shuddered. She had no reason to sympathize with the ingenuous blonde woman who had repeatedly failed to heed her warnings, but she couldn't help feeling sorry for Caroline.

The meals that Clara Lou Hadley served were the key magnets that drew prosperous people to her gaming tables, so she planned her menus with care, supervised the work of her cook, and always prepared some of each day's dishes herself. She spent the morning in her kitchen, as usual, and at noon she walked into the empty dining room, wiping her hands on her apron. The cook and his helper were hard at work, and she was free now to meet Chet at the Harry Allen House for dinner.

Preoccupied with the anticipatory pleasure of that meeting, she advanced several steps into the dining room before she became aware of the flashily dressed man, his dark hair smeared with a scented, shiny substance, who was sitting at one of the tables. He rose, his lips parted in a broad, forced smile.

"Dear God, it's you," Clara Lou murmured.

Jerome Hadley advanced toward her.

"Don't touch me," she said, her voice suddenly strident.

He halted, still smiling, but the scar on one side of his face that extended from his forehead to his chin became livid. "What a way to greet your husband after not seeing him for years," he replied, his voice oily.

"How did you get in here?" she demanded.

Jerome took a ring of keys from a pocket and jangled them. "You've forgotten so much about me, it appears. I've always had a way with locks."

Clara Lou studied him closely. He had aged since she had last seen him; his hair was flecked with gray, the lines in his forehead and at the corners of his eyes had deepened, and he looked old and tired, bearing little resemblance to the young dandy who had persuaded her to marry him after a whirlwind courtship. His attire was both ostentatious and immaculate, as it always had been, but she realized that his cuffs were frayed, his suit was somewhat threadbare, and the soles of his shoes were thin. It was obvious that he was down on his luck, and just as plain that he had sought and found her because he wanted money. He had appeared a number of times over the years, more frequently once the saloon and gambling hall she had operated in California had become a success. Clearly she hadn't managed to escape him by coming to Colorado.

"If you've come here for my help," she said, "you can forget it."

Jerome's smile was unwavering. "I've been in town

for several days," he said, "and I've studied your situation in depth. You've been having an even greater success in Denver than you enjoyed in the Sacramento Valley. You've earned your success, dear Clara Lou, and I'm even impressed by the interest being shown in you by one of California's leading citizens. I've gleaned that he's been adding to his substantial fortune by the earnings of his gold mines here."

She resisted the impulse to hit him and instead lowered herself into a chair. "I should have known," she said wearily, "that you'd snoop around before coming to see me."

He remained standing, folding his arms and looking pained. "I'm hurt by your lack of faith in me, dear Clara Lou."

"I must say one thing for you," she said. "You never change from one year to the next. You still have the ability to sicken me." Her tone changed, and she became curt. "Let's not prolong this. What do you want?"

"I regret to say that the cards haven't been kind to me of late."

She laughed without humor. "You mean that some of the players you tried to cheat got wise to you."

"I'll ignore the intended insult. We agree to the extent that our little reunion should be as brief as both of us can make it. You have money, and I need money." He paused and moistened his lips. "Give me a thousand dollars in cash, here and now, and I'll leave Denver at once. I'll clear out of your life."

"Until the next time," Clara Lou said. "In a year or two or three you'll show up again, holding out your delicate hand for still more cash."

"Don't turn me down without thinking of the consequences," Jerome said. "For both our sakes I prefer not to move in with you, although I have the legal right to do so. But short of going to that extreme, there are so many ways that I can put a crimp in your new romance."

She stood and glared at him. "Are you threatening me with blackmail, Jerome?"

"Call it what you will, but I urge you to do nothing hasty. Think about my offer, which I consider generous in the extreme, and I'll return for your answer later in the day. I'm sure you'll see things in a different light after you've thought about it." He bowed deeply but quickly, and left.

Clara Lou continued to sit until the chiming of a clock reminded her she would be late for her engagement with Chet unless she hurried. She raced to her apartment, where she changed into a more becoming dress, brushed her hair, and added a touch of rouge to her lips.

Chet was waiting for her in the lobby of the hotel and smiled as she approached. "You're always so prompt I was beginning to be concerned," he said.

"I know I'm late, but it couldn't be helped." She offered no explanation.

He glanced at her obliquely as they followed the head waiter to their table; it was apparent that she was upset.

She confirmed his guess when she waved away the menu that was offered to her. "You order for both of us, Chet. I don't care what I eat."

Remembering what she liked, he placed the order and then asked quietly, "What's wrong?"

She dreaded telling him the problem. "Who says anything is wrong?"

"It's all too plain to someone who knows you well and is concerned about your welfare."

Steeling herself, Clara Lou knew she had to give in. "Jerome showed up out of nowhere a half-hour ago," she said. Having removed the initial barrier, she repeated the conversation with her husband.

The color had already drained from Chet's face as he listened to her brief recital.

"I hate the thought of giving him a penny," she

concluded, "but it might well be worth a thousand dollars to be rid of him."

"That won't be necessary. You say his name is Jerome?"

Clara Lou nodded.

"Has he ever told you how he acquired the scar that disfigures his face?"

She shook her head, staring at him. "You know Jerome!" she exclaimed.

"Not personally." Chet's smile was grim. "How well did you know Rick Miller and his wife when you were in the Sacramento Valley?"

"I was fairly well acquainted with him when he was the sheriff, but I only met her once."

"I knew Melissa Austin for years before she married him," Chet said, realizing the time had come to reveal his own past. "I was sweet on her back in Oregon, and so was Danny Taylor. Anyway, she joined us in the party that Rick conducted to Texas, before the start of the war with Mexico. Melissa couldn't decide between Danny and me. Well, he got over her during the war and later married Heather, who is still his wife. I was still sweet on Melissa when she was seduced by a professional gambler—Jerome Hadley."

"That sounds like him," Clara Lou said. "I imagine he met this other woman soon after I threw him out. He's always chased after women."

"He took Melissa to California, and she paid all of their expenses. Then he sold her to a brothel owner in the Sacramento Valley."

"My god! Jerome has done many despicable things, but this is the lowest imaginable."

"Many months later," Chet said, "when he showed up at the bordello, Melissa carved his face."

"Good for her!"

Their soup had been served but was growing cold.

"That's about all there is to the story," Chet said. "Hadley disappeared again—"

"As he has a habit of doing."

"Melissa gave evidence against the brothel owner, who was a criminal. She changed back into the person she had been, and after a spell she and Rick were married. She told me the whole story one night when she and Rick were visiting the Blakes in San Francisco, and I happened to be a supper guest, too. We stayed up late into the evening, talking about the past, marveling how well everything had finally turned out for both of us. I hadn't heard Jerome Hadley's name from that evening until you mentioned it a few minutes ago."

Clara Lou looked at him, then averted her gaze. "You were in love with her, Chet."

"I thought I was, but I was still very young." He reached across the table for her hand. "Now I know the difference between puppy love and the real thing."

Her smile of relief lighted her face, and then she sighed. "What should I do about Jerome, Chet?"

"Nothing," he said. "Leave him to me and eat your dinner." He looked confident as he began his soup.

Clara Lou still had no appetite. "What will you do?"

"First off, we're going to have a long, relaxed dinner, and then I'm going back to your place with you. When Hadley shows up, I'll deal with him. Alone." He did not elaborate.

She asked no more questions and found it easier than she had imagined to get rid of her tensions. The mere fact that Chet intended to take care of the situation gave her a new feeling of optimism.

They ate a leisurely meal, and Chet kept Clara Lou's mind off her worries by telling her stories about his adventures in the California gold fields.

As they started back to her gaming house, she became taut again, gripping his arm hard, and he patted her hand reassuringly.

She used her key to let them in and was not surprised when she found Jerome already waiting for her at one of the dining room tables.

Her husband took in the situation at a glance and leaped to his feet. "Ah, Mr. Harris!" he said. "This is a great pleasure, sir. I don't believe our paths have crossed."

"Not directly." Chet ignored the other's outstretched hand and said quietly to Clara Lou, "Don't forget you have some pies to bake for tonight's customers."

She took the cue and went off reluctantly to the kitchen while Chet sat, hooking his thumbs in his waistcoat pockets.

"Thank you for the opportunity to have a little talk in private," Jerome said glibly. "Women are inclined to become emotional, but as men of the world I'm sure we can discuss matters far more rationally."

"Clara Lou tells me you want a thousand dollars to get out of her life," Chet said curtly.

"I'll keep my word, I assure you, Mr. Harris."

"Your offer solves nothing, Mr. Hadley. Clara Lou would still be married to you."

The gambler grasped at the hint. "I can make a far better offer, Mr. Harris, and I'm confident you'll soon see the advantages."

Playing along with him for the moment, Chet raised an eyebrow.

"It didn't occur to me to make this offer to Clara Lou because I realized her funds are limited. But I'm sure a man of your means could easily afford the slight additional expense." Jerome was expert at throwing out attractive bait.

"I'm listening, Mr. Hadley."

Chet's face showed no expression, but he didn't fool the professional gambler, who knew he had swallowed the bait. "A new law passed in the last year or two by the government of the Netherlands permits the granting of divorces in Holland on many different grounds." Jerome studied Chet and, elbows on the table, pressed his fingertips together. "I'd be delighted to accommodate you and Clara Lou, sir, by going myself to Amsterdam and obtaining the decree. Then you and Clara Lou would be free to do as you please."

Chet rose slowly to his feet. "What would this—ah —convenience cost me, Mr. Hadley?"

"A very small sum for a man of your stature, sir. My fee would be five thousand dollars, plus the cost of my first-class travel expenses."

Smiling, Chet put all of his weight and strength behind a short punch to the pit of the other's stomach. "This," he said succinctly, "is for Melissa Austin."

Jerome doubled over, gasping for breath.

"This is for Clara Lou." Chet straightened him with a hard left to the chin.

Jerome staggered backward.

"And this is for me." Chet sent him sprawling on his back with a hard right uppercut to the chin. "This is just a taste of what awaits you if you ever set foot on these premises again or annoy Clara Lou in any way." He went off to the kitchen, rubbing his chafed knuckles.

The dazed Jerome scrambled to his feet, retrieved his hat, and, holding one hand to his bruised chin, ran out into the street. It was just his luck that Harris had known Melissa, and he mumbled a curse under his breath.

He craved a drink, and when he made his way slowly around the corner, the noisy Palace beckoned. It wasn't his kind of place, but he was in no condition to be particular, so he entered, went to the bar, and ordered a whiskey.

The liquor numbed the pain in his chin, and Jerome gradually became conscious of a poker game being played at a nearby table. It quickly became apparent to him that the women who sat on the arms of the players' chairs, occasionally stroking them and allowing themselves to be fondled, were sending signals to the dealer.

To a professional gambler like Jerome, the system was so crude that he felt compelled to join the game, taking the only vacant seat at the table.

A corselet-clad girl appeared beside him. "Buy me a drink, and I'll bring you luck," she said. "I'm Dora."

Jerome handed her a dollar bill from his dwindling supply. "Indeed you will, my dear," he said. "A drink for you and a drink for me."

She went off to the bar, and he bought five dollars' worth of chips from the dealer. Dora returned with the drinks and draped one arm around Jerome's shoulders.

He was dealt a pair of queens and promptly placed a bet of two dollars. The stakes were too high for the others at the table, and they dropped out, losing their initial twenty-five-cent bets.

Certain that the woman rubbing against him had signaled the dealer, Jerome discarded all but his pair of queens. "I'll take three cards," he said.

All three were low, adding nothing to the hand, which he quietly held so the woman could see it clearly.

"I'll raise you a dollar," the dealer said.

Jerome pushed all of his remaining chips forward. "All right, and two more calls you."

The dealer placed his cards faceup on the table. "A pair of aces," he announced.

Sleight of hand was second nature to Jerome Hadley, and he smiled as he laid out his hand. "Three queens and a pair of tens," he said. "You can pay me double for the full house."

The dealer swallowed hard, and Dora looked bewildered.

Jerome played three more hands, then left the game abruptly, his slender nest egg enriched by twenty-five dollars. Shaking off the persistent woman, he wandered around until he found the man who, it was obvious, was the proprietor.

"Sir," Jerome said, "as one who has earned his living at cards, I find your system astonishingly crude. Any experienced player would see through it."

Willie de Berg's eyes narrowed. "Are you objecting?"

"Certainly not. I'm merely observing that you could utilize the services of a dealer who needs no assistance from whores. Allow me to illustrate. I'll bet you a flat one hundred dollars that I can not only win five hands in a row from you but can also name every card you hold."

"Show me," Willie said. He led the way to his office on the second floor, where he cleared a space on his desk.

"We'll use your cards, sir," Jerome said. "Any cards at all."

Willie went to the outer room, returning with two decks.

Jerome put the decks together, then shuffled them swiftly and easily, seemingly not even glancing at the cards.

Willie cut the combined deck. "Deal," he ordered.

Jerome dealt swiftly. "This is child's play," he said. "You hold three nines, a deuce, and a trey. The three nines are enough to persuade a player to bet. As it happens," he went on, laying down his own cards, "I hold three jacks."

"Not bad." Willie hated to admit he was impressed.

Jerome dealt four more hands, identifying all of his opponent's cards before they were displayed and winning all four hands.

"You're damn good," Willie said, handing him two fifty-dollar bills. "I could use you in the high-stakes room."

"Forty dollars a week base pay," Jerome said, "plus

ten percent of the take. Your whores can wheedle drinks out of the customers, but I want no help from them."

"Your rates are high, but they're worth it. You're hired." Willie extended his hand. "De Berg."

"Hadley," Jerome replied, shaking his hand.

Willie was startled. "Hadley, did you say?"

"Ah, the name is familiar to you. My estranged wife owns the place around the corner."

"Does she now." A gleam appeared in Willie's eyes.

"We appear to share the same opinion of the lady, Mr. de Berg." Jerome forgot his aching chin. "This promises to be a mutually profitable association, sir, in many ways."

transferral of that title. Your whores can wheedle
some out of the customers, but I want nothing to

VII

The school at which Sarah Rose Foster taught was
located a considerable distance from the boardinghouse, so she rode to and from work every day. Men
traveling back and forth from the mines west of
Denver used the road, particularly in the afternoons
when she was returning home, but it was safe as long
as she was mounted. At Scott's insistence she always
carried a six-shooter, but she hoped she never would
be forced to use it.

One afternoon she stayed somewhat later than usual at the four-room schoolhouse, grading examination
papers, and by the time she mounted her mare and
started her homeward journey, a number of miners
were coming into the city from the gold fields. She
ignored them, as she always did, making certain that
she kept her horse on the road. She needed no one to
tell her that she would be asking for trouble if she
took shortcuts across patches of barren, open countryside. Soon new buildings would fill in these areas,
thanks to the continuing, phenomenal growth of Denver, but in the meantime she knew it would be wise
not to stray from the road itself.

Looking straight ahead, she paid no attention to the
occasional remarks of miners, knowing that most were

merely playful and that the men intended her no
harm. She couldn't help glancing at a well-dressed
man, still some distance away and coming toward her,
who veered suddenly from the road and rode his
mount across a field of shale. She could not imagine
why any man would choose to ride over such difficult
terrain and looked at him more closely.

All at once Sarah Rose felt as though a bolt of
lightning had struck her. The man's wide-brimmed
hat was pulled low, concealing part of his profile, but
she knew him instantly from the way he carried
himself in the saddle. There was no doubt in her mind
that he was her missing brother, Tracy.

Too far from him to call out, Sarah Rose turned
instinctively to follow him, forcing her mare to cross
the field of loose shale, which caused the horse to
balk. Afraid she would lose sight of her brother, she
spurred forward.

Tracy soon left Denver behind, riding up and down
steep, boulder-strewn hills, and Sarah Rose continued
to follow him grimly. She was tempted to fire her
six-shooter into the air as a way of attracting his
attention but finally decided it might not be wise.
Tracy was riding through an area where there were
no houses, no cabins, and it would be dangerous if
any mounted miners could isolate her.

For the better part of a half-hour, Sarah Rose
managed to keep Tracy in sight, although the gap that
separated them widened gradually. The countryside
was desolate, with no other people in sight, no signs
of human habitation anywhere, and Sarah Rose became increasingly apprehensive. Perhaps, she thought,
she would fire her pistol after all, but as she drew the
weapon, Tracy suddenly disappeared from view.

Knowing she could not wander alone and unpro-
tected, she took careful note of her surroundings so
she could identify them and then reluctantly started
back to Denver for help. As she rode she drew a
mental map of the route she was taking, and when she

finally reached the city, she went straight to the *Tribune* office.

Her appearance there was so unexpected that Susanna Fuller hurriedly crossed the room and heard her telling Scott her story.

"Can you lead me to the spot where Tracy disappeared?" Scott asked, not revealing his suspicions regarding their brother's activities.

Sarah Rose nodded. "I believe so, but where we can search from there I can't imagine. You have no idea how remote and wild the countryside is out there."

"I'll come, too, if I may," Susanna volunteered.

While she and Scott went to the stable behind the newspaper plant to saddle horses, Isaiah Atkins crossed the street from the office he now was renting opposite the *Tribune*. "I saw you just now as I was looking out of the window, and you seemed upset," he told Sarah Rose.

She repeated her story, and Isaiah said, "I don't want to butt in, but I might be able to help. When I was a youngster, I often went out with a posse that Rick Miller was leading, and I haven't forgotten what I learned about following the trails of fugitives."

"I wish you would come," she replied. "It was so strange. One minute I saw Tracy, and the next he was gone."

Isaiah unlooped the reins of his gelding from the hitching post in front of his office. "I'm ready," he said simply, sufficiently aware of her tension to refrain from boasting or making lengthy, idle conversation.

Soon they were joined by Scott and Susanna, and the four young people set out without delay. The day was far advanced, and Sarah Rose looked up at the sky. "I think we can reach the place where I turned back before night comes."

"You set the pace," Scott said.

She rode even more rapidly than she had when she had returned to the city, her mind whirling. Contrary to her expectations, Tracy had not looked like someone suffering from want. His suit and hat had seemed expensive, at least from a distance, and his horse had been groomed. Her fears that he might be starving appeared to be unjustified.

There was little conversation on the ride, and after a while Sarah Rose slowed her mare to a walk. "This is the place where I turned back," she said.

"Where was your brother when you last spotted him?" Isaiah asked quietly.

She pointed.

"Can you lead us there?"

"I—I think so. At least, I hope so." She moved on again cautiously.

Isaiah rode close behind her, saying nothing.

She rode for another quarter of an hour, repeatedly looking back over her shoulder to make certain she was not straying. At last she came to the crest of a hill; ahead was a narrow canyon, its far slope even more steep than the near side. "I could swear I last saw him just about here," she said.

Isaiah dismounted and walked slowly up and down the crest as he peered intently at the ground. After a time he dropped to one knee.

The others dismounted, too, and watched him. He beckoned, waited until they came closer, and then said, "You weren't far off the mark, Sarah Rose. Here are the hoof marks—in the dust—of a single rider who came this way not too long ago."

The women saw nothing, but Scott finally made out the faint signs of hoof prints.

"We'll go on foot from here," Isaiah said. "Scott, you'll oblige me if you'll lead my horse."

They made their way to the bottom of the canyon, where Isaiah again paused. "The rider dismounted here," he said. "There are the prints of a man's boots as well as hoof prints. It may be we're coming to the end of the trail."

The others looked at the steep slope of the canyon

and exchanged bleak looks. The incline seemed totally deserted, like the countryside around it.

Then Scott caught sight of two thin plumes of smoke emanating from the ground above a ledge situated about two-thirds of the way up the slope. "Either there's a volcano smoldering up yonder, which isn't very likely," he said, "or someone is using a fire. Though I can't imagine where it would be."

They left their horses at the bottom of the canyon, and Isaiah led the way up its side, holding Sarah Rose's hand in order to steady her. The independent-minded Susanna tried to negotiate the slope alone but could not, and eventually she consented to allow Scott to assist her.

Isaiah paused and pointed. "There," he said. "Unless I've gone crazy, a wooden door has been built back of that boulder to seal off the entrance to a cave."

They stared in silence. There could be no doubt that a human dwelling was located behind the boulder, and they struggled upward to the ledge.

The door creaked open, and Tracy Foster came into the open, a cocked rifle in his hands. "Go away," he shouted. "I allow no trespassing here."

"Tracy!" The excited Sarah Rose could think only that she had not been mistaken.

Susanna recognized Tracy Foster as the young man with the strangely penetrating gray eyes who had exchanged a few words with her in a Denver restaurant. Now more than ever was she aware of the almost hypnotic power of those eyes, which so many of the gray ghost's victims had mentioned.

Scott managed to sound far calmer than he felt. "Tracy, we've been searching all over for you. Sarah Rose and I came to Colorado to find you."

Tracy remained violently antagonistic. "All right, now you've found me, so I hope you're satisfied. Go away! Leave me to live my own life as I see fit!" He brandished the rifle. "And don't come any closer. I warn you!"

Sarah Rose was on the verge of tears. "No matter what you say, you're our brother. We came to Colorado because we were so worried about you!"

"I'm fine," he said, snarling. "Now you've satisfied your curiosity, so get out! Go back to California, where you belong. I don't have a brother anymore. Or a sister, either!"

It was plain to Scott that he had taken leave of his senses, and his cocked rifle brooked no argument. Sarah Rose, however, was not afraid, and discarding caution, she advanced several paces. "You may disown Scott and me, for whatever your reasons," she said, "but we don't disown you."

Tracy pointed the rifle at her.

"I don't believe for one instant that you'd shoot me," she said. "The brother who did so much for me through all the years we were growing up together wouldn't kill a sister who still loves him."

The rifle wavered, then was lowered. "What do you want?" Tracy asked wearily.

"A few words with you, that's all." She continued to hold her ground without flinching.

Isaiah felt overwhelming admiration for the courage of this quiet young woman.

Tracy considered the request for a moment. "All right," he said grudgingly. "You can come in for a minute. But just you! Not Scott. Not that woman from the newspaper. And not him!"

Isaiah knew Tracy had recognized him, even though he didn't refer to him by name.

Before anyone could halt Sarah Rose, she walked steadily forward and entered the cave, with Tracy close beside her.

"Sit there," he directed. "I'm going to keep facing the entrance. I don't want my house filled with people I don't want to see."

The large cave was illuminated by two oil lamps

and the glow of a small cooking fire, with the smoke escaping through natural holes in the roof that the search party had seen from the outside. Tracy's horse stood at one side, placidly eating from a feed bag, and a stream of clear mountain water ran through the rear. Sarah Rose was astonished when she saw a cot, clothing boxes, a homemade chair, and various provisions, including sacks of flour and beans, two sides of bacon, and a container of some other smoked meat.

"You really live here," she said in wonder.

"Sure." Tracy was torn by conflicting emotions of pride and resentment. "It took me a long time and plenty of hard work to fix up this place for myself."

"But why here, Tracy? Why a cave—when you could live in a house somewhere?"

"I like it better here," he replied defiantly.

She studied him, and aside from the unchanging expression in his eyes and the deep smudges beneath them, he looked more or less as he always had. His worsted suit, white shirt, and dark cravat were impressive, as were his fine boots. "You don't look as though you're having hard times," she said.

"I've got no complaints." Tracy was curt.

"Do you work in the mines?" Sarah Rose asked.

His temper flared. "I mind my own damn business, that's what I do!"

She realized she had erred and tried a different approach. "What you do for a living doesn't matter. Tracy, please come home with us. We want you and need you in the orchards. This no way for anyone to live."

"You and Scott go back," he said harshly. "I like it just fine here. I don't need to answer to anyone but myself—for anything I do."

"After Ma died," Sarah Rose said, speaking very softly, "Pa told us a thousand times that we had to stick together. He always said we had to lean on each other and depend on each other. Remember?"

"I don't want to talk about Pa," he said, and his

voice rose to a near scream as he added, "or Ma, either!"

She paid no attention to his protest. "Pa also told us that in good times it's easy to get along alone, but in bad times everyone needs family. Surely you remember that, too."

"I'm not having bad times," he growled. "And I'm trying to do you and Scott a favor. Stay away from me. For good and all. I'll just cause trouble for you. That's why you've got to get out of my life and stay out!" Jumping to his feet, he brandished his rifle. "We've talked long enough. Clear out!"

Sarah Rose stood, slowly smoothing her skirt. "You aren't the only Foster who is stubborn, Tracy. Now that Scott and I have found you, it would be easy enough for us to give up and go back to California. But we'll stay in Denver for a spell. Just in case you change your mind and decide you want or need us."

Tracy gritted his teeth. "I don't want anything from you and Scott, and I sure don't need you. Forget me! If you know what's good for you, you'll tell yourselves that I've never existed. Now, walk straight out of here. And never come back!"

There were tears in her eyes as she turned from him and made her way back into the open.

Scott was bitterly disappointed when he saw that his sister was alone. "I'll have a word with him," he said, starting toward the cave entrance.

The crack of Tracy's rifle shattered the silence, the bullet whining high over his brother's head. "You know I can aim a heap better than that," he called from the interior of the cave. "Next time I'll shoot to kill."

Tears were sliding down Sarah Rose's lovely face as she touched Scott's arm. "He means it," she said. "We'd best head back to town." She started toward the base of the canyon, stumbling because she was blinded by her tears.

Isaiah put a protective arm around her shoulders to

guide her, and Scott gripped his rifle so hard that his knuckles turned white.

"You can't reason with him," Susanna said, "and it's plain he means his threat. Don't be a martyr. You'll accomplish nothing."

For a long, tense moment Scott continued to face the cave, weighing the risk of storming his brother's strange dwelling. At last he turned away, his shoulders sagging. "I reckon you're right, Sue," he said.

She could understand the deep bruise to the pride of a man who hated to admit defeat. "There was nothing more you could do."

He nodded, taking her hand to help her down the steep slope to the base of the canyon.

Susanna saw that Sarah Rose and Isaiah had already reached the bottom, but she was in no hurry to rejoin them. "I can understand your disappointment, Scott, but this way may be the best."

"How can it be? My brother needs me, and I've failed him!"

"You're wrong. He's the one who has failed you and Sarah Rose."

"I know what you're thinking. A man would have to be a criminal to hide himself in a cave in a godforsaken area where no other human being would want to live."

She nodded, biting her lower lip. Scott needed sympathy, and she would console him as best as she could while remembering that his raw emotions made him vulnerable. She didn't want to mislead him, but she knew no better now than she had when saying good-bye to Andy Brentwood which of them she preferred.

Night fell soon after the ride to town was begun, and Sarah Rose, controlling her feelings to the best of her ability, repeated her conversation with Tracy.

Scott was certain now that their brother had become a criminal, but he decided to tell no one—least of all his sister. It seemed unlikely, but perhaps—just perhaps—there would be a chance to talk some sense into his brother. And maybe if Tracy turned himself in, the authorities would be lenient. "I aim to stay here for a spell," Scott finally said.

"Me, too," his sister replied. "Just in case Tracy changes his mind about going home with us."

Isaiah remained silent, his heart going out to this courageous young woman. Although he was no sooth-sayer who could peer into the future, he was afraid that unpleasantness lay ahead for Tracy Foster, and he vowed to be nearby so he could shield Sarah Rose from pain.

Caroline Brandon stretched like a cat on the four-poster bed, reveling in the sense of power that her nude sensuality gave her. "I'll be waiting for you right here, darling," she said, "so hurry back."

Willie de Berg's smile was bloodless, and as he dressed quickly he averted his gaze so she could not see the chill in his eyes. She had pushed him too far, and now he was ready to retaliate.

"It seems to me," she said, "that we could be married very privately without telling anyone. Then we can wait as long as we like to make the announcement, after most people in Denver have forgotten Luke's murder."

"I'll think about it," Willie said as he started toward the door.

"Give me your answer today," she said, pressing him.

He paused with his hand on the latch. "I'll do just that," he said. "I give you my word." He left, closing the door behind him.

Caroline stretched again, her smile contented. Her handling of Willie had been masterful, and plans filled her head. As soon as they were married, she would persuade him to build a home for her in some part of town far from his place of business. His wealth would enable her to have a spectacular new wardrobe made, and she would see to it that he bought her the diamond ring, bracelet, and necklace that she craved. Certainly his vocation was no more disreputable than those of others who were acquiring fortunes in this boom town, so it wouldn't be too long before she became a leader of Denver society. Money spoke for itself here.

Enveloped in her dreams and satiated after Willie's lovemaking, Caroline dozed.

The crack of a bullwhip only inches from her face awakened her with a start, and she opened her eyes to see Bessie standing above her, the whip in one hand and a bundle in the other.

"No more naps today, sweetie," Bessie said. "First off, Willie sent your final rent payment to the Chinese woman who is the housekeeper at your boardin' house. He also had all your clothes brought here. You'll recognize your dresses from time to time. I got a couple of them in the distribution myself."

Caroline pulled herself to a sitting position and blinked at the stern-faced woman.

Bessie threw the bundle onto the bed. "You'll wear these," she said, "beginning right now."

Her bewilderment increasing, Caroline stared at a skimpy corselet, black net stockings, and high-heeled pumps.

"That's your workin' outfit," Bessie told her. "And until further notice, they're your only wardrobe. You'll have to earn your street clothes, like the rest of us have done, and I'll tell you now that you'll have to work for a long time before you'll earn a stitch. Until you've paid off your debt to Willie—and he keeps count in his own head—you'll turn over every penny you make to him."

"This is outrageous!" Caroline cried.

The bullwhip cracked again, close to her face. "I've

had enough practice that I'm handy with one of these things," Bessie said, "so heed what I say and don't start makin' a fuss."

Looking around the room wildly, Caroline saw that the clothes she had worn to her late-morning rendezvous had vanished, and the sight of the ugly whip, which was writhing in Bessie's grasp like a living snake, made her even more aware of her vulnerability. "I—I don't understand," she murmured.

"It's simple enough. You're the newest member of Willie's stable of whores. Welcome to the club, sweetie. I'd feel sorry for you if I hadn't warned you until I near lost my voice." Bessie adjusted a thin shoulder strap of her snug-fitting evening gown.

"Surely you're joking."

"This whip draws blood, a lot of it, and that's no joke, believe me. If I don't beat you into bein' reasonable, Willie will finish you off himself. But I can do it, take my word for it. I'd rather beat than get beaten any day. I've worked my way up to the high-stakes room, where my cut is bigger, and you ain't sendin' me back downstairs to the mine pits, I can tell you that. We got a lot to do before I turn you loose, so get movin'."

Caroline hesitated. The bed sheet she was clutching would cover her nudity if she were to run past Bessie and flee, but she had no idea what or who she would find out in the hallway. It was certain that Willie de Berg had made up his mind to foil her, and he no doubt had strong-arm men posted around the building to prevent her escape. She was trapped.

The flick of the whip seemed gentle, but it felt like the sting of an angry bee high on one hip. Bessie's eyes were firm and cold. She would use the whip unmercifully if it were necessary.

Scarcely able to control her hysteria, Caroline began to struggle into the corselet.

"That's better," Bessie said approvingly. "Now you're showin' some sense. And never mind feelin' foolish in that outfit. Everybody does. At first. Always be careful you keep the seams straight in them stockings."

Caroline's calves ached as she slipped into the shoes. "I'll fall down in these."

Bessie giggled. "The customers love the way them heels make you walk, so you'll manage. I'm puttin' the whip away now because we don't want the customers to see it. But if you try any funny stuff, the guards will call Willie, and then may God help you. Come on."

"Where—are we—going?" Caroline was so numb from shock that her mind could not function clearly.

"To your new room, first off. The high-stakes room is open for business now, so waggle your rear end good when we walk through." Bessie opened the door.

The desperate Caroline made her way through the outer room, her hips swaying, and felt certain that the half-dozen card players were staring at her.

"Always let your hair hang loose that way," Bessie said, leading her down the corridor where the women slept and worked. "Here we are. This is your new home, so welcome to it."

The cubicle was small, dominated by an oversized bed strewn with cheap satin pillows. There was a small dressing table with a mirror on it, a pail of water and several basins, and in front of the table a stool. "Where—where is the other furniture?" Caroline stammered.

"That there is all you'll need," Bessie told her. "Now listen good while I teach you the signals you'll give the dealers when you read the cards in a customer's hand. The system is simple, easy to learn, but you got to be careful. We had one new girl who got caught by a customer a few days ago, and he raised the roof, claimin' he was cheated. That girl disappeared the same day, and you don't want to meet the fellow we're callin' the executioner."

A chill moved slowly up Caroline's spine. Her situation was even worse than she could have dreamed.

"He's kind of new here himself. Tall, with gray eyes that look like knives slashin' into you. Stay away from him. But if you listen good, you'll never have anythin' to do with him." Bessie launched into an explanation of the system used by the women to tell a dealer the contents of a card player's hand.

Her mind still whirling, her heart heavy, Caroline knew that her success or failure would determine whether she lived or died, so she forced herself to concentrate. She repeated what Bessie told her, then was instructed to pretend she was perched on the arm of a player's chair, giving signal after signal.

"You'll do." Bessie was relieved when the lesson came to an end. "Your makeup is in one of the drawers, along with a spare corselet and stockings. Fix your face, and plaster it heavy."

Caroline moved from the edge of the bed to the stool and obediently went to work with cosmetics.

"Don't get the idea of runnin' away," Bessie told her as she applied kohl, salves, and rouge. "You wouldn't get very far in that outfit, night or day. Men wanderin' the streets would grab hold of you quick because you're fair game. A couple of new girls tried it, and after Willie was done beatin' them, they wished they was bein' raped again out in the alley."

Caroline shuddered.

"Do what you're told, and don't complain—and you'll have no worries. Use the beauty patch on the left side of your face. A mite more salve on your eyelids, and tie that little red ribbon around your throat. You encourage customers to drink, and the minimum fee you charge anybody you bring up here is a dollar. And don't try hidin' any money. The guards will inspect your room every day, and they can smell out any hidin' place you can think of. You ready?"

"I—I guess so." Feeling shamed and degraded, Caroline slowly rose to her feet and submitted to Bessie's critical inspection.

Bessie grinned, then reached out and fondled her breasts. "Shove these out in front of you, like they was bein' carried on a platter. With your hair and looks and body, you'll have the customers fallin' all over each other to get at you."

Afraid that she would faint, Caroline grasped the bedpost for support.

"Don't let it get you down, sweetie," Bessie told her. "There may be better lives, although I can't remember what it was like before I started workin' for Willie. But there's plenty worse, too. We'll have us a little talk after all the customers leave tomorrow mornin'. Meanwhile, keep your chin up, and you'll do great." Bessie embraced her, pinched her buttocks, and took her leave.

Caroline drew in a tremulous breath and forced herself to look in the mirror. She not only resembled the Palace prostitutes, but she had become one.

The fault was Willie's, not her own. She had tried to inveigle him into marrying her, but he had tricked her in return, and now she would be forced to pay the penalty. Hereafter, she would be forced to endure the pawings of card players while she cheated them; she would coax men who needed no coaxing to drink themselves senseless; and, worst of all, she would bring an endless succession of crude lovers to this cubicle.

Afraid of the punishment that awaited her if she tarried, she forced herself to leave the little room and walk down the corridor to the main staircase. The waves of sound that rose from the ground floor told her the Palace's operation was in full swing.

Descending the stairs as best she could in her teetering heels, Caroline knew it would avail her nothing and place her in grave danger if she tried to bolt out the door and go to the *Tribune* office. The guards would catch her before she went far, and in her provocative attire she would attract every man on the street. Besides, even if she miraculously reached the *Tribune*, there was no way she could explain to Scott Foster and Susanna Fulton how she happened to be wearing this flimsy costume. Her credibility was destroyed, the respectable people who lived in the Harris and Wong boardinghouse would shun her, and she would be plagued by the need to earn a living. It was best to stay here and accept her destiny.

Caroline's blood ran cold when she saw Willie de Berg standing near the foot of the stairs, surveying the scene. He glanced in her direction, then studied her, malice gleaming in his eyes. At that moment her love for him—or what she had imagined to be love—turned to icy hatred. This was the man who had seduced her, somehow arranged her husband's murder, and now was repaying her whole-hearted loyalty by forcing her to become a prostitute.

Under no circumstances would she cringe, beg for mercy, or berate him. Her pride took possession of her, and she walked down the stairs with her breasts outthrust, her bearing erect, her hips swaying. She returned Willie's gaze, then allowed one eyelid to drop in a quick wink as she favored him with her most dazzling smile. Sweeping past him, she made her way into the maelstrom of hard-drinking, women-craving men, knowing she was more beautiful, more desirable than any of his other unfortunate prostitutes.

Clara Lou Hadley was surprised when Chet Harris came into her gambling house at closing time, just as the last customers were leaving. They had dined together earlier, before she had opened the establishment for the evening, and she had assumed that he intended to return to his own quarters for the night. The expression in his eyes told her that he had something of importance on his mind, but she decided it could wait.

"You look like a man who could eat a late supper of bacon and scrambled eggs," she said.

"You're a mind reader, as you so often are," Chet replied. "But I'll have supper only on one condition. You've done enough work today, so I'll do the cooking." Not waiting for her reply, he went straight to the kitchen, where the cook and his helper were donning their hats and coats.

Clara Lou followed and found Chet already slicing bacon. "Sit down," he directed, pointing to a chair with the carving knife. "You're now a guest in your own house, ma'am."

She humored him, then reminded the departing cook to lock the front door behind him. She watched Chet put the bacon in a pan to fry, then break several eggs into a bowl, adding a little cream and some scallions he quickly chopped.

"I thought you couldn't cook," she said.

"I can't," he replied, chuckling as he beat the eggs. "Ke is a real cook, but back in the days when we were poor, before we hit paydirt in the California gold fields, he always burned the bacon, so I always cooked it. He taught me to scramble eggs, but I stopped taking lessons from him after that. Where do you keep the bread?"

She was already on her feet. "I'll attend to the bread," she said. "That doesn't count." She went to a cupboard for bread, cut several slices, and brought them to the stove. "Ready for the toast yet?"

"Start it when I put the eggs on the fire." He poured a small amount of bacon grease into a skillet and heated it. "Now," he said as he put the pan on the fire, stirring the contents vigorously with a fork.

Clara Lou put the bread on the grate in a place

where the wood fire had burned low. While the bread was toasting, she removed a crock of butter from an outer container of water that kept it cool.

Chet removed the bacon from the pan, then stirred the eggs again. Within a few more seconds he slid the eggs onto a serving platter.

The toast was done and buttered at almost the same instant.

"We make a first-rate team," Chet said. "If I should go bankrupt sometime, we could hire ourselves out as a couple to work in a hotel kitchen. Or maybe we could get jobs as a butler and housekeeper."

"I can't imagine you ever going bankrupt, the way your empire is still spreading," Clara Lou said, "but I could always find a job for you here. Assuming I'm still in business, too."

"That," he declared, his smile fading, "is precisely what I came back here to discuss with you."

She wasn't yet ready to face whatever reality he had brought here with him. "Take the platters into the dining room while I pour some mugs of hot chocolate."

Chet was surprised. "I didn't see you preparing any chocolate."

"It's one of my secret vices. The cook always leaves a pot for me on the smaller stove, where it stays hot until bedtime."

He carried the food into the dining room, placing the platters on one of the empty tables, and a moment later she joined him, the pot of hot chocolate in one hand, with dishes, mugs, and eating utensils balanced in the other, along with two napkins.

"I was so proud of myself that I plain forgot the plates, knives, and forks," Chet said, giving her a rueful smile. "I reckon you'd better find yourself another assistant."

"Oh, you have the potential to become an efficient worker," she said as he held her chair for her. "So I'll keep you on the staff for a spell."

He seated himself opposite her. "I like this," he said earnestly.

"So do I, but don't delay any longer. Out with it. You have something other than eggs and bacon on your mind."

"How did you know?"

"I've come to know you, Mr. Harris."

He nodded, began to eat, and then frowned. "I made a mistake the day I lost my temper with Jerome Hadley. Instead of hitting him, I should have made certain that he left town."

"I'm not ashamed to say it gave me pleasure to learn that you knocked him down. And you can be sure that by now he's a thousand miles from Denver."

"You're wrong, I'm sorry to say." Chet frowned and grimaced. "I hoped he'd clear out, too, but it isn't that easy to get rid of a bad penny. When I left you after supper tonight, I could have sworn I saw Hadley going into de Berg's place as I was starting to walk back to the boardinghouse. The thought kept niggling at me after I got there, and I knew I wouldn't be able to sleep, so I left the house again and went to de Berg's for a little personal snooping."

"You went to the Palace?" She was surprised and more than a little dismayed. "That was foolish of you, my dear. Willie de Berg not only hates me, but as you well know, he's extended that hatred to you, too. He could have ordered his bullies to knock you senseless!"

"Well," he said, smiling slightly, "the thought did cross my mind that I might be taking something of a personal risk, but I had no choice. I couldn't ask Isaiah Atkins or Scott Foster to do the looking for me because neither of them is acquainted with Jerome Hadley, and even if I'd managed to describe him, we wouldn't have been certain. The only way to handle it was to go myself."

"I wouldn't have permitted it!"

"I reckon you wouldn't." Chet looked at her fondly.

"But I'm not all that big a fool. The way I figured it, de Berg wouldn't take the chance of assaulting one of Colorado's most prominent citizens. He isn't afraid of much, maybe, but my money still holds him at bay. And I was right. He scowled at me, making it pretty plain that I wasn't exactly welcome, but he didn't stop his hired hands from selling me a cup of coffee or letting me wander around the place."

"You're incorrigible!"

"My first shock," he said, "was seeing Caroline Brandon there."

Clara Lou was incredulous. "She was a patron?"

"No. One of de Berg's harlots. Wandering around half-naked, fawning on customers so they'd buy more drinks, and taking those who could meet her price upstairs with her."

"The poor thing. I can't understand how she could have sunk so low so fast."

"You needn't feel too sorry for her. She had certain inclinations, and they finally came out. I've never told you this, but she tried, some time ago, to persuade me to take her to bed."

Clara Lou bristled. "Why, the brazen—"

"Forget her," Chet said. "We have more important problems on our minds. Jerome Hadley is working for de Berg as a card dealer. In the room where they play for big money, as near as I could make out. He was upset when he caught sight of me, but I saw no point in looking him in the eye, and as soon as I saw him at work, I left the place."

Clara Lou lost her appetite for the scrambled eggs and bacon.

"Willie de Berg and Jerome Hadley make a bad combination," Chet said somberly.

Clara Lou nodded, clearly worried.

"Tomorrow," he told her, his voice quiet but firm, "I'm hiring a couple of reliable men who will go with you every time you leave this place. Don't bother to tell me you don't want or need security guards, because I intend to pay no attention to your protests. This is one time when my money is going to be spent for a purpose that's useful."

She sipped her hot chocolate in an effort to compose herself. "For a good many years I relied only on myself, and I thought I had the strength and the ability to handle any situation that might come along. Well, I was wrong. I'm a sharp thorn in Jerome's side—"

"All the sharper after I gave him a drubbing!" Chet still blamed himself for losing his self-control.

"This has nothing to do with you, really," Clara Lou insisted. "Willie de Berg has enough incentive of his own to want to get rid of this place as competition, and now with Jerome to goad him, the desire is twice as strong!"

"Now you know why I insist on hiring guards for you."

"You should hire a couple for yourself, too," she said.

"I can squash the Willie de Bergs and Jerome Hadleys of the world if they come after me." Chet's confidence was unbounded. "You're the primary target, not me. I'm tempted to take steps right off that will drive both of them out of town."

"How?" she demanded.

"I don't know—yet. Fortunately for them, I have a respect for the law, so it won't be all that simple. But I'll talk to Ke about the problem, and maybe, between us, we'll think of something effective. In the meantime, you're going to have full protection every time you walk out your door!"

Chet kept his promise promptly, and the following morning two husky young men, both heavily armed, appeared at Clara Lou's establishment. "Mr. Harris hired us to keep watch over you," the taller of the pair said.

"I appreciate his concern, and I'm grateful to you, too," Clara Lou replied. "It will be a relief to have an escort when I go out on errands. But I'll have no need for your services here. When I'm under this roof, I'm safe."

"Mr. Harris said—"

"Oh, I daresay he did, and I know he's paying your wages. But this place caters to a rather select clientele, and those who come here for a good supper and a few hours of discreet play at the gaming tables would be disturbed if they saw armed guards. The kitchen is too small to keep you cooped up there when the staff is at work, and you'd be too conspicuous in the dining room or gaming room, if you see what I mean."

"You'll have to talk to Mr. Harris about all that," the shorter guard declared. "He hired us to do a job, and we take our orders from him."

"I'll settle all this when I see him," she said, knowing it was useless to argue with them.

When Chet dropped in for a brief visit late in the afternoon, Clara Lou explained the situation to him, and he reluctantly agreed to dispense with the services of the guards in the evenings, when she spent all of her time at the establishment. In return, however, he insisted that she promise not to leave the premises unless he himself was present as her escort. By the time he set off for the boardinghouse, the issue was settled.

Neither had any way of knowing that Willie de Berg was planning on paying Clara Lou a visit of his own. But he was delayed in his departure from the Palace by an extraordinary incident. In the barroom a violent fight threatened to break out when a Southern miner, who was standing drinking at the bar, began fiercely denouncing the North. Another miner, who had come to the Colorado gold fields from Illinois, grabbed the Southerner on the shoulder and called him a snake. Bitter words were exchanged, and both men, who had been drinking hard liquor the better part of the afternoon, threatened to kill each other. Just then an elderly, bearded miner wandered in, accompanied by a small burro, the animal staying close beside its master even though it was not led by as much as a rope around the neck. Suddenly everyone in the saloon, including the two miners, stopped everything and looked on astonished as the miner and the burro came up to the bar.

Willie de Berg was relieved that the two quarreling miners had been distracted, but he still couldn't permit in his bar this ludicrous spectacle of the man and his burro. He accosted the old miner and said angrily, "Get that beast out of here!"

"The name is Bingham," the miner said, fixing watery blue eyes on the proprietor. "And this here burro is Eustace."

"I don't care who or what he is. Animals aren't allowed in a place where people drink!"

Bingham ignored Willie's statement. "You sell beer, don't you?" he asked.

"Of course, but—"

"Good enough." The old miner turned to the burro. "Come along, Eustace." Together they made their way to the bar, with other customers clearing a path for them.

The card game in progress at one of the tables halted, and the corselet-clad women forgot their duties and crowded forward to see the spectacle. The miners, too, seemed to have forgotten their quarrel, and they moved away from each other, looking on at the scene.

"A schooner o' beer for me, and another for Eustace," the old miner said, slapping a coin on the counter.

The bartender grinned. "Do I serve his in a glass?"

The crowd appreciated his humor, but Bingham was not amused. "Don't mock me, young feller," he admonished. "There ain't no way a burro can drink out of a glass. Put his beer in a saucer. No, that ain't big enough. In a nice big soup bowl."

Even Willie forgot his animosity sufficiently to stare at the old man and his burro.

The bartender, chuckling and shaking his head, followed the instructions he had been given.

"Eustace," the old man said, "I been promisin' you a treat all them weeks out in the gold fields. Even when you was mean, ornery, and wouldn't do what you was told. After this, just you remember I always keep my word. So do what I tell you from now on."

The animal was alert, its eyes on its master, and it made no move when the miner placed the bowl of beer on the floor. As nearly as the onlookers could tell, the beast was awaiting an order from the old man.

Paying no attention to the gaping, laughing crowd, Bingham raised his schooner. "Here's mud in your eye, Eustace," he said, then took a large swallow.

That was the signal the burro had awaited. Lowering its head, it began to lap up the beer eagerly.

Caroline Brandon and Bessie stood together, their arms around each other's waists, and stared in astonishment. "I wouldn't believe this if I didn't see it myself."

Bessie curbed a spasm of giggles. "Mr. Bingham," she called, "let me buy you and your friend another round."

The old man drained his schooner, placed it on the bar with a thump, and wiped his mouth with the back of his shirt-sleeve. Leaning on the bar, he turned his watery gaze toward the young woman. "I thank you right kindly, lady," he said, "but me and Eustace can afford to pay for our own. You ready yet, Eustace?" A loud, prolonged belch emphasized his question.

The burro did not raise its head until the last of the beer in the bowl was gone. Then warm, eager eyes were concentrated on the old miner.

"Set 'em up again!" Bingham commanded, the ring of his coin on the bar sounding loudly.

Again the schooner and the bowl were emptied quickly.

Willie saw that all other activity in the Palace had been suspended, but the customers were laughing and joking with the women and ordering drinks. The shrewd proprietor realized that business would boom after the remarkable exhibition came to an end.

"This next round is on the house," he said.

"That's right kind of you, sir," Bingham replied with a courtly bow. "I thought you was downright inhospitable when we first come in here. But me and Eustace is happy to accept your apology. And your beer."

Everyone in the place was joining in the spirit of the occasion, and Willie had to signal to a second bartender to join his colleague, who was deluged with orders.

Before long, the onlookers lost count of the number of beers consumed by the old miner and his companion. It was evident, however, that both had strong thirsts.

Suddenly Bingham called a halt. Draining his schooner and belching, he looked down at the burro, who was lapping more slowly now. "Drink up, Eustace," he said. "We ain't got all night, you know."

The burro emptied the bowl. Then the miner and his four-legged companion began to make their way toward the door, both weaving a trifle unsteadily.

"Come back anytime, Mr. Bingham," Willie called. "You and Eustace are always welcome here!"

The door closed again. At Willie's signal the card games were renewed, and a number of the women led clients up the stairs. The beer-drinking old miner and burro would account for a larger profit than usual for a weekday; and there had been no need to call out the strong-arm men to break up the fight between the two angry miners. So Willie was in good spirits. He looked out at the gathering dusk, glanced at his pocket watch, and decided there was just time for him to pay his visit to Clara Lou Hadley before her supper customers arrived. Leaving word that he would return in a few minutes, he sauntered around the corner.

Clara Lou had not yet opened her doors for the evening, her dealers would not arrive until considerably later, and as always, she was at work in the kitchen with her cook and his helper. The new waiter she had hired to serve the large crowds to whom she now catered answered the rap at the door, then came to the kitchen.

"There's a man here to see you, Mrs. Hadley," he said.

"Who is he?"

"He didn't tell me, ma'am. He's in the dining room."

Wiping her hands on her apron, she opened the swinging door that separated the kitchen and dining room, then stopped short when she saw Willie, very much at home as he lounged in a chair, smoking a cheroot.

She was almost sorry she had persuaded Chet that the security guards were not needed after dark. "What do you want?" she demanded curtly.

"You've turned this into a nice-looking place," he said, undisturbed by her manner. "I hear that folks have to reserve in advance if they want supper here, and I'm told your tables bring you a steady little profit."

"You go out of your way to find out things that are none of your business!" she retorted.

Willie replied to the rebuff with a smile. "It does my heart good when my neighbors prosper. The way Denver is growing, there's plenty for all of us. And when one place in a neighborhood does all right, it helps all the others."

Clara Lou looked at him suspiciously, unimpressed by his display of friendliness. "You and I have different classes of customers," she said. "You can't help me, and I can't help you."

"I didn't come here for a quarrel." He rose and held

a chair for her, his manner that of a host seating an honored guest. "It can't hurt you to have a little chat with me."

"I suppose not," she replied grudgingly, taking the chair he offered her.

"There are all kinds of nasty rumors around town about me," he said, exerting his charm to the utmost. "But I'm not an ogre or a cannibal. I'm in business, just as you are, and I give my customers what they want."

Clara Lou decided not to mention that anyone who played cards at the Palace was probably cheated. She would hold her tongue until she learned the reason for his unexpected visit.

"Last night," he said, "I saw your beau, that rolling-in-money Harris, hanging around my place for a spell, so you probably know by now that your husband is on my payroll. If you hadn't already known it."

She acknowledged the situation with a nod but had no intention of confirming it in words.

"Hadley has told me about the to-do he had here," Willie said. "He seems the kind who talks more than is good for him."

"Why are you mentioning all this?" she demanded.

His grin deepened. "Be a little patient. I like to talk about things in the way that's comfortable for me. Anyway, I don't blame you and Harris for getting riled up. There's nothing that makes me as mad as attempted blackmail, either."

Clara Lou raised an eyebrow but did not reply.

She was tough, Willie reflected. "His offer to go off to Holland for a divorce was crazy. Nobody in his right mind would pay that kind of money. A total of five hundred dollars for travel, lawyers' fees, and a decent payoff would be plenty."

"This is none of your concern," she said, starting to rise.

He grasped her arm in a viselike grip. "Hear me out and don't get uppity. I'm here with a plan that will help everybody."

"Where do you enter the picture?" she asked coldly.

"You'll see in a minute. The way I look at it, you and Harris would get married if Hadley wasn't in the way." He paused and looked at her.

"We might or might not," she replied with spirit.

"Hey, now, you're talking to old Willie de Berg, not some country hayseed. You and I have been through a few mills. Any woman in her right mind would jump at the chance to marry a nice-looking bachelor whose bank account has to be worth a million or two."

"For the sake of argument, suppose you're right. What of it?" She was still belligerent.

"I have Jerome Hadley under my thumb. He's scared of me. So I believe I can talk him into going off to Holland and getting a divorce for five hundred, not five thousand. One hell of a big difference." He refrained from adding that, if persuasion failed, his special strong-arm employee could rid the world of Hadley with dispatch for the same sum.

"What's in it for you?" Clara Lou wanted to know. "Don't tell me you're just being a kind neighbor, either, because I wouldn't swallow that fishing line. There has to be a hook on the end of it."

"I wouldn't insult your intelligence with flim-flam," Willie said earnestly. "Sure, there's plenty in it for me. Once you're Mrs. Harris and start to hobnob with the rich of San Francisco and Denver and wherever, you'll have no use for a little supper house and gaming parlor, even if it is pretty classy. I'm looking for a way to expand, and I'd like to add a place like this—that's so different from the Palace—to my operations."

"I begin to understand." As much as she loathed the man, she had to admit he was clever.

"It wouldn't cost you or Harris one penny in cash. I'm willing to guarantee it. I'll pay all of Hadley's expenses and fees myself, and you can hire a lawyer in Holland to confirm that he's really gone there and has obtained the divorce in a court of law. Then I'll simply deduct the five hundred from my purchase price of this place from you, and nobody will be out anything."

The scheme was so ingenious that Clara Lou smiled.

Willie was encouraged. "Naturally," he said, "we'd have to establish a mutually agreeable price in advance. You'll want your money's worth for it, even if you're going to be a rich lady. And I don't want to be held up. But we should be able to come up with a fair price."

"You're extraordinary," she said.

"I've liked the idea from the minute it first came into my mind," he said. "Hadley will come out a little on the short end, but he won't suffer much. And I don't think anybody will cry over him."

Under no circumstances would Clara Lou make a deal with this man whom she despised, but she wanted to get rid of him without creating complications. "I'll want to think about this, Mr. de Berg," she said.

"Willie to you, Clara Lou."

"Willie." The word seemed to stick in her throat. "I may or may not want to discuss this with Mr. Harris. Either way, I'll get in touch with you if we have a deal."

"How soon will I hear from you?" He was not one to leave matters to chance.

"I can't really say just now."

"Well, don't take too long. Once Hadley collects a little bundle for himself, he might get restless feet." To her astonishment Willie leaned toward her, kissed her boldly full on the mouth, then sauntered out, a picture of confidence.

Clara Lou wiped her lips furiously. She should have known better than to have listened to the man when she had no intention of doing business with him in the first place. Chet would be annoyed when she told him of the meeting, and she had only her insatiable curiosity to blame.

Worst of all, Willie de Berg would become an even deadlier enemy when she turned him down or failed to get in touch with him.

VIII

Denver was shocked when word was received that a
section of a tunnel had collapsed in a gold mine west
of the city owned by an absentee proprietor. Frantic
efforts were made to dig through the rubble in an
attempt to save several men believed trapped there,
but the rocks and dirt had to be carted to the surface
in buckets and wheelbarrows by hand. When an
opening finally was cut, it was too late. Three bodies
were removed, and that of a fourth victim was not
found.

Virtually the entire mining community clamored to
attend the funeral, and in order to accommodate the
huge throng, the entire Apollo was used. The service
was conducted by a newly arrived itinerant clergyman, the Reverend Daniel Webster Lane. Like his
namesake, the distinguished statesman from Massachusetts, the young preacher was a spellbinding ora-
tor. Threatening those who refused to repent with
hellfire and damnation for all eternity, the Reverend
Lane so swayed his audience that grown men wept.
This reaction heartened the minister, and he decided
to settle his pulpit in Denver permanently. For the
time being, until a congregation could be organized,
he decided to conduct regular Sunday services in an

open area near the junction of Cherry Creek and the South Platte River, which a number of the more conscientious citizens were hoping to transform permanently into a public park.

The tragic accident accomplished far more than bringing a new clergyman to town. Chet Harris and Wong Ke set an example for the other mine owners by closing their mines until further notice, then hiring scores of men to shore up their underground tunnels in order to reduce the possibility of further cave-ins. Suspending all their other activities, Chet and Ke set up temporary headquarters in Central City, itself mushrooming into a boom town, and remained there for several weeks.

Shortly before the accident, the *Tribune* had received its second set of new presses from the East, ordered by Scott Foster, and thousands of additional copies of the edition that contained the story of the disaster were sold. Many of the new readers fell into the habit of buying the paper thereafter, and Susanna Fulton was ecstatic.

"Wade," she told her father one morning as she and Scott went into the publisher's office for a conference, "your work of a lifetime is finally paying off. Our circulation is almost as large as that of the New York *Herald* or the Chicago *Tribune*. If we keep growing at this rate, you'll soon become respectable as well as wealthy."

Long accustomed to her irreverence, Wade Fulton smiled. "You two young people are basically responsible for any success we're enjoying," he said. "Scott, I hope you'll give serious consideration to staying on with me permanently after you've solved the problem of how to deal with your brother. You have a natural talent for newspaper work, and that's a gift that few receive."

"I've been thinking about it a great deal lately, Mr. Fulton," Scott replied, actually speaking for Susanna's benefit and looking hard at her.

Conscious of the pressure, she quickly averted her gaze. Only two days earlier she had received a long letter from Andy Brentwood, telling her how much he had enjoyed his visit with his parents and making it plain that he had told them about her at length. Written from the railroad train and mailed from Antioch, Ohio, where he and the Blakes were visiting Beth, Andy had related that General Blake would see the President soon after reaching Washington City. Most of the communication had been devoted to Andy's earnest assurances that he missed her.

Keeping her promise to him, Susanna had written a reply last night, telling him truthfully that she missed him, too, and at the same time realizing that she also would miss Scott if they parted. Confused by her inability to decide which of her suitors she preferred, Susanna tried instead to think about the mission that had brought General Blake to Colorado. Obviously it was a matter of great importance if he was making a personal report to the President.

She continued to wonder about that report during the meeting in her father's office, and as a result Scott caught her off guard as they emerged.

"Since tomorrow's Sunday and we don't have to put out a newspaper, I've taken the chance that you'll have supper with me. I've reserved a table for us at Clara Lou's. Will you?"

She was flustered momentarily. "I don't gamble."

"Neither do I," he said, smiling.

"I—I'd love to go, Scott. Thank you." Hurrying back to her desk, she wondered why she had hesitated. Was it because Andy was gaining a lead over his rival? She didn't think so. But surely her hesitation signified her reluctance to see more of Scott during Andy's absence. No, on the contrary, it meant she actually wanted to spend the evening with him, and only her conscience kept reminding her of Andy.

Her mind whirling, she plunged into her work, and the article she was writing about the efforts of Chet and Ke to promote safety in the gold mines kept her fully occupied.

After she was done for the day, she went upstairs to the apartment, where she bathed, brushed her hair vigorously, and then dressed in a new gown with lace collar and cuffs, made in the East, that Sarah Rose had persuaded her to buy. A long, critical look in her bedroom mirror told her she no longer resembled herself, and feeling uncomfortable in her frilly finery, she wandered into the parlor. Her father, who had just finished the supper he had insisted on preparing for himself, was reading a recently published novel by Harriet Beecher Stowe, author of *Uncle Tom's Cabin,* which had caused a sensation among Americans whose convictions regarding the slavery issue had already reached a fever pitch.

"Mrs. Stowe is a sloppy writer," he said, putting down the book. "I honestly don't know why I read—" He broke off, staring at his daughter. "My, don't you look pretty."

Susanna flushed. "Thank you, Wade, but you're an unmitigated liar."

"Now, now," he said. "I'm telling the truth, child, and you well know it. You look like such a little ragamuffin at work all week that I sometimes forget how attractive you can be."

"You're prejudiced because I resemble Mama, as you've told me thousands of times."

"That may be so, but I have eyes in my head," Wade chuckled. "Anyway, I'm glad you decided to dress up for an evening with Scott. He's a fine young man."

Susanna nodded but preferred not to trust her voice.

"Between you and me," her father went on, "I wouldn't mind in the least if he asks for your hand someday. What with the success of the *Tribune* and the possibility of setting up a sister paper in the Nevada country, now that gold and silver have been discovered there, too, it would be convenient, to say the least. I'd have a son-in-law as well as a daughter to carry on after I retire or die."

Susanna plugged her ears with her index fingers. "I'm not going to listen to you, Wade Fulton!" she cried. "You're trying to influence me unfairly."

He sobered, but there was still a gleam of humor in his eyes. "On the other hand, after seeing you write page after page of a letter last night, it wouldn't upset me if Andy Brentwood came to me and asked to marry you. The life of an army wife is none too easy, especially with a war between the states seeming to be increasingly unavoidable, but no war lasts forever. And I approve of Andy, too."

Susanna rarely was bad tempered, but she surprised her father by stamping her foot in frustration. "Scott is a fine young man! Andy is a fine young man! And Sue is spinning like a top because she leans toward one of them one minute and the other the next! Oh, Wade—whatever am I going to do before I become so dizzy that I'll lose my wits!"

Alarmed by the possibility that she would burst into tears, a spectacle that terrified him and rendered him helpless, Wade pulled himself to his feet. Embracing her, he led her to the horsehair-stuffed sofa, then sat beside her and held her hand. "As a publisher training a young editor, I've done a good job. As a father, however, I have my deficiencies."

"You do not!" Susanna replied fiercely.

He paid no attention to her protest. "If your mother were still here, she could advise you properly, I know. My trouble is that I see your situation from the other side of the fence, the male side. But I'll try."

Ashamed of her outburst, she squeezed his hand. "I bounce back like a ball made of India rubber, Wade, so don't worry about me."

"All I can tell you," he said, ignoring her remark, "is that once, back in Boston many, many years ago, I had two sweethearts."

"You did?" She was delighted. "Just fancy that! Mama won, of course."

"Neither of them was your mother," he said. "I was regarded as highly eligible because I was a successful newspaperman. Both of the young ladies were very pretty, and between them they tore me apart." Knowing he had captured her attention, he paused.

"You're not writing a dramatic news story now, Wade," she said severely. "Tell me straight out what happened."

"Your mother happened, that's what. I met her at a concert one evening, and the very instant I was presented to her, I knew."

Susanna was blank. "What did you know?"

"On occasion, Sue, you can be very obtuse. I knew that I loved her and would marry her, naturally. Not only was I certain of it in my mind, but I felt it in the marrow of my bones."

Susanna was intrigued. "Did Mama react to you in the same way?"

He chuckled. "She was too much of a lady ever to admit it to me in so many words. But she accepted when I proposed to her only two weeks later, and she did a wonderful job of persuading your grandparents to give their consent."

"That's the most romantic story I've ever heard," she said, her own problem momentarily forgotten.

"I didn't tell you about it to entertain you," her father said dryly. "I was trying to make a point. I stewed about two young ladies and married a third. You're in the middle of a tug-of-war between two young men, and you can't make up your mind."

"Are you telling me I'm going to marry someone who hasn't come into my life yet?"

Wade smiled and shook his head. "Not necessarily. All I can tell for sure is that you'll know who is right for you when the time comes. Maybe it will be Scott, maybe it will be Andy, maybe it will be neither of them. Men and women are different in so many ways, as everyone knows, but we're more alike, too, than most people realize. All of us have feelings and sensitivities, just as all of us have the capacity to love and be loved. All of a sudden, perhaps one day when you least expect it, you'll know you're in love, and that man will be the right man for you."

Susanna smiled at him in relief. In her mind, Wade Fulton was the wisest man on earth.

"Until then, stop tormenting yourself, child. Stop insisting that you're the rope in a tug-of-war. Enjoy the luxury of being courted by two suitors. Have a grand time for yourself. Obey only two rules: make no promises you might break, and don't ever knowingly hurt anyone."

She kissed his forehead. "Wade Fulton," she said, "you're an old fraud."

"Well, now. That's a new accusation."

"You know so much, and you pretend to know so little."

"You're the one who appears to be prejudiced. We may be a small family, but we surely do admire each other!"

She laughed, hugging him, then jumped to her feet when the door knocker sounded.

Scott Foster was at ease with his employer in the *Tribune* office, but seeing him here, in his parlor, was a different matter. Scott twisted the brim of his hat in his hands, stammered, and was thoroughly miserable.

Recalling his own youth, Wade took pity on him. "Why don't you two run along to supper? I've got to return to my engagement with Mrs. Stowe."

Scott was relieved to escape. Susanna, far more conscious of her femininity than usual, took his arm as they walked the short distance to Clara Lou's establishment.

"You sure do look nice," he told her

She accepted the compliment with a graceful smile. Her father was right: she would take each day as it came, enjoy herself, and let the future take care of itself.

Scott wondered why he had never been aware of the dimple that appeared on one side of her face when she smiled. "I got to thinking today about whether or not we should increase our advertising rates soon."

"Tonight," Susanna said, tossing her head, "there will be no discussion of business!"

"What will we talk about?" he asked, smiling.

"People. Life. You!"

Clara Lou greeted the young couple warmly, then conducted them to a place in the corner where their conversation could not be overheard by those at neighboring tables. She chatted with them for a few minutes, took their supper order, then left.

"The first order of business is Scott Foster," Susanna said. "I've listened to you worrying about your brother, and I've heard your concerns for your sister's future. The way she and Isaiah are looking at each other, of course, her future may be settled before long."

"It appears that way."

"But you never say anything about yourself."

"There isn't much to say. As the eldest in the family, I feel responsible for the others."

"You enjoy ranching?" she prompted.

"You bet! I grew up in the orchards, and they're home to me." Scott's eyes glowed. "If I ever decide to sell the ranch, I'd still want to own a property where I could grow at least a few fruit trees. I want to keep my hand in, no matter what else I do."

"You seemed to spark when my father mentioned the idea of making a career in newspaper publishing."

"I thought of it even before he brought it up. I've surprised myself by the way I've taken to it—after knowing nothing about the business. But I can't make a decision just yet. Chiefly because I find it hard to concentrate until I can find some way to persuade my brother to reform. Not that I'll necessarily be able to do it, but I've got to try."

"I understand." She reflected that there might be many complications that would stand in the way of Tracy Foster's rehabilitation.

"After I know for sure that he'll be all right, I'll be freer to think about myself. And you," he added pointedly.

"No fair! We agreed to talk about you, so don't bring me into it." The waiter had just brought their soup, and Susanna ate quickly, not looking at him.

"I can't even think about myself without thinking of you, Sue," he said gently. "By now you must have a pretty good notion of the way I feel about you."

"I can guess," she replied hastily, wishing she could find a change of subject.

"I never had much time for girls, what with working in the orchards and helping to guide Sarah Rose. Tracy, too, to the extent that he'd allow anyone to help him. So it took a spell after being here to realize that I've fallen in love with you." He searched her face intently.

It was impossible to escape the inevitable, and Susanna looked up to return his gaze. "I wish I could say that I return your love," she said softly.

Scott seemed crushed. "Then you've decided on Andy Brentwood."

She shook her head vigorously. "No, I have not!" she declared. "I don't believe in teasing or stringing people along, but I can't help it. Just this evening I told my father that I'm not capable of deciding between you and Andy. I can only say to you what I said to Andy. I like both of you enormously, but I'm not in love with anyone. Which isn't to say that I might not wake up tomorrow morning and find out I am! I hate to be indefinite, and if that isn't good enough for you, we'll confine ourselves to a strictly business relationship."

"Hold on," he said, his manner strained in spite of a broad smile. "I never give up easy. As long as I'm still in the running, that's good enough. Well, not really, but I won't quit until you tell me the race has ended and that someone else has won."

Susanna reached for his hand. "You're sweet and understanding, and I appreciate it."

He gripped her hand hard, and Susanna couldn't help wincing. Scott released her instantly. "I'm sorry! Sometimes I don't know my own strength."

"Don't give it a thought," she replied. "I'm the one, remember, who doesn't know her own mind, and that's worse."

They laughed, and the talk flowed smoothly as they ate a leisurely supper. The night was pleasant, with a cool breeze blowing down from the white-capped mountains. Susanna suggested they take a stroll, but Scott demurred.

"The streets aren't all that safe for a lady at this time of night," he said. "And they won't be, either, until the federal government accepts the application of Colorado to become a formal territory."

"That won't happen until next year."

"Let's watch the folks at the gaming tables for a time," he suggested. "I don't know much about cards, and I've never played poker—"

"I'll explain the game to you, provided you don't become an addict."

"Not much chance of that," he said. "I've become too accustomed over the years to stashing away money as fast as I earn it."

They asked Clara Lou's permission to watch one of the card games, and she laughed. "Forgive me, but you're both so naive. Anyone has the right to watch a poker or blackjack game, so help yourselves."

They wandered into the parlor, and for the better part of an hour, they divided their attention between the two tables. "Let's go," Susanna said suddenly. "All at once I need a breath of very fresh air."

"So do I," Scott replied emphatically.

Susanna took his arm when they walked out onto the street. "Card games aren't for me," she said.

He shook his head. "That big man, with the gold nugget on his watch fob, lost over one hundred dollars in the short time we were watching. Think of it—more than most people earn in a month!"

"I'd rather not think about it," Susanna said.

An amiable silence enveloped them as they made their way to the *Tribune* building, and when they climbed the stairs to the second-floor apartment entrance, Susanna knew that Scott intended to kiss her.

She submitted to his firm embrace, and after they parted she was disconcerted to discover that her heart was pounding and her breath was short. Although she had enjoyed the experience, which was fitting in the light of her new approach to life, she had reacted identically to Andy and Scott. She was so perplexed she could not fall asleep for hours.

"I've read your report with great interest, General Blake," President Buchanan said, "and I'm heartened by it. Is it correct that you estimate the Colorado mines will be producing about fifteen million dollars' worth of gold annually, beginning next year?"

"That was Luke Brandon's estimate, Mr. President, not mine." Lee had no need to consult his notes. "He also estimated that by taking the probability of the discovery of new gold fields in the next twelve to eighteen months into consideration, the Colorado yield won't run out for five to ten years."

"I'm heartened, General." Buchanan leaned back in his chair, his exhaustion evident. "No matter what steps I take to heal the rift between the North and South, the situation grows steadily worse. So, given the country's sectional enmities, that gold will be needed for the Union's war chest."

"I hope you're keeping in mind, Mr. President, that

some of the first mines were discovered—and are still owned—by Georgians who are rabid partisans of the South's cause."

"I can't afford to forget it, General, but I'm not overly concerned. I haven't had too much success in the White House, to my eternal regret, but I've been in politics all my life, and I'm still a politician. I've been informed privately by several of those who have applied for an official federal status for the Colorado Territory that Northerners are more numerous there than Southerners by a ratio of four to one."

"From my observations, sir, I'd be inclined to think the percentage is even higher."

"There you are!" Buchanan rallied somewhat and actually seemed enthusiastic. "When a referendum is taken, the citizens of the territory will forbid the practice of slavery within her borders."

"Free-state sentiments are overwhelming there, sir."

"The North has a heavy majority in the House of Representatives, as well as a smaller but still firm majority in the Senate. You can depend on it that the territorial charter granted by the Congress will be certain to exclude slavery."

"That still doesn't solve the problem of the Southern-owned gold mines, Mr. President," Lee said.

"If that fellow Lincoln from Illinois is elected as my successor, there's sure to be a war. The South can't tolerate him. Then he'll have the unpleasant task of expropriating the mines owned by Southerners and ordering federal troops to take possession of them."

Lee didn't envy the officer who would command those troops.

"Only if Senator Douglas is elected will there be a chance to avert war. But the Democrats in the South appear determined to nominate their own candidate, which will lessen the support for Douglas and give the election to Lincoln and the Republicans."

Lee felt sorry for the prematurely aged man who sat opposite him. The President of the United States was sworn to preserve the Union, but no President could accomplish that feat.

"Enough of these matters. I was sad to learn of Luke Brandon's death, and I hope you'll extend my sympathies to his widow."

"Mrs. Brandon decided to remain in Denver, sir. We couldn't persuade her to come East with us."

"Has Luke Brandon's murderer been found yet?"

"Not the last I heard, sir. I'm inclined to believe the motive for the killing was robbery, but I'm afraid we'll never know who the killer was. Colorado is still a lawless country, and it will take a territorial constabulary, supported by federal troops, to establish and maintain order there."

"You've performed your mission admirably, General. If you wish, I'll gladly reward you by giving you command of the troops we'll send there."

"I wouldn't regard it as a reward, Mr. President," Lee said dryly.

"Oh? What post would you like?"

Buchanan had a habit of ignoring military protocol and traditions, Lee thought. It would be a simple matter to request a return to either of the two places he and Cathy had most enjoyed, the Presidio in San Francisco, or Fort Vancouver, across the Columbia River from Portland, in what had become the new Washington Territory several years before Oregon had achieved statehood. But he would be stepping on the toes of immediate superiors in the War Department, and they would not forgive his interference with their prerogatives. Certainly they would block his final promotion to the rank of major general.

"I prefer to take whatever will come my way, sir," he said.

"There is just one more matter I want to mention to you, General," the President said. "The ruse you used in undertaking your Colorado mission may have been fairly transparent. However, it appears that no one has seen through it. Continue to keep your real pur-

pose in going there confidential. I'm sure you realize
you have many colleagues in the War Department
who will resign their commissions and take up arms
for the South when the war comes. And the produc-
tion-potential figures for the Colorado gold mines are
so secret that I shall leave a private memorandum on
the subject for my successor here, to be seen only by
him."

The President's quiet demand was a direct order,
and Lee knew it would be impossible for him to pass
along the true story to Susanna Fulton for publication
in the Denver *Tribune*. In some ways the war already
had started.

When Lee returned to the house at Fort Zachary
Taylor, he found Cathy anxiously awaiting him, and
she came to him as he was hanging his gold-braided
hat and sword belt in the front vestibule.

"Well?" she demanded.

"I saw the President, but I can't tell anyone, not
even you, the substance of what we discussed."

"After two decades as an army wife, General Blake,
I'd be stupid not to know that much."

Lee grinned and kissed her. "I congratulate you on
your wisdom, Mrs. Blake. Your real concern is my
next assignment."

"You're correct, my dear," she said as they walked
to the sitting room.

Lee poured two small glasses of sack. "The President
opened the door to a request," he admitted cautiously,
"but I closed it again."

Cathy frowned slightly as she took the drink from
him but made no comment.

"There are no more than six brigadiers with greater
seniority than mine," he said, "and a couple of them
are long overdue for retirement. If I mind my manners, I'm almost certain to be on the next list for
promotion to the top rank. Then, as a major general,
I'll be pretty much in a position to name my own

assignment. Until then, of course, we'll stay in limbo."

"When will the War Department submit the next list of new major generals to the President and the Congress for approval?" Cathy asked.

"In the next six to eight months, if these were normal times, which they aren't. There's already a squabble for preferment going on between Northern and Southern factions. The Confederates are sure to give a very special place to any officer who is already a major general." He sipped his drink thoughtfully. "It may be as long as a year, and in that case President Buchanan is certain to do his successor the courtesy of allowing him to submit the nominations to the Congress."

"So you'll twiddle your thumbs for the next year?"

"Not precisely," he replied, laughing wryly. "I've been given a temporary spot in the War Department operations section, and such posts tend to become semipermanent because no one really wants them."

Cathy grimaced. "So we'll stay in Washington for at least a year."

"I could do a blamesight worse, so count our blessings, including the fact that we're only two days by train from Beth's college. I could wind up with the command of a garrison in the South, which could be uncomfortable for a man who is known for his firm support of the North's principles. Or I could be made the deputy to General Albert Sidney Johnston, who has been sent to the Great Plains and the Rockies to put down Indian uprisings. General Johnston is sure to resign and join the South when the war comes, and I'd be stuck out in Indian territory for the duration."

"I'm sorry," Cathy said. "I've been spoiled because some of your posts have been so wonderful that I've lost sight of fundamentals. As long as we're together, it doesn't matter where we live."

*   *   *

Work was in progress on the new church being built in Denver for the Reverend Daniel Lane, with dozens of volunteers contributing uncounted hours to the project. Until the church was completed, the Reverend Lane continued to hold Sunday morning services in the open area that was located near the junction of the South Platte River and Cherry Creek. His fame spread, and attendance soared week by week.

People of every class were represented. Entire families came together, mingling in the open with hundreds of miners in rough attire, merchants, restaurant workers, and gambling hall dealers. A sermon in praise of Mary Magdalene thereafter brought out the prostitutes. Wearing heavy makeup, their gaudy dresses covered by dark cloaks and capes, they marched in a body, usually in pairs, their manner solemn as they came onto the field and occupied one entire section of the area.

"Reverend Lane is shrewd," Isaiah Atkins told Sarah Rose Foster. "He knows that most of the bordellos open at noon, so he tailors his sermons accordingly, and the women go to work on time."

On the third Sunday that the prostitutes appeared, Caroline Brandon joined their company for the first time. She had been diligent in the pursuit of her duties, never complaining, and had been duly rewarded with the gift of a dress and a short cloak. Granted that the dress was sleazy and provocative, but the cloak covered it well enough for the services, and any attire was preferable to the corselet she loathed.

Her air sedate, Caroline looked demurely at the ground as she and Bessie walked side by side at the rear of the procession, holding hands. Both ignored the crude remarks of the men who emerged from saloons to call to them, and so did the other women.

Caroline had no real interest in religion, but curiosity and Bessie's urging were responsible for her attendance. Besides, she had been confined in the Palace for so long that she thought of the place as a jail, and any escape, even one of brief duration, was worth taking. What was more, she enjoyed the thought of pleasing Bessie, who had become her protectress and dear friend. They shared a seething, secret hatred of Willie de Berg, Caroline had discovered, and that all-consuming contempt had tightened the bond that had brought them together.

Only because Bessie virtually shouted the opening hymn did Caroline start to sing, too, and to her surprise she found that she liked the feeling. She had been familiar with the hymn as a child, and singing it loudly now gave her a measure of release. The rich, mellifluous voice of the Reverend Lane thrilled her, as it did so many of the other harlots, and her enthusiasm growing, she joined in the responsive prayers, her shoulder and Bessie's touching as they read together from the latter's small Bible.

Caroline didn't realize it, but she was ripe for the sermon. She listened intently as the clergyman expertly played on the emotions of his congregation, his voice soaring to a roar, dying to a dramatic whisper, and then rising again.

It was true, Caroline had to concede, that she was a sinner. Oh, she had been more sinned against than sinning, and her present vocation had been forced on her, so she didn't feel guilty. The cold rage toward Willie that enveloped her night and day was unabated, but she was inspired by the sermon and reflected that she needed to assert herself in some bold manner. The righteous would inherit both the here and the hereafter, the Reverend Lane declared, and Caroline felt compelled to perform some sort of righteous act. She had meekly accepted her fate long enough.

When the minister invited the members of the congregation to kneel and pray for salvation, Caroline almost followed the example of some of the other women. She was deterred by the realization that rain had fallen the previous night, making the ground soft and somewhat muddy, and she had no intention of ruining her only dress, which she had worked so hard to earn. Surely the Almighty would understand.

Caroline sang the closing hymn as loudly as she could, then linked arms with Bessie for the march back to the Palace.

"That preacher man is special," Bessie said.

Still under his spell, Caroline could only nod.

"He got you worked up real good," her friend commented.

"He inspired me!"

"I hope he pays a visit to the high-stakes room," Bessie said, giggling. "I gave him my best wink as we left."

They soon approached the center of town, and when Caroline saw that the *Tribune*'s office was open because the staff was preparing the Monday edition of the newspaper, she knew what had to be done. Abruptly she slowed her pace.

"What's wrong?" Bessie asked.

"Nothing. You go ahead, and I'll be there in a few minutes."

"Don't do nothin' foolish," the concerned Bessie said. "If Willie finds out you ain't there, he'll make me rip off your hide with that awful bullwhip of his."

"He won't know," Caroline assured her. "The place will be a madhouse, what with all the women changing into their costumes, and I'll be there before I'm missed." Slipping away from her friend, she hurriedly entered the newspaper office.

Susanna looked in amazement at the blonde woman with heavy makeup, her cape barely covering her shocking dress. Scott had repeated the story that the residents of the boardinghouse had heard from Chet Harris, and Caroline's appearance was proof positive that she worked for Willie de Berg.

"I've only got a few seconds, so listen," Caroline

said breathlessly. "The Palace has a system for cheating card players." She quickly related some of the signals that the women gave to the dealers.

Susanna drank in the details, then asked, "What on earth are you doing in that place, Caroline? Why are you there?"

"That's another story. I don't dare tell it to you now." Caroline raced out.

The astonished Susanna went to the windows and watched her entering the side door of the Palace.

Lifting her skirts, Caroline mounted the back stairs two at a time, and by the time she reached her own tiny cubicle, her dress was unhooked. She folded it carefully as she placed it in the wardrobe, glad she had been given no underclothes because she would waste no time removing them. With frantic haste she struggled into her corselet and net stockings and was tying the red satin ribbon around her throat when she heard Bessie's familiar voice in the corridor.

"The door opens in five minutes!" she called repeatedly. "Take your places, ladies!" She opened her friend's door, and her relief made her weak. "I was scared you'd be late," she murmured.

"I told you not to worry, sweetie," Caroline said, then hugged her.

"Why did you dash off like that into the newspaper office?"

Caroline thought rapidly; not even Bessie could be trusted completely. "I—I saw a man in there I knew before I came here," she replied, doing her best to improvise. Necessity made her glib, and she continued. "I'd heard he has a weakness for cards and women, and I know he was sweet on me back when I still had a husband. So I invited him to drop in here for a visit."

Bessie laughed loudly. "I should have guessed! I've never seen any woman take to this work like you have!" She went off to the high-stakes room, spectacular if not elegant in her skin-tight evening gown.

Caroline studied her reflection for a moment in her mirror, decided her makeup needed no patching, and sauntered to the main stairs, ready to take her place when the customers poured in. She had succeeded in striking a hard blow at Willie de Berg, and no one knew it. Now, if the *Tribune* reacted accordingly, Willie would suffer.

Susanna repeated Caroline's story verbatim to her father in his cramped office, then asked, "What do you make of it, Wade?"

"If it's true, you finally have that story you wanted. Why would the Brandon woman betray Willie de Berg?"

"That's an even bigger story, perhaps, and I intend to pursue it in some way. But that will take time. What should I do about this card cheating?"

"You'll need to double-check the facts," Wade said. "You can't just take the Brandon woman's word."

"Obviously."

"It is equally obvious," he went on, "that you can't handle this phase of the story yourself. No decent woman can set foot in the Palace."

Susanna was disappointed but knew he was right. She would create too much attention if she went to the gambling hall and sat down at one of the poker tables.

"I'm afraid our other reporters are too well known and would be recognized as *Tribune* employees. So we have something of a problem."

Susanna thought for a moment. "Scott could do it. All we need is a confirmation of the facts. I'll do the actual writing of the story."

"Not a bad idea. Even if Willie de Berg knows he works here, it isn't likely he'd realize that Scott was gathering material for an article."

Susanna went to Scott's desk. "How would you like to practice your newly acquired skills as a poker

player?" she asked, then told him about her brief talk
with Caroline.

He accepted the assignment, taking ten dollars of
Tribune funds with him.

The ground floor of the Palace had come to life
within minutes of its opening for the day. Scott
threaded his way through the crowd at the bar, ordered a glass of beer, and took it with him as he
strolled toward the gambling tables. He caught a
glimpse of Caroline across the room, her long, blonde
hair immediately attracting his notice, and he tried
not to gape at her in her garish attire.

Caroline saw him, too, and debated whether to
approach him. She guessed his reason for coming
here, and the prospect excited her, but her instinct for
survival, sharpened by her experiences since Willie
had forced her to work for him, prompted her to give
Scott a wide berth. A storm would break when the
Tribune published its story about the Palace, and for
her own protection it would be best if she had no
connection with the newspaper's representative.

Scott saw her turn away without acknowledging his
presence and instantly understood her motive. She
was more shrewd than he had realized.

Within moments a corselet-clad brunette approached him. "Goin' to try the cards, honey?" she
asked, smiling.

This was his first attempt at acting, but he felt at
ease. "I have a few dollars burning a hole in my
pocket," he admitted.

"Buy me a drink, and I'll bring you good luck," she
said. "I'm Helen."

Her drink, which he suspected was tea rather than
whiskey, cost him the stiff price of fifty cents. Then, as
he took a place at one of the poker tables, Helen
promptly sat on the arm of his chair, slid a hand
around the back of his neck, and leaned against
him.

He bought two dollars' worth of chips, and when he

was dealt his first hand, he was quick to note that Helen had deposited her glass on the floor beside her and was fingering her garter, her hand moving swiftly. She was signaling the dealer, precisely as Susanna had said she would, and he felt a surge of elation. His task was proving far easier than he had anticipated.

His wagers were cautious, and he pretended, too, to be captivated by the woman, who relayed the contents of every hand he held to the dealer. He bought Helen a second drink, and soon he was able to anticipate her simple but effective signals. By the time he had lost what was left of the ten dollars, he had obtained all of the hard facts he needed.

"I guess this isn't my day," he said, pushing back his chair.

Helen caught hold of his lapel. "I like you, honey," she said. "How'd you like to come upstairs with me?"

He grinned and turned his pocket inside out.

"Some other time," she said vaguely, then left him for another customer.

Scott walked past Willie de Berg as he left the place but did not look at the man. Returning at once to the *Tribune* office, he told Susanna, "I've confirmed your story."

She questioned him closely, scribbling notes as he carefully explained the signs he had seen Helen give the dealer.

"You can transfer to the editorial department anytime you want," she said. "I'll use everything you've told me except the name of the woman. De Berg might give her a rough time."

The article appeared in the next day's edition of the *Tribune*, filling a full column.

Willie de Berg was thunderstruck when he read the piece at the bar, where he was drinking his morning coffee. He would need to devise a new set of signs for the women and dealers before the gaming tables opened for the day, and he knew so many mistakes would be made that the card tables would bring him vastly reduced profits for the next week. He went to work grimly, writing a complete new list of signals and ordering the entire staff to memorize them.

Trying to analyze the catastrophe that would send many customers elsewhere until the article was forgotten, Willie could not believe that someone from the newspaper had come to the Palace for his own pleasure, only to discover the signaling system for himself. He was certain he had been betrayed, either by a dealer or a woman who held a grudge against him, and he was determined to make the culprit pay.

Tugging at the brim of his hat and opening the flap of the holster in which he carried his six-shooter, Willie stalked out of the Palace and went to the *Tribune*. Not bothering to have himself announced, he walked to the publisher's private office.

"What the hell are you trying to do to me, Fulton— drive me out of business?" he demanded harshly.

Wade Fulton looked up from a document he was reading. "Ah, Mr. de Berg. I had a hunch you might drop in today."

"That pack of lies you printed could ruin me!"

"The *Tribune* stands behind its stories," Wade said. "If you believe you've been unfairly maligned, it will be your privilege to file suit against us as soon as the federal courts are established here."

"To hell with that." Willie became menacing. "I demand to know who came to you with those lies!"

Wade slowly rose to his feet. "No self-respecting newspaper reveals its sources of information, Mr. de Berg," he said calmly.

"You refuse to tell me?" Willie's voice rose to a shout.

"That is correct," Wade replied, his own voice becoming hard.

"You'll regret this, Fulton!"

"Are you threatening me, de Berg?"

"I know how to deal with my enemies!" Willie was livid.

"Get out," Wade told him quietly, "and don't come back here."

Unable to meet the publisher's unwavering gaze, Willie stormed out of the office, cursing as he returned to the Palace. He went straight to his office, put his feet on his desk, and became lost in thought. His dealers, he reflected, had no reason to harm him; the majority had spent years in his employ, and because his profits depended on them, all were handsomely paid and well treated. In addition to wages higher than those paid by anyone else, they received free meals and could avail themselves of the girls' services at a special discount. He had to rule out the dealers.

That left the girls, thirty of them. Most were pleased because their earnings were large and steady, they enjoyed his protection, and no customer was permitted to treat them roughly. A very few were malcontents, but only one had reason to hate him: Caroline Brandon.

His feet thumping on the floor, Willie sent for Bessie.

The young woman had anticipated the call. "I don't know who talked out of turn," she said as she came into his office. "I been stewin' my brains, and I didn't hear a word this morning that would tell us who is guilty."

"Caroline, maybe?" he suggested.

Bessie shook her head. She was well aware that Caroline had rushed into the newspaper office last Sunday, but the woman was her best friend, and she would say nothing to get her in trouble. "She settled down quick, and she's been a good worker. I ain't heard a word of complaint out of her, Willie."

"A strong taste of the bullwhip might loosen her tongue," he suggested.

Bessie sat on the edge of his desk. "We'd be bitin' off our noses to spite our own faces."

"How so?"

"Look at the ledgers. She's the most popular girl in the house. She entertains twice as many customers as any other girl in the place. Give her the kind of beatin' you have in mind, she wouldn't be able to work for three or four weeks. And the scars would make her less attractive to the clients. We stand to lose more than we'd gain."

He knew that Bessie and Caroline had become intimate friends, and he looked at Bessie narrowly. "You're sure she isn't the one who talked to the newspaper?"

"I'd swear to it," she said, hiding her own suspicions. "I think she'd tell me. I'll see what I can find out from her, but I don't expect any solid information."

"All right," he said reluctantly. "But send her in here, anyway. Maybe I can scare an admission out of her."

"I doubt it, Willie," Bessie said as she left.

A few minutes later Caroline came in, her walk seductive, her smile provocative. "I've been wondering how long you could resist me, darling," she said.

"Sit down," Willie told her curtly as he pointed to a chair.

She well knew why he had sent for her but managed to appear bewildered.

"Did you tell our card system to the newspaper people?" he demanded.

Never had she been forced so desperately to play-act, and she looked in astonishment at this creature whom she despised. "Willie," she said, "I was stupid, and I made a nuisance of myself. I deserved what you did to me. And by now I hope I've proved myself to you. Ask any of the bartenders which of us coaxes the most drinks out of the customers. And you know yourself that I bring more of them upstairs than any other woman in the house. Instead of making ugly accusations, you ought to promote me to the high-stakes room—and start giving me a cut on what I bring in!"

If she was innocent, he knew, her demands were justified, and her vigorous defense startled him. "Go back to work," he said gruffly. "If I ever find out that you did it, you'll have a broken neck."

Still smiling, Caroline tossed her head, and her walk was exaggerated as she left. Her heartbeat sounded like thunder, and she was so relieved she was afraid she might faint, but she managed to carry off the deception. All the same, she needed to exercise great caution. She had injured Willie severely, and he surely would resort to violence if he should ever learn the truth.

Willie remained closeted in his office, his own instinct insisting that Caroline was guilty. Well, there were other ways than resorting to the bullwhip to persuade her to talk. He tugged at a bell rope.

One of the women quickly came to the door. "When my special strong-arm man shows up today," he said, "tell him I want a word with him right off."

It was mid-afternoon before the meticulously dressed Tracy Foster appeared at the Palace and received his employer's message.

"Too bad about that story in the *Tribune* today," he said. "It's a bad break, and the place is half-empty, but the customers will start coming back soon."

"It can't be soon enough," Willie replied angrily.

"You have something for me to do?" Tracy cracked his knuckles.

"Maybe. Although it isn't in your usual line." Willie kept his rage under control and spoke smoothly. "You've seen the girls who work for me. What do you think about the blonde with the long, pale hair? I've noticed you watching her."

"Oh. You mean Brandon's—wife." Tracy couldn't force himself to call her a widow. "She's not bad."

"You want her?"

It was difficult for Tracy to admit in so many words that he felt strongly attracted to the woman whose husband he had murdered. Ordinarily he wasn't squeamish, and the killing of a total stranger didn't bother him in the least. But he felt responsible for Caroline Brandon's presence on the Palace staff, and she reminded him of the man he had stabbed.

Willie understood the other man's silence and, reaching for his roll of bills, handed several to the younger man. "Take her for the rest of the day."

"A hundred dollars! I never even knew a woman who could cost that much!"

Willie saw no need to explain that the money would be returned to him, that he was merely transferring the sum of one hundred dollars from one pocket to another. Only Caroline would gain nothing in the transaction.

"I want you to do me one small favor in return," Willie said. "All the girls like you. So turn on the charm with Caroline and see if you can persuade her to take you into her confidence. I have a hunch she was the one who told the newspaper about our card system."

Tracy hoped de Berg didn't want him to dispose of her. Although he couldn't admit it aloud, it would be too much to expect him to murder the woman whose husband he had stabbed to death. "Suppose it turns out that she is," he said.

"We'll move one step at a time." When the time came, Willie thought, this husky young man would be reminded that he was being paid for his services, and like all the others, he would do what he was told. "Enjoy yourself with her. Anything you may find out for me will be a bonus."

Caroline and Tracy made love intermittently through the long hours of the late afternoon and early evening. Occasionally they dozed, and sometimes they chatted, but inevitably they fell into each other's arms again, their mutual desire seemingly insatiable.

At first this ruggedly good-looking young man with the strangely penetrating gray eyes had made Caroline feel uneasy. But, to her surprise, he kept his brute strength in check, and unlike the many others to whom her circumstances had forced her to give herself, he treated her with gentle respect. She was flattered, too, because he had paid her the enormous sum of one hundred dollars. She would be required to relinquish the entire amount, but it was gratifying to know that any man thought that highly of her. Not even Bessie had been paid that much by a client.

Now they rested, enveloped in a light embrace, and Caroline said, laughing, "Eventually we'll have to go downstairs for something to eat."

"Right now, if you're hungry. We can always come back up here."

"I'm in no hurry," she said, yawning. "I like this."

"Me, too." Tracy stroked her long hair. "I've never known a woman like you."

"What's so special about me?"

"You aren't tough or greedy," he replied with great sincerity. "You really like what we do together and don't just pretend, the way the others do. I always know when a woman is pretending, and then I want to choke her. But I couldn't hurt you, no matter what."

Caroline met his earnest gaze and was startled by the expression in his eyes. It was a shock that Willie's strong-arm man appeared to be falling in love with her. "Mostly I pretend, too," she said. "But I couldn't with you."

"Why not?"

"Because you've been so sweet and considerate. I'll be happy to see you anytime, and it won't cost you anything."

He wrenched himself away from her, struggled to a

sitting position, and his eyes became opaque again. "What do you think of de Berg?" he demanded.

The question was so unexpected that Caroline was at a loss for a reply before rallying and choosing her words with care. "I have no complaints," she lied, propping herself on an elbow. "He treats me fine."

"De Berg gave me the hundred for you," Tracy confessed.

It was typical of Willie to play such a trick, and she laughed. "Why are you telling me this?"

"You've been honest with me, and I've got to be the same way with you." She was the most beautiful woman he had ever known, and his eyes devoured her.

His obviously increasing affection for her could cause complications that Caroline preferred not to contemplate, but she did not hesitate to use his feelings for her own ends. "Why do you suppose Willie would do a thing like that?"

"I know why." All at once he became moody. "He wanted me to put you off your guard."

A knot tightened in her stomach. "You're joking!"

"I mean it. Willie thinks maybe you're the one who told the *Tribune* about his card-cheating operation."

She could almost feel the noose being looped around her neck.

"But you couldn't do something rotten like that!" he continued.

"Thank you. Indeed I couldn't."

"That's what I aim to tell him in so many words. Don't let on what I've said to you, but I had to warn you."

"I'm grateful to you," Caroline said. She shivered, and Tracy immediately reached for her and embraced her.

"Don't you worry. Nothing bad is going to happen to you."

"I'm frightened," she admitted.

"You stop that!" he commanded. "You've got me to keep watch over you from now on."

It was helpful to learn she had acquired a protector, but she remained fearful. "You don't know Willie. If he thinks I've done him a bad turn, there are so many ways he could get even with me."

"I'm going to make it plain to him that I'll hold him personally responsible for your safety."

"He won't like that," she said.

"Too bad. Willie knows what I'm capable of doing when I put my mind to it, and you can bet he doesn't want his own body filled with bullets."

There was no doubt in Caroline's mind that this hard-bitten young man, who had taken care not to mention his name, would commit murder for her sake. Or for his own.

Tracy started to make love to her again but stopped abruptly when he realized that she was distraught. "Maybe we'll go downstairs for that food now. We'll eat together in the kitchen."

Caroline rose and reached for her corselet. "All right," she said listlessly.

He began to dress, too. "You've got to believe me," he said fiercely. "Nobody is going to hurt you. Trust me." He stared into space, his eyes remote. "I trust you enough to tell you a couple of secrets. My name is Tracy Foster. And before I leave here tonight, I'm going to tell you where you can find me if you need me. That's something that not even de Berg knows!"

"Thank you for your confidence, Tracy," the young woman said, having completely forgotten about Sarah Rose and Scott Foster's search for their missing brother. "What do you do for Willie? You're never on guard duty here."

"I handle special jobs for him."

"Like finding out if I went to the *Tribune*?"

He shook his head. "Very special jobs."

She stared at him in wonder as he grinned at her, the strange, cold gleam reappearing in his eyes.

Then he slowly drew a finger across his throat.

A chill crept up Caroline's spine, and she had to rub her bare arms. Not only was Willie suspicious of her, but her future depended on the mercurial affections of a professional killer.

"You're the first person who has been good to me," he said, "and I won't forget it."

She gave him her most seductive, tender smile before sitting at her tiny dressing table, where she repaired her makeup and brushed her hair. She had learned more about Tracy than she had wanted to hear, but now she recognized her need to keep him satisfied. Anytime Willie persuaded him to turn against her, that would be the end of her.

They descended together to the kitchen, where they helped themselves to meat and bread. The absence of chairs or benches in the room was a deliberate oversight; Willie knew his employees would return to work more quickly if they had no place to sit.

Holding his food in one hand, Tracy placed his free arm around Caroline's waist and kept it there. In his own way he was making it clear to the security guards, the other women, and the rest of the staff that he had taken a proprietary interest in her. Even the slowest-witted person would have recognized the significance of the gesture.

Bessie came into the kitchen and was relieved when she saw her friend. "I've just been looking for you. One of the customers is asking for you, and you'd better grab him before the emptiness of the place depresses him so much that he'll go elsewhere."

"I've got to go," Caroline told her protector.

He would not release her, however, until he first took her aside and, speaking in a low tone, told her how to reach his cave. Then he insisted that she repeat the directions. "Good," he said. "Now you know where to find me in an emergency. But there won't be one."

"When will you come here again?" She simulated great eagerness to see him again.

"Tomorrow. And every day," he assured her.

"You—don't mind that I'm going back to work now?"

His odd chuckle matched the bleak look in his eyes. "Customers don't count."

Caroline went into the main room, where a middle-aged hotel owner whom she vaguely recognized awaited her. She couldn't help feeling apprehensive as she took the man's arm and started with him toward the stairs. Glancing over her shoulder for a moment, she saw that Tracy had followed her into the main room and was watching every move she made. The protection he was offering her could become a curse as well as a blessing.

Willie de Berg came up beside Tracy, an unlighted cheroot in his mouth. Certainly there was no need to go upstairs for a private word. Thanks to the *Tribune*'s disclosure, the Palace was so deserted that no one else was within earshot.

"Well?" Willie asked.

"It wasn't Caroline who betrayed you," Tracy said flatly.

"What makes you so positive?"

"I know it!" Tracy became more emphatic. "She's too honest and sweet and good to play a dirty trick like that on anybody."

Here was a totally unexpected development. Apparently the hired killer had lost his head over Caroline.

"I don't care about the way she earns her living," Tracy said as he waved in the direction of Caroline and her client, who were climbing the stairs. "But anybody who doesn't treat her right will answer to me. Anybody!" His repetition made his meaning clear.

At some time it might be necessary to deal with this new situation, but Willie refused to become concerned prematurely.

"I'm glad you like her," he said, clapping Tracy on the shoulder. "Now you'll have to put her out of your mind. Later tonight I have some special work I want you to do."

IX

The explosion in the early hours of the morning rocked the neighborhood. The first to reach the scene was Ezekiel, who had been asleep with Patricia in their quarters behind Prudence Adams's general store. Pulling on a shirt and trousers, he ran down the street, discovering that the entire front of the *Tribune* office had been blown away. Curls of smoke were still rising from the debris, and he saw that a portion of the second floor had been destroyed, too, but it was fortunate that the explosion had not started a fire.

Wade Fulton was slightly dazed as he came down the back stairs in night attire and bathrobe, and he was greatly relieved when his daughter followed a few moments later. Susanna had taken the time to change into her shirt and trousers and had inspected the upper story damage, too.

"The parlor is gone," she said. "It just vanished. The ony reason the rear of the apartment hasn't collapsed is because the center beams are still standing. What caused the accident?"

"This was not accident," Ezekiel declared.

Wade nodded. "Someone tried to blow us out of existence," he said. "Whoever it may have been wanted to destroy us—and the *Tribune,* as well."

They made their way across the rubble to the rear, and there was a lift in Susanna's voice as she said, "Thank the Lord! The presses are intact! And the paper supply hasn't been touched."

Others from the neighborhood soon arrived, and a careful examination was made by torchlight. Ezekiel found several charred pieces of hard wood, which he took to Wade, and the publisher studied them carefully.

"There can be little doubt," he said, "that someone placed a keg of gunpowder near the front windows, then set fire to a fuse. Walls and windows and desks don't explode by themselves."

"So this really was deliberate," his daughter declared. "It's hard to believe anyone could be so vicious. I wonder who—"

Her father silenced her with a sharp look; they would discuss the possible perpetrator of the crime later, in private. "We'll need to put the building in shape as quickly as possible," he said. "We have a newspaper to publish."

"I help you!" Ezekiel offered.

Others quickly followed his example, offering their services, and long before dawn, the rubble was being cleared away. When daybreak came and the activity in the center of town increased, growing numbers of people became aware of the attempt to destroy the *Tribune* plant and the publisher's living quarters above it. The newspaper had won the loyalty and affection of Denver's citizens, and their reaction was spontaneous.

Before sunrise horses hitched to wagons and carts were hauling building stones and lumber to the building, and men were giving freely of their time to pitch in as masons and carpenters. The sounds of hammering and sawing echoed up and down the block, and no one worked harder than Ezekiel, who carried large stones by himself and set them in place. When the surprised Scott Foster arrived for his day of work, he removed his coat, rolled up his sleeves, and took an active part in the enterprise, too.

At Wade Fulton's insistence, his daughter and the other members of the editorial staff did not participate in the effort. Instead, using borrowed desks, they set up a temporary office in the pressroom, and even though it was crowded there, they managed to prepare the following day's edition.

The proprietor of the Harry Allen House and the owners of several other hotels insisted that Wade Fulton accept gifts of spare furniture. Chet Harris and Wong Ke made a cash contribution for new rugs, draperies, and desks that either would be ordered from the East or made locally. By nightfall the worst of the damage had been repaired, and it was plain that within days the new plant, more solid than the original structure, would be in full operation.

The banner headline above the article that Susanna wrote told the whole story of the near-catastrophe:

ATTEMPT TO WRECK TRIBUNE FAILS!

Clara Lou Hadley insisted that the tired Wade, his daughter, and Scott come to her dining room as her guests for supper that evening, and she and Chet joined the little group. Only then, relaxing for the first time, did Wade Fulton speculate aloud on the cause of the explosion.

"We've undoubtedly made a number of enemies hereabouts," he said. "But the timing makes me think Willie de Berg was responsible. He threatened me in so many words when I wouldn't tell him our sources for the story about the way he cheats card players in his saloon. I hate to accuse anyone without specific proof, but he's the most likely culprit."

"I know Willie all too well," Clara Lou said, "and I wouldn't put it past him. He's not only mean and vindictive, but he can be ruthless. It wouldn't have bothered him in the least, Wade, if you and Susanna had been killed by the blast."

"I doubt if de Berg actually placed the keg of gunpowder—or whatever the explosive material might have been—outside your front windows and then lighted the fuse himself," Scott said thoughtfully. "He's too shrewd to take the risk that someone might have seen him committing a criminal act."

"There was no need for his personal involvement," Chet said. "He has any number of hired hands who would do the job for him."

"Our immediate problem," Susanna said, "is that we have no way of proving that he paid for the explosion. No one has come forward yet with any information, and without it we're helpless."

"What worries me," Wade declared, "is that de Berg might not be satisfied with the results."

Scott nodded. "I'm afraid you're right, Mr. Fulton. I believe everyone on the *Tribune* staff should carry firearms at all times from now on. That includes you, Sue. You're more vulnerable than anyone else because you wrote the article that exposed de Berg."

"I guess you're right," she replied, "although I hate to let de Berg see he's succeeded in intimidating us."

"It's a matter of common sense," he replied. "When we're dealing with someone unscrupulous, we've got to act accordingly."

"In my opinion," Chet said, "you ought to go a step farther. Security guards should be on duty at the *Tribune* plant night and day until further notice."

"I don't know that we can afford the expense as yet," Wade said. "It would be comforting to know we have full protection, but we've just paid for the new presses, and I don't believe our budget could tolerate the additional cash outlay for the next few months."

"It shouldn't cost you a penny, Wade," Chet replied. "I got the idea from Ezekiel. He's doing guard duty at your office right this minute, and so are a couple of other volunteers. I intend to organize a company of vigilantes who'll work on a regular schedule. The *Tribune* is Denver's only voice for the town's decent element, the only public voice in favor of the establishment of order and obedience of the law. It strikes me the least the citizens of the city can do is offer you protection from criminals who are resorting to violence in an attempt to drive you out of business."

"I don't want people to put themselves out on our account," the publisher said.

"Obviously Ezekiel doesn't feel that way," Chet said forcefully. "Neither do I. Neither do many others. Just leave the organization of a vigilante corps to me. Until the courts are set up here and an effective constabulary is hired, we've got to take the protection of people into our own hands, especially the people who are trying to make Denver a civilized community."

Business at the Palace had been declining steadily after the appearance of the article in the *Tribune*, and in an effort to encourage his customers to return, Willie de Berg had gone to great lengths. Remembering how business had boomed after their first visit, he had arranged with the old miner named Bingham and his beer-drinking burro to make regular appearances at the bar. The old miner had demurred, and even the five-dollar gold piece the saloon owner had offered him was of no interest, but when Willie de Berg had told him that his hired hand in the corral would groom and feed the burro, the old man had agreed.

"Eustace don't get much oats," the old man had said, a smile forming on his toothless mouth. "I think that's right hospitable of you." With this, he had toasted Willie with the schooner of beer the saloon owner had given him, then placed a bowl of beer on the floor for his burro. "I guess we're in for some soft livin', eh, Eustace?" he had said, then swallowed the contents of the schooner as the burro drank from the bowl.

As a result of the miner and his burro, business at the bar had picked up slightly, but most customers were still refusing the gambling tables, wary after the article in the *Tribune*. What was more, the women in Willie de Berg's employ continued to be idle and were becoming increasingly restless and discontent.

When the explosion failed to prevent the continuing publication of the *Tribune*, Willie de Berg was in a cold rage. Leaving word that he wanted to see his special strong-arm man as soon as the fellow showed up, he summoned Bessie to his office. "Have you found out yet who talked out of turn to the newspaper?" he demanded harshly.

She shook her head. "I've had a private word with every girl in the house, Willie, but every last one swears she's innocent."

"Somebody is lying!"

"Maybe so," Bessie replied, shrugging. "But whoever did it—if it was one of the girls—ain't talkin'."

"You'll have to try harder," he told her.

"I can't draw blood from a turnip," she said, her voice plaintive.

"You and I have been together a long time, Bessie," he said. "You finally got promoted to the place you wanted. In the high-stakes room. I'd hate to send you back to the main floor in a corselet."

"You wouldn't do that to me, Willie!" the alarmed young woman protested.

Willie shrugged. "I'll do whatever I have to do. Bear down harder on Caroline. I'm still giving two to one odds that she did it."

Knowing he would make good his threat if she failed to find the guilty party, Bessie went without delay to Caroline, whom she found in her room, preparing to go down to the main floor to start her day's work. "Sweetie," she said, "you and me have got to have us an honest talk."

Caroline turned away from her dressing table, struck by the gravity of her friend's tone.

"We've been pretty close lately," Bessie said. "We get along fine together, and you don't need me to tell you that I like you better than anybody else in the house."

"You know I feel that way about you, too," Caroline replied.

"Well, it ain't enough. Willie is still scalp hunting, and if I don't find out who blabbed to the newspaper, he's puttin' me into a corselet again. But I won't stand for it!"

Caroline began to realize the depth of her friend's anger and frustration.

"So far I haven't said one word to him about the way you went runnin' into the newspaper office on our way home from church on Sunday—"

"But I told you my reason!" A spasm of fear shook Caroline.

"Oh, I know what you told me. But you don't expect Willie to believe that story, do you? He'll make me whip you, and if that don't work, he'll beat the truth out of you himself!"

"You—you're going to tell him, Bessie?"

"It's my scalp or your scalp. I'll give you until tonight to go to him yourself. If you can convince him you're innocent, I'll be glad for you. But the chips are down now, and I've got to look after myself." Bessie left the room quickly, closing the door behind her. Certainly she felt sorry for the naive and impetuous young woman who had become her closest friend, but she couldn't afford to put her own future in jeopardy.

As Bessie walked down the corridor, she saw the handsome strong-arm man entering Willie's office, and his presence confirmed that she was taking the right approach. Willie unhesitatingly utilized the services of ruffians when it suited his purposes.

Tracy Foster was in high spirits as he seated himself opposite his employer's desk. "The explosion must have awakened the whole city," he said. "I was riding hard to get out of town, and the sound almost threw me out of the saddle."

Willie coldly returned the younger man's gaze. "I don't suppose you stopped off there to assess the damage."

Tracy shook his head. "I rode past the *Tribune* just now, and I saw a lot of men building a new front wall, but I didn't want to be too obvious, so I didn't stop or look too hard."

"The damage was minor."

"How could that be?"

"Because you bungled the job." Willie kept his rage under control. "The front wall may have been destroyed, but the presses weren't touched. The newspaper will publish tomorrow, as usual."

Tracy was stunned.

"There was enough powder in the keg to do permanent damage, but all you've accomplished is to win the publisher the sympathy of the whole town."

"It isn't my fault!" Tracy exclaimed. "I took enough of a risk, rolling the keg to the front windows and lighting the fuse without being seen. How was I to know the presses wouldn't be touched?"

"If you had handled the job right, you would have known the presses are located at the rear of the building, with the bedrooms of Fulton and his daughter directly above them. You would have put the keg against the wall closest to the presses, and that would have taken care of the problem."

Tracy was neither chagrined nor upset. "If you knew, you should have told me. It wasn't easy, rolling that keg down the street by myself in the middle of the night."

"When I pay for something to be done," Willie said, his voice rasping, "I expect it to be done right."

"It's your own fault for giving me incomplete information. I'm not repaying you a penny. And if you don't like the way I do things, hire yourself someone else!" A belligerent Tracy rose from his seat.

Willie de Berg was tempted to reach for his six-shooter, but he wanted no violence here, so he waved Tracy back to his chair. "I'm not asking you for repayment," he said. "But I'm going to give you a chance to make up for your failure. You've proved your worth in certain kinds of work, and it wouldn't surprise me if you'll have the opportunity to earn five hundred dollars late tonight."

Tracy slowly clenched and unclenched his fists. "You want me to get rid of someone? Fulton or his daughter, maybe?"

"I'm sure people suspect I'm mixed up in this somehow, what with the article the *Tribune* published about me. If anything happens to either of the Fultons in the near future, I hate to think of what the people of Denver would do to me. No, I have somebody else in mind. A young woman I prefer not to identify by name. You know the one I mean."

Tracy guessed he was referring to Caroline, and swallowing hard, he made no reply. This was not the time to announce that nothing could persuade him to harm the woman who filled his thoughts day and night. Threats wouldn't influence him, and neither would an offer of as much as one thousand dollars.

"I'll let you know for certain this evening," Willie said, "and I'll leave it to you to work out the details in your own way. Do I make myself clear?"

"Sure." Tracy stood again, averting his face so the man wouldn't see the murderous thoughts reflected in his eyes.

"In the meantime," Willie said, "help yourself to any girl you want. We have so few customers coming in, thanks to that damned newspaper, that we're doing no business."

Tracy went straight to Caroline's room at the far end of the second floor, fully intending to warn her of the threat. She was sitting at her dressing table in a state of terror and confusion after hearing Bessie's threat, and she raised her head when Tracy came in but could not force herself to smile at him.

Sensitive to her moods as he was to the feelings of no one else, he looked at her stricken face, then demanded, "What's wrong?"

"I—I'm in trouble."

"What kind of trouble?"

Knowing he had fallen in love with her and desperately needing help, Caroline decided to confide in him. She told him about her brief stop at the newspaper office after attending church services and made a point of insisting that her only purpose had been that of extending an invitation to a man whom she had recognized. "I don't think Bessie believes me, and she says it's her skin or mine. I know Willie will think I've lied, and he'll whip me until I admit anything he wants me to say."

"He'll do worse than that." Tracy told her of the order he had received to be prepared to dispose of a young woman whom Willie had seen no need to identify by name.

Caroline stared at him in open-mouthed horror.

He patted her on her bare shoulder. "Don't you worry," he assured her. "No one is going to hurt you, not with me around."

She realized she was leaning on a slender reed, but there was no one else to whom she could turn for assistance. "What can you do, darling?" she asked.

He took her in his strong arms. "Give me a minute to think." She nestled closer, and Tracy could feel her trembling. "Everything will be all right. I promise.

Which one is the woman who is going to talk out of turn to de Berg?"

Caroline no longer had an alternative and described Bessie in detail, adding, "She's wearing a pale violet evening dress today."

"Um. I reckon I saw her just now as I came through the high-stakes room."

"Yes, that's her station."

He patted her repeatedly as his mind raced. "I'll take care of everything."

She looked up at him, hoping she was simulating an expression of adoration. "How?"

"First off," Tracy said, "I'll have me a little private chat with her. I believe I can persuade her not to say one word to Willie de Berg. Then I'll come here for you, and we'll go away together."

Caroline had no desire to go off with this brute, but even that prospect was preferable to staying here as Willie's prisoner, always at his mercy. "I—I have only one dress," she said, "and it isn't suitable for going anywhere."

He grinned at her. "You leave all that to me. I have enough money to buy you plenty of clothes. I'll bring you a nice dress as a present when I come back for you, and you'll have a gentle mare to ride, too."

"When will you come for me?"

"Tonight."

"It will have to be before Bessie has her talk with Willie. She said she's going to him this evening."

"I'll talk to her first. You can forget her."

"I hope you realize Willie won't allow me to leave."

His eyes burned into her. "To hell with Willie de Berg," he said. "I'm going to take care of you from now on. Just be patient until tonight."

He exuded self-confidence, but Caroline didn't know whether she could rely on him. All the same, she hoped her steady smile encouraged him.

He kissed her, then said brusquely, "I'll be back," and left her room.

Caroline was relieved that there were no customers in the place to be entertained. This was one day she would find it impossible to devote even surface attention to a client.

Tracy walked to the high-stakes room, where the two dealers and several young women were sitting at a table, drinking coffee. Not one card player had shown up, even though the Palace had opened for the day much earlier. He halted, recognized Bessie, and looked hard at her.

She came to him, her walk mincing. "Don't tell me you've already grown tired of our mutual friend," she said.

She was making his task easier, and he nodded. "Something like that."

"Are you suggesting we go to my room together?" Bessie was being coy. "I'll treat you real good like I did that time when Willie hired you and I was your reward."

"That's not exactly what I had in mind." For an instant his mind went blank, and then suddenly he knew how to proceed. "With no customers in the place, I reckon you're free to come and go as you please."

"Of course. Why do you ask?"

"I don't like making love on the same bed that all the clients use. That's why I don't want anything more to do with our friend."

His reason for discarding Caroline seemed logical to her.

Aware that Bessie was accepting his explanation, Tracy became bolder. "Come with me to my house, and I'll make it worth your while."

"How much is that?"

"You name your fee," he said, "and that's what you'll get."

It was far better to be earning money, Bessie told herself, than to fritter away the rest of the day waiting for Caroline to break down and voluntarily admit to

Willie that she had gone to the *Tribune* office. "I'll get my cloak," she said. "I can't go through the street looking like this."

"I'll meet you in the corral out back," Tracy said.

It was a simple matter to persuade the man in charge of the corral to allow him to borrow one of de Berg's mares, and Tracy's self-confidence increased. As he saddled the horse, he reflected that he would present the same mount to Caroline later for their escape.

Bessie took her time, freshening her makeup before donning her long cape and joining him. It was logical that Willie's special strong-arm man had a full wallet, so she would charge him plenty, even though it was flattering to know he had chosen her in place of Caroline. Not until now had it occurred to her that she and the woman she had befriended were rivals, and it was good to know that, in the opinion of a man, she was more attractive.

Tracy moved his horse up beside her, and they rode out of town together. He made only an occasional comment, and as they made their way deeper into the desolate countryside west of the city, he could see her nervousness increasing.

"Where do you live?" she asked.

"It isn't too much farther," he said.

When they dismounted at the bottom of a canyon and started to walk up the far slope, Bessie regretted her decision to come with him. "I can't walk up this hill, not in these heels," she said.

He made no reply but easily picked her up and carried her. Her eyes widened when he unlocked the entrance to his cave and led her into the interior.

"You're the very first person who has ever come here with me," he said, and that was the truth. His sister had forced her way in over his protests.

In spite of her apprehensions Bessie concluded that business was business, and she charged him the outrageous sum of twenty dollars, which was at least four times what she demanded from even the wealthiest customers. She expected him to object, but he paid willingly.

Their lovemaking was perfunctory, and Bessie simulated passion, as she always did. "It'll soon be dark," she said at last. "I don't want to be away from the Palace too long, so maybe we better be gettin' back to town."

Tracy reached for her again.

"You believe in gettin' your money's worth, don't you, sweetie?" she asked, then laughed.

He joined in the laugh. She heard a hard, strident note in his voice but failed to understand the significance of it.

Night had fallen by the time they left the cave, and Bessie hoped that, by now, Caroline had voluntarily made a confession to Willie. She herself would be spared a thoroughly unpleasant evening.

Tracy carefully locked the door behind them, carried Bessie to their waiting horses at the bottom of the canyon, and sat her in her saddle. She found it hard to understand how this silent, moody young man could have become so intimate with the effervescent Caroline. Bessie knew that she herself had been paid lavishly, but she had no intention of coming with this man to this out-of-the-way place again. His cave was a damp, forbidding place.

They reached the top of the slope, but Tracy did not increase his pace, and something in his casual glance made Bessie shiver.

He looked around, making certain there were no other riders in the vicinity. Then, reaching for her reins, he halted both horses. Leaping from his saddle, he lifted Bessie to the ground.

"Don't tell me you want still more lovemakin' here in the open!" Bessie said. "That's not for me, sweetie. I don't aim to ruin my dress."

Tracy put his hands on her shoulders. "You planned to go to Willie de Berg tonight with some tall tales about Caroline," he said. "You were going to get her into trouble with a pack of filthy lies!"

Bessie read his intent in his eyes, and her scream of terror rang out across the plateau.

He clapped a hand over her mouth. She bit him hard, sinking her teeth into the heel of his hand.

Scarcely aware of the pain, Tracy grasped her throat with his free hand, his strong fingers cutting off her supply of air. "You pretended you were Caroline's friend," he said, "but you were going to betray her. For that alone you'll die. And you saw my house. I allow no visitors there."

Bessie struggled furiously, trying to kick him in the groin, her hands clawing frantically at his face, but he held her at arm's length. When he felt her beginning to sag, his other hand moved from her mouth to her throat. Feeling no pity, no compassion for this young woman with whom he had made love only a short time earlier, he squeezed her throat until her life ebbed from her body.

Satisfied at last that she was dead, he allowed her body to fall to the ground and dropped to one knee above her, intending to retrieve the twenty dollars that she had dropped into the top of her low-cut gown.

Sounds behind him told him that a party of horsemen was approaching at a fast clip. He had been careless. Leaping to his feet, he sprinted toward his own horse. Before he could reach the mount, however, the riders caught up with him, and a rifle caught him across the back of the head, sending him sprawling. The blow dazed him, and before he could recover, he realized his ankles and wrists were being bound with leather thongs.

"Look here, Jim!" one of the men called. "You were right! He killed this poor woman with his bare hands!"

The entire group stared at Tracy as though he were an animal.

"He looks familiar, Bob. You know him?"

"Not me, Charlie. But maybe somebody in town will know. We know what needs to be done."

Tracy made no sound as they threw him across the saddle of his own horse, tied Bessie's body to the pommel of her sidesaddle, and with the entire party again mounted, slowly rode in the direction of Denver. All Tracy Foster knew was that his world was coming to an end.

Wade Fulton, Susanna, Scott, and Chet Harris were sitting in Clara Lou's establishment, eating the delicious wild blueberry pie she had baked, when the sounds of loud shouts came from the street outside.

Chet rose and went to the window. "Good Lord," he said. "It looks like a lynching."

Their desserts forgotten, they hurried down the stairs, and in spite of the protests of the men, Susanna and Clara Lou insisted on accompanying them.

By the time they reached the street, they saw that a large crowd had gathered in front of the *Tribune* office, where a beam of stout wood that had not yet been cut to its proper length protruded from the floor of the second story. Over it a length of strong rope had been looped.

A man who had climbed to the top of an unused building stone that had not yet been carted away was addressing the growing throng. "The only reason we didn't shoot the no-good bastard when we saw him in the distance is because we aren't marksmen, any of us, and we were afraid we'd hit the woman. Maybe we should have, at that, because we'd have put her out of her misery sooner. We rushed up on him as fast as we could, but we weren't in time. He had already choked her to death!"

The mob roared, and angry men were shaking their fists.

"Does anybody know him? Look at him good!" the man on the stone called.

"I do," someone in the crowd shouted. "I'll swear he's the gray ghost, the fellow who robbed me about five or six months ago."

Scott Foster began to elbow his way through the crowd. Susanna managed to stay close beside him, and then Ezekiel materialized on her other side.

Scott stopped short as they reached the front ranks.

"That's his brother," Susanna whispered to Ezekiel, and her heart ached for Scott.

"Maybe we fight crowd and get him away," the black giant said.

Scott heard him and shook his head. "Frontier justice is rougher than what's done in a law court, but often it really is justice." He choked and could not continue.

Susanna took his arm in an effort to offer him her sympathy and understanding.

"Maybe he's the gray ghost, and maybe he ain't," the man on the building stone called. "But he's sure as shooting the fellow who killed that poor woman!"

Willie de Berg watched from the entrance of the Palace. He had recognized his special strong-arm man at once and had been stunned and dismayed when he had seen the body of Bessie, too. Now he was standing guard, preventing any of the women or dealers from coming into the open and identifying either. It was imperative that neither be connected with the Palace in any way.

Willie had no idea why the idiot had murdered Bessie, but that was no longer important. He had to keep his own hands clean. In fact, he would be obliged to postpone indefinitely any punishment that he had in mind for Caroline. Even if she came to him and admitted she had betrayed him to the *Tribune*, he would be taking too great a risk if he mistreated her.

And with Bessie gone, he faced a delicate business situation. Caroline was the most popular woman in his stable, and the few customers who came into the Palace would clamor for her services. For the present, at least until business improved, he would be forced to give Caroline the place Bessie had held in the high-stakes room, where she could command higher fees.

"Gents," the man on the building stone called, "I guess you've heard enough. Is the accused innocent or guilty?"

"Guilty!" the crowd responded with one voice.

"What'll we do to him?"

"Hang him!" they roared.

Even though Scott had known what would happen, he couldn't help taking a step forward as his instinctive desire to help his brother asserted itself. Susanna clung to his arm. She realized all too well that, if he interfered, the mob would turn on him and destroy him, too.

Scott became aware of Susanna holding him back, and he stopped straining forward. Tracy had been caught in the act of killing the young woman whose still body was draped over the saddle of the mare that stood nearby, and there was nothing Scott could do for him. Brotherly love could not save him; nothing could save him.

"What have you got to say for yourself, mister?" the man who was the self-appointed judge demanded as he looked sternly at Tracy.

There was no reply.

"Who are you?"

Tracy looked at his brother for an instant, and it was impossible for Scott to determine whether Tracy recognized him. Then the stony, crazed eyes looked off into space.

"I am the gray ghost." Pride and contempt for all humanity were reflected in Tracy Foster's voice and manner.

Scott's shoulders slumped. His once-beloved brother deserved to die.

Caroline Brandon watched the vigilante trial from an open window on the second floor of the Palace. When she had seen Bessie's dead body, she had known she was safe, and now the madman who had preserved her secret would die, too. She couldn't pretend she was sorry that she was not running away with him. Perhaps he would have killed her, too, had she displeased him. For the present she would be content to remain in Willie de Berg's employ. The violence that had taken a toll so close to him would force him to act with discretion for a time.

From her vantage point Caroline saw Clara Lou Hadley bury her face in Chet Harris's shoulder, and as she watched Chet lead the woman from the scene, Caroline knew how she felt. Her own background in orderly, civilized New England had not prepared her for the harsh application of the frontier's crude code of justice, and she moved away from the window, afraid she would become ill.

"You'll hang for your crimes," the man on the building stone declared. "Here and now."

Tracy's face was wooden. Only his eyes showed his blazing, unyielding hatred.

"Do you have any last word?"

An eerie laugh that caused the entire crowd to fall silent was torn from Tracy's throat. The sound, as Susanna would write in the *Tribune*, was like the cry of a coyote that echoed across the mountain wastes in the distance late at night. Many in the mob shivered as the strange, piercing sound died away.

"Hang him!" The man in charge of the proceedings jumped to the ground.

Willing hands lifted Tracy onto the stone, and the noose suspended from the beam above was looped around his neck. The other end was attached to the saddle of his own horse and the saddle of the mare on which the body of Bessie still rested. Then the horses were struck smartly on the flanks, and they moved forward in unison, the crowd parting for them.

Tracy Foster was jerked into the air, his feet flailing, his body turning and twisting. His teeth were bared in a cold, grisly smile of contempt as he died.

Scott stood unmoving, the tears streaming down his face unheeded. Never had he felt such intense, penetrating sorrow, but it relieved him somewhat to know that his sister had been spared the gruesome spectacle.

Sarah Rose Foster first reacted calmly, or so it appeared, to the news that Tracy had been hanged by a vigilante mob after he had strangled a young woman. Scott found her in the parlor of the boardinghouse, where she and Isaiah Atkins were engaging in a spirited discussion, and broke the word to her bluntly but gently, telling her that he had suspected Tracy's criminal involvement for some time.

Color drained from her face, but she remained composed. "It may be best this way," she said, remembering the wild, strange gleam she had seen in Tracy's eyes when she had tried to persuade him to leave his cave dwelling. "None of us will ever know what inner torments he was suffering. He was so unhappy, and I don't believe he knew what he really wanted."

Isaiah sensed that she might dissolve into tears at any moment, and as much as he wanted to console her, he knew she had to fight her own battle.

"I don't want to stay permanently in Colorado," she said. "I'm not asking you to leave tomorrow, Scott. I couldn't myself, because of my obligation to continue teaching until the school finds a replacement for me."

Scott's own future plans were still unsettled, but he could not think of himself. "Do you want to go back to the Sacramento Valley, Sarah Rose?"

She shrugged. "All I know right this minute is that I couldn't find peace of mind here."

"I suggest we make no final decisions now," her brother said. "Let's wait until the initial shock wears off."

"Of course." Suddenly she turned to Isaiah. "Will you come with me to the cave tomorrow? I want to clear out Tracy's belongings. I'd be haunted by the thought that whatever he owned might stay there for years. There may be some way we could break down the door."

"I'll come with you," Isaiah told her. "If need be, I imagine I can shoot the lock off."

Scott realized that she was turning to the young attorney in her travail rather than to him, which was a sure sign of her emotional involvement with Isaiah. Relieved that she had found someone on whom she could lean until she regained her balance, he said good night and left the room.

Isaiah had to use all of his willpower to prevent himself from taking the lovely young woman into his arms. "In the next few months," he said, "Chet and Ke are sending me to the Nevada country. Silver has been discovered there in quantity, and they want me to buy some mining properties for them. Travel won't be easy, what with snow in most of the passes, but I'll be taking a guide and a strong escort, so I'm sure I'll get through without too much trouble. You're welcome to come with me, if you'd like."

Sarah Rose looked at him, her expression grave.

"As my wife," he said.

She drew a deep breath. "Are you proposing because you feel sorry for me?"

"That wouldn't be a sound basis for a marriage. I realize this may be the worst of all possible moments to propose, but I've loved you for a long time, and I don't want you to feel too isolated and bereft."

"I don't understand how this is happening," she said, "but the tragedy of Tracy's death is making it possible for me to see myself—and you—more clearly.

Long ago, when we were children, I admired you, Isaiah, because you always were so self-reliant, so sure of yourself and of what you wanted in life. Now I realize that my admiration has turned to something far stronger." Her smile was tremulous. "I find that I love you, too, and I'll come with you to Nevada, no matter how much snow is piled up in the mountain passes."

He kissed her gently. Now tears filled her eyes, and she clung to him.

"I'll do my best to help you put your sorrow behind you," Isaiah said.

"If the Lord has a grand design for everyone, as I've always believed," Sarah Rose said, "it may be that Tracy—who couldn't have made a happy, useful life for himself anywhere—didn't die in vain. You and I have discovered each other, and this time of mourning will pass."

The Reverend Lane officiated at a simple funeral early in the morning, and Tracy Foster was buried in an unmarked grave in the new cemetery. It was ironic that Bessie, whom no one cared to identify and whose body was unclaimed, was laid to rest only a stone's throw from the man who had murdered her. Chet Harris quietly paid for the cost of her burial. No one lingered at the cemetery. Scott and Susanna went without delay to the *Tribune* office, while Sarah Rose and Isaiah, taking the day off from work, rode out to the barren countryside to dispose of Tracy's belongings.

The clergyman walked back to the center of town with Chet and Clara Lou. "I wonder if these killings will go on for another six months, or however long it takes to establish order when Colorado is made a federal territory."

"We can't allow them to continue, Reverend," Chet

said. "It seems to me that the respectable people, who form an overwhelming majority here, will have to take steps on our own."

"What do you have in mind, Mr. Harris?"

"My partner and I have the experience of what happened in the early days of San Francisco behind us. We're willing to make a substantial financial contribution to the formation of a voluntary citizens' constabulary."

"Are you suggesting an appeal to the public for funds?"

"That's part of it," Chet said. "Those who have the money can contribute for arms, the building of a jail, and the establishment of structures for temporary law courts. Those who don't have the money can volunteer their services as constables. We need a sheriff, someone whose office can investigate crimes and control the lawless elements in Denver and the outlying mining towns. We need qualified, experienced men to serve as judges and bailiffs. In the present situation any man who carries a grudge can kill his enemy. There's a valid place here for honest gaming halls like Mrs. Hadley's, but men like Willie de Berg either should be forced to stop cheating their customers or should be compelled to leave town."

"You make a great deal of sense, Mr. Harris."

"Well, I've had some informal discussions with General Larimer and a number of other civic leaders. All of them feel as I do and are willing to cooperate. Our problem is that we need someone to organize the campaign and take charge of it."

Reverend Lane smiled. "I assume that's a broad hint."

"I hope you'll take it as such," Chet replied.

"I'll be glad to do it, and I'll call an initial meeting in the next day or two. The day has come when the wicked must be prevented from flourishing like the green bay tree."

Chet and Clara Lou parted company with the

clergyman, then went on to a belated breakfast at the boardinghouse. Mei-lo prepared a meal of eggs and ham for them as her helper was busy cleaning the upstairs bedrooms, but she declined their invitation to join them for coffee. "I'm baking today," she said, "and I don't have time."

Chet was hungry, having eaten nothing earlier in the morning, but Clara Lou had little appetite.

"I hope the funeral didn't depress you too much," he said.

"It isn't that," she replied. "After all, I never knew Tracy Foster, although I feel sympathy for his brother and sister. It's my own situation that makes me weary."

"Has Jerome Hadley pestered you?" he demanded, his voice hardening.

"Oh, no. He wouldn't dare come near me again. Jerome is a coward. It's knowing that he is still in town, working for Willie de Berg, that upsets me. It appears that I'll be married to him for the rest of my days."

"Unfortunately, we can't resort to the tactics of the Tracy Fosters of this world and put a bullet into him. Much as I'm tempted." Chet paused and frowned. "I've been opposed in principle to paying Hadley blackmail and sending him off to Holland for a divorce, but it appears to be our only solution."

"No, Chet!" she replied firmly. "I appreciate your generosity, but I know Jerome too well. He'd take the money and disappear—and not to Holland. He'd see your willingness to pay him as a new, easy way to make money. So he'd simply show up again every year or two and keep collecting from you without ever getting the divorce."

"I've been afraid of that. One alternative would be for you to go to Holland yourself. If you're reluctant to make the journey alone, I'd go with you."

"I've thought of that, but it wouldn't do, either. We'd need Jerome's signature on a legal waiver, and the only way we'd get it from him would be by paying him a huge sum of money."

"It would be worth almost any amount to be rid of him permanently."

Clara Lou grimaced. "Jerome would contest the divorce in the American courts. There's no one more slippery. Or more tenacious when he can get his hands on money. I think you and I should go our separate ways, Chet. Just put me out of your mind."

"Is that what you want?" he asked quietly.

"Oh, no! Never, my dear! But I know of no other way to solve our problem."

Mei-lo came into the dining room with their coffee, then went off to the kitchen again. She wasn't eavesdropping intentionally but nevertheless could hear every word they were saying.

"There is one path open to us," Chet said. "I hesitate to suggest it, but I've waited a long time for the right woman, and I have no intention of losing you, now or ever. You could sell your place here and make a tidy profit on it. I'd want you to keep that money for your own use, naturally. Then you and I would leave Denver. Together."

"I see."

"We could go to Nevada for a few months while I supervise the purchase of our mining properties there, and then go on to San Francisco. We can buy a house for ourselves there, as big and as comfortable a mansion as you want, and we'll spend the rest of our lives there together. I think it's absurd to allow the technicality of a divorce to prevent us from achieving the happiness we'll have in life together."

"I've always said that I never would live as any man's mistress, but this situation is so hopeless that perhaps I should reconsider."

"We'd be husband and wife in every sense except the legal aspect," Chet said. "I have too high a regard for you to ask you to do anything that isn't honorable."

"I know." She sipped her coffee in silence. "Let's

think about it for a spell, Chet. We don't have to make any final decision today."

Mei-lo could understand how they felt, but at the same time she was upset by their contemplation of a liaison. Wong Ke had the right to be told what was happening, and her faith in him was so great that she felt certain he would know what to do. Hurrying up the stairs to his room, she tapped at the door.

Ke looked up from the papers that were spread on the small desk where he was working. In her agitation Mei-lo addressed him in Cantonese rather than in English.

Ke listened to her account, thanked her warmly, and then raced down the stairs to the dining room. Ordinarily he was the more diplomatic of the partners, preferring subtlety to force, but he could be blunt when the situation demanded it. "Forgive me for interrupting your private discussion," he said to the couple, who had just poured fresh cups of coffee. "If you wish, tell me to mind my own business. But you have honored me with your confidence in the past, Chet, so I feel you have given me the right to interfere now."

They were startled, looking first at him, then at each other.

"Mei-lo did not listen deliberately to your talk," he said, "but she couldn't help hearing what you were saying, and she was so disturbed that she came to me." He paused, bowed to Clara Lou, then asked his partner, "Do I have your permission to continue?"

"You old curmudgeon," Chet said. "You know blame well that I can't stop you from speaking your mind."

Ke grinned, took a cup and saucer from a sideboard, and poured himself a cup of coffee before joining them at the table. "I cannot blame you for feeling frustrated," he said, "and I can sympathize with your desire to live together."

"Don't tell me, let me guess." Chet was curt. "You're

afraid the people we know in San Francisco will snub Clara Lou."

The Chinese man shook his head. "On the contrary, they will be happy to accept her as the charming lady that she is. Besides, when anyone has accumulated wealth equal to what you and I have acquired, even the biggest prudes will swallow their dislike and greet both of you with smiles."

"That's the way I had it figured," Chet replied, mollified.

"You have failed to take one vital element into consideration," Ke said. "At present you find Jerome Hadley's attempts to blackmail you a nuisance, and it has been a simple matter for you to fend him off. But you hand him a potent weapon if you choose to live together as husband and wife."

Clara Lou grasped his meaning instantly and nodded. "You're right, Ke," she murmured. "We weren't thinking straight."

"Maybe I'm stupid," Chet said, a hint of belligerence in his tone.

"Hadley will follow you to San Francisco," Ke told him. "And he'll have real cause to blackmail you. Some of the less responsible newspapers there thrive on gossip and sensations. And far too many people in this world envy those who are better off. Hadley will back you into a corner. Either you'll pay his blackmail demands, or he'll create a major scandal by presenting himself to the press as Clara Lou's husband."

"He's right, Chet," Clara Lou said. "It's exactly what Jerome would do, and how he'd delight in making us squirm! We can't defy conventions without paying a high price."

Angry and immersed in gloom, Chet clenched his teeth. "What good is all my money if I can't have what I want more than anything else on earth?"

"Money becomes meaningless pieces of gold and silver in matters of this kind," Ke said. "I, too, am wealthy, but my life has been lonely for many years."

"What would you have us do?" his partner demanded, pounding a fist on the table.

"You have not given in to temptation and have lived according to the highest principles of our society. Do not abandon them now, or you'll lose your self-respect —and with it your respect for each other. Do you remember, Chet, how we refused to give up our search for gold when we were hungry and ragged? Show the same determined patience now. Problems sometimes solve themselves in time. It may be that Hadley will give in to you when he learns you cannot be swayed. I possess no magic that enables me to predict the future. You and I have never cheated anyone in business, yet we have prospered. Live according to your code of morality, and ultimately you will not regret it."

Chet made a wry face and took Clara Lou's hand. "My partner should have been a preacher," he said.

Her smile was wan, but she spoke firmly. "He happens to be right."

"I know it, but that doesn't make the medicine any less bitter to swallow."

They rose, and Clara Lou said, "Thanks for your advice, Ke. We'll do our best to follow it."

Wong Ke watched them as they walked out, sharing their feeling of helpless misery. After a time he realized he was not alone and saw that Mei-lo had come into the dining room behind him.

"This time I did eavesdrop," she said. "You were most wonderful. So wise and strong."

"It is not difficult to speak words of wisdom to others," he said. "It is far more difficult to live wisely."

"Those are words that Confucius wrote," she said. "I have been reading the books you gave me."

"Join me in my prayers that Chet and Clara Lou will find happiness together."

"For a long time I have prayed for them each day, just as I have prayed for your happiness," Mei-lo said.

Ke blinked in surprise. "Do I appear to you to be unhappy?"

"Did you not admit to Chet and Clara Lou what I have known for a long time, that you are lonely man?" she countered.

Although his sophistication ordinarily saved him from embarrassment, he became flustered. "You see too much," he said brusquely. "And it does no good to feel sorry for an old man who already has lived the better part of his life."

"You dare to call yourself old?" Mei-lo became derisive.

"I have lived beyond a half-century," he said.

"Age is in the eyes of the beholder. To me you are a man of great vigor, in the prime of life." Afraid she was too bold, she looked down at the floor.

Wong Ke stared at her. He had known for a long time that he had lost his heart to this young woman who was less than half his age, but he had concealed his feelings for fear she would think him foolish. It was true she was good and kind to him, but he was convinced it was out of respect for an elder, not out of love. He had told Chet and Clara Lou only moments earlier that patience was rewarded, often in unexpected ways, but in his case, no amount of patience could make him a young man again.

"Congratulations, Andy. You've been promoted." General Lee Blake removed the gold bars from the shoulders of his nephew's uniform and replaced them with the silver bars of a first lieutenant. "The War Department acted more quickly on my recommendation than I thought they would."

Cathy Blake embraced and kissed her sister's son. "We're proud of you, Andy," she said.

Andy Brentwood was overwhelmed. "I wasn't expecting a promotion for at least another year to a year and a half."

"The whole process has been speeded up lately, especially in the cases of officers who are known to be loyal to the North. The army will grow to several times its present size—almost overnight—when the war comes, so the need for professional soldiers will become much greater."

"I see," Andy said soberly, then smiled. "In any event, I'm grateful to you, sir. This is a pleasant surprise."

"Sit down," Cathy told him. "This is just the beginning of your surprises."

The young officer obediently moved to a sofa in the living room of the Blake house at Fort Zachary Taylor.

"Your formal transfer orders will be coming through in a few days," Lee said, smiling.

Andy started to rise, then forced himself to remain seated. "I'm getting a new assignment?"

"One that you'll like." Lee's smile grew broader. "You've been given command of a cavalry troop that will be stationed temporarily in the Nevada country. In Virginia City, to be precise. I tried to get you assigned to the new Colorado command that will guard the gold being moved to the new mint that the Treasury Department will build in Denver, but all the posts there were already taken. Nevada was the best I could get for you. Your primary duty will be to protect the silver that the U.S. Treasury is buying from the miners."

Andy didn't require a fuller explanation. He well knew, as did his uncle, that Southern partisans would attempt to gain possession of the valuable silver hoard that was beginning to be produced in Nevada. Already in Colorado there had been skirmishes as Southerners protested the acquisition of gold by the United States Treasury Department, and only the swift intervention of the U.S. troops stationed in Denver prevented full-scale riots from breaking out.

"You'll travel by rail to Independence, where Claudia and Sam will be astonished when you show up," Lee said. "The Adjutant General's office is preparing your orders in a way that will make it possible for you to spend a few days at home. Your troop will be waiting for you in St. Joseph, and after you assume the command, you'll travel the overland route via the Great Plains and the Rocky Mountains to Nevada."

All at once Andy understood and became flushed. "I'll be able to travel by way of Denver."

Cathy laughed. "I didn't know you when you were Andy's age, Lee, but I wonder if you were that transparent."

"It isn't likely," her husband replied, the humor in his eyes belying his sober face. "I didn't fall in love until I met you, my dear."

Andy leaped to his feet. "May I be excused for a short time, sir?"

"By all means. You'll have just enough time to write a short note before the mail is collected."

Cathy stifled a laugh as her nephew bolted from the room. She called after him, "Be sure you send our regards to Susanna."

Later that day, when the afternoon mail packet had been delivered to Fort Zachary Taylor, Andy Brentwood returned to the house of his aunt and uncle with letters for them.

"It looks like Andy isn't the only one to get a surprise today." Lee Blake said. "Here's a letter from Whip Holt."

"And I have one from Eulalia! I hope nothing's wrong," Cathy said, hastily opening the letter. "Could it be they're coming to Washington City?"

"I wouldn't think so," Lee answered, opening the letter from Whip. "Not when there's so much trouble brewing in the country."

Cathy raised her hand to silence him as she read. "Toby Holt is going to enlist in the federal army! He intends to leave engineering school, and Eulalia wants our advice."

"Yes," Lee said as he finished reading his letter. "So Whip says. He wonders if his son is doing the right thing."

"What do you think, Lee?" Cathy asked her husband.

"I think any son of Whip and Eulalia Holt will make a fine soldier. When war starts—and I don't think it can be avoided much longer—the Union will need all the good men it can get!"

X

The drive to clean up Denver inaugurated by the
Reverend Daniel Lane was enthusiastically endorsed
by the citizens, and the *Tribune* became the outspo-
ken voice of the campaign. The newspaper printed a
daily list of financial contributors, with the way led
by Chet Harris and Wong Ke, each of them donating
two thousand dollars. Enough funds soon were gathered for the purchase of firearms and the building of a
jail.

A spontaneous movement was under way to elect a
volunteer chief of police who would attend to the
hiring of the constables and direct the force. Not only
did the *Tribune* support the plan, but Susanna suggested Scott Foster for the position in an editorial,
and she paid no attention to his protests.

"You won't be paid, you know," she told him, "and
you can be sure my father will give you whatever
time off you need."

"But I know so little about the needs of the police,"
he said. "We ought to hire a professional."

"So we shall, when we become a federal territory. I
thought that, until then, you'd want the position—
because of your brother's experiences."

"If I'm elected," Scott said curtly, "I'll accept."

His election was assured when the other two candidates dropped out of the race, announcing that they would gladly serve as his deputies. The election became a mere formality, and Scott spent his evenings interviewing men who wanted the fifty full-time places in the constabulary.

Certain elements in the city were opposed to the formation of the force. "We'll police ourselves," Willie de Berg and the proprietors of other gambling halls and brothels said. Willie, whose Palace business was improving steadily as people forgot the article that the *Tribune* had published about him, made a five-hundred-dollar contribution to a war chest.

A number of his colleagues followed his example, and an informal committee led by Willie called on the owners of gaming houses and bordellos to solicit additional funds. Most made contributions because they were afraid of reprisals, and only a few refused. Of these, none was more vehement than Clara Lou Hadley. "De Berg," she said, "I wouldn't give a penny to any cause you represent. What's more, the card games in my place are honest, so I have nothing to fear from the formation of a constabulary."

"Are you trying to revive those lies the newspaper printed about me?" he demanded.

Her smile was tight. "I don't need the *Tribune* to tell me about your saloon. Jerome works for you, and he wouldn't know how to deal a poker hand without cheating."

Thereafter, the full-time constables and the many part-time volunteers, among them Ezekiel, made it a practice to visit Clara Lou's gaming house several times each evening, after the armed guards Chet had hired had departed for the day. As Chief of Police Scott Foster said, "Anyone who has declared war on Willie de Berg needs constant protection."

For the time being, at least, the anger of the gambling hall and brothel owners was directed primarily at the Reverend Lane. Two fires of mysterious origin broke out in his new church, but both were discovered and quickly extinguished before any real harm was done. Then his parishioners formed a group of vigilantes, and every night armed men stood guard duty outside and inside the new church.

Willie tried to retaliate by ordering the women in his employ not to attend services at the church. The following Sunday, however, virtually the entire group attended together, and Caroline Brandon was delegated to explain their position to Willie.

Her spirits had improved since she had been promoted to work in the high-stakes room and was permitted to wear evening gowns rather than the corselet she loathed, and she spoke plainly. "We do what we're told here every day and night of the week, Willie," she said, "but nobody—not even you—can stop us from going to church. If you don't like it, you can throw every last one of us out into the street, but I wouldn't advise it. Without the income we bring you and the help we give your card dealers, you'll soon go out of business."

Aware that he could not win a battle fought in the open, Willie seemingly abandoned his opposition to the forces of law and order. But he confided to Jerome Hadley in private. "We may have to let the customers win more often at poker and blackjack," he said. "But not for long. I've been in this business enough years to know there are all kinds of ways to skin a coyote."

The organization of the new constabulary was virtually completed in this year of 1860, and the murder rate soon declined, as did the robberies and burglaries in the city. Two elderly citizens, one a former United States Congressman from Michigan and the other an attorney from Pittsburgh, consented to act as judges in the "volunteer court" and gave such severe sentences to those found guilty of wrongdoing that, for the first time in two years of Denver's existence, the streets became safe for its residents.

The arrival of a full troop of United States Cavalry,

commanded by First Lieutenant Andrew Jackson Brentwood, was another factor that made it possible to enforce the law. The presence of so many troops also discouraged the Southern partisans in Denver from doing anything to prevent the gold from going to the United States Treasury Department. Andy and his unit, more than one hundred strong, reached Denver only a few days after Susanna received his letter, which had been delayed in the mails.

"My original orders have been amended," Andy told a gathering of his friends at the boardinghouse. "I was supposed to go straight on to Nevada, but there have been severe early snowfalls in the Rockies, and I've been ordered to stay here until the snow clears and offer the services of my troop to the appropriate authorities, whoever they may be."

"I reckon you'll be working with me," Scott told him, grinning.

Their handshake was friendly, even though both were more aware than ever of their rivalry.

Susanna continued to show no preference for one or the other. She was disappointed that Andy had brought no message from General Blake, who had promised to tell her about his secret mission in Colorado. She realized that the mission probably still had to remain top secret and that she would have to bide her time until General Blake was able to write her. Meanwhile, she made no secret of her pleasure when Andy arrived, and she gladly spent his first two evenings in town with him. But the next night she accepted Scott's supper invitation, and she demonstrated her continuing independence by refusing to see either of her suitors the following evening, instead remaining at home with her father and reading a recently published book of poetry by Henry Wadsworth Longfellow.

Sarah Rose and Isaiah had planned to be married immediately prior to their own journey to Nevada, but their departure was delayed by the early heavy snowfalls in the Rockies. Andy graciously agreed to permit the couple to ride with his troop to Nevada and avail themselves of the protection afforded by the cavalry-men.

All at once the prospect of the delay became intol-erable to Sarah Rose. "At first I wanted to delay because of Tracy's death," she told Isaiah. "But I've come to realize that life belongs to the living, and I see nothing to be gained by waiting until spring."

"That suits me fine," he said. "We'll be married as soon as we can make the arrangements."

Reverend Lane agreed to perform the ceremony at his church, and the noon wedding would be followed by a reception that Clara Lou insisted on holding at her establishment. The wedding was delayed for a week while a seamstress made a white dress for Sarah Rose, who confided to Susanna that she was too practical for her own good. She intended to dye the dress a light shade of brown so she would be able to use it as a regular part of her wardrobe.

Scott gave his sister's hand in marriage, Susanna was the maid of honor, and Andy, resplendent in full-dress uniform of blue trimmed with gold, was Isaiah's best man, almost stealing the spotlight from the bridegroom. Prudence Adams, sitting with Ezekiel and Patricia, wept happily throughout the ceremony.

The day was bitterly cold, and only the bride and groom rode in a carriage to Clara Lou's place. A numbing wind chilled the others as they struggled on foot through snowdrifts for several short blocks, but the members of the party were in such high spirits that they paid scant attention to the frigid blasts. Susanna, holding the arms of Scott and Andy, tried to divide her attention in equal parts, quietly marveling at their ability to keep up drumfires of conversation, even though the lower portions of their faces were covered by scarves of heavy wool. Mei-lo shivered unceasingly, but she laughingly refused Ke's offer of his greatcoat.

"You would become ill with the ague," she said, "and I would be obliged to spend weeks nursing you back to health. I prefer to be cold for a short time."

Steaming cups of hot grog awaited the party. Andy gallantly offered the first toast to the bride and groom, and soon the company began to thaw. The younger people surrounded Sarah Rose and Isaiah, with everyone seemingly talking at once, and Ke quietly withdrew to the rear of the dining room, sitting beside his partner when Clara Lou went to check on the progress of the help at work in the kitchen.

"I know your thoughts today, Chet," the Chinese man said. "For your sake and Clara Lou's, I wish we were celebrating your wedding."

"I doubt if that day will ever come," Chet replied. "But I'm doing my damnedest to exercise the patience you insisted I show. One of these days something inside me will snap, and then I don't know what I'll do." He sighed, then changed the subject abruptly. "What about you, Ke?" he asked, nodding in the direction of the animated, tiny Mei-lo, who was straining as she looked up at Andy towering above her.

"Are my feelings so transparent?" Ke asked quietly.

"Well, I've known you so long that they are to me," Chet told him.

"And to me," Clara Lou declared as she seated herself between them. "I saw you falling in love with Mei-lo months ago, perhaps before you knew it yourself."

"I have tried very hard to change my feelings," Wong Ke said. "So far I have had little success, but I shall continue to try."

This was not a moment for delicacy, and the surprised Clara Lou asked, "Why, for heaven's sake?"

"That should be obvious," Ke said. "If I could have afforded to take a wife when I was young, in the Middle Kingdom, before I came to America, I would have had children who are the age of Mei-lo. Perhaps a few years older."

"I don't see why that should matter," she replied.

"Neither do I," Chet said. "You're anything but decrepit, the Lord knows you can afford to support a wife in style, and you have many years of vigorous life ahead of you."

"No man knows the length of his stay on earth," Ke said.

Chet stared at him. "I've never heard you talk in that vein. You're the eternal optimist."

"In some things. Not in this."

"It's irrelevant that Mei-lo is so much younger than you," Clara Lou said briskly. "Take my word for it."

"I wish I could."

"Very well," she said. "Don't take my word. Ask Mei-lo."

The usually urbane Ke became flustered. "That is something I could not bring myself to do!"

She looked at him, then turned to Chet and spoke in wonder. "He's actually afraid she'd reject him!"

Chet laughed heartily.

"I do not share your sense of humor." Wong Ke was miffed.

Clara Lou made an attempt to restore his pride. "Clearly you have very little understanding of women. Accept my assurances that there is nothing that would give Mei-lo greater joy and satisfaction than to become your wife."

"That's right," Chet said. "I'm no authority on women myself, but it's plain from the way she looks at you, the way she lights up like an oil lamp with a long wick every time you speak to her or pay attention to her."

"But how could that be?" Ke asked in bewilderment. "Look at her right now, enjoying herself with members of her own generation."

"I'm going to break my rule of many years' standing," Chet said. "Of course she's having a good time. That's what people do at wedding receptions, and she's become a good friend of Sarah Rose. But I'll bet you one hundred dollars that if you call to her, she'll not only come to you immediately, but she'll smile from ear to ear, and there will be a glow in her eyes."

His partner hesitated for a moment, then drew one hundred dollars from his wallet and handed the money to Clara Lou. "Keep the stakes for us, please."

A grinning Chet gave the same sum. "This is going to be the easiest money I've ever made."

"Give us time to leave the table," Clara Lou suggested, and rising quickly before Wong Ke could reply, she and Chet drifted away.

Ke braced himself, took a deep breath, and, raising his voice only slightly, called to Mei-lo.

She turned, then joined him instantly, her face radiant, her manner eager.

Clara Lou, standing behind Mei-lo, held up the two hundred dollars, then handed the money to Chet, who chuckled as he stuffed it into a pocket.

"I hope I did not interrupt something of importance," Ke said.

"Oh, no," Mei-lo replied. "We were just chatting."

"I did not join the group because the presence of an older person sometimes puts a damper on the spirits of the young."

"No one thinks of you as an older person," she said quickly as she sat beside him.

Although he found it difficult to believe she was being more than polite, he had to admit that what Clara Lou and Chet had said to him might be true. In his business dealings he was firm, quietly aggressive, and he told himself he had to adopt the same approach now. It was preferable to be rejected than to go on indefinitely with a dream unfulfilled.

"Would you like another cup of toddy?" he asked.

She shook her head. "A second cup would make me dizzy."

"I have had only one," Ke said, "and I am already dizzy, although the liquor is not responsible."

Mei-lo looked puzzled.

"A wedding," he said simply, "is a very romantic occasion."

"Of course," she replied politely.

"Even one of my advanced years feels stirrings."

"I will not listen when you speak of yourself that way." Her irritation was genuine. "How old was your father when he died?" she demanded, challenging him.

"Ninety-two." Her vehemence took him by surprise.

"And his father?"

"Ninety-four."

"It is not unusual for subjects of the Emperor of the Middle Kingdom to live until they accumulate many years as well as great wisdom," Mei-lo said thoughtfully. "You are one who lives a life of moderation, so it is reasonable for you to expect that you will spend the better part of another half-century in this world. Is that not true?"

He was forced to accept her logic and nodded. Perhaps she was hinting, in her own subtle way, that she would not be averse to sharing his life with him. He felt compelled to find out, once and for all. "I very much regret," he said hoarsely, "that your father is no longer alive."

Mei-lo was bewildered by the sudden shift in his emphasis and looked at him questioningly.

Ke had to force out the words. "If he still lived, I would apply to him for your hand in marriage."

To his deep chagrin she shook her head. "It would not be possible for me to marry you," she said.

His dream was shattered, Clara Lou and Chet were mistaken, and he appeared doomed to spend the rest of his days alone. "Is it permitted to ask your reason?" He tried not to let her see his distress.

"Wong Ke," she said, "is a man of great stature. There is no other Chinese in America—and few in the Middle Kingdom other than those who are members of the Emperor's family—who have your wealth and influence. You own many gold mines, much property, hotels, and other companies. Mei-lo is poor. I have only the wages that you yourself pay me. I am not able to bring you the dowry that you have every right to expect from the woman you will marry."

Something within Ke had died, or so he had thought, but now it had come alive again, the flames leaping high. "Is that your only reason?"

"It is enough," Mei-lo said, looking miserable. "I have thought long and hard about this matter, and I know of no way to solve the problem."

"There is no problem," he replied, a ring of triumph in his voice. "We live in America, not the Middle Kingdom. We are Americans, and our customs are not those of our ancestors. I require no dowry, and even if you had a family with substantial funds, I would accept no dowry. I have enough wealth for you, for me, for our children, and our children's children."

She returned his gaze briefly, brushed away a tear, and then lowered her head in a gesture of submission. "It is right and proper," she murmured, "that a woman should accept the commands of the man who will become her husband."

Ke gently reached out a hand and lifted her chin. To his astonishment her tears had dissipated, and in her eyes he could see mischief as well as love. Unable to control himself any longer, he jumped to his feet, helped her to rise, and then kissed her soundly.

Chet and Clara Lou led the applause of the whole company. Ke became flustered, and a shy Mei-lo discovered she had no place to hide.

"I offer a toast to our next bride and groom!" Chet said loudly.

Isaiah raised his glass. "I wish Mei-lo and Ke the long life and happiness together that Sarah Rose and I will enjoy!"

Mei-lo's hand found a natural resting place in Ke's hand, and they stood side by side, their shoulders touching, as the others drank to their future.

"Speech!" Clara Lou called.

Ke's reply was succinct. "Nowhere but in America," he said, "are the dreams of mankind fulfilled."

The new constabulary, augmented by the cavalry-men of Lieutenant Brentwood's troop, quickly established a rule of law in the Colorado mining country, but Scott Foster was not satisfied. "For the moment we have the lawless elements on the run," he said at a night meeting of his own immediate police subordinates and the officers of Andy's troop. "Now the time has come to destroy the roots of the problem."

"What do you have in mind, Chief?" one of his deputies asked.

"We'll close down any gambling hall that cheats its customers, and we'll nail shut the doors of any brothel where clients who are drunk or asleep are robbed. When there's a murder, the perpetrator of the crime will be taken into custody at once. Robbers will be thrown into jail and held without bail pending trial, too."

Andy Brentwood whistled softly. "That won't be an easy program to follow, Scott."

"We can do it, Andy, if you'll go all the way with us."

"I'm under War Department orders to cooperate with local authority in every reasonable way. I think your plan is feasible, and I'm all in favor of it. The Congress will be making Colorado a federal territory very shortly, and then you'll have all the help you'll need and want."

"When that happens," Scott replied, grinning, "I aim to resign as volunteer chief of police. This job needs someone with the professional experience of Rick Miller!"

Susanna Fulton wrote a long article for the *Tribune* that outlined the new program, and the law-abiding citizens of Denver were elated, with Chet and Ke making an additional contribution of two thousand dollars each to the new campaign. But there were others who were alarmed, and no one was more disturbed than Willie de Berg.

Calling Caroline Brandon into his office, he flourished a copy of the newspaper. "Have you seen this?" he demanded.

Caroline calmly adjusted a thin shoulder-strap. "If they're successful," she replied, "you may have to close up shop here. You may want to move west to the Nevada country."

"They won't succeed," he said grimly. "As a first step, I want you to seduce either Scott Foster or this Lieutenant Brentwood. I've got to establish control over them."

"It won't work, Willie," she said.

"You refuse?"

"I know Scott—and Andy, too—from the time when I lived in the same boardinghouse. They're not interested in me. Neither of them sparks to me."

"That's hard to believe." Her popularity had made her his largest single source of profit.

"I'd make a play for either or both of them if I thought it would be effective. But if I fail, and the odds are in favor of it, look what would happen. It wouldn't be all that hard to trace my efforts back to you, and then you'd be in even more trouble. So would I." She studied her long fingernails, which were coated with a scarlet lacquer that matched her bright lip rouge. "I'm doing fine these days, and pretty soon you'll have to start paying me what I'm worth to you. I won't be worth a nickel if I'm sent to jail for conspiracy."

Willie had to admit she was right but was annoyed because she was becoming far too independent. He would put her firmly in her right place, but for now, he had to deal with more pressing problems. "Get out!" he ordered.

Caroline concealed her pleasure as she wandered back to the high-stakes room. Willie needed her, and her ability to handle him, the feeling of superiority over him that suffused her, compensated in part for the seeming helplessness of her situation. Ultimately she would get what she wanted from him.

Willie paced his office furiously and had to exert great effort in order to think clearly. This wasn't the first time he had found himself in a dangerous spot, and there always were ways to solve any dilemma.

The weakness of the constabulary, he reflected, lay in its total dependence for wages and upkeep on the contributions made voluntarily by citizens. Cut off the money supply, and the police force would atrophy quickly, then collapse. Now, he thought, he was making progress!

Reaching for the *Tribune*, he read the article more carefully, then turned to an inside page, where the contributors to the constabulary and the amounts of money they had given were listed. By far the largest sums had been offered by that damn Harris and his Chinese partner, each having made a whopping gift of two thousand dollars. At the bottom of the list was a line Willie hadn't noticed previously: Harris was quoted as saying that he and his partner would match their previous contributions for the new campaign.

If he could prevent them from making that new gift, the constabulary would not be able to function.

In such a hurry that he did not bother to don the swallow-tailed coat that concealed the weapon he carried, Willie hurried downstairs to the main saloon. There he paused and became furious when he saw at the bar the ridiculous old miner and his burro, both drinking beer.

"What the hell do you think you're doing here with that goddamn animal!" he shouted at the old man.

"I thought me and Eustace was workin' for you," the miner said, putting down his schooner of beer and turning to look at the saloonkeeper.

"Not anymore," Willie said, grabbing the old man

by the neck and shoving him toward the door. "Now get the hell out. And stay out."

The burro looked up from its bowl of beer and, flicking its ears, followed the miner to the door. Then, as the old man made a show of brushing his soiled clothes, he called out to the retreating saloonkeeper, "We'll go all right. We'll go someplace where we're wanted. Come on, Eustace." And with this the miner and his burro left the Palace.

Willie shook his head in disgust as he returned to the bar. There were two other customers there, miners who had watched the scene with the man and his burro and were smiling as they drank their beer. Suddenly Willie had an idea, and he went up to the two men and offered them a drink on the house.

Unaccustomed to his largess, they grinned and raised their glasses to him.

"You boys have been in these parts for quite a long time," he said.

The miner with a full beard nodded. "Yup. Near a year now."

"Then you must know every mine in the area."

"Just about," the cleanshaven man said.

"Then I reckon you know the new mine that's been opened in the area. Close to town, from what I hear." Willie was casual.

"You got to mean the new Harris and Wong claim. They been hirin' fellers like crazy to dig tunnels, even though they ain't had a strike there yet."

"That doesn't make sense," Willie said, chuckling.

"Them two is crazy like foxes," the bearded miner assured him. "Other folks say there ain't any gold that close to Denver, but Harris and Wong don't hire three hundred fellers to dig all the way to hell and gone without a reason."

"One of these days they'll hit a vein as wide as your hand," the other miner declared, "and then everybody will be claimin' land in them canyons."

Willie signaled his bartender to refill their glasses. "If they really know what they're doing, it might be smart to buy some property nearby. How far from town is this mine?"

"No more'n ten minutes' easy ride," the bearded man said. "The main shaft is close by to No Name Creek, near where it goes into the South Platte. Everybody else was so busy racin' out to Golden and Central City they plumb fergot what's under their noses. But not Harris and Wong."

Willie had learned all he needed to know, but he changed the subject and chatted about inconsequential matters for a time. Then, his easy manner belied by the rock-hard expression in his eyes, he went to the kitchen, where Jerome Hadley was eating his customary late breakfast before taking charge at his regular table in the high-stakes room.

"Come up to my office as soon as you're done," Willie told him.

The request was unusual, so Jerome gulped his food, then bolted up the stairs two at a time. He found his employer with his feet propped on his desk, smoking a cheroot.

"I suppose you've seen today's newspaper," Willie said, "so you know about the campaign to drive us out of business."

The gambler shrugged. "One of the advantages of not working for myself is that I don't have to worry about such things. If I know you, you'll figure some way to beat the holier-than-thou crowd at its own game."

"Maybe that's just what I've done." Willie's smile was cold. "Am I right when I guess that your wife isn't one of your favorite people these days?"

"I'm fonder of a few others," Jerome admitted cautiously.

"How would you like it if she and Chet Harris got what's coming to them—at the same time?"

Jerome grinned, and the long scar on his face turned a deep shade of reddish-purple.

"Harris and his partner are the main contributors to the constabulary," Willie said. "They're so rich that it isn't easy to discredit them and send them running for their lives, but I've worked out a way to do it. They're the great champions of mine safety, you know. Well, they've opened a new mine, very close to town, where a large force of men has been digging tunnels like mad. Suppose there was a bad accident in that mine, with men getting killed and hurt. Harris and Wong would be lucky if they weren't lynched."

Jerome looked at him shrewdly. "How does Clara Lou fit into all this?"

Willie could not admit that he intended to seduce the woman whose rejection had insulted him. "Without Harris to protect her, I can make her sell her place to me. I've been trying to buy it ever since she went into business."

The explanation satisfied Jerome. "Sounds good to me," he said. "How do you arrange for this accident?"

"I don't. You'll do it."

Color drained from Jerome's face. "I'm a card dealer, Willie. I've never been one to get mixed up with rough stuff."

"The risks will be very slight," Willie said soothingly.

"Why me?"

"Because you have a personal stake in the results of this accident. I could hire some bully to do the job, but you can do it with greater skill. And you'll be well paid for your efforts."

"You bet," Jerome said. "But let that part wait for a minute. What would I have to do?"

"Go to the mine late at night, when only a few men are on duty in the tunnels. On a new job like this, there are bound to be many men who aren't acquainted with each other. You'll look like a miner, but instead of the usual gear in the pack on your back, you'll carry a little keg of gunpowder. You'll penetrate as far as possible into the mine, light a fuse, and get out. You'll change back into your own clothes, and no more than thirty minutes after you set out, you'll be dealing cards again. Nobody will see you coming or going, and you'll have a perfect alibi. And you'll make more money in a half-hour than you ordinarily earn in a month."

Greed and caution warred within Jerome Hadley. "How much?" he asked curtly.

"One thousand dollars cash. Payable the minute you walk in here and tell me you planted the charge and lighted the fuse."

"Not enough," Jerome said. "Two thousand. With half paid in advance."

"How do I know you won't disappear?"

"I'm not that foolish, Willie. The only place I could go these days is the Nevada country. You could have me followed there, and my throat would be cut."

Willie grudgingly admitted he was right.

"That's my deal," Jerome said. "Take it or leave it."

Willie went to his safe, opening it with three different keys that he carried on a chain, and slowly counted out one thousand dollars in one-hundred-dollar bills. "We've got to act fast," he said, "because Foster and his police are likely to come snooping around here before they go to any other gambling hall in town. You'll have to do the job tonight."

Jerome spent the better part of the evening presiding at the oval-shaped table that was his domain in the high-stakes room. He glanced at his watch, and when Caroline returned to the floor after entertaining a client in her room, he beckoned to her. "I'm a mite hungrier than usual tonight," he said, "so I'm going downstairs before the kitchen runs out of beef. Get a substitute dealer, please, and attach yourself to a customer so you can send along the signals."

The request was normal, and Caroline complied without dwelling on the matter.

Jerome sauntered off to the back stairs, taking care to wave to several acquaintances. Then he raced down to the alleyway entrance, where Willie de Berg stood waiting, holding a gelding's reins. They exchanged no words, and Jerome pulled his hat low as he cantered off toward the southwest through the quiet streets.

Soon after leaving the town boundary, he came to No Name Creek, and after following it for a short distance, he saw the timbers of the mine's main shaft, with huge mounds of rubble that had been removed from the interior piled in man-made hills nearby. Perhaps, as Willie had indicated, the task would not be difficult to perform. Halting his mount between two of the rubble hills, Jerome quickly changed his appearance. He already was wearing dark trousers, which he stuffed into the tops of his black boots. Next he removed his coat, substituting a high-necked, dark gray sweater for it. The backpack that contained the fuse, keg of gunpowder, a tinderbox, and flint was somewhat heavier than he had anticipated, so he needed several minutes to adjust the straps that slipped over his shoulders. Then he picked up a fat candle attached to a loop that would fit over his hat, clutched the shovel he would carry to fool anyone he encountered, and started forward boldly.

The star-filled sky was clear, with a sliver of new moon providing little illumination, but he breathed more easily when he saw that he was still alone. Apparently no guards would be stationed at the entrance to the shaft until gold was actually discovered in the mine. A small fire burned on the ground near the entrance, which he used to light the candle that he affixed to his hat, and then he entered the shaft.

The downhill slope was very steep, and Jerome descended cautiously into the unfamiliar interior of the earth; the realization that his candle now was providing the only light made him uneasy. But the heavy timbers that held up the roof of the shaft and lined the sides were reassuring.

When he reached the bottom of the shaft, he had no idea how far down he had come, and he wasted no time in speculation. A tunnel stretched out ahead in the gloom, beyond the feeble glare of his candle, and he started down it, instinctively hunching, even though he could have stood erect. Maybe it had been unwise to accept the assignment, he thought, as the stale air stung the insides of his nostrils and made his throat ache. On the other hand, he had been paid half of his fee, and the rest would be safely in his pocket in a short time. He would have been foolish not to accept the money that would make it possible for him to leave Colorado, go off to the Nevada country, and try his luck there. Obviously Clara Lou and Harris were standing pat, refusing to do business with him, and he suspected that Willie de Berg wouldn't insist that he stay in Denver.

To Jerome's surprise the tunnel divided into two, with one part veering toward the left and the other turning sharply to the right. Since he had lost his sense of direction, he didn't care which he followed and chose the tunnel on the right because he would recognize the sharp turn when he headed back. The mere thought of losing his way in this maze made him shiver.

He proceeded slowly, sometimes walking on hard rock, sometimes on dirt, and occasionally traversing pebble-filled flooring. The alien atmosphere made him increasingly nervous, and he decided that soon he would leave the keg, light the fuse, and get out. He had seen no one, and tired of carrying the shovel he had no intention of using, he discarded it.

Suddenly, somewhere ahead in the distance, he

heard the muffled sound of voices. He halted for a moment, then very slowly went forward. Again the tunnel parted, and when he finally realized that the voices were somewhere down the tunnel on his right, Jerome chose to follow the excavation on his left. "First I turned right, then I turned left," he told himself repeatedly.

He was astonished when he noted that one of the rock walls of the tunnel glistened in the light of his candle, and when he touched it experimentally, he felt that it was wet. The dampness and lack of air were stifling, and although the air was chilly, he began to perspire. Never again, he reflected, would he enter a mine.

After he walked another one hundred paces, he discovered that the tunnel came to an abrupt end. A wall of solid earth and rock blocked his passage. He removed the backpack, placed the keg of gunpowder against the end of the tunnel, and attached the fuse to it. Then he moved slowly in the direction from which he had come and was dismayed when he found that the fuse was shorter than he had thought it would be.

Willie had assured him that the fuse would burn slowly, allowing him plenty of time to leave the mine. Well, he had come this far, and he would have to accept Willie's word.

Halting again, he tried to strike a spark with the flint, but the stone had absorbed too much moisture. Dropping the tools impatiently, he removed the candle and loop from his hat and used the flame to light the fuse.

Now he had to hurry, so he did not bother to affix the loop to his hat again. Instead he clutched the candle in his hand, ignoring the hot tallow that dripped down onto his skin, and walked quickly, afraid that the miners whose voices he had heard would become aware of the sound of his feet if he broke into a run.

Suddenly a deep explosion roared behind him at the

rear of the tunnel, the sound echoing through the length of the man-made caverns. Jerome was swept off his feet by the shaking, and then he felt a swift, strong suction of air whistling past him toward the site of the explosion. For a long moment there was no oxygen in the tunnel, and he gasped in vain for breath.

Then, as he scrambled to his feet, he realized that the air suction had extinguished his candle. He had discarded the flint and tinderbox, and there was no way he could light it again.

A sudden panic assailed Jerome, and he broke into a run, only to bump into the damp rock wall. Aware that he had to exert supreme self-control, he reached out in the dark, then had to grope his way down the long tunnel, praying that the ceiling and walls would not collapse and bury him alive.

He inched his way toward the freedom that would await him when he returned to the surface of the earth. He was so intent on reaching safety that only little by little did he become aware of a new danger. Somewhere in the gloom behind him he felt certain he heard the rush of a body of water. His imagination was playing tricks on him, he told himself sternly. There could be no water this far below the ground.

The eleven miners who had been at work on the night shift in the tunnel that extended at a right angle from the one that the gambler was trying to put behind him soon became aware of the extent of their peril. They, too, had been knocked off their feet by the explosion, but they managed to light their candles again, and with one accord they headed toward the entrance.

"What in tarnation could have exploded?" one of them asked.

"Damned if I know," the man trudging beside him replied. "But I ain't aimin' to hang around here long enough to find out!"

"Me, neither," another declared. "Sometimes I think workin' at night ain't worth the pay we get."

The man bringing up the rear halted his comrades when he screamed, "My God! Listen!"

All of them heard the steady roar of a huge quantity of water moving toward them down the tunnel.

"The explosion must have cut through the wall that held the underground part of No Name Creek in its channel," one of the miners shouted. "If we hurry, we can reach that ledge up yonder."

They began to run toward the natural rock ledge that stood about five feet from the floor of the tunnel. Several of the candles were extinguished, but for the moment no one cared. Those at the head of the group reached the ledge, fought their way onto it, and then helped their comrades mount it.

They were obliged to squeeze onto the rock, with the ceiling of the tunnel only inches above them. The roar of the underground river that had been diverted from its channel and was seeking new outlets became so loud that it became impossible to converse.

Then the wall of churning black water, carrying rocks and debris with it, swept past the trapped men, the icy deluge so close that its spray drenched them.

The lips of one man began to move. "Our Father, who art in Heaven . . ."

The others could not hear his voice, but one by one they, too, joined in offering the Lord's Prayer.

Chet Harris was jarred from a sound sleep just as dawn was breaking, and he awakened to find Scott Foster shaking him.

"There's been an accident at your new mine," Scott said. "People on the far side of town claim they heard an explosion."

Still groggy, Chet shook his head. "How could there be an explosion?"

"You know as much as I do. I'm heading out there with as many constables as I can muster, and Andy Brentwood is bringing his whole troop! I just woke up Ke, and he's getting dressed."

Within minutes the partners and the young volunteer chief of police were on their way. A dozen constables joined them in the center of town, and as they rode toward the southwest they discovered that many others were hurrying to the mine, too, some on foot and some mounted.

Too late Scott realized that he should have paused long enough to notify Susanna, who would want the story of the accident for the *Tribune*. Well, he couldn't turn back now, and he felt certain there was so much commotion in town that Susanna soon would make her way out to the mine on her own initiative.

Dozens of men already were at the scene when the mine owners and constables galloped to the main shaft entrance, and there was an angry rumble when Chet and Ke were recognized. "There they are," a man shouted in a deep voice. "The bastards who pretend they're so concerned about mine safety!"

The voices of others were raised, too, and it was clear that the crowd was in an ugly mood.

Ignoring the hubbub, Chet and Ke dismounted, then walked quickly to the shaft entrance, where their superintendent, Chuck Harvey, was already standing. Scott followed a pace behind the pair.

Harvey, who had operated many mines, wasted no words. "There are eleven men of the night shift trapped down there," he said, "and it doesn't look good. Some of the boys started down the main shaft but had to come back. The explosion caved in a retaining wall, and the underground section of No Name Creek is spreading every place where we had dug a tunnel."

"Are the trapped men still alive?" Chet asked.

The superintendent shrugged, pointing at several groups who were spreading out across the hills, pausing to pound the hard ground with sledgehammers. "We're testing now, using the maps of the tunnel routes. If we hear some answering taps, we'll know they've survived. So far."

"What was this explosion?" Ke demanded.

"I have no idea, Mr. Wong," Harvey said. "We've done all of our tunnel-digging by hand. I've forbidden the use of gunpowder, to prevent slides, and we haven't had any on hand."

"Could someone have set off an explosion on purpose?" Scott asked quietly.

"Your guess is as good as mine, Mr. Foster." Harvey hesitated. "A couple of the boys who got there first claim they saw a riderless horse, carrying a saddle, running hell-bent-for-election across the hills. There's been a search, but no one has found the animal yet. And you know how it is. Maybe the boys were just imagining things."

Miners were arriving on the scene in ever-increasing numbers, and several, presumably the spokesmen for their colleagues, pushed past the constables and confronted Chet. "Well, Mr. Rich Man," a self-designated spokesman demanded in a loud voice, "what are you going to do about this mess? How are you going to save the boys who are stuck down there?"

Chet faced him unflinchingly. "Several teams are sending tapping signals directly above the tunnel network right this minute," he replied. "Do you have any other ideas?"

"Not me!" the miner declared. "You and the Chinaman are the ones who didn't shore up your tunnels like you should have done. You made the mess. Now you fix it and get those boys out!"

"I intend to do everything that's humanly possible to save them," Chet replied. "But let's get our facts straight. The ceilings and walls of every last tunnel have been strengthened with timbers, and you blame well know it. I have no idea what caused the explosion down there—if there actually was an explosion.

And instead of standing here squabbling, I suggest that all of us pitch in to help the men who are trapped!"

His firm attitude lessened the belligerence of the miners.

"Each of you take a dozen volunteers," he directed. "Join the parties that are tapping on the surface of the tunnel routes. And if anyone knows a better way to handle this problem, I'll be glad to adopt it immediately."

Turning on his heel, with Ke trudging beside him, he made his way up the slope to take charge of the crude signaling operation.

Scott, who had been braced for trouble, watched the pair in admiration. It was typical of them to take the lead in doing whatever task they asked others to perform.

The leaders of the insurrection hesitated briefly, then began to round up their comrades. Everyone on the site knew that any signals sent by the miners in the tunnels below might be faint, so those who joined in the enterprise maintained a strict silence, and the only sound was the thudding of sledgehammers and other heavy tools on the ground.

The electricity in the air was frightening. The miners were tense, and if the victims of the cave-in were not recovered alive, there was a strong possibility that a lynch mob might try to kill Chet and Ke.

Surveying the scene, Scott knew he faced overwhelming odds. His constables were men of courage, although they lacked experience in controlling riots, but most of the miners, who outnumbered them by at least twenty to one, were armed with pistols, rifles, and old-fashioned muskets, too. Men on both sides would be killed if a nasty fight developed, and the miners were virtually certain to win.

Checking his own rifle and six-shooter, Scott vowed to do his best. He had accepted the post of head of the constabulary, and his duty was plain.

The work of tapping the ground was painstaking and agonizingly slow. Some of the miners, aware of the risks posed in the tunnels by the raging underground river and the lack of oxygen, were inclined to move too quickly. But Chet and Ke tirelessly made their way from one group to the next, urging the men to slow their pace and pause from time to time so they could detect any possible answering signals. How long the miners would remain patient was anyone's guess.

The thunder of approaching hoofbeats broke the quiet, and Scott felt great relief as Andy Brentwood approached the area at the head of his full troop. All carried sabers as well as the new, remarkably accurate rifles being manufactured for the army in New England. Andy called a halt, leaving his unit in formation, and dismounted.

"I've never been so glad to see anyone in my life," Scott told him.

"Sorry it took us so long to get here, but our bivouacs are scattered, and it took time to assemble the entire troop."

"You're here now, and that's what's important. No matter how ugly the miners may become, they know they won't stand a chance in a showdown with more than a hundred experienced soldiers." Scott quickly explained the situation.

The young officer frowned. "You really think that Chet and Ke are in danger?"

"There's no doubt of it."

"Well," Andy said, "I'm reluctant to open fire on fellow Americans, but we can't close our eyes to the murder of prominent citizens." He quickly summoned his three platoon commanders, all of them second lieutenants who had been a year behind him at the military academy. "Hold your formations until further notice," he told them. "If a riot develops, as it well may, we'll go into a spread formation. And I want you to make it crystal clear to every last man in the troop

that we'll use only the flats of our sabers if we're
required to charge. I want no civilian killed or severely injured, so we face the possibility of conduct-
ing a very delicate operation."

The subordinate officers returned to their platoons
to relay the instructions to the cavalrymen, and Andy
took up his vigil beside Scott.

A short time later Susanna Fulton arrived on horseback, wearing boy's attire and riding alone.

Scott brought Susanna up to date on the situation,
then said, "I'm afraid I'll have to ask you to go down
the slope, behind the lines the constables have set up."

She was stunned by the unexpected request. "I've
come here officially as a representative of the *Tribune!*"

"I hardly need remind you that I'm on the *Tribune*'s
payroll, too," Scott said. "But right now I'm acting in
my capacity as chief of police, and it's too dangerous
for you here."

Susanna turned to Andy in silent appeal, but he was
equally adamant. "If anything significant develops,
we'll send down the hill for you so you can get your
story. But there's no telling what may happen up here,
and we can't be responsible for your safety."

"I'll accept responsibility for my own safety!" Susanna said hotly.

"Sorry, but that isn't good enough," Scott told her.
This was one occasion when she would not get her
own way. Andy was equally firm as he shook his head.

Frustrated and irritated, Susanna stamped off, leading her mare partway down the hill.

Both of the young men shifted uncomfortably. Circumstances had forced them to adopt the same position, but neither was happy about it. They took what
little consolation they could from the fact that Susanna was annoyed with both of them.

The task of the men strung out on the slopes
seemed endless, and time dragged. They had worked
the entire day and well into the night, and some

became discouraged, but Chet and Ke cajoled and threatened, sometimes appealing and sometimes becoming scornful as they kept the volunteers at work, the lanterns of the onlookers blazing.

A miner's shout on the far side of the crest sounded loudly. "I hear something down there!" he called.

Men rushed to his side, and then Chet and Ke pushed through the crowd. "Quiet!" the former commanded. "Where did you hear a sound?"

"Right about here," the miner said.

Wong Ke took a sledgehammer from someone in the throng and brought it down on the ground with full force. No one moved, and men scarcely breathed. Then a very faint sound rose from the bowels of the earth and was repeated twice.

The crowd above began to cheer.

Chet took a tunnel map from Harvey, examined it in the light of a torch, then measured the ground with meticulous care. "Hand me a shovel," he said.

One of the miners complied, and Chet shoved the blade into the rocky soil. "We dig here," he said.

Ke waved away the scores of volunteers who would have come to his partner's aid. "Not too many," he said sharply, "or we'll have a bad cave-in from above. We can use four men with strong backs, no more."

Soon the dirt flew as the men chosen for the task went to work in earnest, and Chet, refusing to relinquish his shovel, set the example.

Scott sent a constable for Susanna, and she forgot her pique as she joined the party. "Will it be possible to save the men down there?" she asked anxiously.

A miner replied on behalf of the entire company. "God knows, lady," he said.

Willie de Berg rarely allowed himself the luxury of a stiff drink of hard liquor because the alcohol might cloud his business judgment, but tonight was an exception. His scheme was developing smoothly, precisely as he had planned it. He drained his glass, then refilled it and sipped more slowly, savoring every swallow.

He had not heard the explosion in the new Harris and Wong mine very early that morning, but it had been reported separately by at least a score of customers, so he knew Jerome Hadley had completed his task. Good for you, Hadley, Willie thought as he raised his glass in a silent salute to the gambler—and good-bye, Hadley. The fuse that the poor fool had been given to attach to the keg of gunpowder had been made of loosely woven cotton; anyone familiar with explosives would have known it would burn down in seconds, but Hadley, in his innocence, had been ignorant. There could be little doubt that he had been blown to pieces when the detonation had occurred.

Willie smiled quietly. As much as he regretted the expenditure of one thousand dollars that could not be recovered, he had been saved the loss of another thousand. Even more important, Hadley never would be able to testify in court against him. No one would be able to establish a connection between him and the tragedy in the mine.

Chuckling silently, Willie told himself that all Denver would regard the "accident" as a catastrophe. Every patron who had come into the Palace that day had reported that a number of miners were trapped below the surface of the earth. Willie was supremely indifferent to their number because they were merely the means to his eagerly sought end. By now hundreds of miners were demanding vengeance, and he didn't care whether Chet Harris and Wong Ke were hanged or ridden out of town on rails. The net result was the same: they would be unable to show their faces in Denver again, and without their active financial support, the new constabulary would collapse. The Palace operation would be safe until Colorado officially became a federal territory and a permanent police force was established. The better part of another year would pass before he would be required to pull up stakes and move elsewhere, and by then he would be too wealthy to care. His gambling hall-saloon-brothel was worth more than any gold mine.

On sudden impulse Willie went to the door of his office and summoned Caroline, who was obliged to leave the poker-playing customer to whose crude advances she was submitting.

Never before had he allowed personal considerations to interfere with business, and her limpid eyes were questioning as she came to him.

"Join me in a little drink," he said, again refilling his own glass and splashing whiskey into another for her.

At no previous time had Caroline seen him under the influence of liquor, and she felt uneasy.

"We'll drink to me," he said.

"Why not?" she replied lightly and, clinking glasses with him, carefully took a small sip of whiskey that burned as it slid down.

"A heap of wenches have worked for me," he said, "but you're different." Studying her critically, he knew he spoke the truth. Her ripe figure was provocative beneath her sleek, snug-fitting evening gown, and her expression was seductive. She was a natural trollop.

"I'm glad you're finally realizing my worth," Caroline said.

"Oh, I do," he replied, chuckling dryly. "No woman has ever pushed me around the way you've done. I've got to go now on an errand, and when I come back, you'll have your reward. Your just reward."

She couldn't fathom the look in his eyes and didn't know whether he was promising or threatening.

By the time he returned, Willie told himself, the last of the night's customers would be gone, so he would be free to beat Caroline within an inch of her life. Her beauty would be so marred when he was done with her that she would be of no further use to him, but he didn't care. He no longer needed her—or anyone else.

Gulping the contents of his drink, he fondled her for a moment. "Wait up for me," he said, then sauntered off.

Caroline's instinct told her to leave, but she had nowhere to go. What was more, she was enjoying the respite from her monotonous work, and she looked forward to lounging comfortably in Willie's private rooms.

Willie went out to the street, then made his way around the corner. His timing tonight was perfect. Recently constables had been patrolling the streets in pairs, but there wasn't a law enforcement officer in sight, and he knew that almost every member of the constabulary had been summoned to the site of the Harris and Wong mine for emergency duty. He already had outsmarted everyone.

A few oil lamps were still burning in Clara Lou's establishment, so Willie loitered in the street outside the entrance, but he didn't have long to wait. The last patrons, a half-dozen card players, were leaving in a body.

He grasped the latch when they opened the door and assumed the guise of a security guard. "Good night, gentlemen," he said cheerfully.

They bade him a good night and went on their way.

Slipping inside and going to the card room, where the oil lamps had been extinguished, Willie concealed himself in the dark, smiling silently. This was almost too easy.

A poker dealer and the waiter left together, but Willie made no move. Then the cook and his helper left, and the man in hiding caught a glimpse of Clara Lou, a burning oil lamp in one hand, as she bolted the door.

Moving silently, he followed her into the dining room.

Clara Lou sensed his presence and turned quickly, then gasped. He grinned at her.

"What are you doing here?" she asked sharply. "What do you want?"

"I've been patient for a long time," Willie said, weaving a trifle unsteadily. "But I've run out of patience."

"Leave at once!"

He ignored the command. "First off," he said, "you've lost your protector. Harris is finished in Denver. By now he's either dead or on his way back to San Francisco."

"I don't believe you!"

"Believe what you please," he told her. "You'll soon find out. Look out the windows, why don't you? There isn't a constable on the streets. Or even one army soldier, either."

She couldn't resist the urge to peer out and quickly saw he was right. There were no constables on foot patrol, no mounted cavalrymen anywhere to be seen, the first time in many days that the busy street had been unguarded at this hour. "What have you done, de Berg?" she cried.

"I don't admit to doing anything. All I'll tell you is that the tide has turned. This is my town now, and things will be done my way here." He took several steps toward her.

Clara Lou retreated, putting one of the dining room tables between them. She had left her firearms upstairs in her living quarters, and there was no way she could make a dash now for a pistol.

"I've wanted this place for a long time," Willie said. "I'll give you a thousand for it, in cash. Right now."

"You must be mad," she replied, fighting for calm. "It's worth at least five times that amount, and you know it as well as I do. You also know that I won't sell to you at any price."

"Before I'm finished with you," he said, "you'll be glad to accept a thousand. And that isn't all. I've also wanted you for a long time."

Clara Lou saw he was in earnest, and realizing he had consumed a large amount of liquor, she knew he was even more dangerous than usual. She had dismissed his remark about Chet being dead or forced to leave Denver as gibberish, but now she was less certain. He was so positive, so sure of himself that there had to be grounds of some kind for his confidence.

Well, no matter what might be happening elsewhere, she had to concentrate for the present on her own precarious situation. De Berg was determined to have his way, and her physical strength obviously was no match for his, but her courage did not desert her. "You're trespassing where you're not wanted, and you're threatening me," she said. "If you don't leave instantly, I'll have you hauled into citizens' court, and I'll bring full charges against you."

"Who will haul me into court?" he asked, his voice mocking. "The constables are on their way out of business, and the army troops have no right to arrest civilians unless the police request it. I know my privileges as a citizen!"

Holding her ground, she sucked in her breath.

"Give in to me nicely, act like you're enjoying yourself, and you won't get hurt. Put up a fight, and you'll pay the consequences." Willie lunged across the table and caught hold of her wrist.

With a great effort Clara Lou freed herself and retreated again, this time moving to the far side of the table near the window, on which she had placed the oil lamp.

Willie's face contorted in a grimace. Opening his holster flap, he drew his six-shooter and pointed it at the defiant woman. "I want you right now. Take off your clothes!"

Uncertain whether he actually intended to pull the trigger, she knew she had no choice but to gamble. Reaching out suddenly, Clara Lou caught hold of the

oil lamp and threw it as hard as she could at her
tormentor.

The lamp struck Willie full in the face, spilling oil
everywhere, and when the lamp fell, the glass shield
smashed on the ground. Suddenly the lamp oil, which
had splattered onto the carpets and walls, caught fire,
and flames crept along the floor and up the long
cotton draperies.

"I'm blind!" Willie screamed, holding a hand to his
face and trying desperately to blink away the oil that
was burning in his eyes. "My God! I can't see!"

Clara Lou stared at him in horror.

In his agony and frustration he emptied his six-
shooter, the shots spraying wildly, and then the pistol
clattered to the floor.

Clara Lou started toward the door, escape upper-
most in her mind, and then halted abruptly. Only now
did she become conscious of the fire, which was
spreading rapidly. The tablecloths were going up in
flames, at least one of the wooden tables had caught
fire, and a barrel of trash that the cook had left inside
the door for emptying in the morning was smoldering
nastily.

"Help me!" Willie shrieked as he staggered in cir-
cles, stumbling as he backed away from the heat of
the burning cloth and wood.

Only one thought filled Clara Lou: she had to save
herself, and she didn't know how.

XI

The miners dug steadily, late into the night, their shovels cutting into the hard earth one at a time in a rhythmic pattern, and when one of the men showed signs of tiring, another volunteer came forward to take his place. Chet and Ke stayed close at hand, directing the delicate operation, and consistently refused to permit the hole to be widened beyond a diameter of three feet.

"We don't know what may be eroding down below," Chet explained patiently, repeatedly. "If we make the hole any wider, we'll be running a bigger risk of a large cave-in, and we may do more harm than good."

Only occasionally were the workers encouraged by the sounds of tapping from those who were caught in the tunnel. So far, it appeared that at least some of the victims were alive.

Suddenly a broad-shouldered giant emerged from the still-growing crowd. "Now I dig," Ezekiel announced. Seizing a shovel from a miner, he bent to the task.

Others watched him in awe. The shovel bit into the ground again and again, and huge quantities of earth were removed. In fact, he worked so hard and quickly

326

that a new problem soon arose. Not even his long arms could reach the base of the excavation.

Chet and Ke looked at each other, instantly reaching an unspoken decision. "We'll have to risk a cave-in," Chet announced. "Depending on how accurate the map may be, we'll have to dig at least another six feet."

Additional volunteers stepped forward, at Chet's direction enlarging the excavation as little as was necessary. Only Ezekiel was shoveling dirt and stones from the main portion of the hole now, and he gradually moved lower and lower. In the early hours of the morning, only his head, shoulders, and the upper part of his torso showed above ground level.

Among the many newcomers from town were a number of women, and when Wong Ke caught sight of Mei-lo, who moved to a place beside Susanna, he frowned. He wished she had remained safely at home instead of mingling with this volatile crowd, but he could not divert his attention from the task at hand for a word with her.

As Ezekiel moved still lower, Chet called for a stout length of rope. One end was fastened beneath Ezekiel's armpits, and the other was tied to a stake that was driven into the ground nearby. Now, if a breakthrough should occur, he would not fall to his death in the raging underground torrent.

All at once Ezekiel's shout electrified the throng. "Earth falling into hole now!" he shouted.

A moment later, above the rush of swiftly running water, those on the ground heard feeble cheers from below.

Chet disregarded his own safety and climbed down until he reached a place directly above Ezekiel. "Are you all right?" he called, cupping his hands.

"Thank God for air," was the ghostly reply, and the victims went on to explain that they were trapped on a narrow ledge above the onrushing waters of the underground river.

"We'll lower a line to you," Chet told them. "Then you can come up one at a time."

"Can't move," one of the miners below replied, his voice barely audible.

Chet climbed back up to ground level, quickly explaining the situation. "They've been trapped in there, unable to move, for almost twenty-four hours now. They'll need some assistance."

"We'll have to lower someone on one line," Chuck Harvey said. "Somehow, he'll have to gain a foothold on the ledge and tie a second line to the survivors, one at a time, and we'll haul them up."

"I'll do it," Wong Ke said instantly. "I am smaller than any other man here."

Ropes were fetched, and when Mei-lo realized what Ke intended, she raced forward to him. "You must not do this," she said. "You cannot take such a risk."

"The miners who are trapped down there risked their lives for me," he replied gently as the line was made secure beneath his armpits. "I would be ashamed for the rest of my days if I did not do the same for them."

Since she knew he could not be dissuaded, she accepted his decision. His courage was one of his qualities that she admired most, so she kissed him, then stepped back. Ke smiled at her, and then clutching a second line firmly, he was lowered out of sight.

Few in the crowd moved, and no one spoke; the tension was so great it was a living force.

Wong Ke sized up the situation as best he could in the pale light that filtered down from above. Gaining a precarious foothold on the ledge in the midst of the huddled mass of exhausted miners, he was soaked by the spray of the surging, black water directly beneath him. Not wasting a moment, he looped the spare line beneath the armpits of the nearest miner, then tugged repeatedly at the rope as a signal to the men waiting on the surface.

Chet understood instantly, and Ezekiel took the

lead, pulling hand over hand steadily until the half-conscious victim was safely in the grasp of his deliverers.

"Lower the line again," Chet ordered.

One by one the men trapped in the tunnel directly above the underground river were brought to safety. Ke and Chet worked together with the smooth precision of men whose minds functioned as one, and the assistance rendered by Ezekiel was remarkable, but the task seemed to take an eternity. In actuality, the rescue operation lasted no more than a half-hour.

By the end of that time, Ke was weakening. The icy water that continued to splash him numbed him, his fingers stiffened, and he had to concentrate his total attention on what he was doing. So weary that he almost gave in to the temptation to stretch out on the slippery ledge to rest, he nevertheless tugged at his own rope as soon as the last of the miners was raised to the surface.

The tireless Ezekiel needed no help now as he hauled on the line with a vengeance, and the crowd cheered lustily as Ke was lifted to safety. The animosities toward the owners of the mine that had threatened to spark a riot were forgotten, everyone on the scene well knowing that Harris and Wong were directly responsible for saving the lives of those who had been caught below.

Mei-lo darted forward again to kiss the bone-weary Ke, who was too tired to speak and could only grin at her. Then someone handed her a blanket, and she wrapped him in it, sitting on the ground beside him and cradling him in her arms.

Members of the rescue team exchanged congratulations but were interrupted by a shout from the distance, and then several men hurried up the slope.

"There were more men in the tunnels than we knew," the first up the hill called. "At least one man has drowned!"

The torchbearers led the way, closely followed by

Chet, and neither Andy Brentwood nor Scott Foster
protested when Susanna Fulton accompanied the
group. They headed for the base of another hill,
where No Name Creek emerged from its underground
channel and then flowed about one hundred yards on
the surface before merging with the South Platte.

The raging torrent shot to the surface with great
force, and the limp, crumpled body of a man was
sprawled on the bank several yards from the swift-
moving stream. The torchbearers quickly approached
the dead man, and Chet moved forward to join them,
then halted abruptly.

"Jerome Hadley!" he exclaimed as he stared at the
bloated face of the gambler.

Scott joined Chet and was bewildered. "What was
he doing in your mine?"

Chet shook his head. "Whatever it may have been,
he had no legitimate right to be there."

Susanna found it difficult to look at the body of the
dead man. "Perhaps," she said, "the people who were
so certain they heard an explosion weren't mistaken."

"We may never find out," Chet said grimly. "It
could be he was trying to damage the mine. Whatever
his business may have been, he's paid a terrible price
for his interference." The realization that Clara Lou
was free to live her life as she wished was just
beginning to dawn on him.

The miners, relieved that the man who had
drowned had not been one of their company, moved
the body to higher ground.

Meanwhile, the men who had been trapped in the
tunnel were showing signs of recovery. Supplies had
been fetched from the shack that stood a short distance from the entrance to the main shaft, a fire had
been lighted, and Mei-lo was throwing ingredients
into a kettle. Wong Ke, who had recovered from his
ordeal, stood happily beside her, still wrapped in a
blanket. The victims of the near-catastrophe were

stirring, and a physician who had been present in the throng was assuring them, after subjecting them to hasty, preliminary examinations, that they appeared to have suffered no permanent harm.

One of the miners who had found the body of Jerome Hadley tentatively approached Chet and placed ten one-hundred-dollar bills in his hands. "My buddies and I found this on the body of the dead man. We decided you would know what to do with it."

"One thousand dollars!" Susanna exclaimed. "My guess is that Hadley was being paid off to sabotage the mine."

For a moment Chet said nothing, then he looked up at the miner and thanked him for turning over the money. "We'll put it to good use. It'll go into the fund that's been established for the voluntary constabulary."

"I wonder if Willie de Berg could have been behind this attempt to wreck the mine," Scott said as the miner walked off.

"Do you think he'd dare go that far?" Andy Brentwood asked.

"He has a lot of reasons for hating Chet," Susanna said. "I wouldn't put it past him to hire a man like Jerome Hadley to sabotage the mine."

"It can't do any damage to have a little chat with him after I get back to town," Scott said. "I'll ask Isaiah to come with me. I'll swear him in as a temporary deputy to make it legal. If de Berg has been involved in some shenanigans, he's sure to deny it, but it might be easier for Isaiah to trap him and squeeze the truth out of him. My own experience in catching criminals off guard is too limited."

The crowd began to dissipate, and Chet ordered the mine closed until further notice. "I want us to check into the tunnels that aren't under water," he told his superintendent. "We'll keep them closed until we've had a chance to make a thorough assessment of the damage. When the lives of our men are at stake, we've got to be cautious."

There was no longer any need for the cavalrymen or the constables at the mine site, so both units formed their ranks for the short ride back to Denver. Ke and Mei-lo decided to remain behind for a time with the men who were recuperating from their ordeal and eating the soup that Mei-lo had prepared for them.

Andy and Scott offered Susanna an escort into town, and she accepted with alacrity. Chet decided to ride with them, too, anxious to break the news to Clara Lou about her husband's unexplained drowning in the Harris and Wong mine. The handful of constables took the lead, and it was not accidental that Scott rode on one side of Susanna while Andy, at the head of his troop, flanked her on the other side.

They had gone only a short distance when a rider approached from Denver at a gallop. As he came closer they saw he was wearing one of the red and blue armbands that identified members of the constabulary.

"Chief Foster!" he shouted "There's a bad fire burning out of control!"

"Where?" Scott spurred forward.

"At the Hadley gaming house!"

Chet Harris outdistanced everyone as he galloped toward Denver.

The smoke was so thick that Clara Lou could not make her way to a window. There was no way she could reach the front door through the wall of flames, and she realized that the fire had spread to the kitchen, too, cutting her off there.

"For God's sake, help me!" the hysterical Willie de Berg screamed, stumbling and thrashing as he tried in vain to escape, rendered sightless by the oil in his eyes.

Clara Lou felt no sympathy for him. On the other hand, she could not leave him to die without trying to assist him, even though her own safety had to be her first consideration. "We'll have to try getting out from my living quarters upstairs," she said, the thickening smoke making her cough and causing her eyes to smart.

"But I can't see!"

The cloth that covered the table only a foot or two from him caught fire and began to burn fiercely. Afraid that she could not reach his side in time to be of any help, she called, "Come toward me quickly. You can hear the sound of my voice, so come this way. Then we'll try to reach the staircase."

Even in this moment of supreme peril, Willie de Berg could not trust anyone. "You're just trying to trick me!"

"There's no time to argue! The whole place is on fire!" Clara Lou watched in horror as the flames crept nearer to the crazed, blinded man.

Suddenly Willie laughed maniacally, turned, and raced headlong toward the gaming room, where the flames were soaring.

"No! Don't go that way!" Clara Lou spent precious breath trying to warn him.

He laughed more loudly, lost his balance, and pitched forward into the heart of the fire.

Horrified and sickened, Clara Lou could see his clothes catching fire. There was nothing more she could do for him, and if she lingered any longer on the ground floor, she was certain to lose her life, too. Trying to shut out the sound of Willie's agonized screams of terror and pain, she groped her way toward the stairs.

The smoke was so thick that she could see almost nothing now, and she dropped to her hands and knees, realizing that there was somewhat less smoke near the floor. Gasping for breath, she finally found the bottom stair, and scrambling to her feet, she fled upward.

The thick door to her living quarters was closed, temporarily cutting off the fire, and she managed to open it, squeeze through, and slam it behind her. Considerable smoke had seeped up through the smoldering floorboards, but the air was clearer here, at least for the moment, and as Clara Lou moved through the small vestibule, she was able to organize her thoughts.

Her bedchamber, which stood directly above the gaming room, where the fire was the worst, was the most dangerous place to be, and the floor there ultimately would collapse. For the present, unless the flames shifted, her small parlor offered the best refuge, so she hurried into it, then opened the window wide, letting out smoke and admitting fresh, cool air, which she breathed gratefully.

Fully realizing her respite was temporary, she tried to analyze the options open to her. If she tried to jump to the ground below, she would risk serious injury and might suffer death. There was no way she could climb to the roof and make her way to the roof of the adjoining building; her only hope would be to make a rope of her sheets and blankets and try to climb down to the ground.

Clara Lou opened her bedroom door, then closed it again. It already was filling with smoke, and she was afraid the floor there might give way at any moment. She could not remove the bedclothes, nor could she reach her small linen closet at the far side of the chamber, either. Apparently she had to take the risk of jumping from her parlor window.

A loud shout jarred her. "Clara Lou!"

She peered through the smoke pouring from the ground floor, certain she had recognized the voice. "Is that you, Chet?"

"Yes. How much longer can you hold out up there?"

"I—I don't know. The fire was bad downstairs, and I'm afraid it'll spread fast. Where are you?"

"In the side yard." He wasted no words. "Stay right where you are. I'm coming for you."

She had no idea how he could make his way through the inferno beneath her. "No, Chet! Don't take the chance for my sake. You'll never make it!"

There was no reply.

Apparently he was on his way, and her concern for him was as great as her worry over her own predicament. She had the sense to obey his order, something in a corner of her mind telling her that he would not behave foolishly. In any event, there was nowhere she could go. She felt sure the fire was creeping into her bedroom by this time, and she could see the smoke in the vestibule becoming heavier.

Every moment felt like an eternity. Clara Lou knew there was no hope of saving Willie de Berg, and it was ironic that she, too, might lose her life in the fire that had killed him.

Suddenly the upside-down face of Chet Harris appeared directly in front of her, outside the window. "Quick," he said, grasping her wrists. "Take hold of my wrists, too, and hang on for dear life."

The startled Clara Lou did as she was bidden without stopping to think.

"Trust me," he said.

She felt herself being lifted out of the room, and only their tight, mutual hold prevented her from hurtling to the ground below.

"Now!" Chet shouted.

To Clara Lou's astonishment she felt herself being lifted higher, but her arms felt as though they were being torn from their sockets, and the pain was so great that her mind would not function.

Then, as the roof began to appear, she realized that several men were holding Chet's legs, literally dragging him backward in order to raise her. Strong arms caught hold of her and dragged her onto the roof. She recognized Scott as she lay there, gasping for breath.

Chet scrambled to his feet and helped Clara Lou stand. "This whole roof will give way any second," he said. "Come on!"

The danger was far from ended. Clinging to Chet, Clara Lou saw that two planks had been placed over the open space, about three feet wide, that separated the roof from that of the adjoining building.

"The fire may spread to the place next door before the boys can bring it under control," Scott said.

Chet nodded but saved his breath by not replying.

They reached the planks, and Scott gestured to Clara Lou. "You go first."

She moved toward the edge of the roof, looked down at the gaping space between the buildings, and stopped short. "I—I can't," she said. "I'm afraid I'll fall."

There was no time to reassure and soothe her. Chet lifted her into his arms, and although her weight jeopardized his own sense of balance, he moved boldly across the planks to the next-door building. Several constables and uniformed cavalrymen clustered there began to cheer her, but Scott cut them short. "We've got to get out of here," he told them after he, too, negotiated the planks.

Chet did not release Clara Lou, instead carrying her down the stairs. "I can walk," she protested. He paid no attention and did not place her on her feet until he reached the street.

Her face was grimy and smudged, her clothes had been scorched, and the loose ends of her hair had been burned, but she was truly safe now, and she began to laugh and cry at the same time.

Chet put his arms around her. "You'll be fine now," he said.

Aware for the first time of the activity around them, Clara Lou saw cavalrymen and constables formed in bucket brigades that extended from the wells in sev-

eral nearby yards. Men were pumping water furiously,
and those nearest to the fire were throwing bucket-
fuls at the building adjoining her own, which they
knew could not be saved.

A crash told Clara Lou that the roof of her establishment had collapsed. The flames leaped still higher
for a short time, then began to die down. Everything
she owned was being destroyed, but she was safe, and
nothing else mattered.

She began to babble, telling Chet and Scott about
her confrontation with Willie de Berg. Susanna was
there, too, taking in every word, but Clara Lou was
beyond caring what might be published in the *Tribune.* "De Berg must be dead," she said. "The last I
saw him, his clothes were on fire, and it would have
been impossible for him to get through the front
door."

"That whole side of the building is gone," Chet
said, placing an arm around her shoulders.

"I threw an oil lamp at him," she said, "and I set fire
to my property myself."

"You weren't to blame for anything that's happened," Chet said firmly as he led her away. He
would wait until she regained her equilibrium, he
decided, before he told her that Jerome Hadley had
been drowned.

Someone supplied them with horses, and as they
rode off to the boardinghouse, they saw the bucket
brigades were preventing the fire from spreading.

Chet insisted that Clara Lou drink a small glass of
brandywine when they reached the house, and then
Sarah Rose Atkins took charge. Clara Lou bathed,
then dressed in clothes borrowed from Sarah Rose,
who was taller and far more slender, and when the
older woman looked at her reflection in the mirror,
she realized she had not lost her ability to laugh.

They ate a breakfast prepared by Mei-lo's helper,
and then Chet led Clara Lou into the parlor for a talk.

"I haven't even started to thank you for saving me," she said. "You were far braver than I would have been."

"I want no thanks," he told her. "And after the night you've spent, I don't believe you need to prove your courage to anyone." He looked hard at her. "Sit down. You aren't the only one who had an eventful night."

She lowered herself to the sofa, aware that the borrowed skirt was too long and the waistband too narrow.

Speaking in a low, seemingly calm tone, Chet told her about the reported explosion at the gold mine, the rescue of the miners trapped there, and the appearance of Jerome Hadley's body at the place where the underground river emerged into the open. Then he mentioned the thousand dollars discovered on his body.

She remained silent for a time after he finished speaking, and then she sighed quietly. "Jerome had to have been doing something wrong," she said. "We may never know what it was, but he just wasn't capable of living within the bounds of the law. No man ever rebelled harder against society, but I don't think anyone could have deserved to die in such a horrible way. Or the way that Willie de Berg died, either. I hope their souls will find the peace they denied themselves in this world."

"Amen," Chet said. He had never before known anyone who could be so forgiving.

Clara Lou sat with her hands folded in her lap, looking out the windows at the icy rain that was beginning to fall. "Is that rain or snow?" she asked.

"It's rain, and that's good. That will ensure that the fire won't spread. When we first rode into town, I was afraid the whole downtown area soon would be ablaze."

"You don't suppose I'll be able to salvage much of anything from the ruins?"

"I guess you were still too dazed to see very clearly. The fire gutted the building. There's literally nothing left but the stone portions of the walls."

"It would be too difficult to build again. I suppose I should sell the property."

"Wong Ke and I will buy it from you, so you don't need to look very far for a customer. It's a good location for an office building. Name your price, and we'll meet it. But take your time deciding what you want. This isn't a morning for thinking about finances."

"I guess not, although I'm relieved to know I'll be able to afford a new wardrobe. Every stitch I owned was in that place, along with all my furniture, my dishes—everything I had managed to acquire over the years I've been working."

"I don't think it would be appropriate for me to propose to you once more until Jerome Hadley is buried," Chet said. "But you'll never need to worry about money again."

Her exhaustion had clouded her mind, and she looked at him in wonder, her eyes widening. "I didn't think of it until you mentioned it just now, but the obstacle that prevented our marriage has been removed." He nodded somberly. "Are you quite sure you still want to marry me, Chet?" she demanded.

"That's the most foolish—"

"Hear me out. I—I don't want to stay in Denver. The—the ghosts of Jerome Hadley and Willie de Berg would haunt me here."

"I had already decided we'd leave," he said. "I'll have a talk with Ke, and I'm sure he and Mei-lo won't in the least mind staying on here for a few extra months until we know for certain which of our mines will keep producing and which should be closed down. Isaiah and Sarah Rose will go with the U.S. Cavalry to Virginia City, and I suggest we go there, too. Not to stay. We'll inspect the properties our agents have bought there, and we'll make certain that

Isaiah begins to hire the right miners and gets our company affairs in order. Ke and I have been away from our headquarters too long, so you and I will go on to San Francisco. If you don't find the house you want, we'll build a new one."

"For someone who hasn't exactly been lolling away the night, you've been doing a great deal of planning, my dear."

"Everything except our wedding."

"I'll relieve you of that burden, and in the next few days I'll speak to the Reverend Lane. Before that," Clara Lou added, "I've got to accustom myself to the realization that I'm finally free to do what I want. Buying new clothes, finding a place for us to live, and all the other details are just frosting on the cake. The one thing in this world that matters is that I'm going to be Mrs. Chet Harris—as long as I live."

Susanna spent the whole morning writing and revising the articles that would fill the better part of the next day's *Tribune*, the stories of the events at the Harris and Wong gold mine just outside town and the dramatic fire that had destroyed Clara Lou Hadley's gaming house. Ordinarily she would have found the work exhilarating, but she was troubled, rewriting both stories again and again, and at noon she knew she needed her father's advice.

She went to his cramped office, carrying both articles. "Do you have a few minutes to spare, Wade?" she asked him.

He motioned her to a chair. "I wanted a word with you, Sue. And with Scott. Do you know when he's coming in today?"

"That's anyone's guess. When I last saw him, he was still directing the crews throwing water on the last of the fire at Clara Lou's place. Then he was planning to get an order from one of the citizens' court judges. He was intending to close down the Palace permanently and arrange for auctioning of the bar, kitchen equipment, liquor on hand, and any other assets in the place. Including the property itself."

"The closing of that sleazy saloon will be a godsend. But what will he do with the money he gets at the auction?"

Susanna grinned. "Someone suggested to Scott that the income be added to the fund for the upkeep and preservation of the new constabulary. I plan to write that article this afternoon, after Scott comes in and we know for certain what we already suspect, that Willie de Berg left no legal heirs."

Wade laughed. "I believe I can guess the identity of the person who made that suggestion to Scott."

"I won't mention that in print," she said demurely. "It wouldn't be seemly."

"Well, you won't find many voices raised in protest, although some of the men who were cheated at the Palace's gambling tables might get up the nerve to claim a share. I can't imagine any court upholding such a claim, though." He chuckled again.

His daughter's smile faded. "Wade, I have a problem—"

"Hold on. So have I, which is why I want to see Scott. How do you suppose he'd react if I sent him off to the Nevada country?"

Susanna could only stare at him.

"The *Tribune* is doing better than I had any reason to hope it would. I'm going to add some new people to the staff here, and I believe we'll continue to grow. That success makes me wonder if I can't duplicate it in Nevada. I'd like to install Scott as the publisher, and since his sister and brother-in-law will be leaving soon for Virginia City, I thought the prospect might appeal to him."

"Perhaps it will," Susanna replied. "But there's a complication. Scott has learned enough about the newspaper business to be a competent publisher, but he knows nothing about handling the news. You'll also need an editor."

"I'm well aware of the need," he said with mock solemnity. "Any suggestions?"

"Well, there's a reporter who has been in the business all her life and who would love to become the editor of her own newspaper."

"And who, at the same time, would be able to lead Scott Foster and Andy Brentwood a merry chase."

"You know I never allow personal considerations to interfere with the gathering of news!" she said with great dignity.

"True enough," her father had to concede. "The only reason I hesitate is because Virginia City, from all I've heard, is even rowdier than Denver at its worst."

"I can't imagine coming to any harm there, Wade. Not with Scott and Andy hovering over me."

"That's a valid argument," Wade said, "and I'll think about it before I make a decision. Now, what is your problem?"

"I was reared in a rather special tradition. I was brought up to believe that the news is almost sacred and that there must be no tampering with a news story."

"Quite right. The reader deserves the absolute truth!"

"Exactly. But now I'm wondering if the omission of certain facts is necessarily a disservice to the reader."

"Be more explicit," the publisher said, frowning.

"As I'm sure you realize, it's inevitable now that Clara Lou Hadley and Chet Harris will be getting married. Overnight Clara Lou will become one of the first ladies of the West. It won't be easy for her, you know."

"Go on."

"No one knows that the man who was drowned in Chet's mine was Clara Lou's husband. In order to

spare her an inundation of gossip that's certain to
follow her for the rest of her life—you know how
spiteful jealous women can be—I wonder if it's essen-
tial to mention the whole truth. Jerome Hadley was
known only by his first name when he worked as a
dealer at the Palace. Several of the men out at the
mine recognized him only by that name when they
saw his body." She picked up one of her articles. "I've
tried writing this any number of ways, and I've finally
called him a card dealer known only as Jerome by his
fellow employees and the Palace card players."

"I see." Wade tapped a quill pen on the edge of his
desk.

"Well?"

"Publish it that way," he said. "Identifying Hadley
as Clara Lou's estranged husband doesn't explain why
he was snooping in the mine or what connection he
had with the alleged explosion in one of the tunnels
there."

"I've rounded up enough people who heard the
explosion to know it was real," she said. "I interviewed the miners who were trapped there, and every
last one of them heard it, too. The explosion is more
than hearsay. My theory, which I mentioned in the
article only as a theory attributed to the constabulary,
is that Jerome detonated an explosion for unknown
reasons and was trapped himself when the underground portion of No Name Creek changed its course.
The thousand dollars found on his body could have
been a payoff but also could have been his take at the
gambling tables. But all that is irrelevant to the fact
that he was married to Clara Lou."

"She's a fine woman who has been a credit to
Denver, and she deserves happiness. Omit any mention of the relationship."

"Thanks, Wade," Susanna said. "That solves half of
my problem. The other part is due to my eavesdropping. After Chet and Scott saved Clara Lou, I heard
her explaining to them what had happened. Willie de

Berg wanted to buy her gaming house, threatened her when she refused, and then tried to seduce her. That's when she threw the oil lamp at him. In one of the versions that I wrote, I made no mention of the argument, but that made de Berg appear as a hero who tried to save a neighbor."

"Oh, no!"

"Don't lecture me, Wade. That version stuck in my throat, and I had to throw it away. De Berg was such a vermin that I simply could not tolerate letting the world think he was anything better."

Wade Fulton sat back in his chair.

"The way I've written the story now, I quote Clara Lou saying that de Berg came to her late at night, offered to buy her restaurant-gaming house, and then threatened her when she refused. I quote her as saying that she threw the lamp at him and inadvertently started the fire because she was trying to protect herself from his punches. I've left out the seduction attempt. Again for the sake of protecting Clara Lou from malicious gossip."

Her father laced his fingers. "It strikes me that you haven't really tampered with the facts of the matter. The seduction aspect contributes nothing but a minor element that would titillate some of the readers. Your story is solid without it."

Susanna stood and kissed him on the forehead. "Not only are you a darling who is giving Clara Lou the opportunity to lead a far happier life, but you justify my faith in my own judgment. Please keep that in mind, Wade, when you appoint the editor of the new Virginia City newspaper."

At the Palace the drinkers, the amorous, and the card players had long since left, and the staff, with nothing better to occupy them, went to the roof in the predawn hours to watch the conflagration. The wind was chilly, and the scantily clad women soon went off to their rooms for cloaks to protect them from the cold.

No one had any idea that Willie de Berg had been trapped inside the burning building and had died there. In fact, most of the help failed to realize that he wasn't in their midst.

Caroline Brandon was aware of his absence, as he had told her he had an appointment elsewhere, and she dreaded his return. The expression in his eyes had indicated to her that her days of treating him with superior disdain were coming to a rapid end. But she had no money, her only belongings were the few provocative gowns that comprised her wardrobe, and she told herself she would be forced to tolerate whatever treatment he had in store for her.

Shivering as she huddled beneath her cloak on the roof, she knew she hated Willie as she had never despised any other member of the human race.

Not until Caroline watched the rescue of Clara Lou Hadley did she decide she had seen enough. She opened the trapdoor on the roof, then descended to the second story, leaving the other women, the bartenders, and the dealers behind, still fascinated by the fire. The corridors were deserted, the high-stakes room was empty, and the breeze blowing in through a window that someone had neglected to close had blown open the door of Willie's private suite.

Caroline edged toward it cautiously, peered in, and saw that both the office and the bedchamber beyond it were empty. Obviously Willie had still not returned from the errand that had taken him out of the building. Quietly closing the door behind her, she felt mildly relieved because whatever unpleasantness might await her had been postponed. He could not mistreat her too severely, to be sure, since she earned him far more than any other woman in the establishment. She shrugged, then went down to the kitchen for coffee.

Several members of the kitchen staff had remained

on duty for the simple reason that no one had remembered to send them home. Caroline discovered she was unexpectedly hungry after the long night, so she asked for a breakfast of eggs and toast. Daylight came, and as she poured herself a mug of steaming, black coffee, the others finally trooped down from the roof. They, too, wanted breakfast before they retired for a few hours of rest.

One of the bartenders decided to leave at once. "I've got to reopen the main room in a few hours," he announced, "and I need a little sleep first."

As Caroline sipped her coffee, she reflected that in some ways she was fortunate. Although Willie was not yet paying her a percentage of the income she earned, at least she wasn't required to report for work until noon.

A few minutes after the bartender left the establishment he returned, seething with excitement, his face pale. "I was going past the fire around the corner just now, and the constables and soldiers there said that Willie was caught inside. He's dead!"

Everyone started talking at once, and most of the employees flatly refused to believe the rumor.

Caroline was standing only a few feet from the bartender and moved closer to him. "Are you sure it isn't just a crazy story?" she asked.

"I'm positive," he replied. "As I was walking past Mrs. Hadley's place—what's left of it—that head of the police who works for the *Tribune* identified Willie's body. I saw it myself, and it was one unholy mess."

Others surrounded him, firing questions at him.

Caroline quietly placed her coffee mug on a counter, inched unobtrusively from the kitchen, and, raising her tight skirt so she could move more rapidly, raced up the stairs. Willie's death changed everything, and a daring idea had occurred to her. Now she had to summon the courage to carry it out.

She ran through the deserted high-stakes room to

his suite, bolting the door behind her, and then went to his clothes closet, where she systematically went through the pockets of every suit in his wardrobe. She knew from their earlier intimacy that he possessed two sets of keys to the metal safe that stood in a corner of his office. He invariably carried one set with him, but he always hid a spare set in one of the pockets of a waistcoat he was not wearing.

Beads of perspiration stood out on Caroline's forehead, her heart hammered unmercifully, and she felt faint. She had to hurry! Others would be coming up here at any moment.

Calming herself with a great effort, she looked through every pocket of Willie's many waistcoats, and finally her fingers touched cool metal.

She dropped to her knees in front of the safe, inserted the key in one of the locks, and heard the tumblers click into place when she turned it. Then she turned the keys in the remaining two locks, and the other tumblers gave way. The door was unexpectedly heavy, and she had to tug with both hands in order to open it.

At the rear were a dozen or more small cubicles, most of them containing folded documents to which she paid no attention. She also ignored a small box filled to overflowing with gold and silver coins. Then she saw what she was seeking: a thick stack of paper money, which rested in one of the bottom cubicles. This was the fund that Willie had used daily, taking bills for his needs and adding to the pile from current revenues.

Her hand trembling, Caroline took the money and thrust it into the inner pocket of her cloak. She was grateful she was still wearing it because there would have been no place to conceal the wad beneath her sleek evening gown.

Almost forgetting to close the safe in her haste, she pushed it shut, removed the keys, and dropped them into the first waistcoat pocket she saw. Then, steadying herself, she unbolted the door, opened it a crack, and peered out. So far her luck was good: no one else was in sight yet, but she heard the voices of people mounting the stairs, so she left the door ajar as she raced through the high-stakes room. Then she slowed to a casual saunter as she reached the wing where the women's rooms were located.

A number of her colleagues were gathered in small groups in the hallway, chattering in excitement.

"Have you heard?" a corselet-clad blonde asked Caroline. "Freddy, the main table dealer, and a couple of the bartenders are talking about taking over the management of the Palace. Do you suppose you'll stay on with them?"

"I doubt it," Caroline replied, trying to maintain a surface calm, "but everything is happening so fast that I don't know what I'll do."

"Your men will follow you anywheres," the young woman replied. "Any house in town would be glad to have you."

"If you wanted," another declared, "you could even open your own place. If you do, take me with you, Caroline!"

"Me, too," one of the women wearing an evening dress said. "I'd be happy to give you a percentage. Not as much as Willie took, but a fair split."

"Thanks for your confidence," Caroline replied. "I want to think, and I'll let you know." She escaped from the group and went to her room.

Not until she had carefully bolted the door behind her did she sit on the bed, remove the wad from the pocket of her cloak, and count it. The total astonished and delighted her: she had taken four thousand, six hundred and fifty dollars from the safe! Now, provided she could keep it, leaving the Palace with her theft undetected, she had a small fortune that would enable her to do anything she pleased.

What gave her the greatest satisfaction was the knowledge that she had more than evened her score with Willie. Had he paid her a full fifty percent of her earnings from the day he had first forced her to go to work here, she would not have made this large a sum. It was almost too bad that Willie had not lived long enough for her to savor her ultimate triumph over him.

She had to proceed methodically, she thought, after a glance in the mirror told her that the gown she had been wearing since the preceding day was wrinkled. She changed into another evening dress, sat at her dressing table, and carefully patched her makeup. Then she made a bundle of her only belongings, which consisted of her cosmetics, evening clothes, shoes, and even the two corselets and the net stockings she had loathed. She intended to leave nothing behind.

First, she would take living quarters for herself in the most respectable hotel that would be willing to rent her a room. Next, she would be obliged to buy some ready-made clothes suitable for daytime wear and some undergarments. That would give her enough time to acquire more sensational clothes from the seamstress who previously had made clothes for her.

Above all, she would have the leisure to contemplate and plan carefully for her future. A relatively small part of the money she had stolen would enable her to live in style for a long time, and she would still have a substantial nest egg that would make it possible for her to remain independent.

Her one problem was to make certain that no one found the money. She donned a pair of the black net stockings, then divided the bills into two piles and placed them beneath snug-fitting garters that held them firmly in place. The slits in the sides of her skirt extended only as high as her knees, so the wads of money held in place at her thighs would remain concealed.

When she emerged from her room, she did not look

back. A phase of her existence had come to an end, and a far brighter future beckoned.

Others were hurrying down to the main room, apparently responding to a summons, and Caroline joined them, trying to look inconspicuous. Scott Foster stood in the center of the main room, with several constables posted at the door, and was waiting for all of the employees to assemble.

The police could give Caroline the protection she wanted before she left the place and became truly free, so she smiled at him.

Looking uncomfortable, Scott responded with a solemn nod, then read aloud an order just issued by a judge of the citizens' court. The people of Denver were taking possession of the Palace, effective immediately, he read. Constables already had been posted in Willie de Berg's private quarters and would take charge of his property.

Caroline knew she had made her withdrawal from the safe just in time.

All members of the staff, Scott continued, were ordered to vacate the premises within one hour, taking only their personal belongings with them. All property owned by the house, along with the building itself, would be sold at public auction, with the monies received to be donated to the fund utilized for the upkeep and preservation of the new constabulary.

Several of the bartenders grumbled, and one of the dealers protested aloud, but Scott remained firm. The court order would be observed to the letter, he said.

Most of the women accepted their ejection fatalistically. There was no lack of bordellos in Denver where they could find work.

Several people stopped Scott to ask him questions, which he answered briefly. But he was in a hurry to leave, having learned that Wade Fulton wanted to speak to him regarding the establishment of a new newspaper in the Nevada country.

Caroline made it her business to fall in beside Scott

as he started toward the street. "I never dreamed you'd become the assistant publisher of the Denver newspaper and the volunteer head of the constabulary," she said. "You're quite a distinguished citizen these days."

"I try to serve the community as best I can." Her proximity made him uneasy, and he searched for something polite to say to this once-respectable young woman who had elected to walk down a more notorious path. "You look well, Caroline. Your life must agree with you."

"It hasn't been too easy at times, but there will be a great improvement now." They reached the street, and the stolen money was safe.

"Where will you go now?" he inquired, not knowing what else to say.

Her full lips parted in a provocative smile, and she deliberately flirted with him. One never knew when a man in his position might prove useful to her. "That remains to be seen," she said. "I intend to weigh the future carefully before I make any specific plans."

For a few moments Scott watched her as she went off down the street, her cloak drawn tightly around her, her bundle of belongings under her arms. Her walk was jauntily confident, and he told himself it was too bad that she had chosen an unsavory profession.

The news was sent by telegraph as far as Independence, Missouri, and a special courier carried the word to Denver. The United States Congress had passed a bill making Colorado a federal territory, and President Buchanan, with only a short time left in his term before Abraham Lincoln was inaugurated, had signed the measure into law. A territorial governor would be appointed in the immediate future, as would several federal judges, and funds would be appropriated for the establishment of a government that would assure all citizens full protection under the law. In the rest of the country, war was in the air, and seven Southern states had seceded from the Union, but Colorado had at last become respectable.

Denver duly celebrated, and the constabulary, assisted by Lieutenant Andrew Brentwood's troop of cavalry, found it easy to maintain order. The city that had been so wild in its earlier days was ready to accept its new responsibilities.

Soon thereafter, Chet Harris and Wong Ke were married to Clara Lou and Mei-lo in a double ceremony attended only by a small group of friends. Both couples delayed going off on honeymoons because the improvement in the weather meant that the soldiers soon would be leaving for Virginia City.

Scott Foster pondered for many days, then made the biggest decision of his life. After consulting with Sarah Rose and Isaiah, he wrote to Rick Miller, asking him to sell the Foster ranch. From this time forward, he would spend his life in the newspaper business, and not only would he establish a daily journal in Virginia City, but he also would share in the ownership.

His decision was not based on his personal relationship with Susanna, who took pains to spell out her own position to him. "Accept or reject my father's offer on its own merits," she said. "The fact that we'd be working together in Nevada doesn't mean we'd move any closer, just as we wouldn't be driven apart if you should decide to go back to your orchards. The way you earn your living isn't relevant to my feelings, and neither is Andy's. The risk I run, and I'm perfectly willing to accept it, is that by the time I decide between you—if and when I do—one or both of you may have become interested in some other woman."

Andy was not surprised by Scott's decision but knew that he, too, would be spending the next year in Nevada, so his rival would gain no advantage over him.

Wade Fulton was reluctant to give his daughter the

post of editor of the new newspaper because reports
reaching Denver indicated that Virginia City was
even wilder and more barbaric than the Colorado
country had been at its worst. Sarah Rose and Isaiah
Atkins solved the problem by offering Susanna a home
with them. They intended to buy or rent a house in
the heart of the silver-mining country, and they made
it plain that they would be happy to share a dwelling
with her.

This altered the prospects, and Wade gave his
daughter the appointment. Scott promptly ordered
new presses from a Chicago manufacturer, and they
arrived before the weather became warmer.

Word to the effect that travelers to Nevada would
be protected on the trail by a full troop of United
States Cavalry spread through the community, and a
number of families who had not succeeded in establishing firm roots in Colorado decided to try their luck
in the area where silver was being discovered on an
unprecedented scale. A number of men applied to
Lieutenant Brentwood for permission to accompany
him.

Andy's reply to all of them was the same. "The
more the merrier," he said. "You'll be obliged to supply your own covered wagon, your own food, and
your own teams of horses, mules, or oxen. I'll require
you to submit to my authority in any matters pertain-
ing to safety on the trail, but otherwise, you're free to
do as you please. I'm under orders not to delay in
reaching Virginia City, so you'll run the risk of being
left behind if you don't keep up with us. But I assure
you that I intend to travel at a reasonable pace of no
less than ten miles and no more than fifteen miles per
day."

Wagons and teams were cheap in Denver because
so many immigrants had come to the territory that
way and had no further use for them. The thirty
families who joined the expedition encountered no
difficulties in finding what they needed.

Isaiah bought a snug wagon for himself and Sarah
Rose, and the thrifty young couple decided to sell it as
soon as they reached their destination. Chet Harris
insisted on purchasing a larger, far more luxurious
wagon for Clara Lou, even though she insisted she
would be satisfied with less. They planned to remain
in Virginia City for a limited time, then they would go
on to San Francisco, where they would be joined by
Ke and Mei-lo in no more than six months.

Wade Fulton bought a freight wagon, pulled by six
mules, in which Scott would carry the new press and
supplies of paper and ink. He would sleep in the
wagon, too. It was arranged that Susanna would drive
a far smaller Conestoga wagon, which would be
pulled by a pair of horses.

Spring came, and as soon as scouts brought word
that the snow was melting rapidly in the mountain
passes, a departure date was set. Susanna wrote a final
article for the *Tribune* about the journey, and soon
after dawn the next morning, Andy Brentwood arrived in the street outside the boardinghouse at the
head of his troop. Soon the wagons began to rumble
into place behind the soldiers, and Ke and Mei-lo said
good-bye to their various friends. "I'm glad we're only
staying on here a short time longer," Ke told his
partner. "Denver won't be the same without all of
you."

Prudence Adams was standing outside the boardinghouse, too, accompanied by Ezekiel and Patricia,
and the trio waved as the wagon train began to
rumble off down the road. After it was out of sight,
Prudence wiped at her eyes and blew her nose with
her handkerchief, then said to her helpmates and
friends, "There are a lot of good people on that train.
I do hope they find what they're looking for in Virginia City."

Certainly it was not accidental that Susanna was
given the first place in the caravan, directly behind
the troops. Attired in her boy's clothes, with an added

sweater for warmth, she looked like a wagon train veteran.

Scott grinned at Andy, then moved his larger wagon into place directly behind Susanna's vehicle.

The venturesome young woman had to admit to herself that she enjoyed the continued rivalry.

Andy rode toward the rear to supervise the maneuvering of other wagons into position in the column. Leaving the details to a subordinate, he rode forward again, then stopped short.

Approaching the train was a wagon covered with new, clean canvas, freshly painted, and pulled by a handsome team of matched bay workhorses. Seated on the front was a slender young woman in a snug-fitting, tailored coat and skirt of expensive wool, with a plumed hat above her long, wheat-colored hair. Even from a distance her liberal use of cosmetics identified her as Caroline Brandon.

Andy approached her and politely raised a hand to the brim of his hat.

"I hope you'll have room for me, Andy," she purred, her smile dazzling. "I'm going to Nevada, too, and I'd love to make the journey with you."

It was impossible for the young officer to refuse her request. She had the same rights as other Americans, and it was her privilege to claim the army's protection.

Caroline moved on again, her brilliant smile lighting her face a second time when she saw the freight wagon pulled by the mule team. "How wonderful that you're going to Nevada, too, Scott," she said. "I know you won't mind if I fall into line right behind you. With you nearby I know I'll be safe."

Scott was too polite to ask her to find another position in the caravan.

Susanna seethed. Not only was the brazen wench openly trying to steal her suitors, but Caroline's presence in the wagon train meant there would be problems on the trail and even greater trouble when they reached Virginia City.

The members of the wagon train party were so absorbed in their own thoughts that they failed to notice at the end of the train, holding up the rear, an elderly miner and his burro, wending their way along the trail. The slovenly attired, bearded old man was singing off-key, and the burro ambling alongside him stopped short, raised its ears, and flicked its tail. Suddenly stopping in mid-song, the miner turned to the burro. "Step lively, Eustace," he said. "There's gonna be hell to pay in Nevada, and we don't want to miss all the fun!"

★ WAGONS WEST ★

A series of unforgettable books that trace the lives of a dauntless band of pioneering men, women, and children as they brave the hazards of an untamed land in their trek across America. This legendary caravan of people forge a new link in the wilderness. They are Americans from the North and the South, alongside immigrants, Blacks, and Indians, who wage fierce daily battles for survival on this uncompromising journey—each to their private destinies as they fulfill their greatest dreams.

☐	24408	**INDEPENDENCE! #1**	$3.95
☐	26162	**NEBRASKA! #2**	$4.50
☐	26242	**WYOMING! #3**	$4.50
☐	24088	**OREGON! #4**	$3.95
☐	26070	**TEXAS! #5**	$4.50
☐	26377	**CALIFORNIA! #6**	$4.50
☐	26546	**COLORADO! #7**	$4.50
☐	26069	**NEVADA! #8**	$4.50
☐	26163	**WASHINGTON! #9**	$4.50
☐	22925	**MONTANA! #10**	$3.95
☐	26184	**DAKOTA! #11**	$4.50
☐	26521	**UTAH! #12**	$4.50
☐	26071	**IDAHO! #13**	$4.50
☐	26367	**MISSOURI! #14**	$4.50
☐	24976	**MISSISSIPPI! #15**	$3.95
☐	25247	**LOUISIANA! #16**	$4.50
☐	25622	**TENNESSEE! #17**	$4.50

Prices and availability subject to change without notice.

Buy them at your local bookstore or use this handy coupon:

Special Offer
Buy a Bantam Book
for only 50¢.

Now you can have Bantam's catalog filled with hundreds of titles plus take advantage of our unique and exciting bonus book offer. A special offer which gives you the opportunity to purchase a Bantam book for only 50¢. Here's how!

By ordering any five books at the regular price per order, you can also choose any other single book listed (up to a $4.95 value) for just 50¢. Some restrictions do apply, but for further details why not send for Bantam's catalog of titles today!

Just send us your name and address and we will send you a catalog!